Joe Weber is a former Marine Corps pilot. A native of Oklahoma, he now resides in Colorado Springs where he is a corporate jet captain. He is currently at work on his second novel.

JOE WEBER

Defcon One

GraftonBooks
A Division of HarperCollins*Publishers*

GraftonBooks
A Division of HarperCollins*Publishers*
77–85 Fulham Palace Road,
Hammersmith, London W6 8JB

A Grafton UK Paperback Original 1991

ISBN 0-586-20982-4

Printed and bound in Great Britain by
Collins, Glasgow

Set in Times

As the tree is fertilized by its own broken branches and fallen leaves, and grows out of its own decay, so men and nations are bettered and improved by trial, and refined out of broken hopes and blighted expectations.

– F. W. Robertson

Acknowledgments

I am especially indebted to my wife, Jeannie, who has supported my effort with patience and constructive criticism.

A special thanks to Bob Kane, of Presidio Press, who gave an unknown author an opportunity to become published.

My sincere gratitude goes to Presidio Press Editor Adele Horwitz, who worked tirelessly to assist me in my efforts.

DEFENCE READINESS CONDITION
(DEFCON)

DEFCON Five – normal peacetime activities.

DEFCON Four – increase intelligence watch and increase security.

DEFCON Three – forces on standby, waiting further orders.

DEFCON Two – forces ready for combat.

DEFCON One – forces deployed for combat.

Prologue

Fouad Baqir al-Sadr watched the Aeroflot Ilyushin-62 accelerate down the runway, then climb gracefully into the gray, overcast sky above Moscow's Sheremetyevo Airport.

The stocky Libyan militiaman glanced quickly around the apartment roof, then raised the weapon to his shoulders. An expert in the use of portable air defense missiles, he braced his feet, steadied himself, and aimed the Russian-built SA-14 missile launcher. He carefully set the element sight on the Soviet transport and immediately heard the high-pitched screech that indicated the weapon was tracking.

'What a beautiful flying machine,' the Libyan lieutenant said to himself, then took a breath and held it while he waited patiently, watching the transport's landing gear disappear into the fuselage. Three seconds later, the militiaman gently squeezed the trigger.

The launcher kicked slightly as the projectile arced away, nosed-over for a split second, then curved skyward toward its unsuspecting prey.

Baqir al-Sadr lowered the launcher, then watched, fascinated, as the lethal missile pursued the climbing jet. The thin wisp of the weapon's exhaust trail blended perfectly into the leaden overcast.

Almost instantly the quiet morning was shattered by a deafening explosion. The lieutenant stared, transfixed, as the huge Aeroflot transport shed an engine, then a wing, and tumbled out of the sky, trailing flaming debris.

The Ilyushin-62 crashed on the perimeter of the airport

in a horrendous fireball, showering nearby traffic in blazing jet fuel.

Lieutenant Baqir al-Sadr turned away from the inferno, smiled, then dropped the missile launcher down a ventilation shaft.

The general secretary had made his last trip. The era of *glasnost* was over.

1

USS *DWIGHT D. EISENHOWER*, North Atlantic –
January

The Nimitz-class carrier plunged through foaming
troughs, sending showers of cold spray over the bow, as
dawn began to light the gray sky.

The constant rolling motion of the mammoth ship sent
torrents of icy seawater pouring through open flight deck
elevator doors. A river of water flowed the length of the
hangar deck, mixing with oil and hydraulic fluid, before
returning to the open sea from the aft elevator platforms.

The aircraft handling crews were having difficulty keeping their footing as they attempted to secure aircraft sent
below at the completion of flight operations.

Lt Cmdr Frank Stevens leaned closer to the radar plot
in the CIC, the Combat Information Center. The Hawkeye early warning aircraft, nicknamed 'Hummer', had
just informed him of unidentified 'bogies' approaching
the battle group.

Frowning, Stevens watched the radar blips approaching
from the northeast on a direct course to the battle group.
He strained harder to focus on the images displayed by
the luminescent scope. The tension was stretching his
nerves. Unidentified, in this region, meant Russian.

CIC, the brains of the 'Ike' during any hostile action,
was a myriad of radar scopes, cathode ray tubes, and see-
through luminescent plotting boards. The room was lit by
soft red light. A group of enlisted men stood behind a
transparent plastic screen, writing backwards with yellow

greasepencils, providing constant updates on the status of aircraft and escort ships. The glowing letters and numerals, seeming to appear by magic, changed continually as various commands checked in with fuel and ordnance reports.

Stevens stared at the glowing scope. The radar repeater cast a sallow, green reflection on his taut face as he pressed his microphone transmission button.

'Stingray, this is Tango Fox,' Stevens radioed the Grumman E-2C Hawkeye.

'Roger, Tango Fox. Stand by,' replied the officer in command of the Hawkeye's airborne tactical data system team.

The 'Miniwacs' Hawkeye, always the first fixed-wing aircraft airborne and the last one to land, had been circling the *Eisenhower* at 24,000 feet for two and a half hours. The big twin-turboprop, with its enormous rotodome, was absolutely critical to the carrier and accompanying battle group.

The Hawkeye's radar provided the capability to detect approaching aircraft and cruise missiles, in addition to surface craft, at ranges up to 260 miles, thus making it difficult for aggressors to penetrate the defenses of the fleet.

Stevens paused, a trickle of perspiration running down the inside of his right arm. 'Navigation, CIC. What is our position?' Stevens requested through the intercom system.

'Sir, our present position is seventy nautical miles due north of Faeroe Island, two hundred ten miles below the Arctic Circle,' replied the navigation watch officer, roused from his paperback by the unexpected request.

Stevens was debating his options when the Hawkeye commander responded.

'Tango Fox, Tango Fox, this is Stingray,' the voice

exploded from the overhead speakers. 'We have confirmation on the bogies. Appears to be two Russian Backfire bombers, bearing zero-two-zero, two hundred forty at angels four-three. They're descending with a fighter escort of three, possibly four, aircraft. Acknowledge.'

'Roger, Stingray,' replied Stevens. 'We're launching Ready CAP One at this time, call sign "Gunfighter" on button seven.'

'Okay, Tango Fox, better have 'em move it out. These guys are closing at the speed of heat!'

The standby combat air patrol (CAP) pilots, Lt Cmdr Doug 'Frogman' Karns, Gunfighter One, and Lt (jg) Steve Hershberger, along with their radar intercept officers (RIOs), reacted swiftly to the urgent blaring of the launch signal in their ready room.

The aircrew ready rooms, directly below the flight deck, were adjacent to the F-14D Tomcat fighter planes poised for launch on the two forward catapults.

Lt Rick Bonicelli, the RIO for Karns, and Lt Cmdr Gordon 'Gator' Kavanaugh scrambled into the rear cockpits of their respective jets and began the demanding task of spinning-up the navigation and armament panels.

As the RIOs worked on the complex weapons systems, Karns and Hershberger were strapping in and starting their twin General Electric turbofans. The new generation engines, collectively producing over fifty-eight thousand pounds of thrust, could power the Grumman multirole fighters past Mach 2 plus – over 1,600 miles per hour.

Each Tomcat was equipped with six advanced air-to-air missiles, along with a 20-mm M61 Vulcan cannon for hosing-down targets at close range.

'Launch the CAP! Launch the CAP!' the hollow voice reverberated over the flight deck.

'Jesus, Bone, why didn't we go to medical school like

13

normal people?' Karns laughed over the intercom (ICS) to Bonicelli. 'Canopy coming down.'

'Yeah, Froggy, this is another fine mess you've gotten us into,' responded Bonicelli with a nervous laugh. 'I've got a bulletin for you, Frog. Our radar isn't comin' up.'

'Figures. Only works when we don't need it,' replied Karns in his usual, relaxed manner. 'If it goes tits up, Bone, we'll pass the lead to Hersh and go visual.'

'Rog.'

The sophisticated AWG-9 weapons control system in the Tomcat, augmented by the supersensitive radar, could detect and count engine turbine fan blades in approaching aircraft at a range of over a hundred miles.

'You up, Two?' Karns called over the radio to Hershberger, flying Gunfighter Two.

'Oh yeah, Frog, we're go.' Hershberger glanced at the forbidding sky and angry sea. 'Beautiful day for flying.'

The fighter pilots and their RIOs, racing to get airborne, had no idea who or what the adversary might be. Their mission was to 'scramble' off the carrier as quickly as possible, then confront the unknown gomers. The anxiety level was high and the aircrews tried to dispel their apprehension with light banter.

The Ike was straining and groaning in the turbulent ocean to maintain a twenty-seven-knot speed into the wind. The fighters had to take off and land into the wind, as they would from a shore-base runway, and the carrier steamed as fast as possible to assist the aircraft in getting airborne.

The enormous collisions between ship and thirty-foot ocean swells sent cold spray raining down on the F-14 canopies, obscuring the pilots' vision in the semidawn and low cloud cover. The flying conditions were abominable.

The yellow-shirted catapult officer signaled for the

deck-edge operator to take tension on the F-14 piloted by Karns. At the same time a green light from PRI-FLY, the control tower of the carrier, indicated clearance to launch the two fighters.

'You ready, Bone?' Karns asked as he advanced the twin throttles to military power, then into afterburner. The aircraft was straining and vibrating under the tremendous thrust of the big GE turbofans.

'Actually, I was really looking forward to breakfast,' Bonicelli responded with a chuckle.

'I s'pose you want me to call room service,' laughed Karns as he snapped off a salute to the cat officer, signifying that his Tomcat was developing full power and ready for launch. The catapult blast deflectors, now raised behind the F-14s, were glowing cherry red from the tremendous heat of the powerful engines.

'Naw, I want – '

The statement abruptly ended as the cat officer leaned forward and touched the flight deck, sending a signal to the deck-edge operator, who pressed the launch button.

The Tomcat, engulfed in swirling clouds of superheated steam, exploded down the catapult track in a thundering roar.

Helmets pressed back into head restraints. Breathing was impossible, even with masks supplying 100 percent oxygen. Eyeballs flattened, causing momentary tunnel vision and a graying-out effect. The excruciating G-forces rendered the crew semi-conscious during the violent launch.

The catapult stroke hurled the 70,000-pound fighter plane from zero to 170 miles per hour in two and a half seconds. The sensation was impossible to imagine without experiencing it firsthand.

'Good shot,' Karns said, snapping the landing gear

handle up. His breathing and pulse rates were returning to normal.

'Are we still alive?' Bonicelli asked, happy to have lived through another launch in abysmal weather conditions.

The Tomcat continued to accelerate in afterburner as Bonicelli looked back over his left shoulder. He glimpsed Dash Two accelerating down the catapult.

'I've got a visual on Hersh – off the cat, closing,' reported Bonicelli, as Karns cleaned up the Tomcat and swept back the variable-geometry wings.

'Okay, Gunfighters, let's go button seven and talk with the saucer,' Karns said into his radio as his wingman smoothly slid into a loose parade formation.

'Two,' replied Hershberger in the abbreviated style the fighter jocks had developed during the Korean conflict.

'Stingray, Gunfighter One up, flight of two, six missiles each, state seventeen point two,' Karns said as he advanced the throttles to continue the climb now that his wingman was aboard.

'Roger, Gunfighter. Initial heading zero-two-two at one hundred ninety-five. Bogies descending out of angels three-eight and indicating four hundred sixty knots.'

'Okay, Stingray, we're outa' twenty-one and a half. Stand by one.

'You got anything on the radar?' Karns queried Bonicelli, hoping the gremlins had vanished from the intricate black boxes required to see the enemy at long range.

'Sorry, boss. The tube is down for the count,' Bonicelli replied, thinking about all the imbroglios the flight crews had gone through with avionic technicians.

'Hersh, you and Gator have a lock?' Karns urgently asked.

'That's affirm, Frog. Want us to take the lead?' replied

Hershberger, realizing the flight would rendezvous with the Soviet aircraft in eight minutes.

'Yeah, Hersh, take the lead and let's go combat spread,' Karns directed, as he passed control of the intercept to the Tomcat with the functioning radar system.

'Stingray, we've switched the lead to Dash Two. Our radar is bogus,' Karns stated with a trace of irritation in his normally relaxed voice.

'Understand, Gunfighter.' The Hawkeye coordinator had a tense, controlled voice. 'Targets at zero-two-four, one hundred ninety, descending out of angels three-four. We confirm two Backfires and a flight of four fighters.'

From the repeater television screen in CIC, Lieutenant Commander Stevens had watched the CAP Tomcats roar off the pitching deck, shrouded in clouds of catapult steam.

Stevens, lifting his phone handset, swiveled in his chair and punched the code to connect him with the commanding officer.

The CO, Capt. Greg Linnemeyer, was exhausted. He had fallen into a deep sleep after a strenuous night supervising air operations.

'Captain,' a groggy voice responded.

'Captain, this is Frank Stevens, the watch officer in CIC. We have a situation developing that I believe you need to be aware of.'

'Alright, Frank,' replied Linnemeyer in a raspy voice, 'what's the problem?'

'Well, sir, we launched the CAP. They are intercepting two Russian Backfire bombers and four escort fighters. We haven't had any conf –'

'Goddamn,' Linnemeyer interrupted tersely, 'go to

general quarters, launch Ready Two CAP, and notify the battle group commander. I'll be in CIC in five minutes.'

Linnemeyer juggled the phone, almost dropping it, as he transferred the receiver to his left ear, the ear not so damaged by years of jet engine noise. 'How far out are the Russian aircraft?'

'Sir, the bogies are . . .' Stevens leaned over to see the latest plot, 'one hundred eighty at zero-two-two, descending from three-three-zer – '

'Move it, Frank!' Linnemeyer brusquely concluded the conversation, slamming the phone receiver down and reaching for his work khakis.

'I've got a tally,' Karns radioed to Hershberger and Kavanaugh. Stingray was also monitoring the frequency.

The F-14s had broken out of the overcast, rain-filled clouds into a bright blue sky blazing with early morning sunlight. Karns could see the Russian aircraft seven miles ahead.

'Looks as if Ivan is angling slightly away from the carrier,' Karns said as the Tomcats rapidly closed the distance between the Soviet and American aircraft.

'I've got the lead,' Karns radioed Hershberger as he resumed command of the flight.

'Rodney,' replied Gunfighter Two, deliberately foregoing the traditional 'Roger'.

'Two, you fall in behind the shooters and we'll take the heavies,' Karns instructed his wingman.

'Good plan, Frog,' responded Hershberger, apprehension straining his voice. 'I'm glad we've got 'em surrounded.'

Gunfighter Two gently moved to a position behind and to the left of the Soviet fighters. Hershberger never took his eyes off the MiGs as his thumb caressed the control stick firing button.

'Just like in the movies,' Kavanaugh said over the ICS to the pilot of Gunfighter Two.

'These Russkies are stubborn,' Karns reported to the *Eisenhower*'s Combat Information Center.

Stevens paused, frowning. 'Gunfighter, Tango Fox, say again.' The CIC officer, noticing his palms were wet, waited for a reply from the CAP pilots.

'Ahh, we joined on the inside and they keep turning into us. It's barely discernible, a degree or two at a time,' Karns replied as he quickly looked over at the Soviet aircraft. 'This isn't their normal style. With four shooters tagging along, this could turn into a real furball.'

The F-14 flown by Karns and Bonicelli inched closer to the huge, menacing bombers as Karns felt a warm, damp sensation spreading across his forehead under the padded helmet liner.

'Bone, I think these guys are serious,' the pilot said to his radar intercept officer.

'No shit!'

'Okay, Gunfighters, check switches safe,' Karns radioed his wingman. 'Can't afford a screwup and trigger an international flap.'

'Yeah,' Bonicelli replied over the intercom, 'let alone get our asses smoked.'

'Two's safe,' responded Hershberger as he slowly drifted back and forth behind the four MiG-29 fighters, NATO codenamed Fulcrum.

The Russians had begun deployment of the Mach 2 Mikoyan-Gurevich-29 advanced fighters in 1985 and by 1990 the Fulcrum, along with the newest MiG-31 Foxhound, were formidable opponents for the American pilots and their fighter-interceptors.

The new generation Russian fighters, and their highly

trained pilots, were a serious concern at 'Top Gun' and 'Red Flag' fighter weapons schools.

TUPOLEV Tu-26 'BACKFIRE' BOMBER

Col Istvan I. Torgovnik nervously watched the American fighter plane off his left wing as he deftly used his flight controls to swing the Backfire bomber slowly toward the American fleet.

'Ah, Comrade Colonel, you appear tentative. We must remember our orders from Air Marshal Khatchadovrian.' The small man with the large, scraggly mustache leaned closer to the pilot as he spoke.

'Do not worry. The inept Americans will not interfere,' boasted Maj. Fulvio Fedorovich Vladyka, the political officer assigned to this sensitive mission.

'An assumption, Fulvio Fedorovich,' replied the command pilot. 'We have never tested the Americans in this manner. We cannot guess their response.'

Torgovnik watched the major out of the corner of his eye, testing his own convictions. The political officer did not respond.

'This action, Comrade Major, is not within our defined operating doctrine. In addition,' continued Torgovnik, thinking about the implications of his actions as reported by this insubordinate and thoroughly disgusting *zampolit*, 'I have the responsibility for our six aircraft and these superior aircrews to think – '

'You will remember, Comrade Colonel, it is I who have responsibility for the success of this mission. You will obey the orders to probe the American defensive reactions.'

Torgovnik inwardly flinched, despising Vladyka for

20

talking down to him in front of his crew. The offensive little political officer went on in his deriding manner.

'Besides, Comrade Colonel, this operation, if successfully conducted, could see you achieve general officer status. Perhaps your own car and a dacha near your operational sector.'

'Yes, Fulvio Fedorovich, I realize the significance of this task,' replied Torgovnik, thinking about the onerous situation that would develop if he was deemed responsible for botching the operation. Besides, Torgovnik smiled, when I am a general offficer, I will crush this impudent bastard.

Captain Linnemeyer rushed into CIC, slightly disheveled, and requested a cup of coffee.

'What's the current status?' the captain asked the distraught CIC officer.

'The CAP has rendezvoused with the Soviet aircraft. They are approaching the one hundred-ten-mile mark, sir,' responded Stevens.

'The Ready Two CAP is airborne, closing on . . . should be joining Cap One in two minutes,' he added nervously. 'Also, sir, we have a tanker airborne and a spare Viking on the number one cat. Two more Fourteens are ready.'

Stevens paused to look at his status boards. 'The escort ships are closing in, sir. No sub activity detected at this time.'

'Sounds good,' Linnemeyer replied, sipping the scalding coffee, while he observed that all hands were at their respective battle stations.

The CO, a qualified naval aviator, had come up the hard way. A former enlisted man, Linnemeyer left the Navy after his initial hitch and returned to college. After

21

graduating summa cum laude from Northwestern University, the short, wiry, twenty-five-year-old placed his hard-earned business degree on the shelf and returned to the Navy.

Rear Adm. Donald S. G. McKenna, the task force commander, embarked aboard the Ike, had been awakened by the general quarters alarm and was now in Flag Plot. A steady stream of information was being digested by the carrier's skipper and McKenna.

'Ivan is setting a new precedent,' Admiral McKenna said to Captain Linnemeyer as a steward knocked quietly on the door, then entered the spacious staff cabin reserved for the battle group commander.

'Greg, they are obviously trying to provoke us, test our defenses and reactions. I'll get off a Flash Message to the commander-in-chief of the Atlantic Fleet and the NATO commander. We don't have a lot of time.'

The admiral paused, waiting for a response.

'You agree, Greg?'

'Yes, sir,' replied the skipper of the Ike, 'but we'd better show some resolve if they break fifty miles.'

'I concur. How do you think CINCLANT will respond?' the admiral asked.

'Order us to fire a warning shot. Shoot a missile in front of the lead bomber at fifty nautical miles, and, if they don't break off by thirty, to blow their asses out of the sky,' Linnemeyer responded in a dry, matter-of-fact statement, void of any emotion.

'I hope so. We simply can not, should not, knuckle under to those arrogant bastards. Alert CIC,' the admiral directed as he reached for the phone to send an instant Flash Message to his superiors.

* * *

The Russian Tu-26 Backfire bombers continued to turn into the carrier slowly, a degree at a time. The tension was beginning to have an impact in the cockpits of Gunfighter One and Two. If the Soviet bombers, or their escort fighters, made any overt move, the Fox-Fourteen jockeys had no recourse. They had to wait for confirmation to destroy the invading aircraft, and, as the pilots knew, the order to kill could arrive too late.

This was not a routine, unescorted, flyover by a lone Bear bomber. This was an entirely new approach. A potential disaster in need of revised rules.

Gunfighter One was experiencing difficulty maintaining position on the Russian bombers. The flight of eight aircraft, bouncing around in turbulent air, had descended through a dense cloud cover. The weather conditions made formation flying difficult.

'Let's spread out a little,' Karns radioed.

'Two,' replied Hershberger, as he drifted back another twenty yards behind the MiGs.

'They're closing on our landing platform,' Karns said to his RIO, 'and I don't like it.'

'I read you,' responded Bonicelli. 'That water looks colder every time I think about this gaggle.'

The backseater looked closely at the Russian bomber. 'Let's move in a little closer and I'll "moon" the bastards.'

'Right,' Karns replied with a laugh. 'Why don't you snap a few photos for our State Department people. This should be a real icebreaker on the cocktail circuit.'

Karns gently banked his Tomcat into the Soviet aircraft as Bonicelli shot a dozen pictures of the menacing warplanes approaching the American battle group.

McKenna turned to the Ike's skipper. 'Greg, who is the pilot in Gunfighter One?'

'Lieutenant Commander Doug Karns, sir. One of our

23

best pilots and very experienced. He is the XO of One-forty-two and a fighter weapons grad,' replied Linnemeyer.

'Very good,' Admiral McKenna responded. 'A Top Gun alumnus from the "Ghostriders".'

'We may have to place him in an awkward position, Greg,' the admiral continued as he glanced down at the activity on the busy flight deck.

'Comrade Colonel, now is the time to execute our penetration of the American fleet,' Major Vladyka urged from the cramped seat behind the command pilot.

'Yes, I agree, Fulvio Fedorovich,' Colonel Torgovnik replied tentatively. 'We are inside one hundred kilometers from the carrier battle group. We must commit if this operation is to be successful.'

Torgovnik tried to sound and appear very much the party man and professional soldier to the political officer seated next to his ear, but the command pilot was confused about the sudden change in Soviet military doctrine. Kremlin policy, under *glasnost* and *perestroika*, asserted that military posture would be 'defensive' in character.

Force levels had been maintained at a 'reasonable sufficiency'. Why, Torgovnik thought, after the shocking change in party leadership, were they probing the Americans? Was it simply *pokazuka*, confronting US forces for show?

The Soviet bomber pilot looked at his solemn copilot, then keyed his microphone. 'Prepare to alter course.'

As Karns concentrated on maintaining position on the Soviet bombers, Animals One and Two, the Ready Two CAP, joined on Hershberger's F-14D.

'Gunfighter lead, Animal Flight is aboard and the

Texaco is airborne, two-three-zero for one ten, angels two-six. We have a full bag. Looks like you have 'em cornered,' Capt. Vince Cangemi, United States Marine Corps, checked in with Karns.

Cangemi, an exchange pilot, was spending a tour in a Navy fighter squadron, ostensibly to show the 'squids' how to fly. He was flying lead in a second flight of Tomcats. The Marine fighter pilot, who normally flew the potent F/A-18 Hornet, enjoyed flying the big Grumman Tomcat. The F-14 had been a new challenge for him.

'Rog, Animal. Glad the cavalry could make it,' Karns chuckled, recognizing the call sign of Cangemi. 'Thought you "jar-heads" were s'posed to be the first to fight.'

The marine started to respond, then changed his mind as he focused on the Soviet aircraft.

'Back off about three hundred yards and confirm guns off, switches safe,' Karns instructed the Animals.

'That's affirm, off and safe,' Cangemi answered.

'Two,' Lt Tom Chaffee, USN, responded.

At that precise moment, the Russian bombers abruptly turned into the American fighters, forcing Karns to spiral inward or risk collision. Reacting with remarkable dexterity, Karns simultaneously rolled his fighter away from the bombers and radioed CIC.

'Tango Fox, Tango Fox, Gunfighter One! These crazy sons-a-bitches are makin' a run at the battle group,' Karns shouted into his mask microphone. 'I need permission to fire! Repeat, I need permission to splash 'em.'

'Roger, Gunfighter. Stand by,' the distant voice responded through Karns's padded earphones.

Karns waited uncomfortably for a response to his urgent request, visualizing the odd group of individuals in the decision-making process.

'Guess the operator put us on ignore,' Bonicelli said over the intercom, breathing more rapidly than normal.

'Gunfighter, Tango Fox,' the staccato voice blurted. 'You have permission to fire a warning shot at fifty DME. I repeat, you have permission to fire a Sidewinder in front of the bombers.

'If the Russians break thirty miles, shoot 'em down. Do you copy?' Linnemeyer asked.

'Roger, Tango Fox. Copy warning shot and plug 'em if they break thirty, three-zero from mother,' Karns replied with a strange mixture of relief and adrenaline-pumping emotion.

'That's affirm, Gunfighter,' the captain replied. 'Let me know when you fire.'

'Wilco, Tango Fox,' Karns responded. 'Okay, Hersh, you ease back on Animal's wing. You guys be in position to take these clowns out if they stuff one up our ass.'

Karns waited tensely for Hershberger and Animal Flight to reposition themselves. The Tomcats slowly drifted behind the Russian formation.

'Animals in place,' Cangemi stated. 'Okay, guys, looks like this is the main event. Let's go master arm on and ease back a tad.'

Cangemi slowly dropped back into a good firing position – low and looking at the tailpipes of the Russian fighter planes. Feeling a tightness in his throat, Cangemi took a quick look at his instrument panel, then concentrated on the MiG flight leader.

'Gun One is movin' up under uncle Ivan's left wing. I want the friggin' son of a bitch to see me. These idiots can't be very bright,' Karns radioed CIC and his fellow pilots as he inched the throttles forward, moving under and forward of the left wing of the behemoth.

Karns noted the bright red star painted on the huge jet intake as he jockeyed his Tomcat into view of the Russian pilot.

The fighter pilot had never been so close to any Russian

bomber, let alone a Backfire. It was colossal in size. The bomber weighed 270,000 pounds and stretched 130 feet. Its size alone was intimidating, without considering the tremendous firepower it possessed.

'Okay, comradski, look over here,' Karns said, speaking softly over the radio. 'Come on, you son-of-a-bitch, I don't want to fire any hot lead.'

'Yeah,' Cangemi agreed. 'If we get wrapped around the axle this close in, it'll be a knife fight in a telephone booth.'

Torgovnik glanced briefly at the American fighter plane, wincing at the proximity of the crazy American. The bomber commander judged the Navy fighter plane to be no more than twenty meters from his craft. Keeping his head straight forward, Torgovnik formulated his thoughts as he kept the Tomcat in his periphery.

'Comrade Major,' Torgovnik said quietly, his mind sounding a warning about the danger of this clearly provocative confrontation. 'These Americans . . . we are pushing too hard. Remember what they did to the Libyans.'

'Nonsense,' replied Vladyka, in his familiar conciliatory manner.

'You overestimate the Americans. They will not risk a confrontation unless we openly provoke them,' continued the ingratiating political officer, firmly entrenched in his belief of American conformity to nonaggressive acts.

'I am not so sure, Major,' Torgovnik replied in a hesitant manner. 'We have not attempted to fly a multiaircraft group over an American carrier before.'

Vladyka smiled his most condescending smile. 'Do not worry, Colonel.'

* * *

27

'Aw-right, goddamn it!' Karns said with marked vehemence as his Distance Measuring Equipment (DME) indicated fifty nautical miles from the *Eisenhower*.

'I'm movin' out to the side. Everything is cookin' and looks good. Here we go,' Karns stated as he gently pressed the right rudder and squeezed the firing button.

The F-14 shuddered as the AIM-9M Sidewinder heat-seeking missile flashed from under the right wing, accelerating with startling speed. The missile tracked squarely in front of the lead bomber's cockpit, crossing left to right at a twenty-degree angle, spewing red-orange flame and trailing a shroud of billowing white smoke.

'Fox Two!' Karns yelled as he reduced power and rapidly dropped astern, glancing back to see what action the Russian fighters would take, if any.

The MiG-29s immediately moved closer to the bombers. The MiG flight leader was bouncing all over the sky – in and out of burner – a million synapses taking place as his charges settled down from the shock.

'That was a tad close, old chap,' Cangemi said with a trace of anxiety in his voice.

The lead Russian bomber began a shallow turn to the right as the Backfires flew through the plume of white smoke generated by the air-to-air missile.

'Perhaps so,' Karns replied, nerves keyed in anticipation of a retaliatory action. 'It appears as if Ivan got the message, the dense bastards.'

'Just another fun day at the office,' Hershberger chimed in as he closed on his flight leader.

The six Soviet warplanes slowly turned in the direction of the Barents Sea, as the four Tomcats escorted the intruders away from the battle group. The Russians would return to their base at Olenegorsk, near Murmansk, on Kola Peninsula.

Captain Linnemeyer heard the radio transmissions

from Gunfighter One and began to breathe quietly. He raised his microphone, paused a moment, then spoke to the pilots.

'Nice work,' the CO said to the pilots and RIOs, a smile spreading across his unshaven face. 'Stay with them until the two-hundred mark and RTB.'

'Rog, two hundred and return to base,' Karns acknowledged as the F-14s slowly drifted into combat spread one mile astern of the withdrawing Russian aircraft.

Linnemeyer turned toward Admiral McKenna, who had joined him in CIC only moments before, and gave a thumbs up signal.

'Good job, Captain,' McKenna said. 'How about joining me for breakfast?'

Linnemeyer smiled. 'Yessir.'

'Well, Comrade Major Vladyka,' Torgovnik said in a controlled and barely audible voice, 'that should dispel the myth of American nonconfrontational behav – '

'It is not a myth, Comrade. We have well-researched intelligence from reliable sources,' Vladyka blurted in a voice two octaves higher than normal.

The *zampolit* was trying to digest the unexpected missile encounter.

'I assure you, Colonel Torgovnik, the Americans will be tested to the limit in the forthcoming days.'

Torgovnik and his copilot exchanged concerned looks but didn't reply.

The CO and Admiral McKenna were just sitting down in the Flag Bridge, about to enjoy breakfast and discuss the recent Soviet encounter, when an aide discreetly informed the two officers of the impending recovery of the Tomcats.

'Great,' Admiral McKenna said to the lieutenant. 'Greg, what say we step outside and watch them land?'

'Yessir. Helluva job this morning,' replied Linnemeyer.

The Tomcats, joined in a flight of four, passed off the starboard side of the ship at 400 knots as they approached the break.

Both men, smiling to themselves, noticed the F-14s were in perfect formation. The morning sun, creeping through the ragged rain clouds, glinted off the canopies.

'Nice,' McKenna remarked.

'I can't believe Frog found the boat again,' Cangemi chided the flight leader, Karns.

Everyone respected Karns and liked his sense of humor. Although he was an excellent aviator, his friends still enjoyed kidding him about the time when he was still a lieutenant (junior grade) and he screwed up a terrain reconnaissance mission off the USS *Coral Sea*, missed the rendezvous point with the 'boat', ran out of fuel, and ditched five miles astern of the carrier.

Thus, 'Frogman' became his nickname as a nugget pilot in the fleet. His trip to Fighter Town USA, Top Gun School, had earned him the call sign 'Gunfighter'.

'You marines never change,' Karns replied to Cangemi, 'years and years of tradition, unhampered by progress.

'Gun One, four for the break,' Karns radioed PRI-FLY, the carrier's control tower.

'Cleared for the break, Guns,' responded the assistant air boss. 'Good show.'

Karns slapped the Tomcat's control stick hard left, pulling 4.5-Gs, as he eased back on the twin throttles and swept the wings forward for landing.

Each succeeding F-14 snapped into a 'fangs-out' knife-edge break at four-second intervals – a beautiful display

30

of precision flying by some of the best-trained pilots in the world.

'Well, Animal, think you can get that beauty aboard in one piece?' Karns laughed over the radio as he started his descent out of 800 feet and turned toward the carrier.

'Oh yeah, if you don't foul the deck with your wreckage,' responded Cangemi, laughter in his voice.

'Tomcat, ball, three point seven,' Karns radioed the landing signal officer as he rechecked gear down, flaps down, and tailhook down.

The mandatory radio call informed the LSO of the approaching aircraft type, whether the pilot spotted the bright yellow 'ball' of light reflected in the Fresnel lens (the primary visual aid to assist the pilot in maintaining the proper glide path/descent rate) and the fuel state of the aircraft. Fuel was always a critical item during inclement weather and night landings. A missed 'trap', resulting in a go-around, could cost a pilot hundreds of pounds of the precious jet fuel and reduce his options dramatically.

The LSO would monitor each approach, offer advice if things went awry, and, if need be, wave off a pilot if his approach got completely out of shape.

'Roger, ball, keep it comin',' the LSO said to Karns, a fellow squadron pilot and close friend.

'Hang on, Bone,' Karns said to his RIO as the Tomcat whistled over the round-down of the carrier at 140 miles per hour.

'I'll never get used to this . . .' replied Bonicelli as the F-14 slammed onto the flight deck and stopped in less than 250 feet. Karns moved the throttles to military power at the moment of touchdown, in case the tailhook skipped the arresting wires. A missed wire would necessitate a go-around, a 'bolter' in naval aviation terminology.

A trap aboard an aircraft carrier was so nerve-racking and violent that many pilots compared the experience to having a fantastic sexual encounter and a car wreck simultaneously.

As the last fighter hit the deck and screeched to a halt, the Ike started a turn toward a northwesterly heading.

'Well, Greg, how about breakfast, before it gets too cold?' Admiral McKenna asked Linnemeyer.

'Sure, I'm famished,' the CO responded, knowing he needed a shave and shower. 'Short night.'

As Linnemeyer and McKenna sat down to the fresh pineapple, ham, eggs, and toast, the CIC discreet phone rang.

Linnemeyer watched as the admiral answered the phone, listened a moment, frowned, and said, 'I'll be there in a minute.'

The admiral looked at Linnemeyer. 'Damnit, Greg. The Viking has picked up two subs, both with Russian signatures. One is twelve miles off our port bow, and the other one is seven miles astern.'

McKenna stood up, tossed his napkin on the table, then reached for his cover. 'Let's go back to general quarters and find out what the hell is going on out here.'

The admiral's Irish temper was beginning to flare.

2

MOSCOW

Large snowflakes, mixed with freezing rain, floated gently down and enshrouded the street lamps in ice-fog as darkness settled over the city.

The new party general secretary had called a plenary session of the Central Committee to establish his authority and set priorities. At least the colloquy, on the outside, would appear to accomplish those objectives.

Soviet society, from the ruling hierarchy to the impoverished peasants in remote regions, had suffered years of economic, political and social deprivation.

The general secretary, along with the eleven members of the Politicheskoye Buro, desperately wanted to regain the favor of the Central Committee and the eighteen million members of the Communist party. The new ruler and his Politburo needed the support of their depressed society. The hierarchy needed the support of the masses and the general secretary was ready to placate the Russian people in any way possible. He needed time for his scheme to come to fruition.

The new leader, and a few select Politburo members, had arranged a grazing party for 302 leading representatives of the Central Committee. A few elderly members were unable to attend the festivities because of poor health – the only plausible excuse for not attending a plenum called by the general secretary.

The idea of the grazing party, a Russian cultural tradition, was to soothe feelings, loosen talk, and foster an atmosphere of comradeship between the men of the Central Committee. Many relationships had been strained over the past four years and an opportunity to have fun, relax, and enjoy an evening of frivolity would help renew old friendships and heal damaged pride. Tomorrow would be soon enough to discuss serious matters. This was a night of revelry for the communist leaders.

The main dining room and adjoining bar in the Great Building were cavernous and could easily accommodate the Politburo and Central Committee contingent.

An ornate interior, nineteenth century furnishings, and a warm fireplace at each end of the massive dining room, promoted a convivial feeling in contrast to the snow piled high outside and the temperature registering minus eighteen degrees centigrade.

Zakuska was spread on the vast tables. The array consisted of sliced beef vinaigrette, piroshki, button mushrooms in spicy marinade, pelmeni, smoked fish, stuffed cabbage, pickled herring, dark bread, caviar, and Stolichnaya vodka.

The bar was crowded as the Central Committee members congregated to talk about old times and the promise of the Party's future. The evening was progressing very smoothly.

Three members of the Politburo, greeting old acquaintances at the bar, discreetly caught the eye of the new general secretary. The four men exchanged a brief smile.

They had every reason for celebration. The new leader, ousted from the Politburo in 1988 for being combative and unyielding, had returned to power with a flourish.

WASHINGTON, D.C.

The former chief of naval operations, Adm. Edward Robinson Chambers, set the *Washington Post* on the edge of his seat and reached for his leather briefcase. The navy blue limousine braked evenly and slowed to a smooth stop at the entrance to the JCS headquarters in the imposing Pentagon Building.

Admiral Chambers, chairman of the Joint Chiefs of Staff, was of medium height and weight with a trace of a limp. The limp resulted from injuries sustained in a crash landing aboard the carrier *Midway* after a tough sortie over Vietnam.

Chambers kept his light gray hair trimmed short and wore distinguished tortoiseshell-frame glasses to correct the near vision in his hazel eyes.

'Good morning, Admiral,' Capt. Mike Trenton, the admiral's aide, greeted Chambers.

'What the devil do you make of all this, Mike?' the admiral asked as the captain took the briefcase in hand, thinking it unusual for the genial admiral not to respond to a greeting.

'Sir, the information we have, as of thirty minutes ago, indicates a full-court press by the Soviets,' Trenton replied. 'Sorry to awaken you so early, Admiral, but CINCLANT was absolutely insistent.'

'No problem, Mike. Are the other members on their way?'

'Yes, sir,' Trenton paused, 'with the exception of General Hollingsworth. He is on an inspection tour of Camp Pendleton and should be here in approximately three hours.'

'How is General Seecroft?' Chambers asked, referring to the assistant chairman of the Joint Chiefs of Staff, Army General 'Mick' Seecroft.

'He is mending rapidly, Admiral,' Trenton responded, switching the briefcase to his other hand. 'I talked with the general yesterday, and he assured me that his career as an equestrian is over. Something spooked the horse and it tossed the general onto a tree stump.'

Chambers chuckled. 'Bet I know where we could pick up a good Appaloosa for a song.'

'No doubt.'

Trenton, a tall, thin, red-haired submariner, had been an aide to the admiral for seven months. This assignment, though unexciting to the former sub skipper, was necessary to his career development. He genuinely liked the friendly chairman and had grown used to his quirks.

'Has the president been notified?' Chambers asked as he passed through the door being held open by Trenton.

'He is aware of some unusual events, but not the particulars, sir. The chief of staff has requested, on behalf of the president, a full briefing as soon as the Joint Chiefs convene.'

'Okay, Mike,' the admiral responded, thinking about the simplicity of life twenty-four hours ago. Chambers and his wife, Mariam, had entertained old friends from the Naval Academy with a champagne brunch.

THE KREMLIN

'Good morning, comrades,' General Secretary Viktor Pavlovich Zhilinkhov addressed the Central Committee members.

'It is a pleasure to be with you again. I trust everyone enjoyed the activities of last evening,' the general secretary continued, a warm smile spreading across his craggy face.

A murmur spread throughout the vast meeting hall.

Smiles and soft laughter rose from the contingent of party members as everyone thought about the previous boisterous evening. Formulating a thought, for some red-eyed attendees, was a difficult task at this early hour.

The Central Committee, joined by the Politburo members, had been served a sumptuous breakfast of eggs, beef, pork, dark bread, gravy, and steaming coffee, strong and rich in flavor.

Now it was time to grapple with the multitude of problems facing the Motherland and her leaders. It was time, as Zhilinkhov had stated so vociferously the previous evening, for a return to hard-line Marxist-Leninist orientation. The Gorbachev Doctrine had not strengthened the Soviet economy or restructured Russian society.

The Reagan Doctrine, providing support for anticommunist guerrillas in the far-reaching Soviet empire, had pressured the former general secretary into capitulation on many fronts. The Soviet Union, during the late eighties and early nineties, had been forced to retreat from Afghanistan, Cambodia, Angola, and Nicaragua.

The present American administration, to Soviet consternation, had kept the pressure concentrated on Russian outposts of communism. The ensuing political confrontations in the Politburo had led to the demise of the previous general secretary. Zhilinkhov had been one of the chief conspirators who had planned the transfer of power.

'We have much to accomplish, my fellow countrymen,' Zhilinkhov smiled again. 'I have important news for you. News that will change our country for the better. News that will revolutionize our Motherland.'

THE PENTAGON

The Joint Chiefs, with the exception of Marine General Hollingsworth, sat down and opened the hastily prepared briefing folders.

Soft light fell on the conference table from overhead fixtures. The room was totally void of noise or movement as the service chiefs reviewed the situation briefs.

Admiral Chambers spoke first. 'Gentlemen, it would appear the new Russian boss is an expediter. Why, with all their internal troubles, would Zhilinkhov choose to antagonize the US?'

The chairman paused, waiting for a possible explanation from the other chiefs. No offers were extended.

'It is inexplicable, at least to me,' he continued, 'why they would push us so soon. Zhilinkhov has been in power for less than four weeks. One would think, logically, gentlemen, that he needs all the help he can muster, especially from us.'

The chairman slowly shook his head. 'It just doesn't track, at least not in my mind.'

Silence surrounded the massive oak table and gleaming furnishings.

Gen. Forrest Milton Ridenour III, United States Air Force chief of staff, always a listener, broke the silence.

'I believe the good comrade is trying to muscle us into a position of capitulation through confrontation. The Soviets are totally perplexed, in regard to SDI, and now our Stealth bomber is coming on line. Zhilinkhov needs to make his mark soon. His country is progressively decaying.'

Ridenour allowed his words to have an impact and continued. 'Think about this: Why would they bring back an aging Politburo member, considered too aggressive under the previous regime, to reform the Party?'

The chiefs digested this scenario as the Air Force chief of staff sipped his water and continued.

'The man is in ragged health. Zhilinkhov knows he doesn't have a lot of time. He has to perform. What has he got to lose?

'His reputation and the future of his country, his ideology, is on the line. He must demonstrate to his supporters that he can bring the Americans to the bargaining table, that he can make us, through a thinly veiled threat of war, bow and acquiesce.'

The Air Force general looked around, leaned back in his chair, and continued.

'I believe Zhilinkhov is being manipulated. The Politburo ruling class, the conservative elite, are becoming dinosaurs in a crumbling society. They are becoming desperate. These recent incidents are reminiscent of old-style Soviet tactics.'

Admiral Chambers interrupted in a quiet manner. 'Milt, what do you see as the bottom line?'

Ridenour, looking relaxed, responded. 'I really – it would be pure conjecture to project an absolute.'

The general paused to form his reply. 'I don't know if they, and I emphasize "they", are desperate or deranged. How far would Zhilinkhov push? We don't have any way to gauge.'

Ridenour, seeing Chambers didn't have a question, continued. 'The incidents could continue to escalate to the point where no rationale remains. Desperate people do desperate deeds, as we've seen many times.

'Zhilinkhov has proved to be overly aggressive and reactionary in the past. He openly celebrated the death of President Zia in eighty-eight. Zhilinkhov's display deeply embarrassed the Kremlin.

'That incident and his record of opposing Gorbachev were the fundamental reasons for his removal from the

Politburo during the shake-up. Shortly afterward, as I'm sure all of you will recall, Zhilinkhov publicly criticized Gorbachev for allowing Andrei Sakharov to travel to the United States. So, we can anticipate the worst from the general secretary, in my opinion,' General Ridenour concluded.

'Let me pose a question,' the Army chief of staff, Gen. Warren Kinlaw Vandermeer, said as he leaned over the table. 'Does anyone believe the former general secretary died in a purely accidental crash?'

Vandermeer handed a picture and biography of Zhilinkhov to General Ridenour.

'No,' replied Adm. Martin Grabow, chief of Naval Operations. 'The circumstances are very suspect, what with the short mourning period and the new players in the starting blocks.

'In addition,' the admiral continued, 'there is every indication, according to our operatives, that a ground-launched missile hit the airplane as it lifted off the runway at Sheremetyevo.'

General Ridenour passed Zhilinkhov's biography to Chambers. 'We have a real problem on our hands.'

'I'm afraid you're right, Milt,' Chambers concluded, studying the somber, puffy face of the Soviet president and general secretary.

USS *CARL VINSON*

The Third Fleet carrier and its battle group, recently conducting operations in the Bering Sea north of the Aleutian Islands, had received orders to steam at flank speed toward the Sea of Okhotsk.

The 93,000-ton *Vinson* and her escort ships would join the Seventh Fleet battle group, spearheaded by the carrier USS *Constellation*, to prowl the waters adjacent to Kamchatka Peninsula. The USS *Ranger* and her carrier task force, enjoying a port call to Anchorage, Alaska, were being hurriedly dispatched to replace the *Vinson* in the Bering Sea.

The past thirty-six hours had been marked by significant increases in Soviet air and naval activity near Alaska and the Aleutian Islands, along with an unusual number of Russian submarine deployments from the port of Petropavlovsk-Kamchatski on the Kamchatka Peninsula. The Russian submarine base was the only Soviet seaport with direct, year-round access to the open ocean.

Aboard the *Vinson*, Rear Adm. Thomas R. Brinkman was meeting with his Flag Staff to coordinate the combined efforts of the two battle groups.

'We have seen an alarming and growing threat from the Russian sector in the past four days.' The admiral paused while a color slide of recent Soviet movements was projected on a screen to his left.

'Our intelligence community hasn't come to grips with the actual purpose of this sudden activity; however, we can assume it has to do with the political swing brought about by the untimely death of the former general secretary.'

The portly task force commander glanced at his staff intelligence officer, Capt. Jack Sinclair.

'I believe Jack can give us a better picture of the current situation, at least what we know to be factual at the moment. Jack?'

'The Russians are mobilizing their ground forces in these areas of Eastern bloc countries,' Sinclair paused, pointing to different sections on the slide, 'and they have been moving their fighter air wings to forward operating bases west of the Urals.'

Sinclair placed a different graphic on the projector.

41

'Also, the carrier *Kiev* has left port in the past sixteen hours, presumably to dog the *Eisenhower*. It has a complement of twenty-three Yak-36 "Forgers" on board and three escort ships, two Sovremenny-class missile destroyers, and a guided missile cruiser, the *Slava*. The *Brezhnev* is preparing to get underway from Nikolayev shipyard with a full load of various aircraft.'

Sinclair reached for another slide and continued. 'Every operable sub has left the bases at Polyarnyy and Petropavlovsk-Kamchatski. The waters we are currently traversing are crawling with Russian subs. Intelligence estimates at least twelve Soviet submarines in a three-hundred-mile radius of the Kuril Islands. Satellite reconnaissance confirms seven Russian submarines have ducked under the ice cap from the Beaufort Sea to the Laptev Sea, big boomers.

'This is where we stand at the moment.' Sinclair waited until the other staff officers perused the slide depicting American and NATO movements. It was clear that a major Soviet military buildup was underway.

'What we don't know is the why,' Sinclair continued. 'The general consensus is this: The new regime is sending a strong signal to indicate they want to realign the Soviet and American power base. The Russians apparently believe they can achieve this result through intimidation and military pressure. As you are well aware, the new Soviet government has a basketful of problems, and they haven't had much success at the bargaining table the past few years. The SDI issue had them frothing at the mouth in ninety, and they are aware that our final link to the basic space defense system is about to be launched aboard *Columbia*. Another big rub is the pending deployment of the Stealth bombers. They're already mad as hell about our "no-see-um" fighters.'

42

The intelligence officer set his papers down, removed his glasses, rubbed his eyes, and continued.

'Pressure, gentlemen. The Soviets are under tremendous pressure. The only leverage they have is the strength of their military and, apparently, the newly formed powers believe it is their last recourse. So it's back to MAD, the mutual assured destruction doctrine, before we place them in a position of impotence with the SDI technology,' Sinclair concluded, waiting for questions.

Admiral Brinkman spoke first. 'Jack, do you have any indication the Soviets will actually start, not provoke, but start a skirmish?'

'No, sir. We really don't anticipate that, unless it happens by accident. We're in a holding pattern at the present time, Admiral,' the intelligence officer replied, wishing he had a better answer.

There wasn't any way to predict what the Russians would do, given the desultory circumstances and the character of the new Soviet fugleman and his Politburo. These were ideologically driven people in a very precarious position. The situation could, conceivably, be out of control before anyone could intervene.

CAPE CANAVERAL, FLORIDA

The space shuttle *Columbia*, sitting on Launch Pad 39B, was in the final process of being readied for flight to place the three SDI (Space Defense Initiative) satellites into orbit.

Previous SDI satellites had been deployed in polar orbit from Vandenburg Air Force Base, linking the defensive network in a multilayered lattice. NASA would be in charge of the launch and Space Command would take responsibility once the satellites were operational.

The day and precise time of the scheduled launch were classified Top Secret, as was the sensitive cargo in the three sealed containers aboard the shuttle.

Security was tight at the cape on this cold, blustery day in January.

Rex Hays, Ph.D., was standing at his office window, impeccably tailored, casual in manner, gazing out at the sparkling white space shuttle framed by the aqua blue Atlantic Ocean. He never ceased to be amazed by the grandeur of the space machine built by man.

As the new chief of NASA, Hays, fifty-six, a grandfather and amateur boat builder, exuded confidence and was well-respected by his staff. The astrophysicist was slowly adjusting to his new position at the Kennedy Space Center.

'Dr Hays, you have an urgent call on line two,' the female voice sounded from his phone speaker.

The NASA boss punched line two. 'Dr Hays.'

'Rex, Dave Miller.'

'Morning, Dave,' Hays responded, a flash thought crossing his mind as to the reason David Miller, in the White House Situation Room, would be calling him directly.

'What can I do for you?' Hays was cautious.

'Rex, I'm sure you've been following this Russian push-an'-shove match the past couple of days.' Miller slowed to breathe. He lived under constant stress and was a heavy smoker with the beginning stages of emphysema.

'Yes I have,' Hays answered, an uneasy feeling in his stomach.

'Well, we believe the primary thrust of all this crap is the "Star Wars" dilemma they're facing.' Miller paused again.

'And?' Hays scratched on his desk pad, contemplating a myriad of possibilities for disaster.

'The powers-that-be think the Russians may try to take it out before we –'

'Take what out?' Hays interrupted, thinking about the disdain he had for the unkempt bureaucrat.

'The goddamn shuttle, that's what!' Miller responded with his usual harshness.

'Would you care to elaborate?' Hays asked in a controlled and businesslike manner.

'Intelligence has confirmed three subs, three Russian subs, lyin' off the coast in a direct line with the shuttle trajectory.'

Miller continued when he received no response. 'The closest one is fourteen miles off shore.' Miller coughed twice. 'Our ASW boys are goin' absolutely ape-shit down there.'

Hays queried the excitable White House aide. 'You're telling me the intelligence people believe the Russians may attempt to destroy *Columbia* on the ground, or after the launch?'

'You got it. Even a possibility of covert troops, commandos, from a sub coming ashore and destroying the shuttle and surrounding facilities.' Miller wheezed and continued his scenario. 'Hell, they could be all over the place right now. Could have been picked up by a yacht, everyone in tourist civies, and roaming 'round the cape this very minute.'

'Okay, Dave. What do you propose?' Hays asked as he glanced through his window at *Columbia* and thought about security measures for *Discovery*, *Endeavor*, and *Atlantis*.

'Not much for your folks, Rex. Just be aware, and alert everyone to the possibility of sabotage.' Miller coughed, then continued. 'The Army is going to surround the complex and beef up security at the gates. The Marines are securing the beach, and,' Miller paused, lighting

45

another unfiltered cigarette, 'they will have six Cobra gunships there in – ' Miller checked his watch ' – 'bout forty-five minutes.'

'What about overflights by civilian airplanes?' Hays asked.

'The FAA has been notified. They're issuing a Notice to Airmen immediately. It'll be effective from now until further notice and designates the airspace for twenty miles 'round the launch complex, from the ground to infinity, as a prohibited area.'

'What is the penalty for violating the airspace?' Hays thought about a threat from a passive-looking civilian airplane.

'The message clearly states that any unidentified aircraft, civilian or military, traversing the prohibited airspace will be destroyed.'

'Destroyed by what?'

'I 'magine marine gunships or ground-launched missiles,' Miller responded.

'Sounds as if the president is serious,' Hays remarked, probing the possibility of moving the launch time up a day or two.

'Damn right he is! The Navy is sitting all over the subs and the *Saratoga* is in a hum to leave Norfolk. Should be underway in two or three hours.'

Miller paused, then continued. 'Air Force is sending F-16s from Shaw and Homestead. They'll patrol around the clock and operate out of Patrick and the shuttle emergency runway. Navy F-14s from Jacksonville will rendezvous with the *Saratoga* and provide air cover further out to sea. The Navy boys have a squadron of ASW planes over the subs now.'

Miller paused, then continued. 'Listen, Rex, I gotta' run. The boss just flagged me, so if you have any questions, let me know.'

The NASA chief had many questions regarding the safety of the shuttles, but Miller was not the individual to deal with on this matter.

'Okay, Dave. Appreciate the information,' Hays replied, then placed the phone receiver down.

THE KREMLIN

The general secretary, with assistance from the Politburo, had briefed the Central Committee during the morning session about the difficulties the government had experienced in the previous years.

Zhilinkhov sipped at his strong, hot tea and reflected on Soviet history. Periods of Soviet lenience had always been followed by crackdowns, the only effective way to rule a communist country.

The general secretary thought about the mid-eighties when the new policy of glasnost, or openness, had been installed. The deterioration of the party had been obvious and immediate.

Riots had broken out during 1986 in Alma-Ata, the capital of Kazakhstan, over perestroika, reconstruction. The kazakh who had led the republic's Communist party for more than a generation had been retired and replaced by a Russian. The unfortunate riot caused by that action had been made public and demonstrations erupted over the next five years in many outlying regions.

The open society approach resulted in *Pravda*, the Communist party daily, criticizing the Brezhnev era policies. The paper blamed the former general secretary for sending the country into an economic slump. *Pravda* also charged that favoritism had been rampant during the Brezhnev years.

Zhilinkhov had known that such open reporting would

hurt the Party and the country. He had known also that the information was correct. Leonid's friendship for him had paved the way to his becoming chief of the KGB.

The Party's protracted crisis had worsened with the Chernobyl nuclear reactor disaster in 1986. The horrendous catastrophe had been shown in detail by the media. That incident had been one of the primary reasons the Party had begun to falter. Control of the media had been abolished, leading to further erosion of party authority.

The incident that had irritated the former KGB secret service chief the most had happened in 1987. *Pravda* had publicly rebuked a top KGB officer. The loyal agent, hand-picked years earlier by Zhilinkhov, had been fired as head of the unit in the Ukrainian region of Voroshilovgrad.

The policies of glasnost and perestroika had hit party ministers and members of the Politburo very hard.

Zhilinkhov remembered that his Politburo friend, Boris Dichenkovko, had come very close to forced resignation in 1987 for questioning glasnost.

The general secretary looked at his watch. He had twelve minutes left of his solitary lunch break before addressing the Central Committee again.

Zhilinkhov thought about the serious decline of production levels in the late eighties and early nineties. Economic growth had withered, which resulted in shortages of many consumer items, including clothing, shoes, watches, glassware, television sets, washing machines, refrigerators, cars, and motorcycles.

During the same period of economic stagnation and associated political unrest, more stinging attacks had been directed at the former Kremlin leaders, including Brezhnev and Nikita Khrushchev, from state-run periodicals. The articles had been very demoralizing for Soviet leaders and government officialdom.

However, Zhilinkhov, along with his contemporaries in the Politburo, had known in their hearts that it was typical for the Kremlin leadership to denounce its predecessors. Khrushchev had attacked Stalin in 1956, three years after Stalin's death, and his friend Leonid had denounced Khrushchev after he was ousted in 1964.

The real blow to Zhilinkhov had been his dismissal from the Politburo in September 1988, along with Dichenkovko and two other members who were close stalwarts from the Brezhnev era. The four men, all hardliners, had lived with the stinging embarrassment for many months.

Zhilinkhov had retaliated by publicly criticizing Gorbachev's decision to allow Andrei Sakharov to visit the United States. The Nobel laureate had told Western reporters that Gorbachev's political and economic restructuring faced solid domestic opposition that would endanger world peace. Sakharov warned that perestroika and glasnost could result in an extremely dangerous Gorbachev dictatorship.

The Western press had reported that Gorbachev had tried to rejuvenate the Communist party system, and renovate a government, without reforming it. The editorials had predicted that the authoritarian Communist system, lacking momentum and zeal, would slowly degenerate.

Then, during Gorbachev's trip to the United States in December 1988, the Armenian earthquake overshadowed the general secretary's announcement of Soviet troop reductions in Europe. Rushing to Leninakan, Armenia, Gorbachev found total confusion in the Russian rescue and relief efforts. High-level Soviet officials, aided by the media, lambasted the general secretary and his efforts at restructuring. The disorderly earthquake rescue effort, the critics said, was another example of a faltering government.

Gorbachev, beleaguered and harshly defensive, fired back at his critics during January 1989. He alluded to strong political resistance from leaders at the pinnacle of power, and downplayed calls for a return to the authoritarian style of Stalin.

The most alarming aspect of Soviet economic problems had been the unbelievable drop in oil production in 1990. The flow from the rich Tyumen fields of western Siberia had declined eighteen percent from the previous year. The loss in production had had a staggering effect on the country and the military in particular.

The oil minister, Yevgeny F. Sveridoskiy, a solid party member, had been fired and sent into exile, as reported by TASS. Zhilinkhov recalled, however, that Sveridoskiy had never been seen again by family or friends.

The Russian economy, exploited with ruthless means by the military hierarchy for three decades, had turned on its leaders. The perestroika facade had crumpled as waves of protesters rioted throughout major industrial sectors in 1991. The Soviet image of a dynamic, prosperous work force had become a national embarrassment.

The political meddling had escalated to finger-pointing and shouted insults among Politburo members. Longtime political friends wouldn't speak to each other in social settings.

Party hard-liners had demanded a return to basic communist principles. The Politburo, feeling a total loss of control, had split into two factions.

Zhilinkhov recalled the evening he had contacted his Politburo friend, Boris Dichenkovko. That night the two of them had formed the 'inner circle'.

Zhilinkhov and Dichenkovko had invited three current

Politburo members, who openly resisted the former general secretary, to join them in a bold coup d'état.

The three newcomers to the circle had been bolstered by the zeal of Zhilinkhov and Dichenkovko. Their passion had grown as Zhilinkhov outlined the detailed plan in a lengthy secret meeting.

An 'accident' had been arranged to kill the former general secretary. A Libyan militiaman, expert in the use of portable air-defense missiles, had used a Soviet SA-14 to down the Russian transport carrying the Kremlin chief. The recruited Libyan had been murdered less than thirty minutes after the crash by a Dichenkovko loyalist.

The three current Politburo members had acted swiftly to align the other eight members behind Zhilinkhov and Dichenkovko. The group had been at odds over many issues and readily embraced the plan Zhilinkhov presented to restore Communist party principles. The Politburo, with one dissenter, had elected their friend and former Politburo member, Viktor Pavlovich Zhilinkhov, to fill the position of general secretary and president.

After Zhilinkhov had entrenched himself in the position of consummate power, the inner circle had initiated the next phase. The steps necessary to probe the Americans in preparation for a nuclear, chemical, and biological 'first strike' to the United States were begun.

Zhilinkhov had enlisted a longtime friend, Minister of Defense and General of the Army Trofim Filippovich Porfir'yev, in the inner circle.

Porfir'yev, the Russian equivalent of the American secretary of defense and chairman of the Joint Chiefs of Staff combined, had initially been shocked by the magnitude of Zhilinkhov's intent. Although Porfir'yev was fully apprised of the different first-strike scenarios rehearsed by the senior military commanders, he had never discussed the possibilities with the ruling hierarchy.

After meeting with the other members of Zhilinkhov's aggregation, Porfir'yev embraced the bold plan and strongly recommended that the group include Marshal Nicholas Georgiyevich Bogdonoff, chief of the general staff.

The members of Zhilinkhov's circle, although concerned about security, agreed. They didn't want too many individuals, even at the top, to be aware of the secret strike plan.

Bogdonoff had always been a fervent advocate of the preemptive strike theory. He would provide the key military ingredient during the first stages of investigating American reactions.

Zhilinkhov and Porfir'yev approached the marshal of the Soviet Union in the general secretary's private dining room. Bogdonoff, though initially stunned, enthusiastically joined the conspiracy. He immediately set about implementing the military steps to probe the Americans without alarming any leaders in the Soviet military.

The first step had already been completed. Russian bombers with fighter escorts had approached American battle groups.

The inner circle knew they could launch cruise missiles at the US carriers from within 150 kilometers.

Now Soviet submarines would pursue US carrier groups, pressing closer than ever before, to evaluate Russian first-strike capabilities.

The bomber and submarine probes had been carefully designed to appear as normal military operations under the new regime. Zhilinkhov didn't want to create any suspicion in the Kremlin, or the military, prior to giving the order to launch missiles.

If the secret plan leaked out, Zhilinkhov's power to launch a strike on a moment's notice, without question, would be stripped by the eight uninformed Politburo members. Zhilinkhov was one of two men on the planet who could launch a massive, world-threatening nuclear strike, on his own authority.

Zhilinkhov now waited patiently for the next step to take place – sinking the American submarine prowling the Sea of Okhotsk.

The general secretary looked at his watch again, thinking about the afternoon session with the Central Committee. He would tell them of his economic reforms, reorganization of bureaucratic dynasties, industrial incentive plan, and revitalization of the energy industry. His message was simple: the future would restore Russia to her prominence, if the Party would give him the time needed.

'Comrade General Secretary, the members await you. It is past one,' Dimitri, head of the kitchen staff, gently reminded the eighty-six-year-old party leader.

USS *DWIGHT D. EISENHOWER*

Linnemeyer awoke in his cabin as the ship rolled hard to starboard in a 180-degree course reversal. The CO turned over, glanced at his portable alarm clock, blinked a number of times to clear his vision, and read the hour. He had been asleep over seven hours, much longer than his customary four or five hours.

Linnemeyer rubbed his face gingerly, finding the stubble coarse and uncomfortable. He forced his way out of the warm, inviting bunk and reached for his shaving kit, knocking over a glass of water in the semidarkness of his room.

The private stateroom contained a toilet and shower, the size of a small closet, off to the side of a combination sitting room/bedroom.

Linnemeyer brushed his teeth, shaved, and enjoyed a brief, but exhilarating, hot shower. Conservative use of fresh water was mandatory aboard Navy vessels at sea.

He changed into fresh work khakis, smartly laundered and pressed to razor-sharp crispness, and combed his hair. Slipping into his sage green flight jacket, Linnemeyer grabbed his wallet and watch, opened his cabin door and stepped into the soft red glow of the passageway.

CIC was a short walk away and he looked forward to having a hot cup of coffee, along with an update briefing on the latest Soviet activities, before going back to have his dinner. He had slept through lunch and his body was telling him it was past time to eat.

Linnemeyer stepped over the hatch-coaming into the Combat Information Center and was greeted by the senior petty officer of the watch, Jim Puckette, electronics technician first class.

'Good evening, sir.'

'Evening. Where's the watch officer?' Linnemeyer asked, observing the activity in the room.

'Went to the head, sir. Be right back,' Puckette responded, knowing the CO didn't have a lot of patience. 'Care for some hot tea, sir?'

Linnemeyer glanced at the small, fold-out table normally reserved for the battered coffee pot.

'Hot tea? What happened to the coffee?' Linnemeyer asked as he noticed the watch officer, Lt Pete Dyestrom, step back into CTC.

'Coffee pot shelled, sir.' Puckette looked at Dyestrom, seeking approval. 'We deep-sixed it, sir. Graham broke out Wilson's four-cupper. He only drinks tea.'

Puckette reached for the CO's cup hanging on the bulkhead and poured him a steaming cup of strong rosewood tea.

'Sounds great to me. Can't be choosey when ya' come a-bummin',' Linnemeyer responded, noticing the grins on the sailors' faces.

'Well, Pete, what's the picture at the present time?' the CO asked the CIC watch officer.

'Do you want the good news or the bad news first?'

'Let's go with the good. I'm an optimist,' Linnemeyer grinned as he tasted his tea, still too hot to drink comfortably.

'The *Kennedy* is joining us. They're out of the Med now, somewhere off Lisbon – ' Dyestrom abruptly ended the sentence when his intercom rang.

Linnemeyer looked at the ship's position plot as Dyestrom completed his conversation.

'Staff wants to see you, sir. They tried your quarters and figured you'd be here,' Dyestrom hurried. 'The bad news, briefly, is that we still have the two subs trailing along and the *Kiev* is standing off about – ' Dyestrom looked over to the petty officer manning CIC plot.

'One hundred five miles, zero-six-zero, sir.'

'That's about it. No action yet. We have a two-plane Barrier Combat Air Patrol orbiting seventy miles north-east of the ship. As you can see, sir, we've been steaming back and forth over the same course the past six hours,' Dyestrom concluded.

'Okay. Appreciate the tea. What's the deck status?' Linnemeyer asked as he drank the last swallow in his cup.

'Spotted for immediate CAP launch, sir. The pilots are in the cockpits. The Hummer is airborne, along with two Vikings and a tanker. One Viking is on the subs and the other is patrolling around the battle group. Also, we have a LAMPS antisubmarine helo between us and the subs. We are relieving everyone on station at four-hour intervals.' Dyestrom glanced at the twenty-four-hour clock. Another thirty-five minutes before the next launch.

'Sounds mighty fine, Pete. See ya' later.' Linnemeyer rinsed his cup and placed it on a wall peg before stepping into the passageway leading to the ship's bridge.

USS *TENNESSEE*

The Trident II fleet ballistic missile submarine, one of the newest in the inventory, had been fitted with new DS missiles during a dry-dock period in March 1990.

The advanced nuclear sub was now on patrol with the Seventh Fleet and attached to the battle group led by the carrier USS *Constellation*.

The skipper of the *Tennessee*, Capt. Mark McConnell, had received orders to return to the battle group. He had been reconnoitering deep in the Sea of Okhotsk and was underway for the *Constellation* and her escort ships.

Ohio-class 'boomers' normally patrolled the depths of open oceans. However, the *Tennessee* had been given a highly classified mission to reconnoiter the capabilities of the latest Soviet antisubmarine warfare (ASW) technology.

The Russians had launched a number of secret Cosmos satellites in 1991. Each unit contained a 'blue hue' blue-green laser able to penetrate deep below the ocean's surface. The laser system converted ultraviolet light from an xenon laser source to ultrahigh-intensity, narrow-band blue-green laser light.

Soviet scientists, in less than fourteen months, had launched twenty-nine Cosmos satellites with only one failure. The laser aboard the fourteenth satellite had failed to energize.

The Soviet technological breakthrough had caused great concern in the Pentagon. Had the Russians finally been able to make the oceans 'transparent'? Were our submarines being tracked from home port to destination?

If the answer was yes, our worst fears would be true. The Soviets' latest generation bomber, the 'Blackjack', carrying nuclear-tipped cruise missiles, would be able to select and destroy every American submarine. The triad of United States landbased nuclear missiles, bombers, and submarines would be irretrievably weakened.

Another question military planners needed to have answered involved Soviet antiballistic missile defenses. Could an American ballistic missile submarine get close to Russian shores in order to shorten the flight time of their missiles? Senior military strategic planners believed the less time in the air, the less chance of interception by Soviet countermeasure systems.

Fourteen nautical miles inside Severo-Kurilsk, off the southern tip of Kamchatka Peninsula, the *Tennessee* had been intercepted by a Udaloy-class antisubmarine warfare ship carrying two Kamov Ka-27 Helix-A antisub helicopters.

The blue-green laser from *Cosmos Kuybyshev* had indeed detected the United States submarine in the Sea of Okhotsk.

The American sub had been running at two-thirds speed at a depth of 200 feet, generating a loud acoustical signature, when one of the Russian helos spotted it with a sonobuoy trailing in the water.

To exacerbate matters, two Soviet submarines, one Akula-class and one Sierra-class nuclear attack submarine, were positioned between the *Tennessee* and the American battle group. They had been notified by the Russian antisubmarine ship of the exact position of the US nuclear sub.

* * *

'Skipper, I think we've crapped in our mess kit,' Cmdr Ken Houston, the *Tennessee*'s executive officer, said in a hushed voice. The sub was in a state of silent running, descending deeper after being detected and 'pinged' by the helo's mother ship.

'You're right, Ken,' McConnell acknowledged, looking at his watch. 'I should have had the patience to keep us slowed down.'

Both officers knew the Russians would be enraged if they suspected, or knew, how far the *Tennessee* had probed into their territorial waters.

'Well, Ken,' McConnell said in a whisper, 'was it the laser or a chance encounter?'

'I don't know,' Houston replied, slowly shaking his head. 'They were right on top of us.'

'Yes . . .' McConnell said, baffled. 'Still, it could be a coincidence.'

'You think they might drop on us?' CPO Clay Booker, the senior sonarman, asked Houston.

'I don't know. The situation is really strained right now. We were in their backyard,' Houston said, checking the sub's diving rate.

'They shot down a 747 full of civilians with no provocation and full knowledge that it was an airliner. Can't be sure of anything when we're dealing with the Russians,' Houston concluded, as McConnell gave orders to evade the Soviet helicopter.

'Right standard rudder,' the captain commanded.

'Right standard rudder,' the officer of the deck repeated to McConnell.

'All ahead two-thirds. Steady heading one-two-five,' McConnell barked, as the nuclear sub continued deeper and changed course in order to escape the Russian antisubmarine vessel.

'Aye aye, sir.'

Booker leaned over to Houston and asked in a whispered voice, 'Sir, do we have our whale disguise?'

'We may need it,' Houston answered with a slight grin, realizing the Russian was staying on the trail of the *Tennessee*. McConnell would have to use more erratic evasive maneuvers to escape detection.

The encounter with the Soviet antisubmarine warfare forces was becoming a real workout. The Russians apparently wanted to exploit the untidy situation and the Americans needed to get farther out into international waters. They also needed deeper water under the boat in order to escape from the Russians. It was obvious the US missile submarine had been operating in sovereign Russian territorial waters.

3

THE *FRUNZE*

The Russian nuclear-powered guided missile cruiser *Frunze*, armed with SS-N-l9 antiship cruise missiles, was loitering 270 nautical miles east of Komandorskie Island. The Soviet ship was midway between the two American carrier groups operating in the northern Pacific waters.

The Kirov-class missile cruiser, flagship of the Soviet Pacific Ocean Fleet, was the pride of Adm. Yevgeny S. Botschka, the task force commander embarked aboard the 28,000-ton warship.

Admiral Botschka had been in constant communication with the antisubmarine vessel *Akhromeyev*, the Soviet ship pursuing the USS *Tennessee*.

Fleet Admiral Vosoghiyan had been very blunt in his orders to Botschka – orders apparently issued directly from the defense minister – spelling out the necessity to pressure the American forces at every opportunity.

The word had been passed throughout the chain of command that the general secretary was personally directing the operation.

Botschka didn't understand the reason for these unprecedented actions. His job was compliance and execution, not interpretation of orders.

Botschka felt comfortable with his new mission and believed it was the appropriate time and place to punish the treacherous Americans.

Admiral Botschka had other reasons to perform well. Rumors had been carefully circulated suggesting that

Vosoghiyan would retire on Soviet Navy Day, the first Sunday after July 22, leaving the Fleet Admiralty open.

Botschka knew he would be the selectee to replace the Fleet Admiral if he could confirm the sinking of the intruding American submarine. Botschka also felt certain a second Hero of the Soviet Union medal would be placed on his uniform.

USS *TENNESSEE*

Booker concentrated on his sonar panel, waiting for the Russian ship to 'ping' them again. Another forty minutes and they would be in open waters where the *Tennessee* could dive deep to avoid detection.

Ping, PING!

There it was. Closer this time.

'They've really got us bracketed, sir,' Booker said quietly to Captain McConnell.

The sub skipper nodded and glanced at his executive officer.

'What do you think, Ken? Should we set a straight course for the group? It's been over an hour and they haven't done anything but tail us.'

Houston thought a minute, calculating all the contingencies within logic.

'No sense in trying to evade them. We can't go deep enough at this point and we can't outrun the choppers,' Houston replied as another ping sounded through the Trident's hull.

'True. Might as well come to periscope depth. We need to alert the task force of our position and situation,' McConnell said as he glanced at his watch. Thirty-five minutes before the water would be deep enough to use the *Tennessee*'s full capability.

'We better request air-cover back to the battle group,' McConnell said as Houston silently nodded in agreement.

'Steady course zero-eight-zero,' McConnell ordered the helmsman.

'Steady course zero-eight-zero,' the officer of the deck repeated.

'All ahead one-third,' McConnell said quietly.

'Periscope depth.'

'Ahead one-third, coming to periscope depth,' the lieutenant repeated as the sailor manning the diving planes eased back on his controls, changing the deck angle of the *Tennessee*.

'Communications, stand by for a message to *Constellation*,' McConnell ordered as he picked up the microphone to transmit his report to the American carrier.

The communications antenna would be the only piece of hardware protruding above the water. It would be difficult to detect if the sub was going slow, reducing the size of the wake created by the antenna.

'All ahead slow,' McConnell ordered, not wanting to leave a visible marker for the Russians to spot.

If the Soviets detected a wake from the antenna, they would know the American sub had sent a message. That might force the Russians into action since the *Tennessee* was in a vulnerable position. The Soviets apparently wanted to make an issue of the situation, and that meant keeping the American nuclear submarine in a precarious location.

The sub leveled at sixty feet as McConnell prepared to send a message to the *Constellation*.

'I sure hope the "Connie" is listening,' McConnell said to his executive officer.

'Yeah,' Houston answered. 'We're already overdue.'

THE *AKHROMEYEV*

The Udaloy-class antisubmarine ship was pacing the *Tennessee* at a distance of six kilometers. One of the *Akhromeyev*'s ASW helicopters was orbiting over the intruding sub, trailing a sonobuoy, while a sister helo was being refueled on the *Akhromeyev*. Both Kamov Ka-27s were stalking the sleek American submarine, landing aboard their ship to refuel at staggered thirty-minute intervals.

The ship's master, Capt. Myroslaw Surovcik, was listening to the crew of Akhromeyev Two as the helicopter circled the *Tennessee*. Next to his command chair on the port wing of the bridge were a speaker and discreet phone direct to Admiral Botschka aboard the *Frunze*.

Akhromeyev One was lifting off the aft helo-pad, lowering its nose to gain speed, when Surovcik heard the pilot of the other Kamov radio an urgent report.

'Akhromeyev Two, the submarine is slowing, we think surfacing!' the pilot said as he swept low over the *Tennessee*. He could almost see a shadow of the big Trident submarine in the bright midday sunlight.

'Comrade Captain,' the pilot said to Surovcik, 'I see a mast or periscope on the surface.'

'Keep the sub in sight. Stand by, Two,' the Russian radio officer directed the Kamov pilot as Surovcik radioed Admiral Botschka.

'Comrade Admiral, we believe the American is preparing to surface. A periscope was spotted moments ago,' Surovcik reported to the task force commander.

Botschka responded immediately. 'My orders, Captain, originated in the Kremlin. You must keep the submarine from surfacing until one of our subs is in position to torpedo the Americans. This must happen below the surface. No witnesses. Any surface action might be detectable by reconnaissance satellite or spy plane. Do you understand?' Botschka was adamant.

'Yes, Comrade Admiral,' replied Surovcik, shaken by the task force commander's intent.

The *Akhromeyev* captain had not envisioned attacking the American submarine. What would happen to him if he failed to keep the nuclear submarine totally submerged? More importantly, Surovcik thought, what will happen if I inadvertently sink the American? Will the politically inclined admiral back me?

'It is possible, Comrade Captain Surovcik, for the Americans to send a message if they surface. The periscope may be an antenna, too. The submarine must be kept entirely under water.' Admiral Botschka paused. 'Is that clear, Captain?'

'Yes, very clear, Comrade Admiral,' Surovcik replied as he released the microphone transmit button. He looked at his radio officer who had heard the order. The lieutenant's face was ashen, his mouth slightly open, eyes questioning.

'Akhromeyev One and Two, this is Captain Surovcik, acknowledge.'

Both Russian pilots replied immediately to the demanding voice.

'Your orders are to keep the submarine totally submerged. No mast or periscope. Nothing above the water.' Surovcik was absently rubbing his left temple as he stared at the two ASW helicopters circling the American submarine.

'Akhromeyev One, understand.' The pilot sounded as if he might have a question.

'Akhromeyev Two, understand, Comrade Captain. We are cleared to drop depth charges, if any part of the submarine rises from the water?'

'That is correct. You are to keep the submarine under

surveillance until further notice. Use your judgment. The submarine is not to surface or transmit any message. You have your orders,' Surovcik ended the conversation and reached for his binoculars, noting that the radio officer was in stunned silence.

Everyone on the bridge had heard Captain Surovcik tell the pilots to use their judgement. He had a way out, an excuse for whatever might happen.

The pilot of Akhromeyev Two armed his number one conventional H-E depth charge pack and rolled into a dive toward the *Tennessee*, stern to bow, as he lined up with the antenna wake.

He purposely released the charge late, intending to send a message to the captain of the submarine. He had not been ordered to destroy the sub, only keep it below the surface. A failure to carry out orders in a correct manner could end his career, if not his life. Fleet Admiral Vosoghiyan was not a tolerant man.

The depth charge smashed into the water 200 meters in front of the submarine. It was set to detonate at a depth of 150 meters and quickly sank below the *Tennessee*.

The almost invisible wake of the Trident passed directly through the disturbed water where the depth charge entered the sea.

USS *TENNESSEE*

'HANG ON,' Chief Booker yelled across the control room.

'The bastards just dropped on us,' Booker continued as McConnell barked orders and radioed the *Constellation*.

'We're being attacked! *Tennessee* under attack!' McConnell repeated and tossed the microphone down.

'Left full rudder, all ahead flank,' McConnell shouted, as the submarine surged forward and rolled slightly to the right.

'All down on the planes!' The captain reached for his speaker switch. 'Rig for depth charges! Rig for depth charges!'

The boat came alive as all hands went into action, stowing gear and dogging hatches, involuntarily glancing at the overhead, fear swelling inside.

'Right full rudder, make your depth two hundred feet.' McConnell paused. 'Shit . . .'

The captain looked at Houston as the depth charge went off.

KA-WOOOMPH!

The *Tennessee* shuddered violently. Galley pans crashed wildly to the deck in the officers' wardroom.

'Sonuvabitch,' Houston swore as McConnell now ordered a lower depth for the submarine.

'Take her to three hundred feet. Rudder amidship,' McConnell ordered as he completed the second 90-degree turn, placing the *Tennessee* on her original course.

'How much water under the keel, Bob?' McConnell asked the navigator, Lt Comdr Robert Cromwell.

'Forty fathoms, sir.'

'Do you think the Connie heard us, Skipper?' Houston asked as the Trident plunged toward the ocean floor.

'We'll know in a few minutes. I can't believe this,' McConnell said as he watched the depth gauge level at 300 feet. The *Tennessee* was only 140 feet from the bottom.

'Load and arm four fish,' McConnell quietly ordered the officer of the deck.

'If they drop anything else,' McConnell looked at

Houston, 'we'll take out the goddamned ship. The helos will be as good as finished. They'll have to run for land or take a bath.'

USS *CONSTELLATION*

The Combat Information Center had heard the radio transmission from the *Tennessee*. The last few words were garbled and had to be enhanced and repeated several times before the word 'attack' was discernible.

The task force commander aboard *Constellation*, Rear Adm. Benjamin E. Thompson, had been concerned about the lack of communication with the *Tennessee*. He now realized why McConnell had missed a predetermined check-in. The admiral immediately launched the Combat Air Patrol.

Thompson watched the second F-14 Tomcat accelerate down the forward starboard catapult, rotate sharply, then bank steeply to rendezvous with his leader.

'Admiral, your patch to CINCPAC is open,' Cmdr Steve Tyson, Thompson's aide, said as he handed the admiral a handset.

The message was scrambled and transmitted via satellite to Pearl Harbor, where the commander-in-chief of the Pacific Fleet was based.

'Admiral Jones, Ben Thompson,' the task force commander announced.

'Ben, this is Joe Lindsey,' Vice Adm. Joseph Benton Lindsey replied. 'The admiral is in Tripler undergoing gallbladder surgery. The doctors said it couldn't be postponed. I'm acting at the present time.'

'We've got a confrontation brewing here, sir, and I recommend we go on alert,' Thompson paused momentarily, 'the *Tennessee* radioed she was under attack.'

'Under attack?' the acting CINCPAC was incredulous.

'Yes, sir,' replied Thompson.

'How long ago, Ben?'

'Nine minutes, Admiral. The CAP is airborne, two Tomcats, and we've got a Viking en route. As you know, sir, the *Tennessee* was in their kitchen cabinet – off Sakhalin – and most probably detected before they cleared the Kurils.'

Thompson wished Jones were on the line. He had served under the four-star admiral twice in his career and knew Jones to be a decisive and intelligent leader.

'How far is the *Tennessee* from your position, Ben?' Lindsey asked, looking at a detailed wall map indicating the relative position of American Pacific Fleet ships, along with Russian surface ships. The pictorial display was updated regularly using reconnaissance satellites and routine position reports.

'About two hundred fifty miles. The Fourteens will be overhead the *Tennessee* in approximately twelve minutes, sir.' Thompson wanted answers, not questions.

'Okay, Ben, keep me informed. I will alert Washington. The global situation is heating up. We just received word that one of the *Eisenhower*'s escorts, the *Mississippi*, accidentally ran over a Soviet submarine early this morning.' Lindsey looked over at the Top Secret message lying on his desk.

'They sink it?' Thompson asked, wondering what the Russians had in mind for the *Tennessee*.

'No. Apparently the Russian was surfacing in the dark, very close to the *Mississippi*, and didn't anticipate the ship's changing course. They had been steaming straight for over an hour before the collision. We offered to help and they refused, as usual. The sub is currently on the surface, limping to the White Sea. The impact destroyed the sail and heavily damaged the forward third of the sub.'

'What about the *Mississippi*, sir?' Thompson asked.

'Minor damage. Primarily the rudders. She is staying on station for the present time,' Lindsey answered.

Commander Tyson motioned for Thompson to switch his speaker to CIC network.

'I'll keep this net open until we know something, sir,' Thompson concluded his conversation and listened to the reports from the fighter pilots.

THE TOMCATS

The two Grumman fighters had the Russian ASW ship and her Kamov helicopters locked on their radar scopes. They had been supersonic the past eleven minutes and were now slowing for a rendezvous with the *Tennessee*. Both crews knew a KA-6D Texaco was not far behind, so fuel wasn't a critical item at the moment.

Lt Earl 'Mad Dog' Hutchinson, the flight leader of the two VF-154 'Black Knights', radioed his wingman as they rapidly closed on the two Russian helicopters.

'Chuckles, you stay high and cover me. I'll get down low and slow – see what we have,' Hutchinson stated as he reduced power, rolled inverted, deployed his speed brakes and executed a beautiful split-S maneuver. The Tomcat plummeted for the ocean surface, engines spooling down to a whisper, as Hutchinson checked his armament panel.

'Rog, Hutch,' Lt Chuck Powell answered from his F-14, Mad Dog Two.

McConnell looked at his watch for what seemed like the thousandth time. It had been seventeen minutes since the unprovoked depth charge attack. The Russians had stopped pinging the sub as often. They seemed content to sit on the *Tennessee*. McConnell again checked his watch and decided to have a look topside. Friendly aircraft should be in the vicinity by now, providing the *Constellation* had received his message, McConnell thought as he prepared to ascend.

'Ken, I've got a feeling we're going to have to punch our way out of this mess.'

Houston raised his eyebrows, unsmiling. 'I have the same feeling.'

The men exchanged knowing looks as McConnell inhaled deeply, then purged the air as his shoulders sagged.

'Periscope depth,' McConnell ordered.

'Aye aye. Periscope depth,' the lieutenant repeated as the diving planes tilted upward on the captain's command, sending the *Tennessee* toward the surface.

THE *AKHROMEYEV*

The Soviet ASW ship had detected the approaching American fighter planes on radar. Captain Surovcik elected not to inform the Kamov helo pilots. His postulation required that everything remain status quo for a few more minutes. That would be enough time for one of their hunter-killer subs to be in position to destroy the intruding American submarine.

Surovcik thought about Admiral Botschka's orders. He was still nervous, especially with the American fighter planes rapidly approaching. This was not a good situation. It placed him in a vulnerable position. Surovcik had worked diligently to protect his career.

If the sinking was not visible, the Americans could not prove anything. They could only speculate as to what had happened to their spy submarine. A warning to future imperialistic attempts to undermine the Soviet government. Besides, Surovcik thought to himself, a thin smile on his ruddy face, we can take credit for trying to assist the crippled American submarine. Just a few more minutes . . .

USS *TENNESSEE*

Captain McConnell squatted down, preparing to rise with the attack periscope.

'Periscope depth, Skipper,' the officer of the deck reported as the *Tennessee* stabilized at sixty feet.

'All ahead slow,' McConnell ordered, adjusting the periscope handles.

'Aye aye, all ahead slow,' the OD repeated across the control room.

The big Trident missile submarine slowed to a crawl as McConnell raised the small attack periscope to a position two feet lower than normal. Waves crashed over the top of the viewing lens. McConnell raised the scope another foot. Able to see better, he swept the horizon in a quick 360-degree circle, then reversed his sweep thirty degrees.

'DAMN. Dive! Dive!' McConnell ordered as he slammed the handles into the periscope, already retreating from the overhead.

'Left full rudder, all ahead full. Level at four hundred feet,' McConnell barked.

'Aye aye, Captain.' The OD watched intently as the sailors responded to the skipper's orders.

McConnell looked at his navigator, knowing they would only have forty feet of water between the keel and the bottom.

'Hope there aren't any protrusions,' McConnell said, looking at the navigator.

'The helo, at least one of them, is still there. Don't know if he spotted the scope. The ship is approximately five thousand yards off our port beam,' he explained to his exec.

'See any of ours?' Houston asked in a hushed voice.

'No,' McConnell said in a dejected manner. 'I really didn't have time to focus on anything. Jesus, they're right on top of us.'

'Mark,' Houston said under his breath. 'I'm beginning to have a really bad feeling about this.'

KAMOV-27 #TWO

The flight observer saw the telltale wake of the periscope as he glanced across the open water. The midday sun, slightly to his back, helped the airman see the stark wake clearly against the blue background of the relatively placid sea.

'Comrade Leytenant, there!' the observer pointed excitely at the periscope.

'Yes, I see, Sergey,' Starshiy Leytenant Pyotr Lavrov responded as he rolled into a steep bank and armed his number two depth charge pack.

'Akhromeyev Two,' the pilot radioed excitedly. 'The American has broken the surface! Commencing attack,' Lavrov shouted as he lined up with the foaming wake.

The periscope had just descended beneath the water

when the Kamov pilot dropped the second depth charge on the beleaguered *Tennessee*. Again, the explosive packet was directly in line with the sub's course.

'The submarine is diving,' the Kamov pilot reported as he banked his helicopter to circle the *Tennessee*.

'You have performed well,' Captain Surovcik radioed. 'Return for refueling.'

The young pilot suppressed a smile, then keyed his microphone. 'Thank you, Comrade Captain.'

USS *TENNESSEE*

'DEPTH CHARGE,' Booker shouted, as everyone braced for the thundering shockwave. No one on board the US missile sub had been depth-charged before. The experience was as new to the captain as it was to the lowest ranking seaman.

KA-WOOOMPH!

The *Tennessee* lurched sideways and rolled slightly before righting herself. The strain was evident on the faces of the crew.

'Why are they so intent on keeping us submerged?' McConnell asked Houston.

'Rudder amidship, all ahead slow,' he ordered before his executive officer could reply.

'Doesn't make sense. Unless they have something else in mind for us,' Houston said, as he glanced at the chart table.

'Like what?' McConnell challenged his exec for a logical answer.

'Look at this, Mark,' Houston gestured at the chart table.

'They've caught us with our pants down. The bastards have had every opportunity to blow us out of the water, which they haven't. The depth charges have been warnings.' Houston lighted a cigarette before he continued.

'They either want to detain us until a boat full of press photographers arrives, or,' Houston paused, inhaling deeply, 'they are waiting for a sub to get here. A killer sub, Mark.'

The exec looked up at McConnell.

'Makes sense. They haven't done anything like this in aeons,' McConnell responded, trying to envision the worst-case scenario.

'Correct,' Houston continued. 'If the attack is not observed, only speculation and accusations will fly. They can't attack with a surface vessel. The risk of being caught by a recon plane or satellite is too high. That leaves the job to an efficient hunter-killer. Nice and clean,' Houston concluded, his voice only a whisper to McConnell.

'You may be right, Ken.' McConnell looked at his watch and continued, 'If my message didn't reach the *Constellation* – I didn't see any friendlies overhead – then we're on our own.'

'And being depth-charged,' Houston reminded his friend in a quiet voice.

'And being depth-charged,' McConnell acknowledged.

'My first instinct was correct. Blow the friggin' Russian off the planet and get the hell out of here. If they are setting us up for a sub, which seems like a logical conclusion, we don't have a lot of time,' McConnell said as he reaffirmed their position on the chart table.

'Chief, stay close on our sonar,' McConnell ordered Booker, 'we may have a Russian sub stalking us.'

'Aye, Cap'n,' Booker responded, concentrating intently as he turned up the gain on the sonar, listening intently.

The captain ordered the *Tennessee* back to periscope

depth in order to get a visual confirmation on the Soviet ASW ship.

'Give me a solution,' McConnell ordered his exec, now handling the control room as fire control coordinator.

'Aye, Skipper,' Houston responded as he viewed the data input to the Mk-117 fire-control computer.

The *Tennessee*'s Mk-48 torpedos were the most powerful in the US arsenal, wire-guided and capable of homing on a target with its own sonar. Captain McConnell knew that a fifty-knot torpedo would do the job. Two Mk-48 torpedos would be even better.

'Solution, Skipper,' Houston reported, double-checking the computer readout with his own figures.

'Go,' McConnell responded.

'Bearing three-four-zero. Range is five thousand, four hundred yards. Running time four minutes, five seconds,' Houston reported, adrenaline coursing through his veins.

'Stand by tubes three and four,' McConnell ordered as he prepared to raise the main periscope.

The torpedo tubes were flooded down and ready for launch.

'Confirm tubes three and four,' Houston replied, looking around the crowded control room.

No one was breathing, not even blinking. The reality of the imminent assault on the Russian ship was registering.

'I can't believe this,' McConnell said quietly to his exec, as perspiration formed under his ball cap.

'They depth-charged us first, Mark. We have every right to defend ourselves,' Houston said in a steady, even tone.

'Up periscope,' McConnell ordered, as he gripped the hand controls and again swept the horizon through 360 degrees. Stopping on the *Akhromeyev*, McConnell visually and verbally confirmed the Soviet ASW ship.

Stepping back, the captain asked his executive officer to verify the target for decision continuity. The visual confirmation, unless in a declared war, had been instituted after the Iranian Airbus tragedy in 1988.

'Russian Udaloy-class ASW ship, confirmed,' Houston said, noting that one of the Kamov helicopters was refueling on the aft helo-pad.

'Ivan the bombardier is about to receive the surprise of his life,' Houston said quietly as the skipper stepped back to the periscope.

'Fire three,' McConnell ordered.

The *Tennessee* shuddered as the compressed air charge shoved the big Mk-48 out the number three torpedo tube.

'Three fired, sir,' responded the control room speaker after receiving confirmation from the torpedo room.

'Fire four,' McConnell repeated as he slammed the handles upward and stepped back from the descending periscope.

Another shudder. Then the eerie sound of two torpedos generating increasing energy as they reached maximum speed.

'Four fired, sir.'

'Take her down, right full rudder, all ahead flank!' McConnell ordered the helmsman.

'Sonar, what do you have?' the captain queried Chief Booker.

'Both fish running hot and true, sir. Two minutes fifty-five seconds to go on the first torpedo, Skipper.'

'Okay, let me – '

'Depth charges!' Booker interrupted the captain.

'Rudder amidship. Take her to four hundred feet,' McConnell barked, noticing the navigator flinch.

The *Tennessee* plunged ahead as every crew member grabbed for a handhold.

The pilot of Akhromeyev One, Mladshiy Leytenant Nicholas V. Chernoff, was growing weary from his four-teen-hour duty day. One more hot-refueling and back to this endless circling, he thought to himself, and then a new pilot will take over.

Chernoff could see Akhromeyev Two on the helo-pad, refueling once again. He could imagine the reaction his friend would have to the box lunches issued to the crews. Chernoff and his crewmen had thrown their soggy boxes out the window and watched them plummet into the ocean. This ASW duty was terrible, he reflected to himself as he glanced at the water.

Suddenly, Chernoff thought his mind was playing tricks on him. Was that his box lunch on the ocean surface? Couldn't be, it was moving. Chernoff concentrated on the spot. A periscope! His friend really had seen the American submarine.

'Observers, the sub is showing a periscope again!' Chernoff informed his crew as he pushed over into an attack on the American submarine.

He armed his number one depth charge pack and roared low over the *Tennessee*, dropping the charge 100 meters forward and slightly left of the approaching sub.

The submarine appeared to be diving and Chernoff noticed two strange, almost frothy trails leading away from the American sub. Chernoff pulled up in a steep turn and looked down. His depth charge passed five meters off the port side of the menacing sub.

'What do you make of that?' Chernoff asked his forward observer.

'What, sir?' the ryadovoy airman, three days into his first assignment, replied as Chernoff recognized the sign of a torpedo launch.

His spine grew cold as he traced the two trails of frothy water to the *Akhromeyev*.

'BASTARDS!' Chernoff yelled, the crew oblivious as to the cause of his rage.

'Captain Surovcik! The submarine has fired two torpedos at the *Akhromeyev*,' the pilot shouted into his microphone.

'What?' the stunned master replied. 'Report again. Report in, One!'

'The American has fired two torpedos at you . . . your ship, Captain,' the pilot radioed breathlessly.

The *Akhromeyev* did not respond. The ship's master had raced from the bridge to the closest lifeboat.

Chernoff armed all five remaining depth charges and rolled into another attack on the American submarine. He salvoed all five packs on his first pass and pulled up steeply, racing for the *Akhromeyev*.

Chernoff noticed something move in his periphery and glanced to his right. The shocking sight of the onrushing air-to-air missile would be the last picture in Chernoff's young mind. The Kamov exploded into a fireball, raining debris over one square mile of ocean.

THE TOMCATS

Hutchinson pulled hard on the stick, shooting skyward as he rolled the F-14 inverted for a better view of the falling Kamov. He had no doubt the Russian helo was attacking the *Tennessee*. A split-second decision, no time for error or second-guessing.

'Homeplate, Mad Dog One,' Hutchinson radioed the *Constellation*.

'Mad Dog, Homeplate, go,' the voice of CIC answered.

'We're over the . . . GODDAMN! The ship just exploded,' Hutchinson reported, thinking quickly that it couldn't have been his ordnance. He had fired only one missile. Must have been the sub.

'What ship exploded?' CIC responded instantly, not comprehending the report.

'The Russian. The ASW!' Hutchinson sucked in 100 percent oxygen. 'It blew up in my face.'

'Mad Dog, you were not authorized to initiate an – '

'The ship exploded again! Wait,' Hutchinson paused, calling his wingman. 'Two, get down here.'

'Rog, Hutch,' Powell replied, staring at the shock wave spreading across the water. 'Unbelievable.'

'Homeplate, Mad Dog One DID NOT, I repeat, DID NOT, fire on the ship.' Hutchinson, breathing rapidly, gulped more cool oxygen. 'I have a tally on the *Tennessee*. They're surfacing.'

'What is the condition of the Soviet vessel?' CIC asked in a surprised voice.

'It's dead in the water, listing badly,' Mad Dog One replied. 'The stern is slowly sliding under . . . They're definitely going down.'

4

'Mister President, the situation is extremely serious. We are unanimous in our recommendation.' Admiral Chambers looked at the floor, then up to the chief of staff, who nodded in agreement.

Chambers continued, aware of the increasing tension in the Oval Office. 'It is imperative that you declare a Defense Condition-three alert. Immediately, sir.'

The president of the United States started to speak, then fell silent. He turned and stared out his window overlooking the manicured lawn, his mind refusing to accept the recent invasion of his tranquil surroundings.

The tall, athletic leader, educated in the Ivy League, was a cautious man. The president, by nature, didn't overreact to pressure situations. His close friends and advisers knew, however, that he could be tough and relentless if forced into a difficult position.

'Mister President, these gentlemen are correct, sir. They are the experts. The situation is explosive. We haven't been this close to war in decades,' the chief of staff, Grant Wilkinson, paused, glancing at the service chiefs and the secretary of defense.

'I propose, Mister President, that you initiate DEFCON-Three and return the call to Zhilinkhov without delay.'

The president, his back to his advisers, remained quiet a full minute before turning his swivel chair around and addressing the group.

'This is a radical step you are proposing. I'm not certain the incidents that have occurred thus far warrant such measures.' The president looked Chambers squarely in the face and continued. 'Admiral, would you have me jeopardize our latest advances in arms control, our relations with the Kremlin, over these isolated incidents?'

'Mister President, our pleasant relationship with the Kremlin died in the aircraft wreckage at Moscow's Sheremetyevo Airport, along with the former general secretary.'

Chambers knew he had to press the issue. 'Furthermore, sir, these incidents are not isolated or random. They are, quite clearly, premeditated.'

The president looked at Wilkinson. The tall, prematurely white-haired chief of staff was his closest aide and longtime friend. 'Where do we stand, Grant?'

'Sir, the Soviets are pressing us to the wall. We have satellite confirmation of massive tank movements in Europe. The NATO partners are screaming for our response.'

Wilkinson opened his briefing folder, running his eyes down the page, and continued. 'Squadrons of Russian bombers and fighters have been deployed to staging fields. Many sorties have already been flown over allied territory and our battle groups.

'Sir, Zhilinkhov is a different breed of animal. He is the quintessence of Soviet ideological fanaticism, and, he has a nucleus of adherents supporting him. The past Russian leaders pale in comparison.'

Wilkinson paused, while the president opened his briefing folder and skimmed the first and second pages. He looked at Chambers, a question in his mind.

'This reliable information, Admiral?'

'Yessir,' Chambers replied, opening his folder. 'Our underwater detectors have verified six Russian subs off the East Coast, plus three more off the coast of Florida. The subs you have already been briefed on.'

The president pushed his bifocals to a comfortable position before speaking.

'What's the straight scoop on this *Tennessee* fracas?' Not waiting for an answer, the president continued.

'Zhilinkhov was livid, almost incoherent. That's why, gentlemen, I don't want to overreact to all of this. I'd like to let everyone calm down before we proceed to discuss these matters with Zhilinkhov or anyone else.'

The president looked at Chambers, then glanced at Wilkinson, who remained quiet while the admiral replied.

'First, Mister President, the *Tennessee* was fired upon, depth-charged, by the Russians. That is a fact. Captain McConnell, the *Tennessee*'s skipper, tried to evade the Soviet ASW ship and her helicopters, but the water was too shallow to go deep.' Chambers stopped as the president indicated a question.

'Were they in international waters at the time of this incident, by accepted maritime definition?' The president waited for a response.

'Yessir. Barely. It could be argued extensively, but they were in international waters. No question.'

'Okay. Continue, Admiral.'

'McConnell tried to send a signal to the *Constellation* and got depth-charged again, so he followed the only rational decision available to him. Sir, I endorse his actions. McConnell acted to protect his crew and the submarine placed under his command. He deserves a medal and a pat on the back, Mister President.'

The president, looking somber, placed his elbows on the table, hands forming a peak, and thought a moment.

'What's the *Tennessee*'s condition, Admiral?'

'Minor damage. One of the helo drivers salvoed his depth charges on the *Tennessee* before the Tomcat splashed him. Just some bent fittings and a few puckered asses – a few very frightened submariners, sir.'

Chambers waited for the president to speak, aware of the silence surrounding them.

'Zhilinkhov insists we are trying to start a war. Running over one of their subs and attacking a ship. Hell, sinking the goddamn ship!' The president paused, calming before continuing.

'We all know the score, but on the surface . . .' The president looked at Chambers. 'On the surface, it would appear as if he is correct.'

Wilkinson signaled for a coffee service to be sent in, then spoke to the president.

'Sir, if we don't stand up, don't go into an alert status, they are going to continue to push until we make a mistake.

'They're the ones who have broken the rules we've been playing by for the past thirty years. I recommend you initiate DEFCON-Three, then talk with Zhilinkhov. We've got to play hardball with this guy. We don't know what his real game is.'

Wilkinson paused, studying the president, then continued. 'Sir, Zhilinkhov is one tough bastard.'

The chief of staff looked directly into the president's eyes, sensing he had been successful in making his point. The room remained silent as a steward brought in the silver coffee service and quietly departed.

'Okay, Admiral,' the president said, looking toward Chambers. 'Go to DEFCON-Three and brief me in three hours.'

'Yes, sir, Mister President,' Chambers replied as he and the other service chiefs, quiet to this point, rose from their chairs and filed out of the office, leaving their coffee untouched.

The five men huddled in the anteroom adjoining the

Oval Office, then quickly dispersed to oversee their assigned duties. The stakes were rising in the nuclear cat-and-mouse game.

MOSCOW

The general secretary placed the 'secure' phone receiver down, turning slowly to face his four Politburo coconspirators and the minister of defense.

Zhilinkhov's grin spread across his face. 'The American has no idea, comrades.'

The men exchanged pleased looks as the general secretary poured vodka in fresh glasses and pressed the service staff button.

Dimitri Moiseyevich Karpov, standing quietly in the hallway outside the general secretary's quarters, had been listening to the conversation. The kitchen staff director hesitated an appropriate amount of time before responding to the service buzzer.

Zhilinkhov loosened his tie, then unbuttoned his collar.

'They have implemented an alert-three status, their first step in preparation for war. We will continue to push them further, to defense condition two. If we can successfully continue to probe the American defense posture, including their alert-two status, we will enjoy the psychological advantage when we withdraw.'

Zhilinkhov fell silent as Dimitri entered the room to fill his request.

'Dimitri Moiseyevich, we will be served in my quarters this evening. Have something special prepared for dessert. For now, send in the piroshki.'

'Yes, Comrade General Secretary. I will prepare your meal personally. The piroshki will be no longer than five minutes.'

Dimitri exited quietly and the vivacious conversation continued.

'I am concerned,' Dichenkovko said, 'about the loss of our antisubmarine ship. We cannot make any further mistakes.'

Dichenkovko looked into Porfir'yev's eyes, then back to the general secretary. The defense minister cast his gaze toward the floor.

'We cannot afford to underestimate the Americans,' Dichenkovko continued. 'We have the future of the Motherland at stake.'

Zhilinkhov scowled. 'General Bogdonoff has ordered Fleet Admiral Vosoghiyan to submit a full report within twenty-four hours. I will not tolerate any more mistakes . . . by anyone.'

The general secretary smiled unexpectedly, then continued in an upbeat manner. 'Now, we will see what the American reaction will be when we sink their ship *Virginia*.'

The group glanced at each other in concern.

'Actually, my friends,' Zhilinkhov said, ignoring the questioning looks, 'the loss of the *Akhromeyev* gives us the opportunity to press the Americans even closer. If we can confirm a fourteen- to sixteen-minute delay in the American decision and reaction time to our missiles, in their alert-two status, we have positive proof, comrades, that our first-strike initiative will work.'

Zhilinkhov waited for a response. The Politburo members and the defense minister remained silent, contemplating the picture being drawn for them.

Zhilinkhov continued, sipping his vodka. 'If the Americans allow our forces to get any closer, especially in their alert-two status, we won't even need sixteen minutes before the United States reacts to our strike.'

The general secretary wiped his mouth, then discarded

the cloth napkin. 'Our biological and chemical attacks will follow hours after the nuclear strike. We have targeted all major American military installations, including large overseas bases.'

Zhilinkhov turned slightly to face the defense minister. 'Trofim Filippovich, explain the projected results of our preemptive strike.'

Porfir'yev's eyes narrowed as he slid forward in his chair to speak. 'Comrade Doctor Svyatoslav Cheskiy, chief of the Soviet Academy of Sciences, estimates, conservatively, that we can expect to achieve a minimum of sixty-five to seventy-five percent neutralization of the Americans.'

The defense minister paused, squinting even harder. 'That is, comrades, if their Star Wars system is malfunctioning, or incomplete.'

'It is imperative,' Zhilinkhov said slowly and forcefully, 'that we execute our first-strike plan soon if we are to dominate the Americans. We must take each step carefully, and follow our design precisely.'

Snow fell lightly outside the massive double-paned windows as the six men digested the visionary goal. The fireplace emitted a comforting warmth as logs crackled and the embers glowed red and orange.

'Trofim Filippovich,' Dichenkovko addressed the defense minister, 'what did Doctor Cheskiy project our casualties to be? In the final analysis?'

Porfir'yev paused while Dimitri entered the room and placed the six individual servings of piroshki on the low table next to the fireplace.

The young man turned toward Zhilinkhov, standing almost at attention. 'Comrade General Secretary, you wish me to place more logs on the fire?' Dimitri waited, the ever-attentive domestic.

'That will not be necessary,' Zhilinkhov said gruffly. 'I will see to the fire this evening.'

The senior kitchen servant exited as Porfir'yev prepared to answer the question of casualties.

'Doctor Cheskiy has been consulting with Doctor Beryagin Lysinko, chief of the Kyrchatov Atomic Energy Institute. They estimate, at worst, we would receive a twenty-five to thirty percent destruction level. Mainly the cities and military installations. They believe the effects of radiation fallout will dissipate after eight to twelve months.'

'What about the consequences of nuclear winter?' Zhilinkhov asked, chewing a fresh bite of piroshki.

Porfir'yev set his glass on the table and wiped his hands. 'The doctors are convinced the effects of nuclear winter will disappear in forty-five to sixty days. They are confident the upper winds will dissipate the effects of nuclear winter faster than most scientists predict.'

'What is your estimate in regard to Soviet casualties?' Dichenkovko asked.

'My staff expects, at the outside, a thirty-five percent personal casualty loss,' Porfir'yev replied uncomfortably. 'Approximately ninety million people.'

Zhilinkhov paused, leaning over for a cigar and striking a match to it. Inhaling deeply, the Soviet leader spoke in a strong, persuasive manner.

'Comrades, listen to me clearly. The Soviet Union will never have a better opportunity than the present. The American technological advances have offset our numerical advantage. Our empire, along with our satellite countries, will disintegrate unless we strike the United States very soon. No *peredyshka*, no breathing space. Our options are rapidly being depleted.'

Zhilinkhov's cold eyes sought contact with each member of the inner circle. 'If we don't strike the

Americans now, our Motherland will slowly strangle. Russia will die a lingering, agonizing death.'

Zhilinkhov knew the Politburo members, even his detractors, professed fidelity to the revolutionary tradition of world dominance. However, the Kremlin leaders tended to be conservative. They were uncomfortable with uncertainty and unpredictability. The current division in the Politburo had resulted from ambivalence in party planning.

The previous Soviet leader could not resolve the question of how to constrain the American Strategic Defense Initiative. SDI was then, as it had been for several years, the most contentious issue in Soviet-American relations.

'Comrades,' the general secretary said, 'a first strike would enable us to dominate America, Europe, the entire world, overnight. Literally overnight, without incurring unacceptable casualties or massive destruction.

'Besides, our military assets will be dispersed at sea and in the air, except for the ground forces. We will retain sixty to seventy percent of our prestrike military capability. More than enough to handle any combination of adversaries. NATO forces will not present a problem once the Americans are neutralized. And, Saudi oil will flow when we turn the valve.'

Zhilinkhov carefully ashed his thick Cuban cigar, tapping gently on the crystal receptacle.

'We can expect retaliation from the American submarines for a period of . . .' The general secretary sipped his drink, then noisily cleared his throat. 'Well, Marshal Bogdonoff and his staff are fully convinced the air defense and navy forces can deal with the residual effects of random retaliatory strikes.'

The senior Politburo member, Aleksandr F. Pulaev, quiet to this point, interjected a question.

'Viktor Pavlovich, how accurate can we expect the American retaliatory strikes to be?'

Zhilinkhov inhaled deeply, looking up at the ceiling, then slowly released the blue smoke.

'Our new commander of the Strategic Rocket Forces, General Bortnovska, is certain the Americans will only achieve ten to twenty percent accuracy with their missiles, after our massive strike.'

'Because of the satellite destruction?' the senior Politburo member asked, clearly not convinced.

'Absolutely,' Zhilinkhov answered, puffing slowly on his cigar. 'When we launch our first strike, our ground- and space-based lasers should be able to destroy the American communications and navigation satellites. We don't have to hit all the navigation satellites to make their targeting systems unreliable.'

Zhilinkhov swirled the vodka in his glass. 'Just enough to make their guidance systems unstable.'

The elder friend had another question worrying him, a very important political question. 'Viktor Pavlovich, does anyone – does Doctor Cheskiy, General Bortnovska, anyone – besides the six of us, and Marshal Bogdonoff, know anything about this initiative?'

'No, of course not,' Zhilinkhov said in an impatient manner. 'This information is the result of theoretical studies compiled by our most brilliant strategists and tacticians. The first-strike scenario is played every day in our Ministry of Defense. The military commanders believe these actions I have ordered are in response to escalating aggression by the Americans.'

The room remained silent.

'Initiative?' Zhilinkhov said with a question in his eyes as he refilled his glass. 'This is not an initiative. This is an all-out, massive nuclear strike on the United States.'

The fire snapped, reminding the general secretary that

he needed to resupply the grate. He unobtrusively stepped in front of his five friends and gingerly placed two logs on the glowing embers, showering sparks over his freshly shined shoes. Returning to his chair, Zhilinkhov proposed a toast.

'Comrades, we are joined on the eve of the most important event in the history of our Motherland. Our countrymen will hail us for generations. We will provide our people an opportunity for productive and peaceful lives. A nuclear war can be won if we strike first. We will survive to rule the entire globe. World supremacy at last, comrades. We will be revered for all of history as the fathers of a modern Russia. A Russia without boundaries!'

Zhilinkhov raised his glass in a salute to his five friends. 'To the Motherland, my friends.'

The general secretary beamed broadly. The Politburo quartet, accompanied by the defense minister, responded in kind, glancing cautiously at each other.

'To a supreme Russia, comrades.'

The resounding clink of crystal, as well as the entire conversation, had been clearly audible to the quiet figure standing in the hallway.

CAPE CANAVERAL

Rex Hays, alternately jotting notes and doodling, listened intently to the president's chief of staff. He had been surprised when Wilkinson called to brief him personally on the Russian situation.

Hays reflected on the contrast between Dave Miller and Wilkinson. There was an intellectual chasm between the indefatigable Grant Wilkinson and the slovenly Miller.

Hays waited for an opening to ask his first question. 'Mister Wilkinson – '

'Grant, please.' The chief of staff did not care for ceremony or pomposity.

'Grant it is. What do you think about moving the launch time up a day or two, along with an unpublished schedule?' Hays was thinking about an obvious Russian attempt to prevent the SDI satellites from reaching orbit.

'We don't believe it makes any difference at this point,' Wilkinson cleared his throat and continued. 'They know we're in DEFCON-Three and loaded for bear. The intelligence people believe Zhilinkhov is testing our defensive perimeters. Their scrambled message traffic has increased forty percent in the past forty-eight hours.'

'What's the climate between the president and the general secretary, if it isn't classified?' Hays asked, wondering if he was overstepping his bounds.

'It is classified, but that doesn't make much difference. The walls are porous around here. The *Post* receives information faster than I do.' Wilkinson chuckled before continuing his brief. 'The president proposed a meeting, face to face, one on one, at the convenience of the general secretary. That was late last night. Zhilinkhov agreed this morning and suggested a meeting in twenty-four hours in the Azores, at Lajes.'

'I assume the president accepted.' Hays was very curious about the possibility of a meeting between the two super-power leaders. The Soviet leader was still a mystery to most people.

'Oh yes, and he was unusually conciliatory. He liked the location. Great security and isolated, too. *Air Force One* is being prepared now and we expect to leave in . . .' Wilkinson looked at his wall clock, noting the time, 'an hour and a half. Seventeen hundred eastern.'

'How long do you anticipate being there?' Hays asked,

thinking the president might be out of the country when they launched *Columbia*.

'Three, possibly four days. Perhaps longer if we make any progress. The president has some ideas to present. I'm obviously not at liberty to discuss those topics, but you'll be kept apprised.'

Hays doodled continuously, not wanting to interrupt Wilkinson. He was fascinated by the intrigue.

'Better let you off the phone. This place is a madhouse and I've got a plane to catch. Good luck with your launch, Rex.' Wilkinson concluded the conversation as he packed files in his leather attaché case.

'Thanks, Grant, and best of luck in the Azores.'

'We'll need it. So long.'

Hays placed the receiver down, reaching for his coat, as he pictured the meeting in Lajes. He headed directly for the cafeteria, having missed his late lunch waiting for the preplanned call from the White House.

Talking with the president's chief of staff was unusual, Hays thought, but the present circumstances were unusual, too.

USS *VIRGINIA*

The nuclear-powered heavy cruiser, steaming at full speed, pitched and rolled violently in the towering swells. Waves of ice-cold seawater smashed into the base of the bridge as the missile cruiser staggered from trough to trough.

A North Atlantic winter storm was developing and the *Virginia* was dogged tight for heavy seas. Another 240 nautical miles – nine hours – and she would rendezvous with the *Eisenhower* battle group. The mission was to augment her sister ship, the *Mississippi*, until the

DEFCON alert was cancelled. The *Mississippi* would then return to Norfolk for repairs to her damaged rudders.

Cmdr Fred Simpson, skipper of the *Virginia*, automatically swayed back and forth in front of his mirror, compensating for the rolling motion of the ship.

'Damn!' That was the second nick and he still had the other side of his face to shave.

More swearing ensued as Simpson lurched into a towel holder, then banged his elbow on the sink. He had decided to shave and shower before the seas became rougher, as they were predicted to be near the battle group.

Simpson glanced at the brass clock mounted over his stateroom desk. It was 0300 hours, a hell of a time to be shaving, Simpson thought, as he bounced off the bulkhead, nearly losing his balance. The *Virginia* would rendezvous with the Ike at noon and Simpson would be too busy in the early morning hours to refresh himself. Besides, he couldn't sleep, reflecting on the DEFCON-Three alert.

Simpson toweled his face and reached for his comb when the speaker sounded.

'Captain to the bridge! Captain to the bridge!'

Simpson reached for his phone, punching the bridge code.

'Bridge, sir.' The *Virginia*'s officer of the deck answered personally.

'This is the captain, Stan.'

'Sir, sonar has picked up a submarine, Russian signature, two points off the starboard bow, range nine thousand yards and closing.'

'I'll be there in a minute. Meantime, turn twenty degrees to port and we'll see if Ivan follows.' Simpson stopped a moment, thinking.

93

'Stan, we're at DEFCON-Three, so sound general quarters and give me the status of our ASW gear,' Simpson ordered as he placed the receiver back in the cradle. He reached for his shirt as the general quarters alarm sounded.

The loud warning signal reverberated throughout the ship, shocking sleeping crew members awake.

'All hands man your battle stations! All hands man your battle stations! General quarters! General quarters!'

Sailors piled out of racks, clamoring for uniforms and shoes, bewilderment written on the faces of the young men as they raced for their assigned duty stations.

Simpson stepped into the bridge, noting with satisfaction that his officer of the deck, Lt Cmdr Stan Jenkins, was on the new course and slowing. The seas were too rough to remain at full speed while the men were at battle stations.

'Captain, the ASROCS and launchers are up and ready. Torpedoes and tubes ready and standing by.' Jenkins waited for a response from Simpson.

'Very well, Stan. What about the LAMPS helo?'

'Being readied in the hangar. The duty crew is boarding now. The pilot isn't very enthusiastic about this weather, though.' Jenkins knew the skipper didn't care for naval aviators in general.

'Well, get him enthused,' Simpson replied sharply. 'That's why they get flight pay.'

'Aye aye, sir,' Jenkins responded and turned to the radio-man. 'Tell Seahawk Thirty-eight to launch and commence search pattern.'

'Yessir,' replied the petty officer, a question in his eyes.

The pilot, Lt Hector Chaveze, had the LAMPS III helicopter's main rotors up to speed. He was still lashed to the deck and knew when he signaled for release, crazy in this weather, he would have to rise straight up as quickly as possible or risk colliding with the ship as it rolled in the turbulent seas.

Chaveze knew the risky operation was borderline in his NATOPS flight manual, but Simpson made the rules out here. Better to crash the helo than disobey the omnipotent captain.

'Sonar?' Jenkins formed the word into a question.

'Closing on us, sir,' the first class petty officer reported, studying his scope. 'Appears to be on a thirty-degree intercept course . . . no, they're closing the angle of intercept, sir.'

'Flash to CINCLANT, *Eisenhower*, and *Kennedy*,' Simpson ordered, turning to Commander Jenkins. 'Tell Ike we need ASW coverage, on the double! Is the helo up yet?'

'Lifting off at this time, Captain,' Jenkins replied, reaching for the message phone.

Chaveze twisted all the power he could muster from the twin turbine engines, signaled for release from the pitching deck, and grasped the collective firmly.

Rolling waves of frigid water smashed into the side of the helicopter hangar, spraying the LAMPS helo and sodden deck crew.

At the precise instant the hook was released, Chaveze yanked the collective up sharply, popping the helicopter into the turbulent air.

The lieutenant was on instruments immediately. The darkness was absolute, the stars and moon blanked by cloud cover at 3,000 feet. He leveled at 800 feet above the cold, churning ocean. His copilot, Ens. Randy Gill, noted with great satisfaction that both altimeters, radar and pressure, were precisely in agreement.

The LAMPS crew activated the on-board magnetic anomaly detection (MAD) sensors and lowered their sonobuoy into the raging Atlantic. The Soviet hunter-killer submarine immediately registered on their equipment and Chaveze changed course slightly, closing slowly on the Russian.

'Nest Egg, Seahawk Thirty-eight has the submarine,' Chaveze radioed the *Virginia*. 'Signature confirms a Russian hunterkiller. We're making another sweep.'

'Roger, Seahawk.' The captain looked at the sonar operator, then spoke to the LAMPS pilot again. 'Let 'em know you're overhead. We have a Viking on the way.'

The *Virginia*'s skipper, mentally computing the time it would take for the ASW aircraft to reach his position, was extremely edgy. The captain, who had been on board the USS *Vincennes* (CG 49) in the Persian Gulf during July 1988, had every reason to be nervous. The message detailing the *Tennessee* encounter was fresh in his mind.

USS *DWIGHT D. EISENHOWER*

The Flash Message from the *Virginia* had been received only seconds before the carrier battle group made a course change toward the cruiser. The remaining Russian sub trailing the Ike and her escorts made the course change and followed.

The orbiting Hawkeye was directing the CAP Tomcats, 'Buzzard' One and Two, to rendezvous with Viking 706 near the *Virginia*'s location.

A Soviet trawler, sprouting electronic gear and antennas, was shadowing the *Eisenhower* battle group and eavesdropping on their radio conversations. The Russian submarine skipper stalking the *Virginia* was fully aware of the impending arrival of the American antisubmarine aircraft and escort fighters. The Soviet sub commander had his orders, orders issued from the Kremlin.

Admiral McKenna stepped into CIC as Texaco 514, a KA-6D tanker, screeched down number two catapult, shaking the Ike from bow to stern.

'What's up, Greg?' McKenna asked Linnemeyer, as he rubbed his eyes.

The captain had arrived in CIC only a minute before the task force commander.

'Not completely sure, sir. The *Virginia* sent a message indicating they were at general quarters and requesting ASW coverage. A Russian sub is apparently stalking them. Their LAMPS has confirmed the sub and – '

Linnemeyer was interrupted by the admiral. 'They've got a helo up in this weather?'

'Yes, sir. Think the skipper is being overly cautious 'cause of the alert.'

'Greg,' McKenna paused, thinking, 'can they recover the LAMPS aboard the *Virginia* in this kind of weather?'

'Possible, Admiral, if the pilot is red-hot and the recovery crew is sharp.' The CO was on a limb. 'Fifty-fifty, I'd say.'

Linnemeyer could see the concern registering on McKenna's face. The task force commander turned to the CIC duty officer, Lieutenant Dyestrom, and asked to be patched to the LAMPS helicopter.

'Yessir,' Dyestrom replied. 'His call sign is Seahawk Thirty-eight, Admiral.'

'Thanks, Lieutenant,' McKenna responded as he placed the receiver to his ear.

'Seahawk Thirty-eight, Seahawk Thirty-eight, this is Tango Fox One. Do you copy?'

Chaveze heard the message clearly. He was shocked. Tango Fox One was the task force commander, the admiral himself.

'Tango Fox, Seahawk. Five by five, sir.'

'Seahawk, this is Admiral McKenna. Understand you have ferreted an unwelcome guest.'

'Affirmative, sir. We are over him now.'

'Good job, son.' McKenna looked at Linnemeyer. 'How's the weather?'

'I've seen better, Admiral,' Chaveze replied as he leveled the bouncing helicopter.

'Okay, listen closely.' McKenna paused as he looked at Linnemeyer. 'If you have any doubt about landing on your ship safely, any doubt, I want you to head for the carrier and recover here.'

'Yes, sir!' Chaveze grinned at his copilot. 'As soon as the Viking relieves us, we'll be en route to the carrier.'

McKenna smiled. He could hear cheering in the background. Smart young pilot, he thought to himself.

'Okay, son, we'll have breakfast on for your crew.'

McKenna gave the handset back to Dyestrom and turned to Linnemeyer.

'Greg, I don't like the smell of this kettle.' McKenna sipped his steaming coffee. 'Launch another Viking, along with a tanker, and get two more fourteens airborne, with two on the cats and two standing by, manned.'

'Yessir,' Linnemeyer answered, taking the handset from the outstretched arm of Dyestrom.

SEAHAWK THIRTY-EIGHT

Ensign Gill looked over at Chaveze and smiled, slowly shaking his head. 'You must be livin' right. Snatched from the jaws of Simpson with a breakfast invitation from the admiral, no less.'

They both chuckled, along with the crew. This was going to be a piece of cake now.

'Seahawk Thirty-eight, this is Nest Egg,' Simpson called, miffed by the radio exchange between the helicopter and the carrier. It wasn't good to have your judgement questioned by an admiral, especially the *Eisenhower*'s task force commander.

'Roger, Nest Egg,' Chaveze was trying to suppress a grin.

'You are cleared to recover aboard the carrier.' Simpson grimaced. 'Copy?'

'Copy, Nest Egg,' Chaveze replied, thinking how embarrassed Simpson must feel.

'Seahawk, Killer Seven-oh-six has a lock on your friend. Take it to the boat.' The Viking pilot checked in with Chaveze, not able to resist a jab at the non-aviator who ordered a helo out in this weather. 'Man, you shouldn't be out flapping around in weather like this. Insane, brother, especially in a Spam can.'

'Roger, Seven-oh-six,' Chaveze answered in an even tone. He didn't want to fuel Simpson's rage any further.

'Mother is zero-one-zero for two hundred ten,' the Viking pilot radioed. 'Got enough gas, Seahawk?'

'That's affirm, Killer,' Chaveze replied. 'Appreciate the help. Seahawk is off-station.'

Chaveze headed for the *Eisenhower* while the crew raised the sonobuoy and stowed their gear.

THE TOMCATS

'Buzzard flight, Stingray.' The Hawkeye's airborne controller sounded tired and bored.

'Go,' Jim O'Neill, Lieutenant, USN, replied as he strained his eyes in an effort to see below the cloud base.

The radio crackled, startling O'Neill. 'Killer Seven-oh-six is at your ten o'clock, twelve miles.'

'No contact. Seven-oh-six, turn to three-six-zero and flash your lights,' O'Neill ordered as he studied the soft glow of his radar screen. He had the Viking on the scope but not visually.

'I have 'em, Buzzard,' Vince Cangemi, flying Buzzard Two, radioed his leader. The Marine captain was flying wing position on this sortie.

'Rog, I've got a tally at eleven o'clock, low,' O'Neill acknowledged, sneaking a peek at his engine gauges. He had been increasingly worried about his starboard engine. The RPM gauge had been surging at sporadic intervals. If the situation hadn't been so critical, O'Neill would have flown the F-14 directly to the carrier.

'Buzzard flight, Stingray.' Urgent this time.

'Go,' O'Neill answered, watching the right engine surge.

'We've got four pop-ups at your eight o'clock, two hundred twenty out, smokin' like gangbusters.'

'Keep us informed.'

O'Neill looked at his fuel gauges, disregarding the questionable rough-running engine, before making a decision.

'Roger, Buzzard. The bogies are closing at . . . Jesus, nine hundred knots! Either Fulcrums or Foxhounds.'

'Where'd they come from?' O'Neill asked petulantly, his mind racing for answers. 'We're in the middle of nowhere.'

'Came out of a commercial airline corridor,' radioed the surprised controller. 'Boom, just exploded on my screen. Man, they have got some speed on.'

'Rog, looks like a setup.' O'Neill pictured a large Russian transport, disguised as an Aeroflot commercial flight, full of fuel and trailing hoses, lumbering along at night over the open ocean. They could easily stash four fighters in tight formation under the wings. The smaller aircraft wouldn't show on radar.

'Stingray, Buzzard,' O'Neill radioed, watching the right engine surge again. 'Any Russian airliners on the corridor near the point they popped up?'

'Ah, stand by,' the now lively voice answered.

O'Neill checked his instruments, glanced at Cangemi, and watched his clock sweep through twenty seconds. 'Come on Stingray . . . we haven't got much time,' O'Neill said to himself.

'Buzzard, Stingray.'

'Go,' O'Neill said sharply.

'That's affirm.' The controller released the transmit button a split second, then pressed it again. 'Aeroflot flight Seventeen-oh-eight.'

'Where's it going?' O'Neill tensed, knowing the answer in advance. 'Destination?'

'Cuba.'

'Keep us informed,' the flight leader replied, swearing to himself. 'Have Mother send more chicks, mucho hasto!'

'Roger, Buzzard. Two of the "Jolly Rogers" are on the way, call sign "Scooter". We'll switch them to your freq in a couple minutes.'

'Okay.' O'Neill paused. 'Texaco, you copy Buzzard?'

'Roger, Buzzard.' The tanker pilot sounded relaxed. 'We are anchored over the *Virginia* at two-six-oh. Need some gas and a windshield wipe this evening?'

'That's affirm, we're on our way.'

O'Neill looked over at Cangemi's dull gray Tomcat.

'Let's go upstairs, Two.'

'Rajah.'

Simpson had turned back on course directly to the *Eisenhower*, relieved to have the Viking overhead. His relief was short-lived when he became aware of the approaching Russian fighters, now an airborne threat.

'Mister Jenkins, status report on our Sea Sparrows,' Simpson commanded as he nervously paced the bridge.

'Loaded, all systems up, launchers at the ready. Radar tracking indicates up status, Captain.'

'Very well,' Simpson replied, tapping his Naval Academy ring on the rim of his clipboard.

The bridge was hushed as everyone swayed back and forth, contemplating the next few minutes. The *Virginia* was at battle stations, tension coursing through the ship as she topped each wave and plunged into the next abyss, sending tremors reverberating through the hull.

Simpson and the bridge crew listened to the pilots rendezvousing overhead.

'Stingray, Scooter flight has a tally on the Buzzards,' radioed Lt Davey 'Pork' Heimler. 'Going tactical.'

'Copy, Scooter,' answered the fully awake controller.

'Button four.'

'Rog. Goin' four, switch,' the 'Jolly Roger' fighter pilot ordered his wingman.

'Scooter up.'

'Two,' responded Lt (jg) Jeb Graves.

'Buzzards, Scooter flight is aboard. Your seven, easin' in, two hundred fifty indicated.'

'Good show,' O'Neill answered, concentrating on his egress from the KA-6D. 'Better top off.'

'Scooter, Texaco,' the tanker pilot radioed. 'You're cleared to plug.'

'Rog. One is plugging.'

Heimler eased closer to the trailing basket connected

to the fuel hose. He slowed his closure rate to a barely perceptible mating with the bouncing basket.

Night refueling, always difficult because of a lack of depth perception, was not something pilots looked forward to facing.

Heimler glanced at the tanker, then keyed his microphone.

'How much gas you have left?'

''Bout four thousand pounds,' the tanker jock answered nonchalantly. 'Another Tex is on the way.'

'Okay,' Heimler said. 'I'll take two grand and my partner can drain the rest.'

'Fair enough.'

Simpson looked at the sonar repeater. The Soviet sub was holding the same relative position. He lifted his binoculars and scanned the horizon, wishing for dawn to arrive.

The *Virginia*'s captain couldn't distinguish anything in the black, raging storm, but it made him feel more comfortable than sitting idle, waiting.

The radio speaker continued to blare, harsh in the confines of the bridge, as the fighter pilots finished their airborne refueling.

Simpson's disdain for aviators had diminished in the past fifteen minutes.

'Buzzard flight, Stingray.' This was a new voice, apparently the number one quarterback on the Hawkeye team.

'Go,' O'Neill radioed, closely monitoring his right engine gauges.

'The bogies are at your ten o'clock, one hundred out.'

The four Tomcats, with replenished fuel tanks, had been orbiting in a racetrack course over the *Virginia*.

'Rog, Stingray.' O'Neill was breathing faster, tension

straining his voice. The fluctuating engine problem had to be forgotten at this point.

'This is now Buzzard flight,' O'Neill radioed. 'Both sections go combat spread, Three and Four to the right.'

'Two!'

'Three!'

'Four!'

O'Neill could feel rivulets of sweat trickle down his temples as he checked his armament panel. He breathed deeply and forced himself to relax. 'Come port twenty degrees. Let's go switches hot.'

'Two!'

'Three!'

'Four!'

'You okay, Jeff?' O'Neill clicked his intercom button. He hadn't heard a word from his radar intercept officer in five minutes.

'Yeah, doin' fine,' replied a hushed voice. 'I've got a sweet lock.'

The RIO, Lt (jg) Jeffery Barnes was new to the squadron and O'Neill could understand his problem. This was a rude introduction to operational flying.

'Okay, stay alert,' O'Neill said in an encouraging tone.

'This deal is too well-orchestrated to suit me.'

Barnes shifted his gaze outside the canopy. 'I was thinking the same thing.'

Simpson set his third cup of coffee down on a tray, too nervous to taste the black liquid. He repeatedly swallowed involuntarily.

'Captain, sonar.'

'Captain,' Simpson responded immediately, swiveling in his bridge chair.

'Sir, the sub is surfacing,' the operator said quietly. 'Or coming to periscope depth.'

Simpson looked through his binoculars at the black, turbulent ocean. 'You sure?'

'Yessir, they're blowing tanks.' The petty officer waited a moment, then responded to what he was hearing.

'A lot of activity . . . and noise.'

Simpson turned to Jenkins, simultaneously asking a question and giving an order. 'Where's the XO? Tell the Viking to get on top of the sub, or we're going to be shark bait!'

'The exec is in CIC, sir.' Jenkins felt like he was on a treadmill. 'They notified Killer Seven-oh-six.'

'JESUS!'

'WHAT THE HELL!'

Everyone ducked or flinched as a brilliant flash turned night into bright day for a millisecond. There was a streak of light, too fast to follow, accompanied by a resounding crack and low rumble.

'MAY DAY! MAY DAY! Killer Seven-oh-six, we've been hit! We're goin' in! EJECT! EJECT!' The pilot was still transmitting on the radio, forgetting to switch to ICS.

Simpson was in shock as he followed the action over the speaker. Outside, less than a mile from the *Virginia*, a flaming ball of debris was tumbling toward the ocean. Jenkins had to remind Simpson that they needed to take action.

'Captain Simpson, the sub shot down the Viking! What do you want to – ?'

'Commence firing on the sub!' Simpson ordered, throwing off the mental block.

'SAMS! SAMS!' Cangemi radioed, ducking as another flash of light streaked past his canopy. 'The Viking is down!'

'Buzzard flight, hold your fire! Hold your fire!'

O'Neill was waiting for confirmation on the bogies.

The *Virginia* would have to deal with the sub. He had his hands full setting up for the aerial engagement.

'Buzzard, this is Stingray,' the Hawkeye controller radioed. 'Understand the Viking is – '

Suddenly the darkness glowed miles in front of the American fighter planes. A high-pitched warble sounded in the ears of the four pilots and their RIOs. The Russian fighter pilots had launched their air-to-air missiles in unison.

'Buzzard flight, launch missiles!' O'Neill ordered, fumbling with his armament panel. 'Three and Four, break right! One and Two goin' for knots . . . comin' left!'

'Three and Four, FOX ONE!' Heimler radioed as the AIM-7M Sparrow missiles streaked out in front of the Tomcats. 'Going right!'

Heimler snapped into a gut-wrenching 7-G turn, then glanced at the flash below him. 'What the hell . . . is that . . . on the surface?'

'Don't know!' O'Neill was straining to breathe under the 8-G load he forced on the laboring Tomcat. 'One and Two going high,' O'Neill groaned as he pulled back hard on the control stick, sending the big fighter into a supersonic pure vertical climb. The two Tomcats were indicating Mach 1.2 as they rocketed skyward into the sullen clouds. O'Neill's engine problem had been forgotten.

'God, what happened?' Cangemi asked, inching closer to Buzzard One.

O'Neill never had a chance to answer. His fighter exploded in a horrendous fireball, lighting the sky in an eerie yellow-white burst of light.

More explosions lit the night, causing chaos over the aircraft radios.

'Stingray! Stingray! We're going dow – '

'MAY DAY! MAY DAY!' shouted a high-pitched voice.

'WE'RE PUNCHIN'!'

Three seconds later Cangemi felt the impact of a Russian air-to-air missile. He was blinded by the explosion as his Tomcat tumbled toward the icy water, spinning wildly and spewing flaming jet fuel.

The left wing had been blown off and the fuselage was riddled with holes, leaving the young Marine pilot with only one option. Cangemi thumbed the ICS and yelled at his RIO.

'EJECT! EJECT!'

Cangemi could feel his head being bashed violently against the canopy as his body slammed from side to side. Then he noted the altimeter, rapidly spiraling downward, as he reached up over his helmet with both hands and pulled his ejection seat handle.

The protective face curtain had just covered his helmet visor when the blast from the rear seat ejection turned the cockpit into a howling hurricane. One-half second later Cangemi hurtled into space to join his radar intercept officer.

Buzzard One, gravely injured during the ballistic ejection, was already in his parachute, trailing his RIO down to the cold, rolling ocean. O'Neill viewed the devastation in shock and pain as he descended below the cloud base. He could see the *Virginia* in the distance, flames and smoke pouring from the aft section of the cruiser. It appeared to O'Neill as if the entire fantail was ablaze.

The sky was still lit by explosions and parachute flares as O'Neill slowly drifted toward the *Virginia*, suspended by his parachute risers over the flames and falling debris. A sudden flash to his left, followed seconds later by an explosive noise, marked the grave of his Tomcat fighter.

O'Neill ripped off his oxygen mask, tossing it away in

the darkness, and started preparing for his entry into the frigid waters. The pilot knew he would succumb to hypothermia in minutes if he couldn't board his one-man life raft or be plucked from the freezing waters by a rescue helicopter.

Another aircraft hit the water and exploded with a deafening roar, causing O'Neill to involuntarily jerk around in his torso harness. It was impossible to tell if it was a Russian or American aircraft. Debris was raining down all around him. The Navy fighter pilot, battling unconsciousness, fervently hoped all four Russians were in the drink.

Cangemi's parachute opened with shocking force from the high-speed ejection. As the slightly injured Marine aviator descended below the clouds, struggling with his survival gear, another aircraft smashed into the water with a deafening concussion.

Looking in the direction of the *Virginia*, Cangemi thought he saw another parachute descend below the cloud deck. He didn't have time to study the other figure. The sight of whitecaps indicated only seconds to prepare for the shock of entry into freezing waters.

SEAHAWK THIRTY-EIGHT

Hector Chaveze was only twenty miles from the *Virginia* when he heard the melee erupt. The lieutenant wheeled his helicopter around in a 180-degree turn and raced for his ship as fast as the LAMPS would go. He didn't hesitate a second, realizing aircrew members and ship's-company from the *Virginia* might be in the cold, turbulent ocean. Chaveze and his crew would be their only hope in these conditions.

The LAMPS pilot thought about the fact he was

committed to land on the *Virginia* after all. Not enough fuel for multiple rescue attempts and a flight to the carrier.

Chaveze briefed his crew and called the Hawkeye.

'Stingray, Stingray, Seahawk Thirty-eight proceeding back to the *Virginia*. Standing by for rescue coordination.'

'Roger, Seahawk,' the surprised Hawkeye controller answered. 'We've gota basket of shit here . . . ah . . . multiple aircraft in the water.'

'Stingray, we have the *Virginia* visual!' Chaveze could feel his heart pounding.

'Roger,' responded the controller, pausing to talk to his assistant. 'We have two Tomcats, a Texaco, and . . . the Viking down. Search all quadrants around the *Virginia*.'

'Wilco, Stingray.'

Chaveze looked at his copilot. 'What the hell happened out here?'

Gill shrugged, indicating it was useless to speculate at this point.

The pilot pressed his radio button again. 'Stingray, Seahawk. Any more Russian aircraft loitering in the area?'

'Negative, Seahawk. Stand by.'

The controller studied two radar scopes, then called the pilot. 'Looks like three of them went down. We are tracking one headed for the coast, slow, probably damaged or conserving fuel. No observed threats at this time. No radar returns in the area, except two Tomcats still on station.'

'Roger, Stingray,' the LAMPS pilot replied, descending toward the burning *Virginia*. 'Thanks.'

Gill tugged on Chaveze and pointed in front of the

helicopter. A pencil flare or flashlight bobbed up and down a quarter mile away in the inky blackness.

'Got it,' Chaveze said as he nosed the LAMPS helo over and ordered the hoist ready.

USS *VIRGINIA*

After the first torpedo explosion rocked the *Virginia*, Simpson fired two ASROC missiles at the Soviet submarine.

'Skipper,' the sonarman shouted, 'I have another torpedo tracking, bearing zero-seven-zero!'

'Right full rudder, all ahead flank!' Simpson looked for Jenkins as he tried to assess the damage to his ship.

'Mister Jenkins, get a damage control report and have the XO . . . have Commander Risone report to the bridge on the double!'

'Aye aye, Captain.'

The *Virginia* was racked by another violent explosion, shattering windows on the bridge. The ship was slowing rapidly and starting to list to starboard.

'Captain,' the sonarman yelled across the bridge. 'We got the sub breaking up, sir!'

'You positive?' Simpson shouted as he stumbled toward the operator.

'Yessir,' the frightened sailor responded in a taut voice. 'No question.'

The sonarman turned the volume up for the captain. The sound of the Soviets' pressure hull, being crushed like eggshells, was eerily clear. Simpson relaxed a moment, realizing the immediate threat was gone. Now to save his stricken ship.

Jenkins spoke from behind. 'Captain, damage control says they can contain the fire. One propulsion system is out of commission and seven compartments are flooded. They can't correct the list, but the ship has watertight integrity.'

'Okay,' Simpson answered, appearing haggard. 'What about casualties?'

'Fourteen confirmed dead, sir, including Commander Risone. No estimate of injured yet. Everyone is too busy at the moment.' Jenkins felt fatigue taking over from the adrenaline.

'Very well, Mister Jenkins,' Simpson sighed, eyes cast downward. The captain paused a moment, then looked back into Jenkins's face. 'Bud was a good man. All of them were good men.'

'Yes, sir,' Jenkins responded, placing a hand on the captain's shoulder. 'The best.'

The radioman quietly interrupted the two grieving officers. 'Captain, Seahawk Thirty-eight is back. They're picking up someone now.'

'What?' Simpson looked toward the starboard side of his damaged ship. 'Okay. Stand by to bring them aboard.'

The *Virginia*'s skipper was glad to have the helicopter back. It would be impossible to put a small boat over the side in heavy seas. The helo was the only hope for the survivors in the frigid, churning ocean.

'What a goddamned nightmare,' Simpson said quietly to himself as the lights of the LAMPS helicopter came into sight. An F-14 roared low over the ship, creating a rolling thunder, as the *Virginia*'s captain tried to piece together what had happened in the last seven and a half minutes.

5

The new Boeing executive-configured 747 was cruising at 41,000 feet, experiencing light turbulence, when Grant Wilkinson, carrying a Flash Message, rushed into the president's private dining room.

'Mister President,' Wilkinson paused a second and continued, 'Sir, the Russians attacked one of our ships. The *Virginia* is – '

'SON-OF-A-BITCH!' The president dropped his utensils in his plate, the early breakfast forgotten, as the color drained from his face.

'When?'

'Approximately twenty minutes ago. The *Virginia* is badly damaged but afloat.'

Wilkinson looked at the message in his hand, then subconsciously crushed the paper. 'Sub got them and shot down an antisub plane from the *Eisenhower*.'

'What about the sub?' the president asked, clearly agitated. He quickly wiped his mouth, then threw the linen napkin on the table.

'The *Virginia* sunk it, sir. Another ASW plane confirmed the sinking.'

'How many casualties, Grant?' The president was intense.

'Too early to tell, sir. Fourteen aboard the *Virginia* estimated killed. They have aircrews in the water and rescue operations are continuing.'

'What are our total losses?' the president asked, standing up from his table.

'Two fighters, a tanker plane, and the antisub aircraft are confirmed at this time.'

'How the hell did we lose that many aircraft?'

'Sir, the Russians had fighters up, came out of nowhere. They shot down two of our Tomcats and the tanker aircraft before our pilots had a – '

'Did we get any of their fighters?'

'Yessir, three.' Wilkinson had never seen his friend this violently mad. 'One limped to the coast, may have bailed out over land.'

'How the hell did they get fighters out there without being detected?'

'No one knows for sure, sir.' Wilkinson paused, choosing his words carefully. 'Our airborne radar plane reported the Russians popped out from a commercial airline track, possibly being camouflaged by a transport plane. There was an Aeroflot aircraft in the area at the time of the attack.'

'What do you think, Grant?'

'Obviously deliberate.' Wilkinson sighed. 'An insane move on the eve of your meeting with Zhilinkhov. Just beyond comprehension.'

'Agree.' The president paused, mulling over various responses to the attack. 'I agree wholeheartedly, Grant.'

The president was regaining his composure. 'How do you think I should approach Zhilinkhov and his staff?'

Wilkinson did not hesitate. 'Sir, you're going to have to take the gloves off with this guy.'

Wilkinson watched as the president, formulating a decision, lightly tapped his fingers on the edge of the table.

'You're absolutely correct, as usual.' The president looked straight into the eyes of his chief of staff. 'Order

DEFCON-Two and notify Lajes that I demand to see Zhilinkhov immediately on arrival.'

'Yessir,' Wilkinson replied as he opened the cabin door.

The president, assimilating the unprovoked attack by the Soviets, attempted to analyze what Zhilinkhov was trying to accomplish with these blatant assaults on the Americans.

The commander-in-chief realized there were too many possibilities to contend with at this juncture. He nibbled absently on a piece of cold dry wheat toast.

The president knew the Soviets well. They would become serious and willing to talk only when threatened by systems that effectively neutralized their own forces. He thought about the new Stealth bombers and fighters.

These new weapons, along with early deployment of the basic Strategic Defense Initiative (SDI) satellites, had apparently unnerved the Soviet leaders.

The Russians had continued to exercise power by brute force, while their political system had become moribund and perfunctory. Soviet technology, while excellent in many areas, lagged far behind the United States. The Union of Soviet Socialist Republics, encompassing an area of 8,649,490 square miles and 266 million inhabitants, would not be a superpower without their arsenal of intercontinental ballistic missiles and space-related capabilities.

The Russians had every reason to be concerned, considering the technological advances in American military defense systems over the past four years. The Soviets were now facing the rapid deployment of these weapons.

The president had thoroughly studied the Soviet theories and aims that constituted their political, social, and economic aspirations. The Kremlin leadership simply did not subscribe to the thesis that a nuclear war cannot be won.

All Russian command and control systems had been increasingly hardened. They had constructed extensive relocation facilities and virtually impregnable underground bunkers for their political hierarchy.

The Soviets had continued to deploy widely dispersed mobile nuclear weapons, along with an ever growing submarine force, to augment the massive Russian army.

The enormous cost of such an undertaking sent a very clear message to the United States government. The Soviet leaders were prepared to engage in, and expected to survive, a nuclear conflict with the Americans and their allies.

A polite knock at the president's cabin door interrupted his thoughts as Wilkinson reentered to brief his boss.

'Mister President, DEFCON-Two has been initiated and Lajes Command is relaying your demand, er, request to Zhilinkhov. We should be on the ground a couple of minutes before his arrival.'

'Excellent, Grant.' The president reached for the phone connecting him with the flight deck of the mammoth jet.

'We need to be there even earlier,' the president said to Wilkinson as he waited for the aircraft commander to respond.

'Colonel Boyd, sir.'

'Colonel, I'd like to arrive in Lajes ahead of our schedule. Think we can do that?'

'Yes, sir. No problem. We'll put another man on the coal shovel.'

The president chuckled, thinking about the dry sense of humor Col Donald Boyd, the commander of *Air Force One*, continually displayed.

'By the way, Colonel, you may inform the crew that we are now in DEFCON-Two status.'

'I know, Mister President. We have been informed that we'll have a fighter escort from the carrier *Eisenhower* in approximately fifty minutes. They're airborne and tanking at this time, sir.'

'Okay, Don. I want to beat the Soviet contingent to the ramp, if possible, by at least fifteen minutes.'

'Yessir, we've got 'er up to Mach-knocker now.'

'Very good,' replied the president as he replaced the handset and turned to his chief of staff.

'Grant, I've been thinking about the Soviet preparedness for nuclear conflict.'

'Yes, sir.' Wilkinson waited for the president to collect his thoughts.

'We all know their belief in surviving a nuclear confrontation, a full-blown war.'

'Yes, sir.'

'We also realize the differences between American and Soviet Union thinking. Both philosophies are deeply rooted and abiding.'

Silence.

The president continued. 'There is no moral equivalence between our nations. The really salient aspect of the Soviet attitude toward nuclear confrontation is widespread preparation for the ensuing consequences. Correct?'

'Absolutely, sir,' Wilkinson responded as he rolled up his shirt sleeves.

'Then let me ask you something, Grant.'

'Yes, sir.'

'If the Russians believe they can survive a nuclear holocaust with the United States, and they believe our new strategic defensive systems will negate their ballistic missiles, would it follow that Soviet leadership would use their first-strike capability to crush us before we render their weapons useless?'

'The logic does track, Mister President.' Wilkinson knew when to be quiet and analytical.

'Then why in hell, assuming the Russians plan to launch an all-out offensive, would they bring us to this state of readiness for a preemptive strike?'

Not waiting for an answer, the president continued, lighting a rum-soaked cigar. 'It's suicidal, Grant. One miscue, one commander gets the wrong word, and BOOM. It's all over. The civilized world will be blown back to the age of the Australopithecus man. If the goddamn planet survives.'

Silence followed as the president puffed on his cigar and blew a smoke ring.

'I'm not so sure man can be labeled civilized, Mister President,' Wilkinson said in a low even tone.

'Point taken,' the president replied, blowing a cloud of sweet-smelling smoke toward the ceiling.

Wilkinson leaned forward. 'Mister President, I wish to offer an opinion and suggestion.'

'I'm open to anything, Grant,' the president responded without a pause, inhaling deeply on his cigar.

'Sir, if Zhilinkhov is becoming senile, or unreliable, a likely assumption at his age, then we can't know where we are.'

'True. Continue.'

'If Zhilinkhov's thinking isn't rational, then we might as well be dealing with a lowerclass primate. A very deadly one, I might add.'

The president leaned back in his chair, gazed at the blue and gold ceiling of the jumbo jet, and looked Wilkinson in the eyes before speaking. 'What do you suggest, Grant?'

'Sir, DEFCON-Two is tantamount to a declaration of

war, or as close as one can get to war before pushing the final button.'

'Agree. Go on.'

'I recommend that we contact our operative in the Kremlin, in the quarters of the general secretary, and see if he can obtain any relevant intelligence for us. He will most likely be sacrificed. We've had him in place for two and a half years, but we need substantive information now, Mister President.'

'I could not agree more.' The president paused. 'How reliable is this agent, Grant?'

'Very reliable, by all indications, sir. He is highly regarded at Langley.'

'Very well. Make contact as quickly as possible, and give me an update on the DEFCON-Two status when you have an opportunity.'

'Will do, sir.'

Wilkinson gently shut the door as he hurried down the corridor to the message center of *Air Force One*.

NORTH AMERICAN AEROSPACE DEFENSE
COMMAND (NORAD)

Gen. Richard 'J. B .' Matuchek, United States Air Force, CINCNORAD, stared in disbelief as the status light on the situation board blinked on and off, accompanied by a loud buzzer, indicating a DEFCON-Two alert.

The general had just returned to his command post, deep in the 100-million-year-old Cheyenne Mountain, from a global situation briefing. This new development was totally unexpected, in view of the pending conference between the two superpowers in Lajes.

Matuchek was trying to grasp the consequences of this latest twist in the rapidly eroding American-Soviet relationship. Absently, the four-star general checked the authenticator code a third time. No question. This alert was real, not a computer glitch.

Matuchek opened the DEFCON-Two orders. The NORAD chief was startled when his command phone rang. He fumbled with the operational orders book and reached for the receiver.

'General Matuchek.'

'Dick, Milt Ridenour.' The Air Force chief of staff continued without waiting for an acknowledgement. 'We are going to move our active East Coast fighter squadrons across the pond. Immediately.'

'Yes, sir,' Matuchek answered, momentarily glancing at a new message placed on his console.

'The Stealth fighters are going to be based with our NATO friends. The movement is underway, along with the B-1 repositioning,' Ridenour concluded.

'Yes, I was just briefed on their status for immediate deployment.'

'Dick, we are going to replace the deployed squadrons in six hours, or less, with reserve and guard units.'

'Yes, sir,' Matuchek responded. 'Most everyone has anticipated that possibility.'

'Good show, Dick.' Ridenour sounded upbeat. 'What is your current readiness condition?'

Matuchek quickly checked the status board before replying. 'Eighty-two point two percent at this time. We can expect, conservatively, eighty-four plus in four hours or less.'

'Appreciate that, Dick.'

'Yes, sir.'

'We've got a hell of a mess in our lap and I know I can count on you and the rest of the NORAD crew.'

'Thanks, Milt. We haven't been to DEFCON-Two in

ages. Afraid we have a few cobwebs to dust off in the mountain.'

'You're not the only one, Dick. SAC has had some minor problems, but we've got the 52s and B-ls deployed and on alert. We did lose one 52 out of Carswell. Crashed on takeoff.'

'Yes, sir,' Matuchek replied, saddened. 'I was informed. Sorry to hear that.'

Ridenour continued without acknowledging. 'The Stealth bombers – the ones we have available – are in the process of being deployed throughout North America. The last one left Whiteman ten minutes ago. We made sure the Russians are aware of that fact, along with the knowledge that some of our B-2s are carrying burrowing missiles. Their underground bunkers aren't going to be of much use to them if they push the button. The Soviets know we have shuffled everything in the inventory.'

'Sounds good, Milt. The Stealth presence is going to confuse the Russian air defense, no question.'

Matuchek glanced up when an aide motioned excitedly to him, pointing out satellite confirmation of massive Soviet bomber groups joining over the Barents Sea.

'Sir,' Matuchek stared at the brightly lighted display, 'we are receiving SAT-INTEL confirming large Russian bomber join-ups over the Barents Sea.'

'Better let you do your job and get on with mine,' Ridenour said in a pleasant, but clipped voice. 'Be in touch soon.'

'Yessir.' The line went dead as Matuchek felt his stomach growl again.

The original DEFCON alert had taken away his appetite and the NORAD boss knew he needed to eat a few bites of something bland.

Matuchek ordered a chicken salad sandwich on white bread and a glass of iced tea. Waiting for his sandwich, the general thought about the NORAD complex. If the 'Big One' ever happened, the underground operations control facility would be as safe as any place receiving a direct strike by a nuclear missile.

Experts believed a twenty-megaton warhead, a massive weapon, dropped on top of Cheyenne Mountain would most likely only pop the eardrums of those personnel inside the tunnels of the solid granite mountain.

The general felt reasonably comfortable with the survival aspects of the air defense, missile warning, and space surveillance control center. It would be very difficult, if not impossible, to destroy the command center.

It was a five-minute drive through the rock-walled entry tunnel to the underground city. Two enormous steel blast doors, weighing twenty-five tons each, provided the final protection from attack.

Matuchek politely acknowledged the delivery of his light meal, sipped his iced tea, and continued to think about the cavernous NORAD complex.

Fifteen freestanding buildings, housing the command post and industrial support equipment, were supported by 1,300 giant steel springs.

The huge shock absorbers, weighing half a ton each, would minimize the effects of tremors resulting from nuclear detonations on the surface of the mountain.

Matuchek, chewing the last bite of his sandwich, was interrupted by the assistant operations officer.

'Excuse me, General. We have received an update from the War Room.'

The lieutenant colonel placed the Top Secret, Eyes Only, folder to the left side of the general's meal tray, next to his reading glasses.

'Thank you, Colonel,' Matuchek said, awkwardly swallowing the final morsel of chicken salad.

'Yes, sir.'

Matuchek reached for his glasses and opened the folder. He glanced down the page quickly, then started over more slowly to glean all the pertinent information in one reading.

CINCNORAD was surprised to see the Navy reacting so swiftly to the DEFCON-Two alert. The vast majority of carrier battle groups were already at sea. The USS *Abraham Lincoln*, commissioned in 1989, was underway with her battle group from Subic Bay Naval Station in the Philippines. The USS *Independence* was preparing to depart Alameda Naval Air Station near Oakland, California.

The USS *Midway*, based in Yokosuka, Japan, would be underway in two hours. The carrier USS *George Washington*, newly commissioned in 1991, was undergoing sea trials in the Atlantic and would supplant the USS *Eisenhower* and the USS *John F. Kennedy*.

Matuchek noted that most Air Force and Navy flying squadrons were in place, or would be in four to six hours. Large Army units were being deployed in predetermined areas utilizing heavy airlift capability provided by the Air Force, along with civilian contractors.

The Marines, both air and ground forces, supported by their own KC-130F heavy airlift squadrons, were in place and ready to react. Their normal inimitable efficiency, reflected the general, as he closed the folder.

'General,' the assistant operations officer politely interrupted. 'The fighters are airborne. They should intercept the Russian bombers north of Frobisher Bay. Soviet fighters are now joining with the bomber groups. It doesn't look very good.'

'Thanks, Colonel,' Matuchek said as he handed the folder back to the tall officer. 'Keep me informed.'

'Yes, sir.'

The lieutenant colonel placed the briefing folder under his left arm and returned to his post.

Matuchek noticed the lighted status board indicated a readiness percentage of eighty-two point seven. Doing the best we can, he thought, as the satellite tracking update flashed on the wide screen.

The tension in the NORAD facility was like a tightly stretched rubberband. Every soul in the room recognized that today might be his or her last day alive. They all realized they might never see their families again, or, worse, they might survive to find the world outside the mountain no longer in existence.

February – MOSCOW

Dimitri Moiseyevich Karpov, the former Leonid Timofeyevich Vochik, was nervously pacing back and forth in his small, barren room, as he ground out one cigarette and lighted another. The last day of January had been agonizingly long for him and he fervently looked forward to the new day. He had to make contact with his American 'connection' as quickly as possible.

He reached behind his footlocker and retrieved the clear canning jar of Stolichnaya vodka, one of the perquisites Dimitri enjoyed as head of the general secretary's kitchen staff.

The large glass container had been full two hours ago when Dimitri was released from kitchen duty. It now contained less than two-thirds of the clear liquid as Dimitri raised it to his lips for another long pull.

He sat down in his only chair, wishing he could be with Svetlana in her warm bed.

He took another swig of the room-temperature vodka, lighted a fresh cigarette, and ached for the Russian woman he loved. She must never know who I really am, Dimitri thought as he planned a way to contact his Central Intelligence Agency control. There wasn't time to wait for the scheduled ritual. There was so much pressure, and he longed to purge himself of the devastating knowledge gained in the hallway outside the general secretary's quarters.

Dimitri reached across his end table and turned the windup alarm clock toward the light. The dim, forty-watt bulb in his table lamp made him squint. One o'clock in the morning. He calculated the effects of the vodka and reasoned that three to four hours of sleep would be sufficient.

Kremlin domestic help was not allowed to leave the compound when the evening shift ended at eleven o'clock. Working-class staff could leave the immediate area only when their rotation placed them on duty from five o'clock in the morning to two o'clock in the afternoon.

Movement in or out of the Kremlin, in regard to the working ranks, was not permitted between the hours of nine o'clock at night and five o'clock in the morning. Those individuals fortunate to be assigned to the early shift could leave at two o'clock. However, they had to be present for duty at five the following morning.

Dimitri, who had received special permission to leave the Kremlin grounds at seven o'clock in the morning, would have only six or seven hours to contact his CIA connection.

His assigned agent was aware that Dimitri would not be eligible to leave the Kremlin compound until his work schedule rotated the following week. Would the American even be in the vicinity?

His unusual behavior, Dimitri realized, would place him in a precarious situation, especially if the KGB noticed his change of pattern. He silently cursed the bad fortune of being on the evening work shift.

Swallowing another two ounces of the crystal clear liquid, Dimitri reconciled himself to the fact that he simply didn't have a choice. He had an obligation to his country – America.

The knowledge he carried caused his mind to reel. Nuclear war. Biological and chemical warfare. He couldn't comprehend the reality. The Soviet leaders had a detailed, step-by-step plan to destroy the United States. He had distinctly heard the party general secretary say he planned to strike the United States without warning.

Now he realized what Zhilinkhov had meant about Saudi Arabia. Russia would control the world's oil supplies after the United States was toppled. No country, or combined countries, could stand up to the Soviet war machine. Nuclear war . . .

The vision of hundreds, perhaps thousands, of nuclear missiles and bombs landing on his friends in America, his home, wouldn't leave his consciousness, regardless of the amount of alcohol.

The vision seemed like a never-ending nightmare. Life had been so pleasurable before the tragic death of the previous general secretary. What had gone wrong? What had changed the world so drastically, so quickly, to one of imminent nuclear destruction? Was the new general secretary crazy?

Dimitri flinched as a searing pain shot up his right arm. The forgotten cigarette had burned the insides of his index and middle fingers.

Forgetting the pain, Dimitri lighted another cigarette, swilled a splash of vodka, and remembered, agonizingly, how he had come to be in this position.

An agent from the Central Intelligence Agency had

fostered a relationship, a friendship, with the young son of Russian emigrants.

Dimitri, a recently certified Mitsubishi automobile mechanic in Hasbrouck Heights, New Jersey, had specifically been requested to work on the blue Mitsubishi towed in for transmission repairs.

Dimitri glanced at the clock again, his vision becoming slightly blurred in the alcoholic stupor. One twenty-five.

His nerves were slowly relaxing with the aid of 100-proof vodka.

Thinking back on his adventure, Dimitri realized he had been very naïve. Oh, what he would give to be Leonid Vochik again. A simple, happy mechanic residing in New Jersey.

His customer, and later, his friend 'Phil' had ridden with him when the necessary transmission repairs had been completed on the Mitsubishi.

Phil had suggested they stop for a beer, noting it was past closing time at the dealership. Dimitri eagerly accepted the invitation since Phil offered to drop him at his apartment. The agent had known Dimitri didn't own a car and rode the bus to work.

After a couple of beers, Phil said he had two tickets to the Yankees game the following evening, and asked if Dimitri would care to join him.

The young Russian emigrant, who had not cultivated many new friends, was ecstatic that his American friend would ask him to a big league baseball game.

Afterwards, over beers again, Phil told Dimitri he was a salesman (true, Dimitri reflected with irony) and traveled in the northeast sector of the United States.

Phil genuinely liked the young Russian. That bond had solidified their friendship and Phil suggested a fishing trip the next weekend to his father's private lake and cabin. Again, Dimitri was full of gratitude and anticipation.

The weather, fishing, and friendly banter had been great that Sunday afternoon. Phil had inquired about Dimitri's background, his immigrant parents, and what he felt in regard to the United States.

Dimitri had described the horrors his parents, classified as dissenters, had suffered at the hands of the Russian KGB officers. He had told, in detail, about the suffering his father had endured in Christopol prison and the relentless interrogations at KGB headquarters in the basement of the Lubyanka.

He had explained why he hated the Russian political system and widespread corruption. He confessed to Phil, after several beers, that he was embarrassed by his Russian heritage. Dimitri expressed love for America and thankfulness for the opportunities in his new land.

Phil had listened intently and suggested that Dimitri meet a friend of his who could offer him an unusual opportunity. Dimitri had been taken aback and remained very excited for three days prior to the meeting with Phil's friend.

The friend, who was in charge of CIA clandestine 'mole' operations, was straightforward with Dimitri. The former Marine lieutenant colonel introduced himself, explained his authority and position, revealed the true identity of Phil, and carefully outlined the opportunity he had for one Leonid Timofeyevich Vochik. The young emigrant would be known henceforth as Dimitri Moiseyevich Karpov, if he accepted the dangerous assignment.

The chief of CIA clandestine operations explained that Dimitri would go to work for the agency as an undercover operative in the heart of the Kremlin. He had been shown photos of the Russian worker he would change places with. Dimitri had been shocked by the apparent twin brother staring back.

The similarities had been incredible, a 'clone' to the

casual observer. The only differences had been blood type, twenty-three months in age, one-quarter inch in height, and the faint scar on Vochik's lower right jaw.

The Central Intelligence Agency, Dimitri had been informed, had searched for seventeen months to find a Russian-speaking clone, one who could be trusted, for this crucial assignment. The agency was willing to pay quite handsomely for his services.

The CIA chief reiterated the importance of the operation, explained the Federal Bureau of Investigation background check conducted without Dimitri's knowledge, the salary, benefits, and rewards at the completion of the mission. He also detailed the guarantee of anonymity and relocation to the western United States after his extraction from Moscow in five years.

The chief agent, along with Phil, who would remain a friend and be in charge of the operation, told Dimitri they needed an answer in twenty-four hours. Period.

They also indicated that Dimitri would need minor cosmetic surgery to eliminate the scar and to flatten his nose slightly.

In addition, Phil explained, three months of intensive and exhaustive training, six and a half days a week, would be required.

Leonid Vochik would become Dimitri Karpov through mimicry and emulation of tapes and recordings of Karpov obtained by highly sophisticated intelligence gathering equipment.

Dimitri looked at his alarm again. One fifty-six. He crushed the empty pack of cigarettes, reached into his top dresser drawer, felt toward the back, and retrieved another pack. Dimitri flicked open the Proshinsky cigarette lighter, staring at the inscription as the flaming tobacco sent smoke curling around him. He recalled the evening Svetlana had given him the lighter, precisely one month after they had become lovers.

Inhaling the acrid smoke, Dimitri thought back to his decision to join the CIA operation. The money, lifetime security (providing he lived through his commitment), and the desire to be respected in the United States. If only he could take Svetlana, the only woman he had ever loved, home with him to his country, America.

The reality of the danger involved, the high-risk factor had not focused for Dimitri until he was in the counterfeit Soviet tractor-trailer leaving Sweden for the Russian border via Finland.

The truck, in fact, had been stolen from the Russian state trucking line, Sovtrans. The Glavnoye Razvedyvatelnoye Upravleniye (GRU), Soviet military intelligence, had used the vehicle for spying on NATO training exercises and maneuvers off the island of Musko, Sweden's most important naval base.

Dimitri had been extensively briefed about his insertion into Russia and the Kremlin headquarters. Taking advantage of the Transport International Routier (TIR) agreement that guarantees sealed trucks customs-free transit en route to final destinations in Eastern bloc countries, the CIA could safely blend Dimitri into Russia near Leningrad.

Dimitri had posed as a codriver learning a new route. The 'driver', a CIA operative, had been the leader of the mission and familiar with the route.

The Soviet tractor-trailer had a new serial number, side numbers, and license – all numbers that corresponded to a truck then in operation by the Russians. It would be in their computer.

From Leningrad, Dimitri and his driver had traveled to Vologda, four hundred kilometers northeast of Moscow, to await the train carrying the real Dimitri Karpov.

Dimitri Karpov, trusted Kremlin domestic, traveled by train twice a year to see his aging mother. His father died when he was a child and his mother had never remarried. She was in poor health and nearly blind.

Tatianna Karpov wasn't expected to live long, and, if she did, she would most likely not recognize the difference in her clone son. The replacement son had practiced speaking precisely like the real Dimitri Karpov and had memorized his life history, along with the family tree.

The trips were predictable and always occurred in early fall and the later part of spring. Karpov traveled from Moscow to the village of Yemetsk, on the shore of the Northern Dvina River, via the city of Vologda. He always stayed in Yemetsk two to three days and returned to Moscow on the evening train.

Dimitri lighted another cigarette and looked at the clock again. Two seventeen. He inhaled the rich smoke and thought about how easily the switch had been made.

The agent/driver had waited for a call from an operative in Moscow when Karpov departed for Yemetsk, then boarded the train during the stop in Vologda.

After the CIA operative left on the train with the unsuspecting Karpov, the former Leonid Vochik had only to wait for a message detailing the train he had to board for Moscow. He never left his hotel room and ate sparingly from his knapsack.

He had not been told how the former Dimitri Karpov had been dispatched, but assumed the 'driver' had killed him on board the train. The former head of the Kremlin kitchen staff was most probably at the bottom of Lake Kubeno, northwest of Vologda.

Dimitri recalled the heavy lead weights the CIA agent had concealed in his bulky clothes. The agent had placed the weights inside his large coat, in heavily sewn pockets, prior to leaving the hotel for the train station.

Dimitri could still envision the agent wrapping the body in rags, and, heavily weighted, tossing it off the long railroad bridge over murky Lake Kubeno. There wasn't any guardrail to contend with. The darkness of late night, and the sound of the train, would conceal the deed. The body had disappeared to the bottom of the lake, where it had decomposed fairly rapidly.

The CIA operative had given Dimitri a package when he joined him in Vologda. After the train was safely en route to Moscow, Leonid Vochik, now Dimitri Moiseyevich Karpov, had completed the transformation by changing into the clothes of his deceased predecessor and reviewing his credentials. He had also noted a lack of blood stains or signs of violence. The clothes were only rumpled. Dimitri had noted, however, that the shoes were a size too large. The CIA had not thought of everything.

Dimitri had been terrified when he first approached the Kremlin. Remembering previous visits to Red Square and recognizing the local landmarks, Dimitri felt more confident.

He presented the authentic credentials of Karpov and entered the Kremlin compound. He was, after all, a clone of his predecessor.

Dimitri knew precisely where to go from months of studying the Kremlin floor plan. There had been some rough spots, but he had adjusted rapidly to his new environment. Dimitri initially felt that his colleagues sensed something different, but they couldn't fathom the subtle change. Routine soon erased fleeting doubts about the head of Kremlin kitchen staff. Everyone assumed Dimitri's slight personality change was the result of worry about the declining health of his mother.

Swallowing the last ounce of vodka, Dimitri ground out his cigarette, set his alarm for six o'clock, and fell asleep almost immediately. He was exhausted from the strain on his nerves. He could not comprehend what was happening to him, or, for that matter, what would happen in the next twenty-four hours. His world had gone mad, spinning out of control in a kaleidoscope of confusion and fear.

6

AIR FORCE ONE

The huge presidential jet, sunlight sparkling from the highly polished silver, white, and blue surface, made a straight-in approach to Lajes do Pico, Azores. The Portuguese island shimmered in the early morning sun.

The aircraft commander, Colonel Boyd, had kept the speed fast throughout the descent, lowering the landing gear and flaps at the last possible moment, a very unusual procedure. However, a request from the president of the United States had precedence over routine, if the request didn't breach the limits of safe operation.

The four F-14s escorting *Air Force One* broke off three miles from touchdown and climbed rapidly to join their tankers en route to the *Eisenhower*. The roar of the F-14s' afterburners was deafening to the observers on the ground.

During the landing roll-out, Grant Wilkinson, with a quick knock, entered the president's private study. The president, adjusting his tie in a full-length mirror, looked out the corner of his eye.

'What is it, Grant?' The president's voice had a slight hesitancy in it.

'Sir, NORAD is now tracking three large Soviet bomber groups, each escorted by fifty or sixty fighters.' Wilkinson paused, seeing the president yank on his tie.

'Where are they located?'

'One group is – '

'What's the status?' The president continued, wrestling with his tie.

'One group – approximately seventy to eighty bombers – is fifty miles north of Nordkapp, Finland. Appears to be comprised of a mixture of Bears and Backfires.'

'The other groups?' The president growled, finished with the burdensome tie adjustment.

'The other groups are split and appear to be converging north of Komandorskie Island.' The chief of staff sounded tired.

'Where?' The president wasn't sure of the location.

'Komandorskie Island, sir. Approximately five hundred miles northwest of Adak, Alaska,' Wilkinson replied as he looked at his notes.

'What the hell is Zhilinkhov trying to do?' The president was exasperated, irritation showing in his voice.

'I wish I could answer that, sir.'

'I know. Sorry, Grant.' The president sat down heavily. 'Go on.'

'Again, this provocation is well-orchestrated, sir.' Wilkinson trailed off, not wanting to expound, unless prompted by his boss.

'How so, Grant?'

'The other bombers – the Backfires and Blackjacks – are operating from forward bases, supported by twenty or more tankers. The planning for mass join-ups had to be in-depth and extensive. Sir, the Soviets have dispersed seven regiment-size bomber units from Alekseyevka to auxiliary airfields at Primorski Krai, Kamchatka Peninsula, and Sakhalin Island.'

Quiet surrounded the two men as the president slowly rolled a pen around in his hand.

'What's been our response?' the president asked in a low voice.

'The Bering Sea join-up is considered the most serious

problem at the present time. They aren't far from our bases in the Aleutian Islands and Alaska.' Wilkinson sat down on the couch, exhausted.

'The bombers are staging from their Arctic airbase at Mys Schmidta, and joining a group from Petropavlovsk-Kamchatski. They are armed with AS-4 Kitchen antiship missiles and cruise missiles. NORAD reports the Alaskan Air Command on full alert, sir. We have Air Force and Navy fighter groups joining the Russian formations.'

'Excellent.' The president visibly stiffened. 'How long until our boys intercept the bombers?'

'About one hour, sir.' Wilkinson consulted the scrawled notes in his hands. 'The Forty-third Tactical Fighter Squadron, based at Elmendorf, has twenty-three F-15s airborne.'

'Will that be sufficient?' the president asked, noticing *Air Force One* was rolling to an imperceptible stop in front of the welcoming committee.

'The Forty-third is being reinforced by two West Coast squadrons, along with the interceptors from the Ranger's carrier group.' Wilkinson looked down at his notes and continued. 'They have two E-3 AWACS planes coordinating the intercept, sir.'

'Okay, Grant. Keep – '

A gentle knock interrupted the two men as an aide announced the arrival of the welcoming delegation.

'Mister President, we are prepared for you to deplane, sir.'

'Very well,' the president responded, 'Mister Wilkinson and I will be along shortly.'

'Yes, sir,' the Navy officer replied, waiting patiently in the hallway.

The lights blinked momentarily, an indication that *Air Force One* had shifted to the auxiliary power unit. The massive turbofan engines spooled down, fan blades quietly slowing in the cool morning breeze.

'When I talk to Zhilinkhov, don't hesitate to inform me of status changes as you receive them,' the president ordered.

'Yes, sir,' Wilkinson said as he rose from the thick leather couch and brushed off his trousers.

'In fact, Grant, the more you interrupt me for quiet updates, the more worried I suspect Zhilinkhov will become.' The president looked up, eyebrows arched, dead serious in manner.

'You're probably right,' Wilkinson responded as the president reached for the cabin door handle.

'Let's meet our greeting party. I want to have all the hand shaking and ceremonial posturing over with when Zhilinkhov steps on the ground.' The president didn't care for officious functions. He referred to the rituals as 'dog-and-pony shows'.

'I intend to blow the air out of his arrival and nail him to the post on the spot.' The president paused for another breath as they started down the hallway. 'Grant, see if you can secure a place close by – a hangar will do, or something similar – so we can kick this off without all the ostentatious bullshit.'

'I'll get right on it, sir.' Wilkinson chuckled at the president's unexpected imprecation.

The two men reached the forward air-stair door simultaneously with Colonel Boyd, who spoke first.

'Mister President, we managed fourteen minutes ahead of the Russian ETA. Best we could do, sir.'

The aircraft commander of *Air Force One* prided himself on being punctual and a perfectionist, along with retaining a sense of humor under demanding conditions.

'Couldn't be better, Don.' The president shook his pilot's hand. 'Enjoyed the flight.'

136

'Thank you, sir.'

The lean colonel snapped a salute as the president and his chief of staff, joined by the secretary of state, departed the 747 and descended the air-stairs.

The president, analyzing the precarious stability of global politics, mindlessly went through the reception line, shaking hands and exchanging pleasantries with dignitaries, bureaucrats, and other officials of various rank.

The president requested that everyone accompany him to the position where the general secretary would deplane.

The contingent, looking confused, followed the American leader to the Soviet reception area, leaving the reviewing podium nearly deserted.

Walking slowly with Wilkinson and Herb Kohlhammer, the president kept an eye turned upward and listened for the sound of the approaching Soviet transport.

THE WHITE HOUSE

Tedford W. Corbin, director of the Central Intelligence Agency, sat next to Marine General Hollingsworth, as the secretary of defense outlined the DEFCON-Two status report in the White House Situation Room.

The vice president of the United States and former Navy lawyer, Susan Luthe Blaylocke, chaired the tense early morning meeting. Firing questions and fielding onslaughts was her forte.

Blaylocke had replaced the sitting vice president, who had resigned under intense political pressure. A series of controversial social and political gaffes had underscored the lack of confidence party leadership had had in his abilities to assume the presidency. When a congressional hearing committee had been convened to investigate questionable financial dealings, the president requested, and received, his resignation.

Blaylocke had been welcomed in the White House in an unusual display of bipartisan acceptance.

She had earned the reputation of being a very business-oriented professional. As a Navy officer, Blaylocke had continually been assigned to greater responsibilities and higher visibility as her law career progressed.

The vice president had been assigned to the Pentagon when she met her husband, Congressman Stephen Blaylocke. The couple had no children but worked tirelessly to assist underprivileged and handicapped children.

Lieutenant Commander Blaylocke left active duty after her marriage and ran successfully for a congressional seat. Name recognition and further visibility followed, marking the intelligent brunette as a rising star in the political arena.

The vice president was always pleasant, if possible, but very demanding of those individuals in positions of responsibility. Susan Blaylocke, without a doubt, was an organized and courageous leader. She had earned the respect of her colleagues at every level of government service, along with the respect of the American people and Western allies.

The vice president had been in Saint Thomas, Virgin Islands, enjoying a working vacation with her husband, when the DEFCON-Three alert was initiated.

Rushing back to Washington, Blaylocke and the president had discussed the global situation via secure air-link. They had decided to launch space shuttle *Columbia* earlier than originally planned. The mutual decision was a tactical gamble.

The Soviet general secretary, visible to the world in

Lajes, would not be in a position to offer much resistance. The DEFCON-Two status was delicate and unpredictable, in view of the scheduled orbiter launch linking the basic stage of SDI.

The vice president had arrived at Andrews Air Force Base three hours after the departure of the president and his staff. Now, with five hours of sleep, Blaylocke was absorbing the most recent events, provided by Cliff Howard, secretary of defense, and requesting solutions from the White House leaders. She did not suffer individuals afflicted with nonlinear thinking, as a number of White House staff had learned.

'Gentlemen, that brings us to date on the global situation, militarily speaking.' Susan Blaylocke looked around the table before continuing. 'Thanks, Cliff.'

'You're welcome, ma'am.'

'Ted, where are we in regard to contacting the Kremlin agent?' Blaylocke asked.

The truculent little CIA director, without hesitating, responded clearly.

'We have two of our best men attempting to make contact at this time, around the clock.'

'Why is it so difficult, Ted?' Blaylocke realized the small, irascible man didn't like being questioned. Especially by a woman.

'The surveillance in and around the Kremlin is very thorough. They – the KGB and GRU – make it almost impossible to contact an operative outside the established pattern.' Director Corbin was being as polite as he had ever been in government service.

'Do you believe, Ted, that your men will succeed in the next twenty-four hours?' The vice president wanted a commitment, a positive answer from the CIA boss.

'Yes.' Corbin inhaled, then exhaled loudly. 'The operative we are trying to contact has a girlfriend, a lover, who has a small apartment by the Taganka Theater. She is a leading dancer and rates an efficiency apartment.'

Corbin sensed the stillness in the room, noticed the sunlight creeping through the windows, then proceeded.

'When Dimitri – '

'Who is Dimitri?' Blaylocke interrupted.

'The agent, the "plant" in the Kremlin,' Corbin responded.

'Please continue.' The vice president listened intently, her coffee forgotten.

'When Dimitri journeys to the woman's apartment, our men observe him from different locations. His visits vary because of his irregular work schedule.'

'How do the agents actually make contact?' Blaylocke asked, attempting to expedite the early meeting.

'If our operative, Dimitri, has anything of significance to report, he folds his arms across his chest,' Corbin demonstrated for the staff members, 'with the left wrist on top of his right wrist.

'If he has nothing to report, the opposite arm fold is used, a very subtle gesture.'

'That seems fairly inconspicuous,' Blaylocke responded, then waited for the diminutive CIA director to continue.

'That part is. If our plant and one of the agents need to communicate, the agent waits at the Central Moscow train station for the operative – our Kremlin resident.'

Corbin paused for a sip of orange juice, then continued the narrative. 'If Dimitri takes his train ticket money out of his right pocket, he is going to Gorkiy. If it's the left pocket, the destination is Kharkov.'

'Doesn't that create suspicion with the KGB goons, if they are watching?' General Vandermeer, the Army chief of staff, queried the civilian administrator.

'Not really, General. They have grown accustomed to

Dimitri's frequent train trips, along with his two sojourns home each year. We have been fortunate his mother can't see and is only semilucid.' Corbin found himself wandering away from the subject.

'So the contact is made on board the train?' Blaylocke had all the information she needed, except the when.

'Yes. The agent buys a ticket to the destination indicated by the plant. When the agent visits the toilet facilities, Dimitri joins him for a brief update.'

The Marine commandant had an observation. 'The train noise, the clanking of the wheels, would make it virtually impossible to record a conversation or eavesdrop at a urinal.'

'Precisely, General.' Corbin leaned back and waited for the vice president to speak.

'So, Ted, we can anticipate information from the Kremlin operative within twenty-four hours?' Blaylocke wanted substantive information as quickly as possible.

'That is correct.' The CIA director could not bring himself to address the woman as Ms. Vice President, let alone ma'am.

Blaylocke wanted to make a judgement on the value of the forthcoming information, if any. 'But we don't know if the information gleaned from the operative will be of any value in the present situation.'

'That is correct.' Corbin fidgeted, uneasiness showing in his demeanor.

'Any questions, gentlemen?' Susan Blaylocke waited to see if the secretary of defense, or any of the Joint Chiefs of Staff, had questions for the director of Central Intelligence. None did.

'Thank you, Ted. You have been very helpful.' The vice president smiled slightly, removed her glasses, and closed her briefing notes.

'You're welcome, and . . . ah, I will inform you of any

141

findings immediately on receipt,' Corbin stammered, being respectful without using a title, or the dreaded ma'am.

Blaylocke faced the other staff members. 'Well, gentlemen, we expect to hear news from Lajes in the next hour,' Blaylocke looked at her wristwatch and noted that it was two minutes past seven, 'so I recommend we adjourn for breakfast and reconvene here at eight o'clock.'

CAPE CANAVERAL

The five astronauts assigned to the SDI satellite placement mission had been awakened early. Breakfast would be later, they were told.

'Plan to attend a briefing in thirty minutes.' End of statement. Door shut.

'Well, I appreciate the guy's candor,' Air Force Col Lowell Crawford, mission commander, joked as he waited his turn at the well-used coffee pot in the NASA briefing room.

'Yeah, Skipper, the guy should get a PR job where his personality could really shine,' chimed in Navy Lt Cmdr Henry 'Hank' Doherty, the mission pilot.

Alan Cressottie, mission payload specialist, struggling into his powder blue flight suit, was the last of the flight crew to enter the small room. He was a popular and jovial member of the astronaut corps.

Cressottie waved to everyone, then threw a sealed cardboard container of doughnuts into the air. 'Gotta be prepared!'

'Is that the Cub Scout or Boy Scout motto?' Doctor Minh Tran, mission payload specialist, asked with a grin spreading across his face.

Doherty, the picture-perfect astronaut, plucked the box of doughnuts from midair as Marine Maj. Ward Culdrew, mission specialist, replied, 'Naw, that's the Marine Corps motto, "Semper Preparedness".'

There was a scramble for the dilapidated microwave as Hank Doherty 'nuked' the dozen old-fashioned glazed doughnuts for one minute.

'Semper preparedness?' Cressottie laughed. 'Drew, you ever finish grade school, or did you get that far?' Cressottie loved to bait his friend, the Marine Corps aviator and rookie astronaut.

'Yeah, sure did,' Culdrew grinned at Cressottie. 'Even went on to junior high school. Pledged the fraternity "I felta thigh."'

The banter ceased as Rex Hays and Mission Controller Ken Stankitze entered the room.

'You'd think NASA could spring for a new microwave,' Doherty mumbled as he pried the door open on the charred and dented oven. He quickly served doughnuts around the cabinet and grabbed his steaming coffee.

Everyone took a seat as Doctor Hays and Stankitze greeted the astronauts. Hays walked to the podium, while the gaunt mission controller had a seat in the front row of the briefing room.

'Well, fellas, hell of a time to get you out of bed, but we've had a change of plans.' Hays wasn't upbeat, nor did he appear dejected.

The astronauts had cautious looks on their faces. Had the mission been scrubbed again? Was all the training down the drain?

'You men are aware of the global tension at the present time, and the increased security here at the cape,' Hays said. 'We have been informed by the secretary of defense to launch the SDI mission at the earliest possible time. Unannounced, no media, middle of the night.'

143

Hays looked at the faces of the crew. Surprise, shock, then relief registered on the five astronauts.

'The president has decided to go for launch early, in view of what happened in the Atlantic. He believes the Russians won't attempt anything with the general secretary under scrutiny in Lajes.'

Hays gave the crew a moment to collect their thoughts. 'We plan to launch this evening, gentlemen.'

Again, surprise registered on the five faces in the audience.

Colonel Crawford, caught off guard, spoke first. 'Can we do that? We haven't completed the preflight checklist yet. The fueling will take – '

Hays raised a hand, quietly silencing the concerned command pilot.

'The final fueling is under way. We are keeping everything low-key. Business as usual. That sort of thing.'

Hays looked at the mission controller. 'I'm going to turn the briefing over to Ken now. He can supply you with the details and I'll meet with you later this morning.'

Hays turned from the battered podium, motioned to Stankitze, and left the room. The mission controller walked around the podium and unfolded his notes.

'As Doctor Hays explained, *Columbia* is being fueled at this time. We anticipate an oh-two-forty-five launch time. The software is being reprogrammed as I speak, and the window will be fifty-five minutes long.'

'What about security?' Culdrew asked.

'Every effort is being made to ensure this day doesn't seem strange in the normal prelaunch cycle. What that means, in a real sense, is the troops are being informed of the change of plans. However, their orders are explicit. They are to remain in a low-profile posture.'

Stankitze saw that Crawford had a question. 'Yes, Colonel?'

'What about the media?' the pilot asked.

'They aren't going to be very happy with us,' Stankitze replied.

Laughter filled the room.

'The media is being informed, during a press conference at noon, that a launch will take place four days from now, as per schedule.'

'They're goin' to love you, Ken.' Culdrew couldn't resist a jab at the serious-minded controller.

'No doubt,' Stankitze chuckled, then continued, 'the media will believe this evening is a dress rehearsal.'

Laughter.

'They will have to leave the launch site at the scheduled time, as usual, so nothing will seem out of the ordinary. We hope.'

Stankitze turned his pad over, then explained the new sequence of events.

'Since the satellites are already on board *Columbia*, the logistics aren't very difficult. You will have breakfast, attend another briefing with Doctor Hays and the launch coordinators at oh-nine-thirty, and meet the press hounds at eleven hundred hours. I don't need to remind you to keep your mouths shut.'

Stankitze glanced at his schedule. 'This afternoon, after lunch, Crawford and Doherty will follow the normal schedule for proficiency flying. The Thirty-eights will be available from thirteen-thirty to fifteen-thirty hours.'

The mission controller looked directly at the pilots. 'Don't bust your asses. The rest of you will report for payload training at fourteen hundred hours. Dinner will be early. We'll call you around midnight, as late as we can. Breakfast will be in orbit. Try to sleep as much as possible.'

'Sleep?' Doherty exclaimed. 'The Russians are getting ready to blow the world to smithereens. I'm getting ready to ride a rocket into space, and the area around the launch pad looks like a "Rambo" movie.'

Laughter.

'Sleep?' Doherty continued. 'The man tells me to sleep! I couldn't go to sleep with a quart of bourbon and a case of tranquilizers!'

Stankitze laughed with the crew, thinking Doherty was right.

The briefing was terminated as everyone piled out of the room, spirits high in their togetherness. The close-knit group proceeded to breakfast, Doherty complaining about Cressottie's 'gut bomb' doughnuts destroying his appetite.

GALENA AIRFIELD, ALASKA, Forward Interceptor Base

The two United States Air Force F-15 Eagles roared off the short airstrip, afterburners blazing in the night. At the controls of Cobra One was Maj. Enrico DiGennaro, a career military pilot and Air Force Academy graduate. Capt. William 'Wild Bill' Parnam, piloting Cobra Two, would join on DiGennaro's right wing in a running rendezvous.

The scramble had been initiated by the E-3 Airborne Warning and Control Aircraft. The aircraft's high-altitude radar had tracked the Soviet bombers and escorts for the previous hour.

The recent Red Flag fighter weapons graduates were temporarily assigned to Galena, one of two forward fighter-interceptor bases in Alaska.

The two Fox-15 pilots had the unenviable task of reconnoitering the Russian bomber groups before the other twenty-three F-15s arrived on station.

KC-10 tankers, operating from Eielson Air Force Base, were en route, along with carrier-based Navy and Marine fighters from the USS *Ranger*. Two Marine KC-130 tankers, operating from Adak, Alaska, would help support the carrier aircraft. This intercept was shaping into a real hardball mission, especially under a DEFCON-Two alert.

The Russians had increasingly been flying strike profiles rather than peripheral reconnaissance missions, but not in these numbers. Seventy or eighty bombers, plus escort fighters and tankers, was an imposing force under any conditions.

'Cobra Two aboard,' Parnam announced as he thumbed his speedbrake closed. He had bled-off forty knots to match his leader's speed.

'Roger, Two,' responded DiGennaro, 'let's go high station and check with Pinwheel.'

'I'm with you, lead.' Parnam inched the throttles forward to remain alongside of DiGennaro as they initiated a cruise climb to 54,000 feet.

'Pinwheel Seven, Cobra One with you outa three-one-oh, flight of two Fox-Fifteens.'

'Copy, Cobra. Come to heading two-four-zero and squawk ident.'

'Roger, two-four-zero and ident.'

Pause.

'Pinwheel has a tally, Cobra.'

The E-3 AWACS airborne controller had the two McDonnell Douglas fighters on radar and was vectoring the heavily laden aircraft toward the Soviet bomber group.

'Pinwheel. How far out are the fifteens behind us?' DiGennaro needed the reference point of the supporting fighters in order to form a tactical battle plan.

'Hawk flight is two hundred eighty miles at your seven o'clock. Stand by.'

'Roger.' DiGennaro eased back on the throttles, reducing power two percent.

The E-3 was silent a few seconds while they checked with the other F-15s from Elmendorf Air Force Base.

'Cobra, Pinwheel.'

'Go.' DiGennaro didn't waste words, on the ground or in the air.

'Leopard flight is five minutes behind the Hawks. They had one turn back with hydraulic problems.'

'Roger.' DiGennaro eased back another one percent of power to reduce fuel consumption and shorten the distance between his two fighters and the joining F-15s.

'Pinwheel, what's the Navy's position?'

'Coming up from the south . . . be a while.' The controller hesitated again. 'The Ranger is six hundred nautical at one-six-zero from your position.'

'Roger, Pinwheel. We're going to slow it up until we have a few more troops.'

DiGennaro didn't want to engage the Soviet bomber group with odds running thirty to one. Not a good tactical decision.

The mission of the Forty-third Tactical Fighter Squadron, up to now, had been to intercept the occasional Russian Bear bomber-surveillance aircraft that strayed too close to the Aleutians or Alaskan coast. This situation was a whole new ball game.

7

MOSCOW

Dimitri, alternately dozing and staring at his clock, was startled when the alarm sounded at six o'clock. He remained in his narrow bed, exhausted after a restless sleep, believing he had been the victim of a bad dream. Actually, it had been an ongoing nightmare. America being obliterated in a firestorm by his native Russia.

Sitting upright, Dimitri surveyed the room, realizing it was not a dream at all. His mind raced as he assembled his toilet articles and walked down the narrow hall to the communal bath-house.

Shaving and bathing quickly, Dimitri dressed in fresh warm clothes, checked his credentials, buttoned his heavy coat, and walked to the security entrance for lower ranking domestic workers.

The guard was a familiar friend who had been posted to his billet three months after Dimitri arrived at the Kremlin. Dimitri had provided the sentry with sumptuous leftovers on more than one occasion.

'Up early, Dimitri,' the uniformed guard said in a friendly greeting.

'Yes, Comrade Alexei Nikolayevich,' Dimitri responded, 'I have many errands to attend to this morning.'

'But the shops are not open for some time, my friend.' The guard was inquisitive at this early hour.

'Yes, but my Svetlana's door is open at any hour,' Dimitri said, forcing a sly smile.

Dimitri didn't have time for small talk. He tried to be calm and appear normal, but his heart was pounding. Dimitri placed his shaking hands inside his coat pockets. He was sure the Kremlin guard had seen them trembling.

'You will be busy, my friend,' the guard said, waving Dimitri through. 'Have fun shopping.'

'Thank you, Alexei Nikolayevich.'

Dimitri walked across Red Square, passing the eight domes of Saint Basil's, and turned down the side street leading to Svetlana's tiny apartment. Along the way, he peered into shop windows, trying to effect a slow, casual stroll down the narrow, rough street. Dimitri passed the small, dingy cafe where he and Svetlana occasionally had a warm beer. They always laughed about having to drink fast before the paper cup soaked through.

Dimitri could almost sense the presence of KGB agents in the vicinity. No one knew where they would appear next. He forced himself to relax, his breath turning to white mist in the cold February air.

The young Russian-American thought about the conversation he had overheard in the general secretary's quarters.

Would his CIA contact believe the incredible information he possessed? The general secretary planned to strike America with nuclear and chemical weapons.

Could he even make contact at this unusual time of the day? He had no idea the American agents were desperately trying to locate him.

Dimitri rounded a corner and almost walked into his most frequent CIA connection.

'Excuse me. I-I'm sorry,' Dimitri blurted, shocked by the unexpected encounter.

'No harm, Comrade,' the American agent responded in flawless Russian, surprise registering on his face, too.

Steve Wickham, the senior CIA agent in Moscow,

stepped off the sidewalk and around Dimitri. He continued down Kuybisheva Street, nonchalant in attitude and casual in his gait. Inside, however, his mind was whirling from the sudden and unexpected meeting.

'Christ Almighty,' the CIA operative said under his breath. 'Now what?'

The American agent stopped, apparently gazing at fresh bread being placed in a shop window. Actually, he was staring at Dimitri in the reflection of the glass.

The Kremlin 'mole' was slowly strolling by the shop windows, his arms folded, left over right.

'Damn, I've gotta go for it,' Wickham said to himself. He had been instructed to contact the plant as quickly as possible. He sensed the urgency in the operative, too. His superiors, he thought quietly, had been correct about the immediacy of establishing contact. There wasn't time to go through all the steps and take all the usual precautions.

Dimitri, adrenaline surging through his body, slowly continued toward the apartment. He felt weak, fear turning to nausea. Dimitri was sure his connection had seen his arms crossed, left over right. He had a moment of panic. Did I inadvertently reverse the procedure? No, he convinced himself, and repeated the arm crossing.

Dimitri glanced in a window, no matter the dark curtain was drawn, and saw the CIA agent retracing his steps, a loaf of bread tucked under his left arm.

The former Leonid Vochik, on the verge of panic, continued his slow pace. He noted the increase in early morning pedestrian traffic and saw nothing that would indicate a sinister presence.

The CIA agent, nearly abreast of Dimitri, quickened his pace slightly. As he passed the Kremlin mole, the American spoke to him in Russian, his hand covering his mouth as he appeared to inhale from his cigarette. 'Meet me at Chlebnikow Restaurant.' The statement, short and clear, was an order.

Dimitri, knowing better, didn't utter a sound as the American continued down the street, looking very Russian in his heavy coat and fur cap.

LAJES, AZORES

The president, Grant Wilkinson, and the secretary of state, Herbert Kohlhammer, watched as the large Ilyushin 11–76 transport circled over the airfield and turned downwind in preparation for landing.

The powerful Soloviev turbofan engines increased in sound when the flaps and massive landing gear were extended. The president watched the huge Russian jet turn toward the runway, landing lights blazing, and thought how far Russia had come in the past seventy years toward the announced communist goal of global conquest.

The jet touched down, rolled half the length of the runway, then turned toward the flight line. The president watched the aircraft taxi to a stop.

'Let's be first in line, gentlemen,' the president stated as the three Americans walked to the front of the red carpet being placed beside the Soviet jet.

The powerful engines slowly droned to a halt, leaving a peaceful quiet as the forward passenger door opened on the gleaming Aeroflot transport.

The band played, flags were presented, and cameras clicked as the Russian general secretary deplaned, followed by the Soviet foreign minister, the Central Committee secretary, the military chief of staff, and various aides and functionaries.

As General Secretary Zhilinkhov reached the bottom

of the stairs, the American president raised his hand for a perfunctory handshake. The Soviet leader weakly returned the gesture. The atmosphere was definitely cool and restrained at this juncture.

'Secretary Zhilinkhov,' the president confronted the Soviet general secretary, 'we need to talk immediately.' The president was calm, matter-of-fact, but demanding.

The general secretary spoke in Russian, then smiled thinly. He understood English well enough to follow what the president was saying, but not well enough to speak the language.

'Mister President,' the Soviet interpreter repeated, 'we are scheduled for discussions this afternoon. We have scarcely arrived and our hosts have planned a welcome.'

'Secretary Zhilinkhov, recent events dictate that we dispense with protocol and address the urgent issues at hand,' the president said firmly.

The imposing Soviet head of state, his black suit bedecked with medals, was clearly perplexed and moderately ruffled. He had not anticipated the American being so bold, especially in public.

'Mister President,' the interpreter continued, 'I will discuss this – '

'We, General Secretary Zhilinkhov, need to discuss this situation now,' the president said slowly and deliberately, clearly enunciating every word.

The Soviet leader looked resigned to the inevitable confrontation as the president continued without pause.

'Many of our fine young military people are dead as a result of Soviet aggression. In recent hours, a Russian submarine heavily damaged one of our ships, and Soviet fighters shot down several of our aircraft, without provocation.'

Tempers flared.

Zhilinkhov spoke forcefully, then waited while the

interpreter responded. 'The general secretary warns you –'

'You're not on Soviet soil, Mister Zhilinkhov,' the president said, ignoring the interpreter. 'It would serve you well to remember that one fact. You don't warn, or threaten, anyone here.'

The Russian leader was flustered, off guard, and visibly agitated. The crowd was hushed, tension mounting, as the two world leaders stared intently at one another. No one had anticipated this situation.

The Soviet leader spoke loudly, then listened as the interpreter addressed the American. 'Where do you propose we talk?'

The general secretary was openly embarrassed and seething with rage. He had underestimated his adversary in the development of his scheme.

Staff members of both delegations, caught off guard by the unexpected confrontation, were ill at ease. The band had stopped playing and soldiers, scheduled to pass in review, were halted in front of the reviewing stand, bewilderment written on their faces.

'We have arranged a space in the large hangar across the ramp.' The president gestured toward the hangar used for itinerant aircraft. It was already surrounded by security personnel.

'Let's walk together,' the president suggested, then added, 'I'll have refreshments sent over.'

'That will be greatly appreciated,' the short, thin aide replied. 'We had a long and strenuous flight.'

The general secretary of the Soviet Union knew he had to be conciliatory and not let anger or impatience put his entire plan in jeopardy.

The president didn't reply, or encourage conversation, as the two leaders walked the short distance to the hangar.

The president stepped close to Wilkinson, talking in a hushed voice. 'Let's turn this into a working lunch. I want to press Zhilinkhov, not let him have time to formulate a new strategy.'

'Yes, sir. I will take care of the arrangements.' The chief of staff was pleased to see the president place the communist leader in a compromising position.

The president turned to the Soviet delegation and motioned them to join him at the center table.

'Secretary Zhilinkhov, let's sit at the head table, across from each other, with two each of our staff. Six total, plus your interpreter.'

The Russians were clearly confused.

'Secretary Zhilinkhov, my chief of staff, Grant Wilkinson, and our secretary of state, Herb Kohlhammer.'

The general secretary responded in kind.

'Foreign Minister Vladimir Vuyosekiev and Central Committee Secretary Yakov Toporovsky.'

The men awkwardly shook hands around the table, no smiles or small talk.

The Soviet leader was forced to leave his senior military representative, General Bogdonoff, out of the discussions, a step he reluctantly went along with under the circumstances. Two large sheets had hurriedly been placed over the stained surface of the scarred banquet table. The president, along with Wilkinson and Kohlhammer, sat down. The Soviet contingent hesitated a moment, then slowly sat down with the Americans.

'General Secretary Zhilinkhov, I want to make one statement. All the meetings, arms control negotiations, endless diplomatic conferences, et cetera, aren't going to accomplish anything if we, you and I, can't come to some agreement that we can both live with.

'Agreements, Secretary Zhilinkhov, known to the

whole world. Agreements we must honor, or be judged by the entire globe as untrustworthy and reprehensible.'

The president sat back, arms folded across his chest.

'Mister President, I am in agreement with you. Totally. As the new leader of the Soviet people, I am prepared to travel a different path from my esteemed predecessors.'

The interpreter waited while Zhilinkhov completed his statement.

'I wish to cooperate with the United States to make this world a better and safer place in which to live, for all humanity.'

Zhilinkhov extended his hand to the president, catching him off guard.

'I'm very pleased, Mister Secretary. Very pleased indeed,' the president said as he extended his hand in return. The two men shook hands warmly, then opened briefs supplied by aides.

A stir of subdued voices quietly discussed the unprecedented event, sounding openly skeptical and suspicious of the agreement.

Zhilinkhov, following the pause, continued his discourse.

'We, the Russian people, Mister President, don't want a war with the United States, or anyone, for that matter. We are a peaceful country, offering – '

'General Secretary Zhilinkhov,' the president interrupted the interpreter, 'I have no doubt the Russian people don't want a war with anyone. Our dispute is not with the people of Russia, but with its totalitarian, expansionist policies, which violate international law.'

The short honeymoon was over, resentment again invading the conversation.

Zhilinkhov, unprepared for the frontal assault by the tenacious American leader, took the offensive.

'Mister President,' the Russian interpreter hesitated,

clearly uncomfortable, 'I must remind you that your country has been responsible for sinking two Soviet Union vessels, a submarine and a ship of the Soviet Pacific Fleet.'

The president responded immediately, his neck becoming rigid.

'Unbridled Soviet militarism is bringing the globe closer to catastrophe. Annihilation, Mister Zhilinkhov. You are fully aware, as everyone at this table is aware, that Soviet aggression caused us to respond in kind.'

The president continued, speaking over Zhilinkhov's attempted rebuttal.

'Secretary Zhilinkhov, your actions have brought us to the brink of war. That is why, Mister General Secretary, we are meeting here.'

The Kremlin leader became distant, not attempting to refute the American president. Zhilinkhov was visibly irritated and gulped his iced tea.

'Mister Zhilinkhov, let me assure you of one thing, a very important point for you to remember. Don't underestimate the American resolve, our dedication to freedom. We are a civilized nation, but we mean what we say.'

The president hit a nerve and the Kremlin leader's jaw muscles tightened. Both men stared at each other in silence.

COBRA FLIGHT

DiGennaro looked at his altimeter and then his twenty-four-hour clock. His F-15 was climbing through flight level 470 – forty-seven thousand feet – over a cold ocean at eleven o'clock at night.

157

The flight leader looked over his right shoulder at his wingman, Cobra Two.

Captain Parnam could see DiGennaro's head turn in the soft, eerie glow of his cockpit lights. The fighter pilot appeared luminescent, floating in a black void of time and space, Parnam thought as he pressed his radio transmission button.

'I'm with you, Major.'

'Roger, we'll stay high for awhile, then drop down for a drink when the rest of the team is in sight.'

DiGennaro had no intention, without backup fighters, of going in for a close look at the Russian bomber group.

'Two.' Parnam was trying to concentrate on the task at hand, but a picture of his wife and seven-month-old daughter kept creeping into his consciousness. They were home in Tallahassee, Florida, where the sun would rise in less than an hour. The fighter pilot could see them clearly in his mind.

Shelly feeding breakfast to Meredith, laughing as the baby gurgled gleefully, squashed bananas running down her chin.

'Cobra, Pinwheel Seven.'

'Go, Pinwheel.' DiGennaro's nerves involuntarily twitched when the radio startled him.

'The rest of the players will be with us in twelve minutes.' The E-3 coordinator, relaxed and clear-voiced, knew his job well.

'Roger, Pinwheel. We'd like to gas-up before everyone hits the tankers.' DiGennaro always stacked the odds in his favor, if possible. Airborne refueling would be necessary for the fighters joining the group.

'Stand by, Cobra.'

'Rog.'

These AWACS crews are sharp, DiGennaro thought as the radio crackled to life again.

'Cobra flight, go tact two. The tanker, Nightrider Four, is waiting for you at flight level two-seven-oh, zero-eight-zero for twenty-three.'

The E-3 had told the fighters the tanker would give them fuel at 27,000 feet, almost due east at a distance of twenty-three nautical miles.

'Cobras going tact two,' DiGennaro responded as he simultaneously reduced power, switched radio channels, lowered the nose, and rolled into a left turn.

'Two up,' Parnam checked in as he followed his leader into the descent, remaining in perfect position throughout the transition.

'Rog, Bill,' DiGennaro acknowledged before he contacted the tanker.

'Nightrider Four, Cobra One, flight of two Fox-Fifteens.'

'Bring it on in, Cobras,' the friendly tanker pilot radioed.

'You're cleared to the stabilized position. One plug first and call stabilized. We have you on radar.'

'Roger, Cobra flight five out, closing from your seven o'clock.' DiGennaro had the big tanker visually at this close range.

'Okay, check nav and form lights, Cobras.'

'Copy.' DiGennaro responded automatically, having practiced this task countless times.

'Pinwheel Seven to all tactical one and two aircraft. Be advised Pinwheel Two will be channel eight controlling the carrier-based fighters, copy?'

'Nightrider Four.'

'Nightrider Five.'

'Cobras.'

'Hawks copy.'

'Leopard flight.'

DiGennaro knew the tankers would be as critical as

the AWACS aircraft to the mission. He was surprised the carrier-based fighters weren't being supported by their own E-2C Hawkeyes.

The Russian bomber group, besides the Bears and Backfires, had a large contingent of tankers including the Tupolev Badger, the Myasishchev Bison, and the recently operational Ilyushin Midas.

The Soviet force would pose a serious threat, especially with their long-range AS-15 cruise missiles. The nuclear armed cruise missiles, traveling at 0.74 Mach, had a range of over 3,000 kilometers. They could easily target all major US West Coast cities and military bases.

The large Soviet fighter escort, DiGennaro decided, would be last in priority. First fighter wave go for the bombers, second for the tankers, and high cover take the Russian fighters.

This would be a real treat at night, DiGennaro thought, his mouth dry from the pure oxygen, as he plugged into the KC-10 tanker.

MOSCOW

The interior of the Chlebnikow Restaurant was warm and somewhat comforting to Dimitri as he sat down at a vacant table, lighted a cigarette, and ordered hot tea.

Dimitri rubbed his shaking hands together, as if to warm them, and stirred his steaming tea, glancing nervously at his watch. He paid the small Russian woman who brought him a refill and waited for his connection to arrive.

The CIA agent walked boldly through the door and announced, in Russian, that he was a KGB officer and wanted to see Dimitri's papers. A very brash move in the heart of Moscow.

Everyone was shocked into silence, including Dimitri, who looked at the American in wide-eyed disbelief – the exact effect the CIA agent wanted to convey.

Two patrons, an old man and a young woman, left a couple of rubles on their tables and went out the front door with their coats not fully buttoned. The handful of other early morning customers hunkered down, trying to be as inconspicuous as possible in the confines of the small restaurant.

The American ordered Dimitri to the kitchen, where the agent told the small Russian woman and her young helper to leave them alone for five minutes. The two women were more than relieved to disappear from the compact room and the dreaded KGB officer.

'Your report. Quickly,' Wickham said, speaking in English.

'Zhilinkhov plans . . . they plan to launch nuclear missiles on . . . at the United States!' Dimitri struggled to be articulate.

'WHAT?' The CIA operative blinked twice, grabbed Dimitri by the shoulders, and stared intently into his face. The grip was like a vise, sending an excruciating pain through Dimitri's upper body.

'Yes. I heard the general secretary talk at length last night with three Politburo members and a former member of the Politburo – '

'When?' the agent asked, stunned.

'Just before he left on – '

'No!' the tall agent said angrily. 'When is he planning to initiate the preemptive strike?'

'I'm not sure of the exact time,' Dimitri responded, talking rapidly. 'He said very soon.'

'Slow down,' the American said, lowering his voice to where it was almost inaudible. 'Exactly what was said?'

'They have planned for the Americans to be off guard
. . . something about an alert being over.'

Dimitri was trying to rush, searching for the best way
to explain something unbelievable.

'Go on,' Wickham ordered.

'They talked about survival statistics. I couldn't hear
all of it – the conversation.'

'What exactly did you hear, regarding the missile
strike?' The CIA agent was adamant. He also found the
disclosure incredulous. Would his superiors think he had
lost his faculties?

'He – Secretary Zhilinkhov – used the term "first
strike" more than once. He said when the military
withdraws, when the alert is over . . . then the strike will
happen.'

'Anything else?'

'Yes. They – the six of them, including the defense
minister – talked about dominating the world and . . .
acceptable casualties.'

'Then what?'

'They drank a toast . . . and celebrated,' Dimitri said,
more sure of himself.

'Do you recall any other pertinent information?' The
agent was insistent.

'No,' Dimitri replied, trying to remember the details of
the secret plan. His mind still couldn't accept the horrible
fact.

'Okay, now we've – '

Wickham was cut off abruptly when Dimitri remembered an important point. It would have been easier if he
had written everything down, but one of his first lessons
at the CIA was to never leave a record of anything, ever.

'They talked about a delay or reaction time they
needed to test. How long it would take the Americans to
react to a missile launch from the Soviet Union. The

general secretary said if the Russians have a sixteen-minute period of time before the United States reacts, then they can successfully destroy America.'

'Anything else?' the agent asked, knowing they needed to leave the restaurant.

'Only that they discussed how they would go about occupying America and Europe . . . and having all the oil they needed.'

Dimitri paused, trying to collect his thoughts.

'Only the six of them know of the plan . . . plus the chief of the general staff. They intend to sink an American ship, escalate . . . I believe they said defense conditions to stage two, then withdraw. When the Americans withdraw, Zhilinkhov is going to launch all the Soviet missiles.'

Dimitri waited as the agent glanced through the thin curtain stretched across the door to the kitchen. 'Go on.'

'They definitely said "first strike" . . . on America. I know that for sure,' Dimitri said, sounding exhausted.

'Alright, Dimitri, can you continue in your capacity, or do you want out?'

Wickham could see that Dimitri, the agency's only Kremlin in-house operative, was on the threshold of breaking. That was the last thing they could afford to have happen to him inside the Russian headquarters. He had done a great job, under constant tension, but this astonishing revelation had fractured his mettle.

'I want out,' Dimitri said in a resigned whisper. 'I can't stay here . . . knowing what they are going to – '

'This will be tough, understand?' Wickham didn't have much time for explanations.

'Yes.'

Dimitri thought about Svetlana, his mouth dry, as he tried to grasp the enormity of the task ahead.

163

'Tell them your mother is worse. Explain that you have to leave now to see her one last time.'

'Yes, sir,' Dimitri responded, openly fidgeting in the small room.

'You must be bold, Dimitri. You understand? You've got to keep it together. You must give us a little time to organize your trip out, okay?'

'Yes, sir. I can do it.'

Dimitri saw a flash of Svetlana and the New York City skyline – incongruous under the circumstances – his mind trying to deal with too many changes too quickly.

'Take the train to Yemetsk, see the old woman, and wait to hear from us. We'll be in touch soon.'

'I will leave this afternoon.'

Dimitri could feel relief surging through him, his fears quelled by the need for clear thinking.

'Make it appear normal. Don't take anything out of the ordinary. Understand?'

'Yes . . . but,' Dimitri paused, trying to decide how to approach the subject of Svetlana.

'But what? We don't have much time.'

The agent nervously looked at the front entrance.

'What about my girl? Svetlana Grishinakov. We plan to marry when my commitment is – '

'Impossible!'

Silence filled the small room before Wickham, in a pleasant voice, spoke again.

'Look, we will be lucky to get you out alive, under the circumstances.' The American gently squeezed Dimitri's shoulders. 'I'm sorry. It's just too risky. You must understand?'

Dimitri nodded, frightened and dejected. 'I understand.'

'We've got to get out of here. You walk in front of me to the front door.'

The Central Intelligence expert was pressing his luck. Changing back to fluent Russian, the covert operative gave Dimitri an order.

'You report back to work immediately! You will be contacted soon. Your papers are not in compliance.'

The ruse might have convinced everyone except the beefy, bald-headed man sitting alone in the corner. He didn't even glance up as the two men passed his table.

'Yes, comrade,' Dimitri replied in a weak voice.

Turning to the two women, the American agent bellowed in Russian. 'Your kitchen is a disgrace. Have it cleaned before I send the inspector.'

The women trembled but didn't utter a sound as they huddled in a corner.

Dimitri walked into the street, trying to sort out his trip to Yemetsk and what he would tell Svetlana. He had to find a way to get her out of Russia. Dimitri knew if he could arrange for his beautiful Svetlana to go to Yemetsk with him, or meet him there, it might work. First, he must tell her the truth.

Dimitri looked over his still-aching shoulder as he crossed the street and saw the CIA agent disappear down a side street next to the restaurant.

The Kremlin operative also saw something else from the corner of his eye.

Panic gripped him when the black Volga, bearing KGB tags, turned down the same side street behind the American.

Dimitri froze, confused, not comprehending the gravity of the situation. The desire to flee almost overpowered his reasoning. He looked around, sensing other KGB agents near. Nothing appeared abnormal.

Dimitri made a snap decision. His contact, his only connection to the outside world, was in jeopardy. He had to do something. Now.

Think, he told himself. The words 'be bold' came back to him. That's what the American agent said he must be in order to survive and escape.

Dimitri hurried back across the street and followed the black car down the side street. Ahead he could see Wickham, hands shoved deep in the pockets of his heavy coat, stepping off the sidewalk to cross the narrow street. Did the American have any idea the KGB officers were following him?

'There must have been an informant in the restaurant,' Dimitri absently said to himself. 'Someone who knew the American wasn't KGB.'

Dimitri slowed his walk. At that very instant the Volga stopped twenty meters from the CIA agent. The two occupants got out of the car and approached the lone man. The American, if he did notice the car, or agents, didn't react to the KGB pressure. He continued his normal pace, stepping onto the opposite sidewalk as the two Russian agents confronted him.

The three men then stepped into a concealed space between two rusted, peeling buildings. Dimitri moved forward cautiously, trying to suppress the gnawing fear overcoming him. He looked up and down the street. No trace of anything unordinary.

Dimitri could see the three men clearly now. The American presented his credentials to the KGB officers and stepped back. The Soviet agents looked at the papers, then told Wickham to turn around and place his hands over his head, forehead against the rough wall.

The taller of the two Russians then pulled a snub-nosed gun from his coat as his companion placed the American's credentials in his vest pocket.

Dimitri reacted without thinking. Running at full speed into the narrow space, Dimitri barreled into the two KGB agents. The impact knocked all four men down in a thundering crash of rubbish containers and egg cartons.

The American leaped to his feet, whirled around and solidly kicked the taller Russian under the chin, breaking his neck and crushing his larynx.

Dimitri, struggling to regain his footing, saw only a blur as Wickham slung a rubbish can lid into the skull of the other supine KGB agent, rendering him unconscious.

The American yanked Dimitri to his feet, grabbed the snub-nosed revolver, retrieved his credentials, and ushered the frightened young spy into the street.

'Follow me! We've got to leave Moscow immediately.'

Dimitri was amazed at the self-control demonstrated by the CIA operative.

'Yessir,' Dimitri responded automatically, so frightened he was shaking uncontrollably.

POW! The backhand caught Dimitri completely by surprise, the result being instantaneous. He stopped shaking and his mind snapped to reality.

'Sorry, but you've got to get it together or we're both dead,' Wickham said in a menacing tone. 'Too many people have seen this. The KGB will have our descriptions in minutes.'

'Yes . . . I'm okay,' Dimitri replied, rubbing his jaw.

'Follow me,' the agent said, breathing heavily. 'Stay twenty meters behind and keep your eyes open.'

'Yessir,' Dimitri paused, looking around for signs of more KGB officers.

The two men walked at a steady pace, slightly separated, as a shocked crowd gathered around the inert Soviet agents. No one attacked KGB officers.

8

NORAD

General Matuchek watched the continuously changing status graphics at his control module and contemplated the approaching Soviet bomber fleets. He thought about the American concept of layered defenses and fervently wished the Space Defense Initiative system were fully operational.

The NORAD commander knew the SDI system had faults. Scientists and engineers, during the previous three months, had argued various theorems, trying to correct the deficiencies in pointing and tracking.

SDI had been designed to recognize instantly the plume of smoke and fire from a hostile missile launch. The object of the sophisticated deterrent was to destroy the weapons as they rose from their silos or broke the surface of the water.

If the enemy knew, or believed, their missiles would explode over their own territory, they would presumably not risk that option.

The exasperated SDI experts had been working feverishly to eliminate the problems of wavefront control. Atmospheric distortion wreaked havoc with the pointing and tracking ability of the SDI satellites already in orbit. Various experiments had recently improved the system's capability.

Astronauts and scientists, working in orbit from *Starlab*, had been achieving great success firing lasers at test missiles launched from ground-based sites.

However, the final solution escaped the scientists as they continued to rework the optics in the equation. Everyone felt a breakthrough was imminent. A 100 percent reliable system of nuclear missile defense was only months, if not weeks, away.

The real concern, in both the scientific and military communities, was the vulnerability of our SDI satellites to Soviet laser attacks. The Soviets had previously damaged the Indigo Lacrosse spy satellite, which used radar to view through clouds or bad weather. The satellite, crucial for guiding the B-2 Stealth bombers over Russia during a nuclear war, would have to be replaced.

'Excuse me, General.' The assistant operations officer handed Matuchek a folder.

'Another Top Secret, huh?' CINCNORAD replied, reaching for the packet.

'Yes, sir. Your eyes only.'

'Appreciate it, Colonel.'

'Yes, sir,' replied the lieutenant colonel.

Matuchek watched the lanky officer as he returned to his central command post, then read the contents of the secret message.

Z010532ZFEB
TOP SECRET
FROM: AIR FORCE SPACE COMMAND
TO   : CONSOLIDATED SPACE OPERATIONS
        CENTER
SUBJ : STRATEGIC DEFENSE INITIATIVE
REF : CHAIRMAN JCS MSG Z010405ZFEB
INFO : CINCNORAD
        SATELLITE TEST CENTER
1. FINAL SDI DEPLOYMENT RESCHEDULED FOR 010645ZFEB. WINDOW 0645Z THROUGH 0740Z. COORDINATE TRACKING WITH HOUSTON AND NORAD. ESTABLISH ON-LINE TAP AT 010600ZFEB. CALL COLUMBIA FIFTY-SEVEN.

2. RESUME NORMOPS AT COMPLETION OF SEV-
ENTH ORBIT. AWAIT REPLY.

Matuchek looked at the twenty-four-hour clock on the
wall and compared the time to his wristwatch. Less than
one hour before launch.

'Christ,' he muttered quietly as he punched the code
for Lt Gen. Jonathan R. Honeycutt, his Canadian vice
commander.

'General Honeycutt,' replied the three-star officer in
his usual crisp manner.

'John, J. B. When you have a minute, I need to speak
with you privately.'

'Yes, sir,' Honeycutt replied. 'Right away.'

MOSCOW

Dimitri and the tall CIA agent rounded the first street
corner and ducked into a narrow walkway. The American
had not said a word since they had left the chaotic
confrontation with the KGB agents.

Dimitri, his pulse racing, broke into a half run as the
CIA operative quickened the pace.

'Move it out, Dimitri,' the agent ordered as he placed
his hands on a small wooden fence and catapulted himself
over the rickety structure.

Dimitri didn't answer. His breathing was already
ragged, his mouth tasted like cotton, and his right hand
throbbed with pain.

Wickham continued to instruct Dimitri as the two men
hurried down walkways and back streets.

'Hang on, Dimitri. Two more minutes and we'll be in
my apartment.'

'Okay. I'm not – '

'Don't talk,' barked the agent. 'Just listen!'

Dimitri didn't respond as he tried to quicken his pace behind the fast-moving American.

'When we get to the apartment,' the CIA agent paused while he reconnoitered Cherkasskiy street, 'we will change into disguises to facilitate our escape.'

The American slowed to a normal walk as they approached his apartment.

'No need to draw unwanted attention or suspicion. Just be casual,' the agent cautioned as they neared the Novaya apartment complex, 'and speak in Russian at all times.'

'Da,' Dimitri replied as he glanced from side to side, then down to his aching hand.

The CIA operative looked up at his apartment window, then continued talking to Dimitri.

'We will become Soviet bureaucrats. Agriculture inspectors traveling to Leningrad to examine the truck farming administrative center. The credentials are flawless.'

Dimitri knew, at this point, to listen, not respond to the American.

'I will brief you on the train,' Wickham continued as they started up the steps to the apartment building. 'The area around Leningrad is full of state-run farms producing potatoes, vegetables, dairy products, and they also raise hogs and livestock.'

'Okay.' Dimitri ventured a tentative reply.

The CIA agent, noticing the long hallway was empty, continued summarizing the escape plan.

'The KGB will be circulating our descriptions through-out the city in a matter of minutes. You'll be missed at the Kremlin by midafternoon.'

'Yes. Before, probably,' replied the frightened young auto mechanic, wishing he could be with Svetlana in New

171

Jersey. His mind raced as the events of the morning caught up with him. No turning back.

'We have some time, not a lot, but enough to prepare adequately for our trip.'

Dimitri nodded, thinking about Svetlana.

The agent, reaching for his keys, continued. 'We have to catch the ten-thirty train to Leningrad. The KGB will be everywhere, but our disguises and credentials will obviate any suspicion. Understand?'

'Y-Yes,' Dimitri stammered, not accepting the necessity for the sudden departure from Moscow. He ached for Svetlana and the passion-filled nights they had shared. Would he ever see her again? Could he ever explain?

The CIA agent unlocked the door and the two men stepped inside. The American immediately went to the window and peered into the street. A black Volga containing three KGB agents drove slowly down the street, stopping in the intersection.

'The KGB is already out in force,' the CIA operative reported, slowly turning his head to view the opposite direction.

'Dimitri, I hope you can appreciate how serious this is.' The agent released the window curtain and turned to face Dimitri.

'Sorry, the wheels just fell off and we've got – '

Wickham stopped in midsentence, horrified. His eyes widened and he swallowed twice before speaking, pointing his finger, arm outstretched, at Dimitri's right hand.

'Dimitri, your hand is bleeding!'

Both men stared at the bright red blood steadily dripping on the floor. The two agents realized they had left a clearly marked trail to the apartment. Their sanctuary was now a deathtrap.

COBRA FLIGHT

Major DiGennaro concentrated on flying perfect formation while he glanced at his fuel gauges. Two minutes
passed before he saw the refueling light wink out on the
huge KC-10, checked his fuel load, and prepared to
unplug from the tanker.

'Cobra One,' announced the fueling boom operator,
'you're cleared down and to the left.'

'Roger, One is down and left,' DiGennaro replied,
easing back on his throttles.

The sleek F-15 disengaged from the tanker cleanly,
dropped astern twenty feet, and slowly moved below and
to the left of the mammoth flying gas station.

Now it was Parnam's turn to take on fuel before the
other thirsty F-15s arrived on station. DiGennaro knew
their flight leader would be anxious to have his troops
topped off before confronting the Russians.

DiGennaro watched as Parnam made an abortive
attempt to mate with the KC-10, then smoothly plugged
into the tanker on his second try.

'How ya doin', Bill?' DiGennaro asked in a conver-
sational tone, noticing the pilot induced oscillations were
dampening.

'Mighty fine, boss,' Parnam responded, intently concentrating on his formation flying, 'and the price isn't bad
either.'

DiGennaro chuckled to himself, knowing his wingman
was damn good. He checked his fuel gauges once more,
glanced at his armament panel, and called the AWACS.

'Pinwheel, Cobra with you.'

'Cobra, Pinwheel.'

'I'm topped and Two will be off the tanker in a minute.
Where are the other fifteens?'

'They're thirty out, Cobra, descending on the tankers.' The voice was calm, reassuring.

'Roger, Pinwheel. Point us toward the bogies,' DiGennaro replied, checking Parnam's F-15.

'Two eighty-five, blocking three-three-zero to four-one-oh, one hundred forty out.'

'One with a copy,' responded the flight leader, waiting for his wingman to finish refueling.

'Two shows full,' Parnam announced in a quiet, steady voice.

'Nightrider confirms,' the boom operator verified the load, 'cleared down and to the right.'

'Down and right,' Parnam repeated, easing the F-15 back to the right of the tanker. He looked over to his flight leader on the left.

'Good hunting, Cobras,' radioed the pilot of the lumbering KC-10.

'Thanks, Nightrider. Appreciate the drink,' replied DiGennaro as he watched his wingman slide into position on his right wing.

'Our pleasure, guys,' responded the KC-10 pilot. The tanker was already turning to remain in the racetrack refueling pattern.

'Cobras, go combat spread,' ordered DiGennaro. 'Check your panel; we're goin' upstairs.'

'Roger, lead. Clean and green,' replied Parnam, inching his throttles forward while he scanned his radar.

The Russian bomber group and fighter escorts were approaching the American fighter pilots at a combined closure rate of over 1,000 miles per hour.

MOSCOW

The CIA agent shoved Dimitri toward the tiny bathroom, shouting orders, as he hurried to effect their escape. No time now for a full transformation or disguise. Their options were dwindling rapidly.

'Wash your hand off and wrap it with gauze,' Wickham said, yanking open drawers. 'Keep your gloves on.'

The American agent quickly combed white powder through his hair, creating an instant aging effect. Wickham, donning different trousers, white shirt, conservative dark tie, and long black topcoat, began to look like a Soviet bureaucrat, an agriculture inspector. He topped off the ensemble with a black, Russian-made, medium-brimmed hat.

Racing back to the window, the agent tossed Dimitri a pair of pants, long coat, and similar black hat.

'Get into those quick! Remember how to use this?' Wickham asked, tossing Dimitri a 9-mm Beretta.

'Yes,' Dimitri responded, dancing on one leg while he tried to get the pants over his shoes. The pistol bounced off his left knee as Dimitri simultaneously lost his balance and fell against the bed.

'Don't, unless you absolutely have to,' the agent said, holding the window curtain open half an inch. 'We've gotta move fast!'

The American thrust a package of credentials into Dimitri's inside coat pocket, peered out the window, and quickly stepped back.

'Aw, shit! They're on us, Dimitri. Let's go.'

The two men raced down the hallway, clambered through a window, went part way down a fire escape, and leaped over a fence into an adjoining courtyard.

Dimitri stumbled and fell forward on his knees, knocking his hat off. Wickham picked him up, slamming Dimitri's hat down over his ears.

Together the men raced toward the Moscow suburb of Barviha, where the CIA operatives had a Volga. The car was registered in the name of a United States embassy official, but reserved for this type of contingency, a quick escape from Moscow proper.

'Hurry, Dimitri! We can't outrun their dogs.' Wickham's breathing was becoming labored.

Dimitri's response was a gasp, a croak, 'Ahh – 'kay.'

The two men emerged from a narrow passage between two buildings, 150 meters from the waiting Volga, and started walking across the street.

Suddenly, the American pushed Dimitri into a row of shrub trees, again knocking his hat askew. Wickham pointed down Kazabova street, visibly straining to slow his breathing, his lips parched dry.

Dimitri could see the black KGB car 200 meters past the Volga, their escape vehicle. Two GRU officers, one holding the leash of a Doberman pinscher, were talking with the driver.

The American quietly motioned to Dimitri. 'Follow me and stay alert.'

Dimitri responded by grabbing the back of the agent's coat as they forced their way through the shrubs and hedges until they were in a small yard.

'We'll cut between the buildings, then try to approach from the dacha directly in front of the car.'

The two men crept across three small private yards in the posh suburb and stealthily approached the side of the dacha in front of the parked Volga.

Wickham motioned Dimitri to kneel down. They moved quietly to the side of the front porch, removing their hats. Dimitri could feel the Beretta gouging him between his back and belt.

'Listen,' Wickham whispered. 'The keys are in a special container under the left rear fender.'

Dimitri listened intently, nodding his head in under-standing. His hand still hurt, hot and stinging, but the pain was almost forgotten in his near-panic.

'I'm going to head for the car, get the keys, and unlock the driver's door. Then – and only then – you walk casually out and get in the other side. Understand, Dimitri? Clearly?'

'Yes,' Dimitri said, fear written on his face. 'I understand.'

Wickham nervously looked around the corner of the porch. The GRU officers and their Doberman were slowly crossing the street, approaching the row of dachas in front of the Volga.

The KGB men were still in their car with the passenger door open.

'Dimitri, it's very simple. We have no other choice. If we stay here, I guarantee you we will be dead, or imprisoned and tortured, very shortly.'

'Yes, sir,' Dimitri replied, regaining his confidence.

'Then do as I say. Put your weapon in your outside coat pocket. If we need them, we'll damn sure use 'em.'

Dimitri nodded, gently placing the Beretta in his right coat pocket.

'Here we go,' Wickham said as he walked from the side of the porch, shocking Dimitri with his boldness.

The American stepped between a tall hedge and the outside door of the dacha, pretending to be leaving the residence. He opened, then slammed the outside door, casually strolling down the short steps, carefully fitting his hat to his head.

'Good morning, comrades,' the American agent said in perfect Russian.

Dimitri was petrified as he watched the agent talk to the KGB officers.

'Morning,' came the brusque reply. The black Doberman growled menacingly, straining on his leash.

Wickham reached for the keys as the GRU officers started back across the street.

Dimitri watched as the American unlocked the driver's door. The young Kremlin operative stood upright and started toward the car. Every step was filled with agonizing terror. Every fiber in his being cried out in alarm.

Without warning, the door to the dacha opened, startling Dimitri. A pretty Russian woman appeared, thinking someone had knocked on her door.

'What do you want?' she cried out, alarmed at the presence of GRU officers across the street.

The two officers stopped, turned around, a quizzical look on their faces.

Before Dimitri could respond to the frightened woman, the American turned and spoke to her in Russian.

'We apologize,' Wickham said loudly, 'we knocked at the wrong dacha. Yevgeny Govorko, we have the wrong address.'

Dimitri hesitated, then started for the car.

'Keep moving, Dimitri,' Wickham said under his breath.

'Halt!' the GRU senior officer commanded. 'Stop where you are!'

'Run, Dimitri!' the American ordered. 'Get in the car.'

As Dimitri rounded the corner of the car, a black object hit him from the side. He felt searing pain in his right ear, then heard a loud shot close to him.

Wickham had shot the Doberman when he glanced off Dimitri, catching the vicious beast as he leaped off the pavement for another assault.

'GET IN,' the American shouted as he leaped into the driver's seat and inserted the key.

Dimitri plunged headlong into the car as Wickham floorboarded the Volga and careened into traffic.

The black KGB car made a U-turn and was recklessly pursuing the two CIA men, swerving wildly to miss oncoming vehicles.

The two agents had to lose the Russians quickly if they had any chance for survival.

Wickham yelled at Dimitri to keep his head down, then glanced in the rearview mirror at the pursuing auto-mobile. At that precise instant the rear window was shattered by three rounds from a KGB submachine gun.

9

THE WHITE HOUSE

The vice president, surrounded by Cliff Howard, secretary of defense, and the Joint Chiefs of Staff, waited patiently for Ted Corbin to enter the Situation Room.

The director of the Central Intelligence Agency had called the vice president only minutes before to report an 'irregularity' in Moscow.

Susan Blaylocke, sensing a major problem developing, ordered the CIA director to report in person, then called a meeting of her staff.

Corbin entered the room, tie askew, and sat down.

The vice president spoke first. 'What, precisely, is the problem in Moscow, Ted?'

The director seemed flustered, hesitating before he answered. 'The information I have at the present time is preliminary and doesn't accurately reflect appro –'

'Ted,' Blaylocke impatiently interrupted, 'just state the problem, clearly and concisely.'

Corbin's face flushed, turning almost crimson.

'Something has gone wrong in Moscow. We only know, at this juncture, that our senior field operative and the Kremlin plant have been involved in an altercation with the KGB. Our mole was apparently on to something. He violated the normal procedure for contacting the senior agent, and, we believe, that initiated the screwup.'

Every face in the room was staring at Corbin, unnerving the intelligence director.

'Altercation?' The vice president looked puzzled. 'Could you be more specific, Ted?'

The director averted his eyes. 'We don't know the details as of yet. We do know there was some sort of scuffle. Our senior agent in Moscow, Steve Wickham, has disappeared, along with Dimitri. Our belief is that both men have been pla – '

'What do you mean by disappeared? Does the KGB have them in custody?' Blaylocke, irritated, watched the director closely, measuring him.

'We don't believe the KGB has them,' Corbin responded, wetting his lips. 'At least not at the moment.'

'Go on,' Cliff Howard prodded.

'As I started to say previously, our other senior field agent – he works closely with Wickham covering the Kremlin – reported the incident and the disappearance.'

Corbin glanced at his notes as he fumbled with his attaché case, then continued. 'Apparently, from preliminary reports, Wickham and Dimitri escaped on foot from the incident with the KGB. We don't know where they are at this time. They're probably en – '

'Wait a minute,' Blaylocke said, her hand slightly raised. 'How did the incident come about? It was our understanding, at least my understanding, that everything was under control. What happened?'

Corbin took a deep breath. 'I – we don't know. Our other agent sent a brief message saying that Soviet television and newspapers, *Izvestia* and *Moskovski Komsomolyets*, are reporting fatalities, including KGB officers.'

The CIA director, eyes cast downward at his briefing sheet, continued. 'The other Moscow agent suspects the KGB knew about Wickham and may have been waiting for an opportunity to seize him. They, the KGB, had never been able to link Wickham to Dimitri before the unplanned rendezvous. They made a cardinal error in deviating from standard operating procedures, perhaps because of the nature of the information.'

Silence followed that disclosure, then murmurs filled the quiet room.

Cliff Howard broke the silence. 'I don't intend to be the harbinger of doom, but this is the last thing we need with the president in Lajes.'

'Ted,' the vice president spoke quietly, 'if I understand this correctly, our agents are on the run, being pursued by the whole of Moscow.'

Corbin nodded silently.

'Do we have a contingency plan to get them out of Russia without creating an international embarrassment?'

'Yes,' Corbin responded, 'providing, of course, that our senior agent, Wickham, still has his satellite transmitter.'

Blaylocke looked straight into the director's eyes, then spoke slowly. 'Again, you'll have to be more specific, Ted. Many of us are not completely aware of the CIA's capabilities.'

Blaylocke paused, then spoke in the same deliberate manner. 'Also, as a reminder, any operation, in the magnitude you refer to, will need my personal approval.'

'I am fully aware of that fact, Ms. Blaylocke.'

'Please continue,' the vice president replied.

'The original plan was to have the agents return to Leningrad, disguised as Soviet agricultural inspectors, then cross the border with –'

'Ted,' the vice president sighed, 'I would think the original plan is no longer applicable. Their descriptions will be posted at every crossing. What are your plans for retrieving the agents under these conditions?'

The condescending remark almost caused the CIA

director to become apoplectic. Corbin's face blanched, then reddened again.

'Ms. Blaylocke, if the operatives are alive, if they have the transmitter, then we intend to rescue them with high-speed helicopters,' Corbin said, darting a look at the chairman of the Joint Chiefs. 'When we know their location.'

'That's pretty risky,' Admiral Chambers responded in a reserved manner.

'Yes, Admiral, it is. But we have sufficient reason to believe it is imperative that we extract the agents.'

'Okay, Ted, back to the helicopter rescue plan. Explain the operation to us,' Blaylocke ordered, taking notes on a legal pad.

'We have three Sikorsky S-70 Night Hawk helicopters – they're combat rescue helos – camouflaged in Russian livery, in the hold of a cargo ship in the Baltic Sea near Stockholm. When we know the location of our agents, the helos will take off at night from the Porkkala Peninsula, refuel in Lovisa, Finland, then proceed to the pickup point. We hope, as the original helicopter rescue plan outlines, that our agents can make it by train to Novgorod, which is about a hundred thirty miles south of Leningrad. We have a prearranged site, outside of Novgorod, to land the rescue helicopter. It will be on the ground only for a few seconds, just long enough for our agents to leap aboard.'

'Then what?' Howard asked, running a hand through his unruly hair.

'Then two helicopters will fly diversionary routes while the helo containing our agents will fly at treetop level straight over the Gulf of Riga and recover on the cargo container ship.'

'From there?' Chambers asked.

'After refueling, the helicopter will fly our agents to

Stockholm, where we will place them aboard an Air Force transport plane bound for Washington.'

'What about the other two helicopters?' Chambers asked, uncomfortable with the entire rescue plan.

'They will race for the Gulf of Finland, one hundred miles west of Leningrad, then proceed back to Lovisa for refueling. After they depar – '

'What is the bottom line chance for a successful helicopter rescue, as you've outlined?' Blaylocke asked, adjusting her glasses.

'Ms Blaylocke, that's like predicting what a roulette wheel will do. Half is black, half is red.'

The vice president glared at the contentious CIA boss, then spoke slowly, her voice rising ever so slightly. 'When I ask you a question, Ted, I will appreciate a straightforward, forthright answer.'

Silence filled the room.

'The chances are fifty-fifty,' Corbin shot back, thoroughly miffed by the tall, slender woman.

'Thank you,' Blaylocke responded, unruffled. 'I will take your information under advisement.'

The vice president shifted slightly in her chair and addressed Admiral Chambers and the other chiefs of staff.

'Admiral, what is the current military status?'

Chambers looked at the Army chief of staff, General Vandermeer.

'Warren, where do you stand with the airlift?'

'All buttoned and ready to go on immediate notice,' replied the four-star general.

'Excellent,' Chambers responded as he turned back to Blaylocke. 'All services are at projected manning levels for Defense Condition-Two.'

Blaylocke turned to the secretary of defense. 'Cliff, what's the status of the shuttle?'

Howard replied in a voice that echoed weariness.

'Final stages, ma'am. The countdown has started. No reports of security problems. Actually, no significant problems at all, so far.'

'Okay,' Blaylocke looked around the conference table, 'let's take a break, gentlemen.'

The vice president faced the CIA director. 'Ted, I expect an immediate response when you receive any further information.'

The intelligence agency boss didn't respond, only nodding yes to the imposing woman.

SHUTTLE *COLUMBIA*

The 4.4-million-pound space shuttle, poised for flight, was bathed in soft moonlight.

The handover/ingress personnel had already spent several hours in *Columbia* checking every detail in preparation for the early morning launch.

The tempo was picking up as the flight crew settled into their launch positions.

On the flight deck, Colonel Crawford, Hank Doherty, Alan Cressottie, and Doctor Tran were strapped into their seats. The astronauts were on their backs in a sitting position. Ward Culdrew was seated in the middeck cabin, apprehensive at not having any controls of his own.

The liquid oxygen and liquid hydrogen had already been pumped into the orbiter. Mission Control now acknowledged the final countdown.

'*Columbia*, this is Launch Control. Radio check, over.'

'Roger,' Crawford answered, switching to Mission Control and repeating the radio check.

The crew continued with the preflight checks, including abort advisory, side hatch closure, and cabin leak check.

'Control, *Columbia* shows cabin pressure nominal,' Crawford reported.

'Roger, nominal.'

Crawford continued with the preflight preparations, carefully monitoring the checklist.

'Control, IMU alignment complete.' Crawford looked at the Inertial Measurement Unit and continued. 'We show two-eight degrees, three-six minutes, three-zero point three-two seconds north, by eight-zero degrees, three-six minutes one-four point eight-eight seconds west. Over.'

'Concur, *Columbia*.'

'Houston, commander's voice check.'

'Copy,' replied the distant voice.

'Pilot voice check,' Doherty reported.

'Roger, Hank.'

Five minutes passed as the flight plan was loaded into the computers. The flight deck CRTs would now indicate any guidance navigation or control system faults, along with the launch trajectory.

Mission Control performed a mandatory check at T-minus fifteen minutes.

'*Columbia*, we are conducting the abort check, over.'

Crawford glanced at the blinking annunciator lights, then looked at Doherty. The pilot acknowledged the abort signal as Crawford keyed his microphone.

'Looks good, Houston.'

Crawford then copied the latest landing weather data for a return to launch site abort, or abort down range.

At the same time, three Marine Cobra gunship helicopters lifted off the shuttle runway. The trio made two sweeps down the beach and then settled into a racetrack pattern around the orbiter.

'Houston, *Columbia*. Event timer started.'

'Roger.'

'*Columbia*, initiate APU pre-start.'

'Roger, Houston,' Crawford replied. 'Powering up APUs.'

'*Columbia*, you are on internal power.'

'Copy internal,' Crawford read back, checking the movement of the flight control surfaces and exercising the hydraulic systems.

At T-minus three minutes the orbiter's main engines swiveled to their launch positions.

'*Columbia*, main engine gimbal complete.'

'Copy, Houston.'

'*Columbia*, H-two tank pressurization okay. You are go for launch at this time.'

'Go for launch,' Crawford responded, adrenaline pumping more rapidly in his veins.

At T-minus twenty-five seconds the shuttle countdown switched over to onboard computers.

'Fifteen seconds and counting,' Houston reported in a calm, relaxed voice.

There was no reply from the shuttle crew.

'Five, four – we have main engine start – two, one, zero. SRB ignition, lift off! We have lift off!'

At T-plus 2.64 seconds the shuttle's solid rocket boosters ignited.

'The tower has been cleared. All engines look good,' Houston informed the orbiter crew.

'Roger, Houston. Lookin' good here.'

'Instituting roll maneuver,' Houston reported to Crawford.

'Roger, rolling,' Crawford responded, closely watching his attitude direction indicator (ADI).

The mammoth shuttle, belching clouds of billowing white smoke, thundering like a thousand jets, began a slow 120-degree roll to a 'heads down' crew position. The ground shook for miles in every direction.

The circling helicopter gunships spread out and descended to two hundred feet.

'Roll completed, *Columbia*. You're looking good.'

Approximately forty-five seconds into the flight, at the speed of sound (Mach One), the main engines throttled down from 100 percent to 65 percent.

'Houston, main engines at sixty-five percent.'

'Copy, *Columbia*.'

Twenty-eight seconds elapsed before the shuttle reached maximum dynamic pressure.

'Houston, Max Q,' Crawford radioed in a tense voice.

'Throttle up to one hundred percent.'

Everyone in Mission Control crossed their fingers, remembering this point in the *Challenger* disaster.

Crawford, breathing easier, looked over at Hank Doherty.

The orbiter pilot replied with a thumbs up gesture. 'So far, so good, boss.'

'Houston, we have SRB burnout.'

'Roger, *Columbia*,' the relieved voice responded.

'Stand by for separation.'

The solid rocket boosters exploded off the shuttle, falling smoothly in a graceful arc.

'Houston, we have separation,' Crawford reported.

'We can see that. Looks good, *Columbia*.'

'*Columbia*, you are negative return. Copy?'

'Roger, negative return,' Crawford replied, realizing the cape could not be used for an emergency return.

Crawford, aware of the tension in his voice, checked with each crewman over the intercom system.

'Drew, you okay down there?'

'My ass is so puckered, you couldn't drive a knittin' needle up it!'

'Next mission, Drew,' Crawford said with a chuckle, 'we'll place a stick down there so you can help drive.'

'Thanks, boss,' the Marine pilot replied. 'You figure the news people are awake yet?'

Laughter filled the flight deck while Crawford checked his instrument panel. They could reach orbit even if two main engines failed. 'Houston, we are single engine press to MECO.'

'Roger, *Columbia*. Press to MECO.'

The main engines began to throttle down to keep acceleration below 3-G.

'*Columbia*, main engine throttle down.'

'Copy, Houston,' Crawford responded, intently watching the instrument panel.

Another minute passed before Mission Control talked with Crawford. '*Columbia*, go for main engine cut-off.'

'Roger, main engine cut-off on schedule,' Crawford replied in a more relaxed voice.

'*Columbia*, go for external tank separation.'

The huge orange tank fell away, tumbling to its destruction in the ocean far below.

'We have separation; looks clean,' Crawford radioed.

The shuttle rapidly approached orbital insertion.

'*Columbia*, you are go for OMS-one burn.'

'Roger, cleared for orbital maneuvering system burn number one.'

The APUs were shut down and the external tank umbilical doors were closed.

'*Columbia*, coming up on OMS-two.'

'Roger, Houston.'

Less than a minute passed before Crawford spoke to Mission Control.

'OMS-two cut-off. We have achieved orbit, Houston.'

'Congratulations, *Columbia*. Time to go to work.'

Dimitri stared, frozen in horror, at the Volga's blood-splattered windshield.

'WIPE OFF MY WINDOW!' The American agent was shouting above the roar of the engine. His right arm was hanging limp, blood coursing down his sleeve.

Dimitri used his forearm to clear a section of the windshield, losing his balance as the car skidded through a corner and bounced off a curb.

'Return their fire. NOW, GODDAMNIT!' The CIA agent's face was ashen white.

Dimitri, shaking from shock, glanced out the rear window. The glass was completely gone, save a few shards sticking out of the lower molding.

'Shoot at the grill!' Wickham ordered, knowing Dimitri would probably yank on the trigger, causing the round to go high, and, hopefully, hit the driver.

Dimitri fumbled for his Beretta. As he turned in his seat, knees drawn up, the Volga bounced through an intersection, throwing Dimitri against the passenger door.

BOOM!!

Dimitri accidentally pulled the trigger, sending a round into the seat next to the CIA agent.

'GODDAMN! SHOOT THEM, NOT ME, FOR CHRISSAKE!'

Dimitri, shaking violently, placed the Beretta over the front seat, staring at the black KGB car seventy meters in trail.

'Grab it with both hands, like you were taught! Rest the weapon on top of the seat and aim for the grill.' Wickham was yelling over the screaming engine.

BOOM! . . . BOOM! BOOM!

The windshield of the KGB car shattered in an explosion of glass particles and metal fragments.

Dimitri stared, fascinated, as the pursuing automobile swerved to the right and crashed into the back of a parked truck. The entire upper body of the Volga was torn off as it nose-dived under the huge truck, decapitating the two Russians.

'Outstanding,' Wickham yelled. 'Hold on for just three minutes, okay?'

'Okay,' Dimitri responded, looking closely at the American for the first time since he had been shot.

Dimitri could see the agent had a streak of blood across the right side of his head, slightly above his ear, where a round had grazed his skull. Blood was running down the side of his head, saturating his coat collar.

What frightened Dimitri most was the gaping wound in the agent's right shoulder. Most of the flesh, along with his coat sleeve, had been torn away on the outside.

'Dimitri, take off your belt . . . Make a tourniquet under my armpit and over my shoulder.' The agent groaned. 'As close to my neck as possible.'

Wickham slowed to a speed consistent with traffic and made two turns, one left and one right, then blended into the flow of vehicles on Spasskaya Boulevard.

As Dimitri applied the tourniquet, the CIA agent briefed him. 'We are going to steal a car, a bureaucrat's car, and drive to an outlying train station.'

Dimitri gave the American an incredulous look as he twisted the tourniquet tighter.

'The best disguise, under the circumstances. We have our credentials,' the agent groaned again, 'and I can camouflage my shoulder and head.'

Dimitri remained silent, brooding.

'You with me, Dimitri?'

'Yes. I am with you.'

'Okay, let's move it!'

191

Dimitri nodded, still in shock. His mind was working slowly, mechanically.

'Reach in the glove box and reload your weapon. Put some extra rounds in your coat pocket.'

Dimitri complied as they turned a corner next to a government building by the Hotel Minsk. Wickham drove past the parking area and turned into a narrow alley.

Dimitri stared at Wickham, thinking he was insane. Every KGB and GRU officer in Moscow was after them and the American was going to steal a Soviet government vehicle.

The Russian immigrant now understood what the CIA director of clandestine operations had meant when he said Stephen Wickham was the best in the business.

Wickham, a former Marine captain and decorated combat veteran of the Grenada invasion, was regarded as a real-life hero throughout the Central Intelligence Agency.

Wickham stopped the car, ripped off his undershirt, wrapped his head, then jammed his hat over the make-shift bandage. The American then relocated the tourni-quet under his topcoat and turned to the young spy.

'Dimitri, walk across the street and wait for me by the row of trees next to the corner.'

'Yessir,' Dimitri replied, glancing up and down the alley.

'I'll pick you up in five minutes. Don't do anything to draw attention.' Wickham looked down at his shoulder. 'Understand?'

'Yes,' Dimitri said. 'By the row of trees.'

'Okay, here we go.'

The two men got out of the car. Dimitri walked across the busy street while the American proceeded toward the parking area.

'Cobra, Pinwheel. You have multiple bogies at eleven o'clock, thirty-five out, blocking three-three-zero to four-one-oh.'

'Roger, Pinwheel,' DiGennaro replied, scanning his radar scope and instrument panel.

'Time, Bill. Let's climb to forty-three-oh until we have a visual.'

'Roger, forty-three,' Parnam responded quietly, checking his radar and armament switches.

'Cobras,' the voice was cautious and tense, 'looks like a couple of fighters in trail. Say 'bout five miles at four-one-oh.'

'Copy, Pinwheel,' DiGennaro replied as he leveled his fighter at 43,000 feet.

Fifteen seconds passed as the two F-15 pilots strained to see the massive Soviet bomber group.

'Two has a tally,' Parnam simultaneously informed DiGennaro and the AWACS aircraft. 'Ten o'clock, low.'

'Roger. I've got 'em, Bill,' DiGennaro radioed. 'We'll go down this side, past the tail-end charlies, then do a one-eighty and join in trail.'

'Copy, boss. You wanna stay here, or descend?'

'We'll go down to four-one-oh when we reverse. I'll call the descent.'

'Roger,' Parnam replied, surveying the large Russian group in the moonlight. 'Be hard to miss, firing into that gaggle.'

'Yeah,' DiGennaro answered, then added, 'be like stomping on Godzilla's foot. He'd eat you for breakfast.'

Pinwheel broke in as the two F-15s streaked past the two Soviet MiG-31 Foxhounds trailing the bomber group.

'Cobras, Hawk flight is on the tankers. Leopard flight will be aboard in four minutes.'

'Roger, Wheel. We're comin' around and descending to four-one-oh, in trail.'

'Copy, Cobra. The flight leader of the Hawks will be up your freq when they're off the tanker. He's the tactical commander.'

'Roger,' DiGennaro replied, uncomfortable with not knowing who the flight leader was. Placing the thought aside, he concentrated on lowering his nose and reducing power as the two F-15s turned to join the Russians.

'Pinwheel, the group is staggered in different layers, altitudewise, and flanked by fighters.' DiGennaro silently counted the Soviet aircraft.

'Roger. The Hawks are on the way. Be up your freq in a couple of seconds.'

'Okay, Pinwheel. Looks like the Russians continually rotate the fighters off the tankers.'

No reply.

'Cobra, Hawk One up.'

'Roger, Hawk,' DiGennaro replied, not recognizing the flat voice.

'Hawk flight is taking high cover. The Leopards are taking low,' the Hawk flight leader ordered.

'Cobra One,' DiGennaro responded.

'Cobra flight, deploy on each side of the lead bomber,' the Hawk leader ordered.

DiGennaro hesitated, thinking that was the last place he wanted to be.

'Copy, Cobra?'

'Ah, roger, Hawk. We're movin' forward now,' DiGennaro replied, looking over at Parnam, happy his wingman hadn't made a snide comment. He couldn't see his face in the dark, but he knew what Parnam was thinking.

'Two, you take the right side. I'll go left.'

'Super,' Parnam responded, irritation clearly evident in his speech.

'Hawk, Pinwheel,' the AWACS controller interjected. 'The Navy troops are one hundred out. Recommend we wait until they're on station.'

'Copy, Pinwheel.'

The radios were silent for a few seconds.

'Cobra flight, Hawk One,' the flat voice radioed.

'Hold your position for the moment.'

'Holding,' DiGennaro answered, looking over at the Russian pilots in their MiG-31s.

'Great,' DiGennaro said to himself. 'Absolutely fantastic.'

LAJES

The president knew he had to de-escalate the confrontation, without backing down, and rescind the DEFCON-Two condition before a major military crisis developed, a crisis that could be the decisive turning point in the survival of mankind.

The hangar was quiet. Zhilinkhov spoke in a low, controlled voice.

'The American government,' the interpreter said slowly, 'has continued to build a vast array of weapons, while – '

'In response to your massive military buildup,' the president shot back.

'Is your Star Wars system not designed to control the world, to hold the Russian people and our friends under your thumb?' Zhilinkhov responded, trying to regain the offensive.

'Secretary Zhilinkhov,' the president sighed heavily, 'our philosophy has never changed, never will. We

195

believe that weapons in the hands of free people discourage war. Weapons held by free people deter attacks by aggressive enemies and keep the free world safe.'

Zhilinkhov started to respond, then fell silent as the president continued.

'Secretary Zhilinkhov, before we can proceed with any meaningful dialogue, I have to insist on a condition.' The president looked straight into Zhilinkhov's eyes. 'Now. Immediately, Secretary Zhilinkhov.'

'What is this, you say, condition?' Zhilinkhov was no longer smiling.

'Turn back your bomber groups. Now, Mister Secretary. The groups approaching our east and west coasts. We cannot talk under a cloud of threats and provocations.'

The president stared, unblinking, at Zhilinkhov. The Russian clamped his jaws together, looked down at his briefing notes, then back to the president.

The room grew quiet, everyone waiting for the Soviet leader's reply.

Zhilinkhov, without speaking to the president, turned to his foreign minister, Vladimir Vuyosekiev. 'Send the message. The groups are to turn back immediately.'

'Yes, Comrade Secretary,' the burly Vuyosekiev replied, rising from his chair, motioning for an aide.

'Report back,' Zhilinkhov ordered as the foreign minister and his top aide conferred at the end of the table.

The crowd was hushed while the two men spoke in low tones. The military officer snapped to attention, saluted Vuyosekiev, turned on his heel, then briskly walked out of the hangar.

The president, inwardly pleased and relieved, waited for Zhilinkhov to speak.

'It is done, Mister President, in good faith. I am a

reasonable man, as you can see.' Zhilinkhov beamed a deceptive smile.

'Your quick response is sincerely appreciated, General Secretary Zhilinkhov. A step in the direction of peace.'

Zhilinkhov only nodded, smiling.

The president turned to Herb Kohlhammer, his secretary of state. 'Herb, downgrade to Defense Condition-Three immediately. On my authority.'

'Yes, Mister President,' Kohlhammer replied, turning to his aide.

Zhilinkhov smiled at the president. It made no difference to him if the Americans went to their condition-three status. He already had the information he needed. The Americans were honest and gullible. They would react to the threats. The plan would work. Russia would soon rule the world.

The Kremlin boss continued smiling, genuinely this time. 'Mister President, your initiative is gratifying to the people of Russia. We have made a great beginning working together.'

The president returned the smile. 'Let us hope we can resolve our other differences too, General Secretary Zhilinkhov.'

'Oh, we can, Mister President. I assure you that every effort will be made to correct the current situation.'

The general secretary of the Union of Soviet Socialist Republics Communist party felt pride in not lying to the naïve American. Deception was not regarded as lying in the Soviet government.

10

NORAD

General Matuchek sat in the briefing room listening to the operations officer and the intelligence chief. The staff intel officer was speaking.

'General, the French Spot Earth resources satellite has photographed five Soviet Typhoon submarines leaving their secret base at Gremikha, on the Kola Peninsula. All of this activity has taken place in the past fourteen hours.'

'Go on, Colonel,' Matuchek urged.

'These subs, General, are the largest in the world. They're five hundred fifty-eight feet long and carry twenty SS-N-20 ballistic missiles, which have a range of more than five thousand miles.'

'Where are these subs now?' Matuchek asked, writing notes on his briefing folder.

'We don't know, sir. Probably headed for the center of the northern Atlantic. Each missile carries six to nine multiple independently targetable nuclear warheads.'

The officer paused, seeing Matuchek leafing through his folder. 'General, they are capable of striking North America and Western Europe even when docked at their home port in Gremikha.'

'Please continue, Colonel,' Matuchek requested, looking at the last page of the report.

'At least eleven other subs – mostly Delta – and Yankee-class boats – have left port too. Another Typhoon, in the final stages of construction, is preparing to leave the shipyard at Severomorsk. Sir, missiles have already been loaded on that particular Typhoon and the boat has never been to sea.'

'What do you read from this?' Matuchek placed his pen on the table and folded his arms.

'Sir, the submarine bases at Polyarnyy and Petropavlovsk are empty, along with the secret base at Gremikha. The Soviets protect their fleet, especially the Typhoons, like mother hens. I believe, sir, they're going to use these weapons on us.'

Matuchek glanced at his watch, keeping in mind his briefing with the Joint Chiefs of Staff in eight minutes.

'Colonel,' Matuchek hesitated, 'you may be absolutely correct. However, our immediate threat is the approaching Soviet bombers. They can do a lot of damage with their nuclear cruise missiles.'

'I couldn't agree more, General. Their long-range airborne missiles do constitute a tremendous threat to our major coast cities, especially if they're used in conjunction with nuclear weapons launched from submarines.'

'What is your recommendation, Colonel?' Matuchek continued, not waiting for a reply. 'The submarine problem is not a NORAD priority, as you well know, until the missiles break the surface of the water.'

'I recognize that, General. My recommendation is to push the Joint Chiefs to focus more ASW coverage in the North Atlantic. The Russians can sit out there, with near impunity, and blast the hell out of Europe and North America. We really need all the naval air coverage we can concentrate in the North Atlantic.'

The small briefing room remained quiet while Matuchek organized his thoughts. 'Okay, Colonel, I'll suggest a stepped-up effort. The Navy isn't going to appreciate the Air Force recommending any . . .' Matuchek paused. 'You get the picture?'

'Yessir. We need a more concerted naval effort, though, or we're going to be vulnerable in the midsection.'

'Alright, Jim. I appreciate all the work you and Matt have done. Keep me informed.'

'Yes, sir.'

Matuchek reached for the door handle leading to the private, sealed room where he would confer with the Joint Chiefs in three minutes.

As he swung the door open, a loud horn blared, startling him. The raucous sound signified a change in the Defense Condition.

Matuchek changed course, almost jogging, as he stepped onto a narrow threshold overlooking the central operations room. The two briefing officers followed closely behind.

CINCNORAD stared at the status board, then audibly sighed. A large DEFCON-Three display had replaced the Defense Condition-Two light.

'Well, things are looking up,' Matuchek said as he turned to reenter the sealed briefing room.

The two younger officers were visibly relieved, grins creasing their faces.

MOSCOW

Dimitri stood by the row of trees, nervously glancing up and down the street. He shifted his weight from one foot to the other, then back again while he watched the parking area where the American had disappeared.

His numbed mind tried to sort out what had happened in the past two hours. It seemed like ages since he had slept in his bed, or, more importantly, had a cigarette.

He had left them in Wickham's apartment in their hasty escape.

Dimitri thought about Svetlana momentarily, then snapped back to the present when the dark Lada, bearing government markings, pulled alongside the curb.

'LET'S GO,' the American shouted in Russian, barely stopping the car.

Dimitri bolted into the automobile, catching his coat in the door. Wickham roared into traffic as Dimitri opened the door and freed his coat.

'Where are we going?' Dimitri asked, his eyes darting back and forth, searching for possible threats.

'To Kalinin to catch the train. Two-hour drive, at most. We will turn off the highway at Khimki and follow the road to Kalinin. I'll explain more when we get out of traffic. They probably won't miss this car for a couple of hours.'

Dimitri sat quietly, watching the CIA agent drive with his left hand. His right arm remained motionless with the hand through his coat front, providing a sling.

As the Lada reached the outskirts of Moscow, both men breathed easier. Each kilometer spelled safety, more security for the agents.

'Dimitri, our original plan won't work now.'

'What are we going to do?' the young agent blurted, in a small voice, tension tightening his throat.

'I'll need your help, so listen closely.'

Dimitri nodded, rising in his seat to look behind the automobile. His heart still pounded. What would they do to Svetlana? He ached to go back to her, then realized he could never return.

'When we get to Kalinin, we'll submerge the car in the river. Then we'll separate to enter the train station a few minutes apart.'

Dimitri's eyes appeared glazed.

'Are you listening, goddamnit?'

'Yessir,' Dimitri replied, focusing on Wickham's face.

'When we enter the station, Dimitri, you go into the john, the men's room, and enter a stall. Stay in there until the train arrives. I'll come and get you when it's time to board.'

'I understand. Where are we going?'

The agent checked in every direction, awkwardly downshifted for a corner, then continued.

'The train will take us close to Leningrad. We'll get off outside Novgorod, next to the Volkhov River.'

'Then we go by truck again . . .?' Dimitri interjected, hoping their escape would be in a familiar, nonthreatening environment.

'No, that's too risky. Intelligence has informed us the Soviets are on to the ruse. We lost two men eight months ago. The Russian border guards knew precisely where our agents were concealed in the truck. We had to resort to hiding our people inside the trucks a few months after your insertion.'

'How then – ?' Dimitri stopped himself, seeing the look on the American's face.

'When we get off the train near Novgorod, at night, I'll send a prearranged signal via satellite. That will set the rescue operation in motion.'

The American braked for another turn and continued his brief to Dimitri. 'I have a satellite transmitter sewn inside my topcoat. We can send only coded messages. No voice.'

Without hesitating, the agent continued. 'When we are in place, at the pickup point, I'll send a coded message and the helos will be en route almost immediately.'

'Helicopters?' Dimitri was astonished.

'That's correct. The extraction procedure has been rehearsed many times. I have a UHF radio built into the satellite transmitter. I will be able to talk with the pilots when they are within fifteen or twenty miles of our position.'

The Lada rounded a corner and the American continued his explanation to the frightened young operative. 'Dimitri, when we get close to Kal – OH SHIT!'

Both men saw the checkpoint simultaneously. The guard house and closed gate were only four hundred meters away as the American started slowing the Lada.

'Dimitri, quick, grab the scarf from my right coat pocket and wrap it once around my neck.'

Dimitri complied, initially fumbling to unfold the brown knit fabric.

'Make sure it covers the blood around my collar.'

'It's covered,' Dimitri responded, his voice again choked in near panic.

'Drape the end over my torn shoulder.' Wickham squirmed as a sharp pain shot through his shoulder. 'Got it?'

'It's completely covered,' Dimitri said as he spread the scarf over the agent's wound.

'Okay, Dimitri, I'll talk. We're agriculture inspectors, so act like one.' Wickham motioned to Dimitri. 'Get out your credentials.'

The Lada slowed as the American glanced at himself in the rearview mirror. No trace of blood visible, at least from the left side.

Two guards, one with a Kalashnikov rifle and the other brandishing a submachine gun, stood in front of the closed gate.

Both Russian guards raised their hands, motioning for the Lada to stop.

'Get a hold on yourself, Dimitri, or we're both dead. Act the part you're supposed to be.' Wickham lowered his voice. 'Official.'

The American brought the automobile to a smooth stop as the guards approached the Lada, one on each side.

'Greetings, comrades,' the American said, displaying his credentials.

The guard studied the papers closely, then looked at the American and Dimitri.

'Step out and open the trunk,' the Soviet guard sternly ordered.

'Yes, comrade,' the American replied, opening the door gingerly with his left arm.

Wickham's mind raced, knowing he didn't have a key to the trunk. He had hot-wired the ignition to start the car.

The American rounded the end of the automobile, appearing to search for a key.

'What is wrong with your arm, Comrade Inspector?' the Russian holding the Kalashnikov rifle asked, suspicion written on his face.

'Farming accident, comrade.' Wickham appeared nonchalant. 'Many years ago in Groznyy.'

The American was in pain and he hoped it didn't show on his face.

'Comrade Inspector, this is not an Agriculture Bureau automobile. This is registered to the State Medical Department.'

'That is true, comrade. Our vehicle was in for routine service and inspection. The Bureau Directorate procured this automobile for our trip.'

The other guard, listening to the conversation, was examining Dimitri's credentials through the open passenger window.

'Open the trunk, Comrade Inspector,' the guard again ordered, tapping the metal with the barrel of his weapon.

'I'm afraid they didn't give me a key to the trunk. The

204

inept blunderheads,' responded the American as he noticed the other guard carrying Dimitri's credentials into the guard house. If he got on the phone with the false papers, it was all over.

'Comrade Inspector, let me have your key to the ignition,' the guard ordered in a loud voice, raising the barrel of the rifle strapped over his shoulder.

'Yes, of course,' Wickham replied as he approached the open driver's door. He reached inside, as if to retrieve the key, and noticed the other guard dialing the wall-mounted phone.

SHUTTLE *COLUMBIA*

The orbiter drifted effortlessly over the azure Pacific Ocean, inverted, top facing the planet, as the crew prepared to extend the remote manipulator arm.

Maj. Ward Culdrew, the mission specialist, looked through the aft crew station windows. The three satellites appeared unharmed after the rocket flight into space.

Doctor Minh Tran, mission payload specialist, stood at the payload handler station. Tran was preparing to operate the remote manipulator system.

Hank Doherty was at the pilot's position in the center of the aft crew station. His job would entail maneuvering *Columbia* during the satellite deployment procedure.

Alan Cressottie manned the other mission payload specialist position, ready to assist any crew member, while Colonel Crawford supervised the operation from the forward flight deck.

The shuttle was parked in orbit in the lower Van Allen belt. The crew could not spend long periods at this altitude because of the radiation hazard.

'Stand by to deploy the RMS,' Culdrew ordered.

The cargo-bay floodlights were on, creating eerie shadows toward the rear of the compartment, along with the television cameras and viewing monitors.

'Okay, Minh, do your stuff,' Culdrew said in a quiet, respectful tone.

Doctor Tran turned his switch to the orbiter unloaded position. He then selected shoulder and pitch on the joint switch.

Everyone watched intently as the diminutive Tran maneuvered the remote arm to a position to extract the first satellite. The mission payload specialist then switched to orbiter loaded and approached the first SDI satellite, using a television camera mounted on the end of the remote control arm.

'Looks good, *Columbia*,' Houston radioed.

Mission Control was monitoring the deployment via television downlink.

'We hope so,' Crawford replied tentatively. He knew what hung in the balance.

A collective sigh announced the end effector mating with the satellite package grapple.

'Got it, Houston,' Crawford radioed.

'Copy. You're go for deployment.'

Tran suppressed a grin and prepared to lift the anti-missile satellite out of the cargo bay.

'Hold your breath, boys,' Culdrew whispered.

Tran gently raised the satellite package, stopped momentarily, flexed his fingers, and regripped the rotational hand controller.

'Nice and easy, Doc,' Culdrew said in a soothing, quiet voice. 'You're doing great.'

Tran manipulated the satellite out of the cargo bay, then stopped the arm, frozen in place.

'Okay, Doc, let me know when you're ready,' Doherty

announced as he prepared to maneuver the shuttle clear of the satellite.

'Stand by,' Tran replied, checking his switches. Everything looked normal to the small physicist.

'*Columbia*, Houston. Looks mighty fine, guys. You're ahead of schedule.'

'Roger,' Crawford replied, watching Doherty's every move. This was a critical maneuver. The first of three in the next thirty-five minutes, Crawford thought as he watched the crew work in total harmony.

Tran, making sure the satellite was stable, announced he was ready for deployment. 'Ready for payload release in fifteen seconds.'

'Set,' Doherty answered, checking his reaction control system (RCS) thrusters.

Tran made one last check and released the satellite from the arm. 'Released.' The astronaut stared, transfixed.

'Roger,' Doherty replied, deftly maneuvering *Columbia* away from the satellite.

'Outstanding, *Columbia*. Two to go,' Houston radioed as the orbiter moved slowly away from the satellite.

LAJES

The last of the dessert plates were being cleared when the president addressed the Soviet leader again.

'We are not naïve, Secretary Zhilinkhov. We realize your space-based antisatellite weapons, kinetic-energy shrapnel weapons, and powerful lasers are in place for one reason, to defeat us in space. The sole intent is to reduce, if not eliminate, our ability to communicate and navigate. Our effectiveness to defend ourselves. We have reason, Mister Secretary, to believe your government has used the powerful laser at Sary Shagan to damage two American satellites.'

The president noticed Zhilinkhov's eye twitch.

'The most recent incident happened during the past two months.'

'What is your point, Mister President?' the interpreter asked in a pleasant manner. Zhilinkhov was strained, but businesslike.

'The point, Secretary Zhilinkhov, is that we are not a threat to you or the Soviet people. We can achieve, working together, a peaceful coexistence through de-escalation of arms. We must exchange our collective technical knowledge. Two powers working together for the enrichment of all people.'

The president again waited for a response. The Russian remained quiet.

A disturbance at the entrance to the hangar startled the delegation.

The Soviet foreign minister, who had left the room to receive a message, barged through the door and strode angrily toward Zhilinkhov, gesturing for the general secretary to join him in conference.

Grant Wilkinson looked over at the president, then removed his glasses and slowly rubbed the bridge of his nose. When he looked up, the president was shaking his head in resignation.

The president, apprehension gnawing at his stomach, watched the agitated foreign minister confer with Zhilink-hov. The general secretary's face blotched, then turned a deep red, almost purple color.

Wilkinsor leaned over to the president. 'Here comes the space shuttle broadside. You might as well enjoy a rum crook and relax.'

'Good advice,' the president responded as he withdrew

a cigar. His eyes squinted behind the match, making him appear tired.

'Wish I were enjoying this someplace else,' the president said quietly, closely watching the Soviet leaders.

The Kremlin boss, obviously upset, was marching back to his seat opposite the American. He reached his chair and launched into a loud harangue. The bombastic, ranting speech was mostly incoherent to the American delegation. The Russian interpreter stepped away from the general secretary, not sure how to react.

Wilkinson made the first move, then sat back as he observed his boss lean forward.

The president spoke forcefully to Zhilinkhov, projecting his voice from the diaphragm. 'Secretary Zhilinkhov! We can't understand you. Calm down!'

Both men were talking simultaneously, causing further confusion.

Suddenly, without warning, Zhilinkhov stopped shouting. He pointed his finger at the American and started talking slowly, in a low, controlled tone. The interpreter tentatively stepped closer to the general secretary. 'You have deceived us. Tricked us again with – '

'I'm not following you, Mister Zhilinkhov. We, as a government, have never – '

'You lied about your space war defense!' Zhilinkhov spat, thoroughly incensed.

Every person in the hangar was frozen in silence, shock registering on their faces. The usual pomp and pageantry, with the pretentious behavior, had started to evaporate when the general secretary stepped off the Ilyushin transport. The diplomatic reservoir was now bone-dry.

'We haven't lied about anything, Mister Secretary,' the president replied in a normal, controlled voice, exhaling cigar smoke.

Zhilinkhov, still standing in front of the table, pointed

his finger at the president again. 'You launched your shuttle craft without warning – ahead of schedule! Even your own newspeople did not know of the secret launch.'

Zhilinkhov was livid, trembling slightly in a half crouch, knuckles on the table.

The president bolted from his chair, knocking ashes across the table. 'It is OUR prerogative to launch OUR shuttle when WE deem it appropriate. WE don't need the permission of the Soviet government, or, for that matter, the American news media.'

Zhilinkhov was beginning to perspire in the stagnant air.

'I thought, when I talked with you from Moscow,' the interpreter continued, 'that we had an agreement to discuss your space defense satellites on a foundation of mutual trust.'

'Oh, we did, sir, and I'm happy to discuss them n – '

The president was abruptly cut off when the burly Russian leader slammed his fist on the table, spilling three glasses of water.

'Before you launched them,' Zhilinkhov bellowed. 'You changed the date! We can not trust the Americans again. Ever!'

The president realized Zhilinkhov's real concern was the SDI satellites. Everything else was simply window dressing. He decided to let Zhilinkhov talk himself out. The meeting was a fiasco anyway. The outcome would be futile. Back to square one, with immediate escalation of tensions.

'Also,' Zhilinkhov continued, a smile spreading across his craggy face, 'two of your spies have been exposed in Moscow.'

The president reacted with a surprised look, questioning the interpreter, then glanced at Wilkinson.

The chief of staff, anticipating some type of surprise, spoke out. 'That isn't anything new. We expelled three of your KGB operatives – spies, Mister Zhilinkhov – less than two months ago.'

The Communist leader smiled again. A shiver ran down the spines of the president and his chief advisor. They both had a premonition.

'One of the spies,' Zhilinkhov paused for theatrical effect, leaving the interpreter in midsentence, 'was in charge of my kitchen help.'

That information did shock both Americans. The president and his closest advisor looked at each other, dismay and sadness in their eyes.

'The bastard traitor could have poisoned me,' Zhilinkhov hissed, pounding the table again as his aides began to assemble their papers.

'Too bad he didn't,' Wilkinson uttered softly to the president.

'What is your response!?' Zhilinkhov snapped back.

'I asked if you have the men in custody? Are they all right?' Wilkinson responded, unperturbed.

Zhilinkhov smiled again, then spoke in harsh tones. 'No, we don't have them – yet,' he spat, 'but we will soon. They have killed at least four of our men. They won't make it to trial. I have ordered execution on the spot. Don't forget that!'

Zhilinkhov was yelling again. 'What do you have to say?'

The president waited, puffing on his rum crook, looking upward at the hangar ceiling.

'Well?' Zhilinkhov leaned toward the president, frightening his own aides and interpreter.

'Mister Zhilinkhov, we have nothing else to say, given the circumstances and your state of mind. I will, however, give you a piece of personal advice.'

Zhilinkhov exploded. 'We – I don't need any advice from American liars!'

The Soviet general secretary stalked out of the hangar with the Russian contingent close behind. The Russian faces, to a man, reflected anguish and surprise.

'What a disaster . . .' The president paused. 'Grant, reestablish DEFCON-Two, then find out what the hell happened in Moscow.'

'Yes, sir,' Wilkinson responded, then added, 'Mister President, I suggest you reboard *Air Force One* for security reasons.'

'Okay, Grant,' the president responded, grinding his cigar to pulp, 'on my way.'

The two men, along with a shocked Herb Kohlhammer and two aides, walked through the commotion and boarded the big Boeing. Crew members were scurrying in every direction, caught off guard by the rapid change of events.

Air Force One, shining brightly in the sun, had been refueled and restocked immediately after landing, as always, in the event of an emergency departure.

The president, quiet and contemplative, boarded the 747 and walked to his private quarters. He sat down, removed his tie and unbuttoned his shirt collar.

The president glanced out a window and noticed a disturbance on the ramp adjacent to the Soviet transport. He reached for his phone and called the flight deck.

'Colonel Boyd, sir,' the aircraft commander responded immediately.

'Colonel, how soon will we be ready to roll?'

''Bout seven minutes, Mister President.'

'Okay,' the president said, looking out his window a second time. 'What's the problem with the Soviet transport?'

'No problem with the aircraft, sir. The pilots were over at the club having a vodka and they couldn't locate them.

They'll be pounding stakes in Siberia, if they don't get their heads lopped off.'

The president half-turned as Grant Wilkinson knocked, then entered the cabin.

'I can believe that. Sorry to have to turn the crew around so quickly.'

'That's our job, sir. No problem,' Colonel Boyd replied.

'Thanks.' The president placed the handset down and sighed. 'What's the situation, Grant?'

'The agents, including our Kremlin mole, have eluded the Russians thus far.' The chief of staff looked forlorn and tired. 'How the lash-up came about is unknown at this point, sir.'

'Grant,' the president exclaimed, 'we've got to get it together.'

Wilkinson folded a message in his hand. 'The vice president has authorized a rescue attempt, sir. The one I briefed you about. The operation using three helicopters for a night pickup.'

The president looked up. 'Yes, I remember. What are the chances for success?'

Wilkinson shrugged. 'I can't say. Especially after what has transpired in the last two hours.'

'Should we call it off, Grant, under the circumstances?' the president questioned, looking very concerned.

'I don't believe so, sir. There is something going on we don't know about, something essential, or the operation wouldn't have unwound so quickly.'

Wilkinson again looked at the message report, then back to the president. He was hesitant, then spoke calmly to the commander-in-chief. 'Sir, the shuttle has a problem. However, the fir – '

'WHAT?' the president responded in disbelief.

'NASA has two satellites out in fine shape. The third one is slightly damaged. Apparently jammed, somehow.'

'I need a drink,' the president replied, rising to walk to the cabinet bar.

Wilkinson continued his brief. 'The mission commander believes they can repair and launch the satellite. Just take a little time.'

'Okay. What's the military posture?' the president asked, yanking a decanter of Tennessee whiskey from the teak holders.

'DEFCON-Two is being reinstated, sir. The order is being sent now. No reported incidents at the present time.'

'Good. I'm going to finish this,' the president held up a tumbler containing three fingers of Jack Daniel's, 'and take a nap.'

'Yes, sir,' Wilkinson replied, reaching for the door-knob. 'I'll wake you if anything negative develops.'

'Thanks, Grant,' the president responded as Wilkinson closed the door.

The president sat down, exhausted, disheartened. As he stared at the presidential seal on the opposite wall, he felt like an enormous failure. His eyelids sagged as he felt *Air Force One* begin to roll.

THE WHITE HOUSE

The Joint Chiefs, relief showing on their faces, waited while the vice president conferred with Secretary of Defense Cliff Howard.

Up-to-the-minute briefing folders had been placed on the conference table.

The vice president turned in her seat and opened her

folder. 'Although we have downgraded to Defense Condition-Three, prudence and logic tell me our forces need to remain ready for any contingency. Do you agree, gentlemen?'

Admiral Chambers spoke for the Joint Chiefs.

'Unequivocally, Ms. Blaylocke. We believe it is imperative, and certainly appropriate, that our military remain poised for any threat. We are cautiously optimistic at this juncture, but the continued instability has us worried.'

The vice president looked at the secretary of defense. 'Cliff?'

Howard replied in a clipped manner. 'The Soviet bomber groups have changed course toward Russian territory. They have elected to hold their positions approximately two hundred miles farther away from us. That's the upside. On the negative side is the sudden departure of the new Soviet carrier Tbilisi. The ship is loaded with various strike aircraft and presents a tremendous threat to our northern Atlantic fleet.'

Howard looked at the chairman of the Joint Chiefs. 'What bothers me most is the continued submarine threat.'

Chambers responded. 'That is of the utmost concern to us too, Mister Howard. Even CINCNORAD, General Matuchek, was anxious in regard to the submarines, and he has enough other variables to contend with at the moment.'

The admiral removed a page from his folder before continuing. 'We are going to keep our bombers on station, using aerial refueling, for the next few hours. The fighters will rotate fresh pilots during ground fueling.'

Chambers cleared his throat and resumed his outline. 'The Navy is remaining in a high state of readiness and will be conducting around-the-clock sorties from the carriers, concentrating the ASW efforts. The Army has

215

completed most of the troop relocation needed at this time, freeing sixty percent of our heavy airlift capability.

'The Marines are in place at strategic locations, aboard ship, in the air, and at land installations, to effect amphibious landings or secure sensitive areas quickly.'

General Ridenour, Air Force chief of staff, motioned to Chambers.

'Milt,' the admiral responded.

'One point. We have elected to keep our Stealth aircraft on the ground, camouflaged and guarded, unless they absolutely have to be launched. The technology is too advanced to take the chance of having one fall into Soviet hands.' Ridenour sat back, waiting for a response.

The room remained quiet.

'That is our status to the moment, Ms. Blaylocke,' Chambers concluded, readjusting his glasses.

'Thank you, Admiral.' Blaylocke used her thumb to rotate the petite diamond ring on her right hand. 'I wish to make a suggestion in regard to countering the Soviet intimidation.'

No one spoke in the quiet room.

'I propose, gentlemen, that any further Soviet attacks be met with swift and decisive consequences, strong military retaliation in whatever form it takes.'

Cliff Howard seconded the order. 'I agree, on behalf of the president and the chief of staff.'

'We appreciate your endorsement, Ms. Vice President,' Admiral Chambers said, noticing the nods of the service chiefs. 'We will respond accordingly, I assure you.'

'I know you will, Admiral,' Susan Blaylocke said, turning to reach her notes. 'I have been informed by Ted Corbin, minutes ago, that our agents in Moscow are not in custody. They have apparently escaped, killing an unknown number of Soviets in the process. Nothing has been verified, but Corbin believes the information is accurate.'

Blaylocke looked around the table, then added a comment. 'I've had enough shocks today, gentlemen. This information isn't going to serve the president well in Lajes.'

The Joint Chiefs were solemn.

Blaylocke again looked at Cliff Howard. 'I believe you have some information concerning the shuttle.'

The defense secretary frowned. 'I don't want to be the bearer of bad news, but they are having some difficulty launching the satellites. NASA reported a – '

'Is the mission threatened?' Chambers was stunned.

'Not at the moment,' Howard said wearily. 'Apparently, from what I gleaned from Doctor Hays, two satellites have been launched. The third one is jammed somehow. At any rate, an antenna on the satellite was twisted, or bent, and they will have to send one of the crew out to fix the problem.'

'Damn! What next?' General Hollingsworth blurted, frustration showing in his voice. 'Sorry, ma'am.'

'No apology necessary, General. I couldn't have said it better. Anyone else have anything?'

No one responded, their faces showing disappointment. 'Then we'll take a break and reconvene in twenty minutes.'

Blaylocke looked around the table. 'Thank you, gentlemen.'

The speaker-phone next to the vice president buzzed softly. 'Yes,' Blaylocke answered.

'Ms. Vice President,' the male voice said, 'DEFCON-Two has been reinstated.'

COBRA FLIGHT

Major DiGennaro and his wingman, Wild Bill Parnam, had been amazed when the Soviet bomber group suddenly turned ninety degrees to the right.

The pilots, along with Hawk flight and the Leopards, had listened in relieved silence to the AWACS coordinator. The Russians were turning back and DEFCON-Three would be implemented when the order could be verified.

'Cobra and Leopard flight, return to base,' the controller ordered.

'Cobras RTB,' DiGennaro replied.

He looked over at the moonlight reflecting off Parnam's canopy, then smiled.

'Cobras and Leopards, go tactical four. Have a nice trip.'

'Tact four, switching,' DiGennaro responded as he rapidly added power to the F-15 Eagle. He waited for the other flight to check in, then called, 'Cobra is up, flight of two.'

'Roger,' the controller answered immediately. 'Initial heading zero-three-zero. We'll switch you to Gator Control shortly.'

'Cobra One,' DiGennaro replied, scanning his cockpit. Engine parameters, hydraulics, weapons systems, avionics, and navigation instruments all looked normal.

'Two,' DiGennaro radioed, 'you might want to turn on your lights before someone runs over us.'

'Sorry, boss,' Parnam replied, flipping on his formation and navigation lights.

The lead pilot flew without lights, save the small, dull formation lights, so he wouldn't blind his wingman.

'Cobras, contact Gator Control.'

'Switching,' DiGennaro replied, relieved to be so close to home base.

The two pilots, emotionally drained, were slowly winding down from the gut-wrenching tension of the previous hour.

'Gator, Cobra flight. Two Fox-Fifteens and we're fat on fuel.'

'Roger. When you rollout, follow the wagon to refueling. Be prepared for hot-refueling and crew changes.'

'Understand hot-pumping and pilot changes.'

Twenty-five minutes later the two sleek McDonnell Douglas fighters turned off the Galena runway and fell in behind the 'Follow Me' cart.

The F-15s eased to a stop, canopies raised, in front of the fueling pits. The engines would remain running while ground crew members quickly topped off the fuel tanks and checked the armament and missiles.

Both pilots glanced over in the semilight to see their replacements. They couldn't see the pilots' faces but knew their stances, two experienced flight leaders, including a former Thunderbird pilot.

DiGennaro was in the process of unstrapping and removing his helmet when his crew chief scrambled up the side of the cockpit.

'Major, the shit has hit the fan again!'

The crew chief was a grizzled veteran of sixteen years in the Air Force. DiGennaro knew he could take the sergeant's word to the bank.

'Wha . . . I don't understand,' DiGennaro replied, trying to remove his sweat-soaked gloves.

'The Russians turned back okay, but now they are holding in an eighty-mile-long pattern, sir. The latest skinny is we might be going back to DEF-Two,' the sergeant said breathlessly. 'It's the goddamnedest mess I ever seen, Major.'

'Thanks, Red,' DiGennaro replied, slapping the sergeant on the shoulder as he climbed over the side of the canopy. Reaching the pavement, DiGennaro turned toward the advancing pilots. Both of the fighter jocks simultaneously saluted their deputy detachment commander. DiGennaro smartly returned their snappy salutes and began unzipping his uncomfortable g-suit.

The major felt the tremendous burden of being the frontal West Coast fighter defense against the Soviet bomber groups.

11

THE AGENTS

The American CIA agent knew he didn't have a second to waste. One of the Soviet guards, standing in the open door of the guard shack, not seven meters away, was clearly ringing a number on the wall phone.

The guard who had asked for the ignition key was behind him, near the back of the automobile.

Wickham didn't hesitate as he straightened his body and half-turned toward the Russian guard.

'Oh, how dumb of me, comrade. The keys are here in my coat pocket,' Wickham said as he squeezed the trigger of the Beretta twice.

Two small holes appeared near the bottom of the CIA agent's left coat pocket, accompanied by two explosive reports.

The shocked Soviet guard, eyes bulging, staggered sideways clutching his groin, then fell headfirst into the side of the vehicle. His body convulsed twice, then quivered for over a minute.

During that period of time, the American had pumped two rounds into the other guard. Wickham had fired three times, striking the door casing with one round.

His aim wasn't the same with his left hand.

Dimitri stared, transfixed, as the American ran to the guard shack, retrieved the critical credentials, then opened the road gate.

The Russian soldier in the guard shack, mortally wounded, crawled to the edge of the open door as the

Lada sped away. He rolled onto his side, grasped his ballpoint pen, and scratched the tag number and description of the bureau car on the wooden floor. He then collapsed in a pool of his own blood.

'Snap out of it, Dimitri. I told you that I'm going to need your assistance.' The American glanced at Dimitri, then the rearview mirror, then back to the road ahead.

'Dimitri, listen,' Wickham said in a calm, reassuring voice. 'Is your weapon fully loaded?'

'Yes,' Dimitri replied tentatively, 'it's loaded all the way.' The only thing Leonid Vochik, aka Dimitri Moiseyevich Karpov, had ever shot before today was a target with a human silhouette outlined.

'Then change with me and reload mine. You still have rounds in your coat pocket?' Wickham asked, watching the road closely.

No answer.

'Dimitri,' the American said slowly, 'that was a question. Do you have more ammo in your pocket?'

'Yes,' Dimitri replied in a hushed voice. The young man was dazed, his coordination slowed by shock and confusion.

'Then get on with it.'

Wickham slowed the Lada to a reasonable speed, then continued his dialogue in an upbeat manner. 'Dimitri, hang in there. We're in pretty good shape, overall.'

Dimitri nodded, quietly loading the Beretta, as he stared with blank eyes.

'It will be a while before the guards are found, Dimitri, and there isn't any traceable evidence to link us. The KGB won't know what kind of car to look for.'

The American looked over at Dimitri. 'Come on, cheer up. We'll be out of Russia tomorrow morning. We're almost home, Dimitri.'

The agent returned a faint smile.

'By the way, here are your credentials,' Wickham said as he handed the papers to his charge. 'There was nothing left behind to implicate us. Relax, Dimitri. Breathe slowly.'

Twenty kilometers behind the gray green Lada, a KGB officer raced into the guard shack and turned the Russian soldier over. The KGB agent checked for a pulse. He could see it was useless. The officer walked to the door and waved his companion, who was checking the other slain guard, into the guard shack. Then he reached for the phone, noticing the dead guard had a ballpoint pen clutched in his hand. He leaned down and saw scratch marks, lightly colored in black, across the wooden floor.

AIR FORCE ONE

The jumbo jet cruised serenely at 39,000 feet. Two miles off the right wing of the 747, slightly astern, four F-14 Tomcats flew in loose formation.

Directly behind the presidential jet, and slightly above, two additional F-14s trailed the big Boeing. One of the pilots in the flight of two was Capt. Vince Cangemi, United States Marine Corps. His flight leader was the *Eisenhower*'s air group commander (CAG), Peyton Reynolds.

Captain Reynolds, USN, reasoned that he should lead the flight of six Tomcats assigned to escort the president of the United States.

Reynolds had selected Cangemi to be his wingman. The Marine aviator had been the only American pilot rescued – after the ambush over the USS *Virginia*. Cangemi was fighting mad and had fire in his eyes when he volunteered to fly the escort mission.

Reynolds was concerned but knew the Marine pilot

was well-disciplined and would respond accordingly. He had great respect for the young fighter pilot.

Reynolds looked over at Cangemi, then took in the other four fighters. 'Tuck it in, gents.'

'Roger, Kingpin,' came the reply from the leader of the four F-14 Tomcats.

Reynolds scanned the sky, then checked his fuel gauges and glanced at his watch. Twenty minutes to feeding time for the thirsty fighters.

He and Cangemi could see their tankers on the horizon. The two KA-6D Intruders were full of fuel and standing by to gas the F-14s. Two more tankers, from the USS *America*, would rendezvous with the Tomcats in slightly more than an hour.

The president, though groggy, opened his eyes and sat up. He focused on the presidential seal, then stood up and walked into his private half-bath, the water closet, as he referred to the inclosure.

The president splashed cool water on his face and reached for a toothbrush. After applying the toothgel, he looked in the mirror, noted the bloodshot eyes, then began to brush his teeth slowly.

A knock on the door interrupted the ritual as Grant Wilkinson stepped in.

'Umph – with-oo-n-mome . . .' the president mumbled, toothpaste dripping from the corner of his mouth.

'Sorry, sir,' Wilkinson said, closing the door behind him. 'Take your time. Nothing that important at the moment.'

The president finished, rinsed his mouth, then tossed the disposable toothbrush into a waste can.

'What's up, Grant?'

'The shuttle crew is getting ready to go outside – EVA, I believe they call it – and see if they can free the satellite.

It took some time for the astronauts to get into their suits.'

'Good. We're makin' progress at least,' the president responded as he toweled his hands dry.

The president poured another splash of whiskey into a fresh tumbler, dropped two cubes of ice into the liquid, and offered Wilkinson a drink.

'Thank you. It has been a long day,' Wilkinson replied as the president turned around to the bar.

'Please sit down, sir. I'll fend for myself.'

The president sat on the couch and posed a question to his closest aide. 'Grant, what do you think about the outcome of the meeting with Zhilinkhov?'

'Sir, we accomplished what we wanted. Our satellites were being deployed while we placated Zhilinkhov. He is, by the way, completely unbalanced, in my estimation.'

The president, taking a sip, nodded. 'I could see that in his smile. Frightening.' The president shuddered.

'Also,' Wilkinson continued, 'we know he is very upset about our SDI capability.'

'Yes,' the president reflected out loud, 'that's what bothers me most. Zhilinkhov knows the last pieces are in place. SDI is breathing.'

'Almost in place, sir.' Wilkinson sipped his Chivas and soda, then sat down in the single chair by the cabin door.

'Right. Soon to be in place. I hope,' the president said quietly, twirling the ice in his drink. 'I believe Zhilinkhov is truly afraid we are going to use SDI as an offensive weapon against the Soviet Union.'

A flicker lighted the darkened room as the president placed a match to his rum-soaked cigar.

'Grant,' the president looked up, his eyes twinkling behind the flame, 'what is Zhilinkhov going to do, in your opinion?'

'Sir, with respect, only Zhilinkhov knows the answer

to that question, and I'm not sure he feels certain from minute to minute.'

'Again, that's what frightens me, Grant,' the president replied, extinguishing the match. 'Really frightens me.'

'Sir, my recommendation,' Wilkinson paused, searching for the proper word, 'is that you meet each provocation with retaliation. If Zhilinkhov continues to attack our forces, you need to counterattack with a bigger club.'

'I agree,' the president responded, clenching his fist. 'That's the only message Zhilinkhov understands.'

NORAD

The command post was a beehive of activity after the DEFCON-Two alert was reinstated.

General Matuchek sat at his control console, intently watching the surge of airborne activity. He had forgotten about the cup of lukewarm coffee at his elbow. His tie was undone and the strain was evident on his face.

His vice commander, Lt Gen. John Honeycutt, was at his side providing a situation update.

'J.B., the AOA aircraft is airborne and the standby Boeing will be up in twenty-five minutes,' the jovial Canadian reported in his normal, chipper manner.

'Okay, John. Thanks,' Matuchek replied, thinking about the Airborne Optical Adjunct Boeing 767s. The specially modified planes, sporting elongated cupolas, contained SDI missile detectors and worked in conjunction with the strategically deployed satellites.

The airborne sensors could acquire and track attacking missiles' reentry vehicles, predict their impact points, and hand over data to ground-based radar for terminal intercept and destruction.

The airborne sensor system had been on-line less than

two years. The AOA provided a wide field of view and high resolution for intercepting attacking missiles. However, the SDI satellite network was absolutely essential for the AOA program to function correctly.

Matuchek was concerned about the airborne instability in so many regions of the Northern Hemisphere, along with the frailties of the SDI system. The skies were crawling with Soviet and American warplanes.

'John, if this alert blows over without a major confrontation, if we survive this insane mess, I'm going to retire early and dig out my fishing gear.'

'J.B.,' the surprised Canadian responded, 'you can't be serious. You've been selected to become vice chief of staff the first of April.'

'John, I've had it. The kids are grown. Alice is supportive of my desire. I'm developing, or have developed, a bleeding ulcer.'

Matuchek looked up at Honeycutt. 'Alice and I want to retire on a lake somewhere – not sure where and take the pack off. If the idiots and lunatics of the world want to blow it to smithereens, John, I don't want to be the first to know. I want to be fishing with Alice when the switch is pulled.'

'J.B., you need to take some time off. Two weeks, at minimal, and relax with Alice. You deserve some rest.'

'No. My decision has been made, John. It's over. Time to retire.'

The NORAD commander and his deputy were interrupted by the alert and warning alarm. The startled generals looked at the airspace situation display.

The massive Soviet bomber groups had altered course again, closing on the territorial waters and shores of the United States.

Most alarming were two new threats. A third Soviet group of bombers had become airborne heading over

Taymyr Peninsula, due north, directly over the North Pole. Their flight path, if not altered, would take the Russian nuclear bombers over Thule, Greenland, and northern Canada.

The fourth group of Soviet warplanes was flying parallel to the Koryak Range, just off-shore in the Bering Sea, headed for Alaska.

The NORAD leaders looked at each other and made simultaneous decisions.

'Let's get everything up, John,' Matuchek stated as he actuated the fighter scramble order for all Air Force Tactical Fighter Wings deployed in the high-threat areas.

Matuchek pressed another switch, then a third. He waited, then pressed two more alarm switches. Status and tracking displays illuminated instantaneously, changing colors and formats.

Satisfied, CINCNORAD pressed another button which displayed an overview of all space and satellite activity. Nothing unusual at this point, Matuchek noted, punching his intercom.

'Colonel Griffin, what is the real-time status of the orbiter?'

The assistant operations officer replied without hesitation. 'One of the crew members is preparing to enter the airlock at this time, General.'

'Good. Keep me informed on their progress.'

'Will do, sir,' Griffin responded, scratching event/time notes on his pad.

'One other thing, Bob.'

'Yes, General,' Griffin replied, placing his pen on his console.

'Are the two deployed satellites working satisfactorily?'

Matuchek would be ecstatic to have the basic SDI system in place and functioning correctly.

'Yes, sir. We haven't seen any anomalies in the data procurement.'

'Excellent.' Matuchek looked relieved. 'How about the down-link channels for the two satellites they've already deployed?'

'We see no problem, sir. Okay status on all SDI downlinks checks with Space Command,' Colonel Griffin replied as he rechecked both reporting systems.

'Good work, Bob. Keep me informed.'

'Yes, sir.'

Matuchek looked at his Canadian friend. Honeycutt's normally relaxed face wasn't smiling.

THE AGENTS

The two agents were approaching Staraya, near their pickup point at Novgorod. Wickham had decided against taking the train. Too many risks and too much exposure.

The Lada had just rounded a curve when the two men heard the sounds. Wickham cocked his head to one side, motioning Dimitri to be silent. The CIA agent pulled the vehicle to the side of the road and stopped under a grove of barren trees. His shoulder continued to throb and he felt light-headed from the loss of blood.

Wickham released the 'hot-wire' switch, killing the engine, and rolled down the window. The staccato sound was still unclear, almost muffled.

'What is it?' Dimitri whispered.

'Sh-sh,' the American hissed, straining to interpret the alarming sound.

Wickham opened the door of the Lada and stepped out into the cold air. He listened intently, then walked closer to the roadside, hesitated a moment, then jumped back in terror. His mind could not comprehend what his eyes were seeing.

Low on each side of the road, less than three kilometers away, were two Soviet Mil Mi-28 advanced combat helicopters. It was obvious they were conducting a methodical search-and-destroy mission.

The Russian helicopters remained low and moved slowly, checking every square dekameter of ground.

The American agent now understood why the engine and rotor blade sounds had been muffled. The trees and rolling terrain had distorted and masked the sounds of the approaching gunships.

No question about their purpose. The two CIA operatives were being stalked in a deadly game of persistent pressure. Fatigue and panic would take their toll eventually.

The stunned American yelled at Dimitri. 'Get some tree branches for camouflage. Move! Move!'

Dimitri leaped into action, stumbling through the brush. Wickham jumped back into the Lada and started the engine.

The two Mi-28s, NATO code name HAVOC, were only two kilometers away when Wickham ran the Lada under the base of the trees, smashing the right front fender.

The sound of the helos was becoming distinct and loud as Wickham and Dimitri yanked down tree branches and limbs to cover the car. The trees were practically void of foliage in the cold February winter. Both men, in desperation, threw dirt and branches on the Lada.

'Come on, Dimitri,' the American yelled, holding his right shoulder with his left hand.

The two hunched figures raced down the adjacent embankment and splashed through a narrow stream.

Their progress was impeded by thin ice and slush along the bank. The footprints wouldn't be hard to follow.

Wickham struggled up the other side of the narrow stream and motioned for Dimitri to follow. It was imperative that the two men find a hiding place in the next few seconds.

Wickham turned and sprinted toward some large mounds of earth piled next to a field. A rubbish dump was only two meters from the knolls. Dimitri rushed after the American, scrambling along in a renewed effort.

'We'll have to dig in for now and hope the helos keep moving,' Wickham stated as both men dove behind the earthen mounds and crawled into the edge of the rubbish.

Their spot was precarious, under the circumstances. The only good cover was a ragged tree line two hundred meters away. They couldn't reach that concealment until the helicopters passed.

'Listen, Dimitri, not a word, not a single move. Don't even blink.'

Dimitri lay sprawled in the garbage dump, paralyzed with fear. He could actually feel his heart palpitating. The adrenaline shock to his cardiovascular system was exacting its levy. Dimitri felt faint and nauseated as he lay in the garbage, staring at a rat crawling under a pile of rotting trash.

'Stay down. It'll be okay, Dimitri,' the CIA agent soothed the terrified young man.

Both men watched the approaching Russian gunships, camouflaged in brown and sand colors. The Mi-28s sprouted 57mm rockets and a nose-mounted 30mm gun. The helicopters represented the state of the art in Soviet rotor-wing assault aircraft.

'Don't look up, Dimitri. Don't do anything.'

The American agent watched the nearest Mi-28 pass directly over the camouflaged Lada, then continue on.

231

'So far, so good. Easy,' Wickham comforted Dimitri, while he surveyed their surroundings. The only movement was his eyeballs.

The second gunship was across the road and approaching the wrecked Lada. Wickham stopped breathing as the helicopter passed the vehicle, climbed slightly, and continued down the road.

The agent could clearly see the pilot and nose gunner.

Wickham slowly let his breath out and turned toward Dimitri, studying his face. 'Think you can travel in a few minutes? On foot?'

'Yes,' Dimitri said, regaining a bit of confidence.

'Dimitri, I'm going to go ahead and send the satellite message.' Wickham pointed the antenna straight up and punched in the various codes. He waited ten seconds and repeated the steps. 'We will have to change our pickup point a ways, but – '

The American saw Dimitri's face turn ashen, then reflect stark terror.

'What's wrong?' Wickham said as he turned his head. The attack helicopter on the far side of the road had indeed spotted the Lada.

The Russian pilot had been looking across the road, at a low angle, and had spotted the stolen Soviet vehicle. The crew had completed a 270-degree turn to the left and now approached the car from across the road. They were coming to a hover ten meters over the pavement.

'Keep down!' the American ordered, yanking on Dimitri's soiled coat sleeve.

The second gunship helicopter was returning also, its nose low as the Mi-28 raced along the roadway.

Admiral Chambers was in the process of briefing the vice president and secretary of defense. The other chiefs were gathered in the Situation Room, as was Ted Corbin.

The group had finished the soup and light sandwiches, along with the hastily prepared dessert. Everyone sipped coffee, or hot tea, and listened intently to the chairman of the Joint Chiefs of Staff.

'Ms. Blaylocke, we are in a state of readiness unparalleled in the history of our military. Every ship, aircraft, and ground unit is at the ready.'

Chambers looked at the Air Force chief, General Ridenour, and received a nod before he continued.

'The Stealth aircraft are in the air, too. We are going to stay in this condition until the SDI system is fully online.'

Chambers turned to Cliff Howard. 'Perhaps the secretary of defense will provide us an update on *Columbia*. Mister Secretary?'

Howard, eyes bloodshot and baggy, responded slowly to the request. 'Doctor Hays told me they expect to have the problem solved inside of two hours. Actually, an hour and forty-five minutes from now.' Howard leaned back, not really focusing on Chambers.

'Ms. Blaylocke,' Chambers continued, 'it is the considered opinion of the Joint Chiefs that you, or your designate from this staff, be on board the airborne command post until we downgrade to DEFCON-Three. The E-Four, as you well know, has nonjammable communications.'

Chambers spread his hands on the table, fingers outstretched. 'We believe, in the event of a full-scale Soviet preemptive strike, that someone from the White House should be in the airborne command post. There simply won't be time to transport a staff member, or yourself, ma'am, if the Soviets push the button.'

Blaylocke, hands clasped together on the table, did not respond immediately. The room remained quiet while the vice president pondered the recommendation.

'Admiral, I believe it is my duty to remain in the White House until the president is physically in this room.'

Blaylocke, poised and radiating confidence, paused a moment and continued. 'It is my opinion, Admiral, that General Ridenour, being Air Force, should be the on-site commander in the command post.'

Everyone nodded in agreement, except Cliff Howard, before Chambers spoke. 'Any problem with that, Milt?'

'None whatsoever, Admiral. I'll be on board within the hour.'

Ridenour rose from his seat, reached down for his cover and attaché case, then faced the vice president. 'By your leave, ma'am.'

Blaylocke rose from her seat and offered her hand. 'Good luck, General.'

Ridenour had just departed the White House Situation Room when an aide rushed in and conferred with the CIA director.

The members of the staff stared curiously. The news at first brightened Corbin, then saddened the director. Corbin addressed the group.

'We have heard from the agents. Central communications received the message approximately seven minutes ago. Seems they are alive, but the rendezvous point has been changed. We're not sure why.' Corbin coughed into his fist. 'It's only a matter of fifteen or twenty kilometers.'

Blaylocke didn't understand. 'Was there some kind of trouble after the initial problem in Moscow?'

'Apparently so,' Corbin responded, then cleared his

throat. 'We don't know. The signal just arrived, so it will take some tim – '

'How will the pilots find them in the darkness so far from the prearranged rendezvous, Ted?' Blaylocke was relentless.

Corbin, showing a trace of irritation, responded in a caustic manner. 'Wickham, our senior agent, has a low-powered automatic direction finder for the crews to home on. He also has a limited-distance UHF radio to communicate with the rescue pilots. The transmitter will reach, from the ground, up to twenty miles.'

'Thank you,' Blaylocke replied without emotion. 'I know you will keep us updated.'

12

COLUMBIA

The unscheduled extravehicular activity (EVA) had set the satellite deployment mission hours behind time.

Preparation for an EVA had to begin at least two and a half hours ahead of time. The flight deck of the shuttle, with a cabin atmosphere of seventy-nine percent nitrogen and twenty-one percent oxygen, at a pressure of fourteen-point-seven psi (pounds per square inch), was the same atmosphere as on earth.

The space suits had to be pressurized with pure oxygen at four-point-one psi. The lower pressure was sufficient to sustain life; however, there was one major problem. If an astronaut went directly from the oxygen-nitrogen cabin atmosphere into the pure-oxygen, reduced-pressure environment of the space suit, nitrogen gas dissolved in the blood would bubble out.

The nitrogen gas bubbles, which would collect in the astronaut's joints, would cause a condition known as dysbarism, or more commonly, the bends.

The bends, at the least, would be painful. The condition, as the shuttle's crew knew, could cripple or kill the astronauts.

Doctor Tran and Alan Cressottie had breathed pure oxygen for over two hours before donning their suits. Two hours provided sufficient time to rid the body of all traceable nitrogen.

Crawford was becoming anxious about the lost time. NASA was growing more nervous by the minute.

'*Columbia*, Houston.'

The mission commander answered, irritated by the constant intrusions. 'Go, Houston.'

'We've lost video. What's the status?'

Crawford, the archetypal fighter pilot, was growing even more exasperated with the NASA controllers.

'Houston,' Crawford asked in a pleasant manner, 'are we on closed audio?'

'That's affirm, *Columbia*,' replied the controller, without inflection.

'Good.' Crawford waited a second, then continued. 'I wish to explain to you that we are not playing gin rummy up here. We're working on the problem as quickly and safely as possible.'

Long pause.

'Roger, *Columbia*.' The voice had become more friendly, showing a thread of emotion. 'Understand.'

Absolute quiet followed for the next three minutes.

'Houston, *Columbia*,' Crawford radioed. 'Doctor Tran is ready to enter the airlock.'

'Roger. Copy entering the airlock. We have video again.'

The airlock, a small cylindrical chamber, allowed the astronauts to perform an EVA without depressurizing the entire crew compartment.

Doctor Tran checked the airlock's life-support system, gave a thumbs up signal to his fellow crew members, and closed the entry hatch behind him.

Cressottie had suited also, as a backup, but did not enter the airlock.

'Houston, Minh is donning his maneuvering unit and pressurizing the airlock,' Crawford reported, waiting for the astronaut to check in via radio.

'Roger, *Columbia*. Looks good.'

Tran waited for the pressure to reach zero-point-two

237

psi, then checked in by radio. 'Ready for EVA. Good pressure in here.'

'Copy, Minh. Cleared,' Crawford looked out the viewing port, 'and good luck.'

'Thanks, Skipper.'

Tran opened the outer hatch and floated effortlessly into the cargo bay. He used his maneuvering unit to propel himself toward the aft section of the bay. Tran could clearly see the satellite from his vantage point.

'Houston, I see our problem,' the astronaut reported as he slowly floated toward the satellite.

'Can the package be salvaged?' the mission controller asked in a worried voice.

'Let me get a closer look,' Tran radioed as he moved to a position directly over the satellite.

'Looks as if the tracking and data relay antenna is twisted,' Tran reported as he circled above the high-gain antenna. 'Houston, the antenna is broken. It's actually twisted in half.'

'Copy, *Columbia*,' the controller paused, conferring with a NASA engineer. 'Stand by.'

'Roger,' Tran replied, breathing deeply.

Tran continued his inspection of the missile tracking satellite. He could see no other apparent damage. The satellite pallet had shifted, probably during the launch sequence, and pressed the antenna against the aft bulkhead of the cargo bay. That action had caused the package to jam under the ridge of the cargo bay doors.

'*Columbia*, Houston. Can you effect a repair that will allow the satellite to function?'

Another pause followed.

'At least until we can provide a replacement antenna?'

'Houston, I'm skeptical,' Tran replied, looking closely at the bent antenna, 'but I'll give it a try.'

Crawford and his crew watched Doctor Tran as he worked on the antenna.

Six minutes. Seven minutes. NASA staff members grew impatient again, pressure flowing down from the top. Doctor Hays, absently massaging his chin, was standing next to the mission communicator.

'*Columbia*, Houston,' Rex Hays radioed, talking on his own headset. 'Any luck?'

'Not yet,' Tran answered, working under duress. 'I'm going to have to splice the antenna. It may take a few minutes . . . it's bent ninety degrees.'

'Roger,' Hays replied in an irritated voice.

Crawford spoke to the payload specialist. 'Minh, if it looks unsalvageable to you, let's forget the job.'

'Skipper, I don't believe this is going to work, but I'd like to lash the antenna together. Take a shot . . .'

'Okay, Minh. Use your judgement. No pressure,' Crawford replied as he watched the physicist work on the satellite.

'Roger,' Tran replied, breathing deeply.

Without warning, a brilliant flash stunned the astronauts, partially blinding them for a second.

'WHAT THE HELL!!'

Everyone instinctively flinched as they tried to adjust their minds to what was happening.

SNAP!! Flash!

Another bright light, like the flash of sunlight off a mirror, shocked the crew.

'LOOK!!'

Crawford and Cressottie reacted at the same instant, leaping back to the aft viewing port, blinking their eyes to clear the dots floating before their pupils.

'Oh, God . . . No . . .' Crawford said, emotion and pain tearing his guts out. He could feel the visceral impact of the sight in front of him.

All the crew members crowded the two viewing windows. They could not believe their eyes when they surveyed the carnage in the cargo bay.

Doctor Minh Tran had disappeared. Literally disappeared in the jumble of pieces gently floating away from the orbiter. Part of the vertical stabilizer was missing, along with a section of the right cargo door. Debris covered the cargo bay from the midsection aft to the damaged tail.

'Houston! *Columbia*! We've been hit by something,' Crawford radioed, staring at the annunciator panel. It was lighted like a Christmas tree. 'We've got an emergency!'

'Copy, *Columbia*. State your emergency.' The voice seemed removed from the extreme situation.

'Shit, we've been hit by something! I don't know what it was . . . just a huge flash.'

Crawford was still in shock, along with his crew staring in disbelief at the wreckage in the cargo bay.

'*Columbia*, do you have cabin integrity?' asked the hollow voice, strained with anxiety.

'Yeah, we seem to . . . at the moment.' Crawford looked at the cabin environmental gauges. Everything looked normal.

'Cabin pressure holding, Houston.'

A different voice emitted from Mission Control.

'*Columbia*, recommend crew don their suits. What is the nature of your emergency?'

Crawford responded, looking aft through the shattered cargo bay. 'Something hit us. I don't know what it was, but it destroyed the aft section of the cargo bay and part of the stabilizer.'

'Roger, *Columbia*. Get Doctor Tran inside the cabin and descend to lower orbit.'

'We can't, Houston.' Crawford's voice cracked.

'What do you mean you can't?'

Crawford took a deep breath, then replied slowly. 'We can change to low orbit, but Doctor Tran is dead.'

'Oh, no . . . You're positive?'

'That's affirm, Houston,' Crawford responded, tasting bile in his throat.

'Send Alan to retrieve him and descend to lower orbit. We're analyzing the data now.'

Crawford swallowed, then breathed deeply and slowly. 'We can't retrieve Doctor Tran. His body disintegrated. He isn't aboard *Columbia*.'

'Oh, Jesus . . .' the controller replied, then – keyed his microphone again. 'Okay, get down to recovery orbit as soon as practical.'

'Roger,' Crawford replied, turning to face the crew. 'Let's suit up and descend before we lo – '

Another blinding flash cut him short.

'OH . . . ,' Cressottie said, panic in his voice as he pointed to the annunciator panel. 'FIRE!'

All eyes turned to the emergency annunciator panel. Two smoke detector panel lights were brightly illuminated, along with a left main gear unsafe light. Two more emergency lights illuminated, glowing intensely, as the crew stared in horror.

The flightdeck was chaotic as the astronauts scrambled to complete emergency procedures. Colonel Crawford, with the assistance of Ward Culdrew, began donning his space suit.

Hank Doherty took command of the shuttle and initiated an emergency orbital change. Alan Cressottie, standing behind Doherty, read the emergency checklist to the shuttle pilot during the hasty descent.

'*Columbia*, Houston,' the radio crackled.

'*Columbia*,' Doherty replied, glancing at the array of twinkling lights on the annunciator panel.

'What's your status?'

'We have . . . ah, we have nominal cabin pressure, and the electrical fires appear to be contained. No primary threat indications at present.'

'Roger, *Columbia*. Stand by.'

'Houston,' Doherty replied calmly, 'we do have a major problem with the main hydraulic system.'

'What's your problem, *Columbia*?'

'We've lost complete system integrity. Must have ruptured a main line,' Doherty explained, then added, 'We don't want to use the auxiliary system until we enter the lower atmosphere.'

'Copy, *Columbia*.'

Crawford climbed into his seat, strapped in, then keyed his microphone. 'Houston, we've got another problem. Our left main gear indicates unsafe.'

'We're working on the anomalies, *Columbia*.'

Crawford didn't acknowledge the transmission. He turned to the crew, hesitated momentarily, then spoke quietly and slowly.

'We are in deep kim chi. We have never addressed the problem of ricocheting back into the earth's atmosphere with extensive structural damage, and, God help us, our hydraulically boosted controls shot to shit.'

'*Columbia*, Houston. We've got some valid data for you on the secure net.'

'Stand by, Houston,' Crawford radioed, switching to the discreet frequency, then addressing his crew on the intercom. 'It'll be like skipping a flat stone across a mill pond. Depends on how many times we bounce.'

Crawford flipped the secure net switch. 'Houston, *Columbia*. Radio check.'

'Five by – . Preliminary telemetry indicates you were hit by a particle-beam weapon. We're ready to commence the recovery at this time.'

'Well, the Russians have got our number,' Crawford replied, watching the deorbit burn count down to one minute.

'We're set.'

'Copy, *Columbia*.'

The flight deck was quiet as Crawford programmed the shuttle for reentry.

'Autopilot to manual,' Crawford said to himself, checking the programmed roll, pitch, and yaw axis. All parameters appeared normal.

'You're doing great, Skipper,' Doherty said as he watched the number one CRT.

'Yeah . . . like building a soup sandwich,' Crawford replied, watching the orbiter rotate into the nose-forward, thirty-degree pitch-up attitude.

'Houston,' Crawford glanced at the CRT again, 'we're in entry attitude, ready to do it.'

'Copy, *Columbia*,' the mission controller responded.

'Antiskid,' Doherty stated.

'On,' Crawford replied tersely.

'Nose wheel steering.'

Crawford checked the switch. 'Off.'

'Speedbrake – throttle controls.'

'Full forward,' Crawford responded, checking the controls.

The checklist continued, concluding with the acknowledgement that the functioning emergency hydraulic system was operating normally.

'Houston, entry checklist complete,' Crawford reported, then typed in a new set of instructions for the computer to handle. The CRT screen lighted, followed by an acknowledgment beep.

The mission controller reported the weather. '*Columbia*, the Edwards weather looks good. Ten thousand scattered, forty miles vis, temperature sixty-seven, wind out of the southwest at twelve, gusting to twenty.'

'Copy, Houston,' Crawford replied as he moved the orbiter's aerodynamic control surfaces to exercise the emergency hydraulic system.

'Hank, this is going to be difficult,' Crawford said to the shuttle pilot.

'Yeah, looks like you're struggling a bit.'

'They're stiff as hell,' Crawford responded, 'and there isn't any air resistance at this point.' The pilot rolled the controls in the opposite direction, using a considerable amount of force. 'Wait 'til we blast into the lower atmosphere.'

'Yeah,' Culdrew replied, 'take a gorilla to move 'em.'

Crawford entered a code to dump the forward reaction control system propellants overboard, shifting the orbiter's center of gravity for reentry.

'Houston,' Crawford radioed, then made another entry into the computer. 'RCS dump completed.'

'Copy dump,' Houston acknowledged. 'Our prayers are with you.'

'Thanks,' Crawford responded.

Crawford and Doherty checked the entry attitude a fourth time. The ADI showed no roll, no yaw, and the nose-up pitch now indicated thirty-four degrees. The shuttle, although heavily damaged, was in the ideal position for reentry into the earth's lower atmosphere.

'Looks good, Hank.' Crawford looked at Doherty. 'Let's go for it!'

'Hit it, boss,' the mission pilot replied, watching the instrument panel while he read the checklist.

'Speedbrake-throttle.'

'Auto,' Crawford responded, watching the attitude indicator for the slightest deviation.

'Pitch,' Doherty continued, monitoring the command pilot's moves.

'Auto,' Crawford said as he quickly entered more information into the computer, then watched his CRT for the proper response.

'Yaw and roll,' Doherty challenged.

'Auto,' Crawford said, as he prepared for atmospheric entry to commence at 400,000 feet.

Columbia, hurtling through space at 17,000 miles per hour, was absorbing the effects of the more dense atmosphere. The shuttle was rapidly heating from the thermal shock of reentry.

'Houston,' Crawford radioed, pulse pounding in his neck, 'we're at entry interface, ready for LOS.'

'Roger, *Columbia*. Copy ready for loss of signal.'

The shuttle was approaching an altitude of 315,000 feet, traveling at 16,700 miles per hour, when the communications blackout began. *Columbia* was enveloped by ionized particles during deep atmosphere entry.

Crawford tensely watched the flight instruments. When sensors detected an atmospheric pressure of ten pounds per square foot, the roll thrusters would be turned off. The elevons would then supply roll control, providing the low-pressure emergency hydraulic system could move the flight controls.

'Oh, shit!' Crawford exclaimed as the orbiter decelerated to 15,000 miles per hour in the lower, denser atmosphere. 'I don't like this stiff feeling in the controls.'

Crawford was intently concentrating on the flight instruments, fixating on a few. 'The vibration is beginning to make this very diffic – '

'Watch your roll, boss,' Doherty reminded Crawford, noting the right wing had dropped seven degrees.

'Got it!' Crawford answered, then stared at the RCS

245

pitch thrusters deactivated light. The bright light winked on, startling the shuttle commander.

The elevons now controlled pitch, as well as roll, with limited hydraulic pressure to activate the aerodynamic flight controls. *Columbia* was crippled and entering a dangerous transition zone.

'Hang on, guys!' Crawford said as the shuttle, over the Pacific Ocean off the coast of Baja California, neared 230,000 feet of altitude at 14,000 miles an hour.

This would be the time of maximum heating to the orbiter as atmospheric drag dissipated the kinetic energy of the shuttle. The nose and wing leading edges, heavily covered in thermal protecting tiles, would reach temperatures above 2,800 degrees Fahrenheit.

Maj. Ward Culdrew, sitting in Minh Tran's seat, tightened his straps and keyed his intercom. 'Please extinguish all smoking material, and bring your stewardess to an upright position.'

Columbia started to buffet, then oscillated in roll and pitch.

'I don't like this . . .' Crawford, obviously strained, said over the intercom.

'Stay with it,' Doherty replied in a tense, low voice.

The shuttle began to yaw, increasing in magnitude, with each roll. The emergency boosted flight controls could not react rapidly enough to stabilize the orbiter.

Crawford fought the controls, breathing heavily. 'I'm losing it . . . oh, God . . . I've lost it . . .'

THE AGENTS

Dimitri and Wickham stared with terror-filled eyes as the other Russian gunship landed fifty meters from the first helicopter.

The gunner from the first Mi-28 crawled out of the helicopter and cautiously approached the Lada. He carried a handgun and had another weapon slung over his shoulder.

After carefully reconnoitering the stolen vehicle, the gunner returned to confer with the gunship pilot. After two or three minutes, an eternity to the CIA agents, the second helicopter added power and hovered approximately ten meters over the pavement.

The Russian gunner remained close to the first gunship as the second Mi-28 began to circle slowly in the area around the Lada. After two complete circles the second helicopter departed in the direction they had arrived from, following the road.

The first gunship remained stationary as the big rotors wound down. The huge Isotov turboshafts idled noisily, masking any conversation for a hundred meters.

'Dimitri, we've got a break,' Wickham whispered. 'The choppers don't have much range. I'm sure the other bastard went after fuel. When he gets back – who knows how long – then this guy will go.'

Dimitri nodded his head in understanding, feeling more confident.

Wickham slid next to Dimitri. 'They know we're in the vicinity. After they're both full of fuel, and, probably, have reinforcements on the way, then they'll begin the hunt in earnest.'

Wickham looked around the area, then turned back to his charge. 'We've got to move now, get as much real estate between us and them as soon as possible.'

Dimitri, calming himself, responded positively. 'Okay, I'm ready. I'll . . . I'll be okay.'

'Good. Follow me and stay on your stomach. We're going to crawl to that tree line,' Wickham pointed in the direction, 'and then cut back across the road to – '

'Across the road? They . . .' Dimitri stopped, eyes enlarged, expressing his worry about the open road.

'Dimitri, they're going to find our footprints by the stream and figure we headed straight across the field. That's natural. They'll lose our prints in this rubble. If we crawl through this crap, we won't leave any signs. They won't expect us to backtrack and cross the road. Besides, the road curves. We'll just go to a point where we can't see the chopper and then cross. Got it?'

'Yes,' Dimitri replied, brushing himself off.

'Let's go. Real slow and easy, no quick movements,' the American coached as the two agents belly-crawled toward the distant tree line.

Wickham struggled after Dimitri, hiding the pain in his arm. Every shift of his body, using only his left arm, sent a throbbing ache through his shoulder.

After fifteen minutes, punctuated by frequent stops to listen and look around, the two men reached the scraggly tree line.

They stopped and listened again, then crawled to the edge of the small stream. The American led Dimitri across the stream, leaping over the ice and landing on thick, brown winter grass. Dimitri followed, landing in the same spot.

The agents crouched down and walked to the edge of the road. Wickham spoke quietly to Dimitri. 'Stay put and I'll check the road.'

The American, creeping on his hands and knees, ventured to the edge of the roadway. Standing half-upright, Wickham edged toward the center of the road.

Both men heard the sound at the same instant.

WHOP-WHOP-WHOP-WHOP.

Wickham dove back into the sparse shrubbery as the other gunship, flying extremely low, rounded the curve at high speed.

248

'That was close!' the American said, catching his breath. 'Dimitri, let's go before the other guy gets off the ground.'

The agents darted across the bare pavement as the arriving helicopter slowed to a hover. They could hear the engine of the first helicopter begin to develop take-off power.

'Come on, Dimitri,' Wickham ordered, holding his right shoulder. 'Follow me.'

13

THE WHITE HOUSE

The White House Situation Room was in upheaval when the vice president walked into the chaos.

'Gentlemen.' All conversations stopped, heads turning toward Blaylocke.

'The president has landed at Andrews and he is boarding *Marine One* at this time. I believe it would be prudent for us to await his arrival before we initiate any contact with the Kremlin.'

Everyone agreed, standing by their seats until the vice president sat down at the head of the conference table.

Blaylocke surveyed the situation status displays, then turned to the group. 'Cliff, can you give us an update on *Columbia*?'

The secretary of defense paused momentarily, then addressed the staff.

'NASA scientists, along with Doctor Hays, believe the Russians used an antisatellite killer, one of their new ASAT satellites, to hit the space shuttle.'

'How so?' asked General Vandermeer.

'The source of energy – the brilliant light – combined with the destruction, points to a laser beam. Nothing else would have the same effect, or the same properties.'

Blaylocke interrupted. 'What about the crew? Can the shuttle make a safe descent, considering the damage it sustained?'

Howard half-turned toward the vice president. 'Mission Control isn't sure at this point. The crew used emergency extinguishers to put out two small electrical fires. Their hydraulic systems were damaged, too. The commander also reported a slight loss in cabin pressure.'

Howard lifted his water glass, sipping two swallows, then continued. 'To make matters worse, NASA engineers aren't sure the shuttle has the structural integrity to survive the reentry.'

'What's the primary reason?' Blaylocke asked, weariness showing in her eyes.

'They aren't sure if the vertical stabilizer, the tail, will remain intact when they penetrate the lower, denser atmosphere.'

The room was totally quiet as Howard continued the brief. 'Also, the structural load on the orbiter will be tremendous because of the damage to the cargo-bay doors. The fuselage section, from the middle of the cargo bay to the tail, is extensively damaged. The big question seems to be whether or not the cargo doors will remain locked and provide the strength to keep *Columbia* in one piece during the high-speed reentry.'

General Vandermeer indicated that he had a question. 'Is it possible to launch one of the other shuttles and rescue the crew in low orbit?'

Howard turned to Vandermeer. 'That really isn't an option, General. In fact, *Columbia* should be reentering now. We should know something soon.'

Blaylocke thanked the secretary and turned to the chairman of the Joint Chiefs. 'Admiral Chambers, will you give us an overview of the global situation to this point?'

'Yes, ma'am,' Chambers replied, spreading three briefing sheets, side by side, on the table.

'The Russian bomber groups have entered large holding patterns. There is a constant shuttle of tanker aircraft supplying the bombers. A large number of the escort fighters have returned to coastal bases. We anticipate they'll be returning to the bombers soon.'

'What about the submarines?' Blaylocke asked, looking at her watch.

'Their big boomers, at least the ones we've detected, have moved into firing positions. They are well spaced to inflict the maximum damage. We've got every operable sub stalking them, along with the P-3s, Vikings, and our ASW helicopters.'

Chambers reached for a different briefing sheet. 'Our bombers, including the Stealth aircraft, are cycling on and off station. Our missile forces, both ground- and submarine-based, are at the ready. Also,' Chambers continued, scanning the third sheet of paper, 'the activated reserve and guard units are ready for immediate deployment.'

Chambers looked up at Blaylocke. 'Our F-117As, the Stealth fighters, are strategically stationed at NATO bases. We are keeping six airborne around the clock until this crisis is over. The Navy carrier groups are in excellent positions to respond to any hostility. They have over twenty squadrons of Navy and Marine Corps aircraft at coast bases standing by to supplement the air wings on board the carriers.'

An aide stepped into the room and announced the arrival of *Marine One*.

'Thank you, Commander,' Blaylocke replied, then addressed Chambers. 'How long can we keep this up? What's your estimate?'

Chambers frowned, then placed his papers in a neat stack.

'We can remain in this posture for a protracted period of time, no question. The primary problem, as we see it, is the inevitable encounter that will lead to further escalations, and, possibly, a nuclear showdown.'

Another aide, wearing the uniform of an Army lieutenant colonel, entered the room. He approached the vice president and handed her a message.

Blaylocke read the contents, then sighed in despair, and removed her glasses. 'Gentlemen, we've lost another SDI satellite.'

The group sat stunned as Blaylocke turned to the defense secretary. 'Cliff, your recommendation.'

'It's time to take action,' Cliff Howard said, balling a piece of paper in his hand. 'Past time. The Soviets know we don't need SDI to win a nuclear war. It only lessens our casualty rate. Our conventional and nuclear delivery systems are much more accurate and reliable than theirs.'

'The former general secretary,' Chambers politely interrupted, 'didn't believe we needed SDI to win. That's why he was so willing to compromise. Zhilinkhov on the other hand, well, we simply don't know what he believes.'

'True,' Howard continued, 'we don't know. However, the Soviets are aware of our standoff strike capability, the accuracy of our weapons. Also, in my opinion, what they fear most is our Stealth bomber.'

Chambers looked at Blaylocke. 'That's true, to a degree. The Soviets know any massive strike to Russia would be evident on radar scopes very quickly. They would have time to respond in kind. What they are most concerned about is having thirty or forty B-2 bombers, loaded with nuclear weapons, undetected on radar, over the Soviet Union. They wouldn't have any warning time.'

'My point,' Howard broke in. 'I think the recent deployment of the Stealth aircraft, both the fighter/attack airplane and the bomber, has caused Zhilinkhov to react. I don't think his primary concern is SDI. I may be wrong.'

Zhilinkhov, tired from his trip to Lajes, waited while the cardiologist closed his bag, retrieved his topcoat, and walked through the huge doors of the Kremlin residence.

The general secretary looked at the capsule of blood pressure medicine, then decided he needed a Stolichnaya on ice.

'Well, comrades, the American space defense system is no longer fully operable. Our plan will work, without question. We will pull back, then mount a massive first strike as soon as the Americans return to a normal status.' Zhilinkhov smiled, pleased with his efforts.

The Politburo members, along with Defense Minister Trofim Porfir'yev, did not appear convinced. The men remained quiet, each with a vodka in his hand.

'Well,' Zhilinkhov asked, 'what is your opinion, my friends? You do not seem to share my joy.'

The senior Politburo member, Pulaev, carefully placed his glass on the end table, inhaled his cigar, ashed, then looked at Zhilinkhov. 'Viktor Pavlovich, we are very concerned.'

'Concerned?' Zhilinkhov replied, a quizzical look on his puffy red face. 'Concerned about what?'

'The spy, the CIA agent planted here in your quarters. How did the blundering idiots at KGB allow that to happen?' The elder politician, jaw set, was loudly grinding his teeth.

'Calm yourself, my friend, or you'll be needing this medicine, too.'

Zhilinkhov's attempt at humor fell on deaf ears. 'There is no need to worry. Colonel General Vranesevic, the GRU commander, assures me they have the spies contained. It is only a matter of time, comrades.'

'What about the rest of your staff, Viktor Pavlovich?

How many other spies have infiltrated our walls?' The Politburo chief drank the last of his vodka while he waited for the general secretary to answer.

Zhilinkhov scowled. 'They have been checked, all of them, and interrogated. There are no other spies, believe me. Colonel General Vranesevic does not believe the American agent knows anything valuable. The KGB didn't find any electronic eavesdropping equipment or transmitters anywhere on or around the – '

'Our present KGB, with respect, Viktor Pavlovich, couldn't track a hemorrhaging elephant in a snow field.'

Zhilinkhov sat back, pulled out a fresh cigar, chewed on the end, then responded. 'I have sent word to KGB headquarters. If the two American spies escape, Chervenok will be relieved of command. Does that satisfy you, my friends?'

The Politburo members looked shocked. The senior member spoke again.

'Viktor Pavlovich, what in the name of . . .? Chervenok is a candidate for the Politburo! He has many influential friends, many ties with leaders in the Central Committee. This is not good, Viktor Pavlovich. Not good . . .'

'It will pass,' Zhilinkhov replied, 'as all things do eventually.'

The general secretary smiled, lighted his cigar, then added to his statement. 'Please relax. The American spy, and our traitor, will be caught. No information will leak out. Chervenok will be spared, and our plan will bear fruit.'

Zhilinkhov puffed on his cigar, then rose to his feet, walking slowly to the open bar. He poured a large quantity of Stolichnaya in a glass, then turned to his friends. 'Comrades, trust me.'

'Just five or six more kilometers, Dimitri. We'll take a break in a few minutes.'

'Okay,' Dimitri replied, breathing hard, his breath condensing in the cold February air.

The late afternoon light was fading under the low overcast as the two men trudged through the deserted fields. Small snowflakes had started falling, drifting lazily through the sparse trees.

'Do you think they got your message?' Dimitri asked, shivering uncontrollably.

'Let's not borrow trouble, huh? We've got enough problems,' Wickham panted.

Both agents walked another kilometer in silence, staying close to a collective farm.

The American broke the silence. 'Dimitri, if we encounter anyone, let me do the talking.'

Wickham glanced at Dimitri, who nodded in return. 'We had an accident and left our car. That's how we got in this shape. We still have our credentials, so – '

The American abruptly stopped, dropping to the ground on his hands and knees. He motioned Dimitri to follow him. The two men sprinted to a tree line and dove into the underbrush, breathing heavily.

'What is it?' Dimitri asked, his grimy face contorted in fear.

'You hear that?' Wickham briefly glanced at Dimitri, then back to the sky. 'The choppers are back!' The American looked back along their path. 'Son-of-a-bitch! They must have found where we crossed the road.'

Dimitri stared at the approaching helicopters, his mind confused and fatigued. He had never been so tired in his life. The agent reeked from crawling through the garbage pile and his hand still ached.

The Soviet Mi-28s were clattering along, hugging the treetops. They looked menacing, even from a distance. Both agents watched the helicopters flow over the landscape, nimble, deadly, probing every foot of terrain.

'Dimitri, they've got infrared sensors. We've got to get out of here!' Wickham grimaced in pain as he bumped his shoulder turning around.

'I don't understand,' Dimitri replied, shivering in the semidarkness. 'What is infrared?'

'They can spot body heat in total darkness. Especially in cold conditions like this.'

The American frantically scanned the terrain in all directions, then motioned for Dimitri to follow him.

After traveling sixty meters in the brush, hugging the tree line, Wickham stopped.

'Dimitri, our only chance is to make a run for those animal pens.' The agent pointed toward two fenced areas next to a feeding trough. 'It's dark enough for us to conceal ourselves in the middle of the pigs and sheep. We've got to blend our body temperatures in with the animals.'

Dimitri nodded in silence.

'Let's go,' the American yelled as they crashed through the brush, stumbling, then vaulted over the fence and sprinted to the edge of the pens.

Both men, panting, lay flat on their stomachs next to the crude fence. They could hear the sound of the helicopters growing closer.

'Okay . . . we've got to move slowly to the edge of the sheep . . . can't scare them.' The American paused to catch his breath. 'Then we ease under the fence and remain still until the choppers are gone.'

Dimitri nodded, then crawled forward on the cold, moist ground. The stench, overpowering, swept both men with revulsion.

The sheep, alarmed by the sound of the approaching helicopters, gave little attention to the two figures lying next to the herd.

The two Soviet gunships, searchlights ablaze, slowly tracked over the collective farm. Both helicopters continually S-turned as they remained on their base course toward Novgorod.

Wickham and Dimitri watched, not moving, not breathing, as the closest Russian helicopter flew directly over the two animal pens. The glare of the spotlight blinded the agents as it slowly crossed the sheep enclosure.

THE WHITE HOUSE

The president stepped off the air-stair door of *Marine One*, smartly saluted the Marine sentry, and walked briskly into the White House. The president's military aide, hurrying to catch the commander-in-chief, struggled with an oversized attaché case and two umbrellas.

Grant Wilkinson and Herb Kohlhammer, followed by a second aide, stepped out of the Marine helicopter and hurried across the lawn.

The weather was cold and dismal. Ice pellets and snow granules fell sporadically, mixed with fog and low clouds. The skies threatened a major winter storm at any moment.

Susan Blaylocke and Cliff Howard greeted the president as he entered the Situation Room.

'Have we heard from the Soviet Ambassador?' the president asked, removing his topcoat and scarf.

'Yes, Mister President. He is on his way here, along with the deputy foreign minister,' Blaylocke responded. 'They should be here in the next five to ten minutes.'

'Good,' the president replied, then looked at Howard.

'Cliff, explain to me, in detail, what happened to our shuttle.'

The secretary of defense waited until the president and the arriving staff members were seated.

'Doctor Hays at NASA has informed me, approximately thirty minutes ago, that *Columbia* was the target of Soviet laser weapons. He – '

'How do they know, Cliff? What . . . How can they substantiate their conclusions?' the president asked, then waited for Howard to compose his thoughts.

'Well, sir, the measuring devices the data NASA receives from the orbiter – indicates the strikes were highly charged beams. Doctor Hays explained, in layman's terms, the possibilities.'

Howard reached for his reading glasses and opened his notes.

'There are, according to Doctor Hays and his associates, only three ways to damage the shuttle in such a fashion. First, and least likely, is a killer satellite, in the same orbit, that destroys its victims with barrages of pellets. Shrapnel lasers, if you will.'

The president frowned, cleaning his glasses.

'Second,' Howard continued, 'is the remote chance that Russia has developed a ground-based laser powerful and accurate enough to pinpoint the orbiter. Doctor Hays has projected a random profile of – '

'Excuse me, Cliff,' Grant Wilkinson interjected, 'but the Soviets do have a laser base at Sary Shagan capable of damaging or destroying our satellites, especially the delicate sensors and solar power cells. They have already damaged a Lacrosse satellite, and knocked out one of the Magnum birds.'

Howard looked directly at Wilkinson. 'That's true, Grant, but the ground-based laser, powerful as it may be,

doesn't have the destructive capability to blast sections
. . . actually disintegrate major structural components of
the orbiter. Besides, the Soviet lasers, ground-based and
space-based, have a difficult time tracking and aiming.
They take a high number of shots for every hit they
achieve. We've been monitoring their efforts – it's
documented.'

'Alright, Cliff,' the president interrupted, 'what is
Doctor Hays's hypothesis?'

'Well, sir, he doesn't consider his conclusions hypo-
thetical beca – '

'I understand,' the president interjected. 'What evidence is Doctor Hays using to support his findings?'

'That is the next point, sir.'

Howard readjusted his glasses, looking over the top of
the frames at his audience. 'Third, and most plausible of
the scenarios, is a space-based laser. We have evidence
that the Soviets have been pouring over a billion dollars
a year into a fast-paced program to develop space
weaponry. Doctor Hays stated – '

'If what you're saying is true,' the president interrupted, 'then all our satellites, not to mention the shuttles, are now vulnerable to Soviet laser weapons. Right?'

'Not entirely, sir. As you know, we've lost another SDI
satellite, presumably to the same weapon that damaged
the shuttle.' Howard made a note on his pad. 'The Soviets
might be able to damage a number of our satellites, but
it would take a prolonged period of time, much longer
than they could afford. Our missiles would be striking
Moscow before their lasers would make any major
difference.'

Howard waited a couple of seconds before continuing.
'Another important factor in this finding – one we can't
overlook – is the crew. Their observations corroborate

260

the technical information received at Houston when the laser initially struck *Columbia*.'

'What, exactly, did the crew experience, Cliff?' the president asked.

'They were in shock, obviously. But they reported brilliant flashes of light, not unlike lightning, that temporarily blinded them. The destructive force was simply devastating. Sir, this was no chance meeting with meteorites.'

Howard took a deep breath, then continued. 'The Soviets are going to press us to the edge of the abyss, I'm afraid, if we don't respond in a forceful manner.'

The room remained quiet until the president spoke.

'How is the crew, Cliff? What are their chances of surviving the reentry?'

'Doctor Hays said the crew is fine at the moment. They did lose the payload specialist, as I'm sure you are aware.'

'Yes,' the president replied. 'I've sent my condolences to Doctor Tran's widow.'

'No one knows the odds for survival of the crew,' Howard continued. 'Doctor Hays was pessimistic, actually. He indicated NASA was preparing for the worst. They are flying the families to Houston as soon as possible.'

'Susan,' the president asked, 'what about the recovery effort going on in Russia? Our two fleeing CIA operatives?'

'Sir, we haven't been informed of any changes. The only conclusive information is over an hour old. The agents sent the extraction signal and the rescue effort is under way.'

The president lighted his familiar cigar and addressed his staff.

'Lajes was a disaster, to put it succinctly. Grant and I

261

believe Zhilinkhov is not mentally sound,' the president looked around the table, 'and that scares us.'

Blaylocke was surprised. 'How do you mean, sir?'

'Susan,' the president hesitated, forming his thoughts, 'the general secretary vacillates from one extreme to the other, then rants and raves, followed by comic smiles and low guttural accusations. He is clearly schizophrenic, in my estimation.'

'What do you believe is his primary motive for pushing us to the brink of war?' Blaylocke asked, feeling a resurgence in her stamina.

'We're stymied, Susan.' The president looked over to Wilkinson. 'Grant, why don't you explain your theory about Zhilinkhov.'

Wilkinson placed his pen on his desk pad.

'At first, it appeared as if Zhilinkhov wanted to pressure us into compromising the SDI program. Then, after the confrontation in Lajes, we were perplexed. Nothing computed. Nothing in the realm of logic, that is.

'When we were informed of the attack on the shuttle, along with the loss of another SDI satellite, the warning lights started glowing.'

The president spoke. 'Grant believes we should plan for the worst even a preemptive strike.'

Loud murmurs filled the room.

The president gestured to Wilkinson. 'Will you run through your event sequence for us?'

'Yes, sir,' Wilkinson responded, opening his glasses. 'The previous general secretary, a man of basic equanimity, died in a mysterious plane crash. Zhilinkhov, from the bowels of obscurity, was in power within hours. The Soviet economy is in complete shambles. The Russians have been deeply embarrassed, twice, by being caught violating the INF Treaty. The United States is about to jump at least a half decade ahead in spacebased missile defense technology.'

Wilkinson waited while everyone grasped his reasoning before continuing.

'Pressure. Real Soviet hard-line pressure from the ruling class. Pressure brought on by the West. The United States, more to the point.'

Wilkinson looked at Chambers. 'Evidence indicates there has been a strong shift, or fragmentation, within the Politburo. The political direction of the Soviet Union has made a complete reversal during the past four weeks.'

Everyone, including Admiral Chambers, listened intently.

'My supposition,' Wilkinson continued, 'is that Zhilinkhov, the majority – or all – of the Politburo, and hand-picked senior military officers, are behind this effort.'

The chief of staff looked at the president, who expressed his approval. 'Go ahead, Grant.'

'The ruling hierarchy has no time left to dispatch officials to plead their case on Capitol Hill. No time for a renewed disinformation campaign. No time for exploiting pacifist sentiment among the religious sector. No time left, gentlemen.' Wilkinson could see a few heads, including Susan Blaylocke's, nod in approval. He looked directly at Admiral Chambers before speaking.

'The Soviet system is falling apart, and further behind, even though they have an ambitious and sophisticated space colonization and exploration program. This past holiday season was terribly bleak for the Soviets, purported to have been the worst in over seventy years. TASS and *Izvestia* reported stores and shelves were virtually empty, provoking an unprecedented public outcry. The Soviet press ignored senior party officials and bitterly criticized perestroika's failure. They published hundreds of reader complaints.'

Wilkinson looked around the table. 'The continuing decline of the Communist party, in my thinking, is why we have seen the drastic changes in the Kremlin. The Party has both feet in the coffin, and they are afraid – paranoid, if you will – that we are going to close the lid.'

Wilkinson paused, then added the bottom line. 'We have a resurrected hard-line fanatic, under tremendous pressure to save the Communist system, holding the match closer and closer to the fuse.

'Zhilinkhov wants to see if we'll flinch and use our extinguishers to put out the flame. If he gets it next to the fuse, as he has now, and we don't do anything, he is home free. Sure, Russia will take some hits, but they'll survive, and we'll be blasted into oblivion. Zhilinkhov will become the Soviet hero of the century, and the Communist party will finally rule the globe.'

Wilkinson cleared his throat. 'Zhilinkhov will blow out the match, laugh, watch us put away the extinguishers, then strike the fuse before we can react,' he concluded, sitting back, ready to field the questions.

Blaylocke spoke first. 'Grant, I'm not the greatest military strategist, but if you are correct, it means we can't downgrade from our current posture and readiness.'

'Precisely,' Wilkinson replied. 'Zhilinkhov holds the match. If he backs away, he knows we'll have to back away, eventually. Zhilinkhov knows we can't tell the American people, and our military personnel, that we'll have to remain in DEFCON-Two indefinitely.'

Admiral Grabow, chief of Naval Operations, quiet to this point, interrupted. 'I'm not sure that is categorically true, Mister Wilkinson.'

'Zhilinkhov realizes, clearly,' Wilkinson paused, directing his words to Grabow, 'that we can't convince our citizens that he is going to blow us to kingdom come.

Zhilinkhov knows that we, this administration, would be the ones to appear insane.'

Wilkinson waited a moment, giving Grabow an opportunity to speak. The admiral remained quiet, though not convinced.

The chief of staff addressed the group. 'I may be off the mark. Then again, there may be more to this than any of us can imagine. I'm only planning for the worst, as I see the picture.'

The president interrupted, a look of frustration on his face. 'Are those goddamn Russians here yet?'

'Yes, sir,' Herb Kohlhammer responded, rising from his chair. 'They're outside. I'll get them.'

'I'm open for recommendations,' the president said, not pleased with his predicament. 'I agree with Susan. We're going to have to respond in a firm manner. We will retaliate militarily to any future Soviet transgressions.'

14

THE EMISSARIES

The gunships continued on their search path, alternately turning forty-five degrees left and right of their base course.

The two Soviet Mi-28s were almost a kilometer away before the American spoke. 'Come on. Easy, don't startle the sheep. We've got to get near the pickup point and dig in.'

Dimitri responded with a grunt, wiping his coat off as he got to his feet.

'Hang on and stay close,' Wickham ordered as they started across the field.

The cold was becoming sharper as the last shades of light disappeared. Light snow continued to fall in the black void of night, chilling the two agents to the marrow.

Wickham and Dimitri, after stumbling in the dark for an hour and a half, finally reached the edge of the partially frozen river. They were as close to Novgorod as they dared venture. Exhausted, the men collapsed on the bank, cold, frightened, and hungry. The American suffered excruciating pain whenever he bumped his right shoulder, but the penetrating cold had partially numbed all sensations.

Wickham collected his thoughts and spoke to Dimitri in whispered tones. 'As soon as you get your breath, we've got to move about a half kilometer upriver and conceal ourselves.'

Dimitri, listening intently to Wickham, heard the approaching trucks first. 'Shh – I hear some – '

'Shut up,' the American snarled, yanking Dimitri flat on the ground next to him.

Both agents, lying on their stomachs, crawled up the embankment to peer down the road through the under-brush. They could see a multitude of lights, twinkling in the dark, reflecting off the falling snowflakes.

'Keep your face down and smear it with dirt,' the CIA agent ordered, spreading the moist, cold semi-mud over his forehead, cheeks, ears, and neck.

'We've got problems . . .' Wickham said, scooting back down the muddy embankment.

'What d – ?' Dimitri's eyes bulged.

'We're close, almost home, but we've got problems,' the American whispered.

Dimitri nodded in the dark, swallowing continuously. He sensed the CIA agent's agitation.

'Dimitri, that has to be the GRU. They've got some very elite troops, the kind they turn loose to locate Kremlin spies. You read me?'

'Y-yes. What are – ?'

'I'm sure they've got dogs with them. You hear them howling?' Wickham was listening with his hand cupped to his left ear. 'That's the same way we came. They're right on our trail. Shit!'

Dimitri remained silent, aware of the sounds of the Russian GRU troops growing closer.

Wickham leaned closer to Dimitri. 'We're going to cross the road, make a large circle, then cross back to this same position.'

Dimitri looked at Wickham as if he were seeing a ghost.

'The dogs will track across the road and become confused by the circle. We'll retrace our steps, then cross the river, make the other side upstream, and head for the rendezvous point.'

Wickham listened a moment, then again spoke to Dimitri. 'We're going to freeze our asses, but it'll throw the dogs off our trail for awhile.'

The American paused, observing no reaction from Dimitri.

'Better than a goddamn firing squad. Let's move out!'

The two men scrambled up the bank, darted across the paved road, ran forty meters into the sparse trees, and completed a large circle. Both agents, stopping momentarily at the edge of the pavement, ran back to their original position, then slid into the ice-cold water as quietly as possible. The numbing cold literally took their breath from them. The respiratory shock was almost overwhelming to the exhausted agents.

'O-kay, Dimitri . . . just dog paddle. S-stay with me . . .'

USS *DWIGHT D. EISENHOWER*

Lt Comdr Doug 'Frogman' Karns snapped a salute and braced his helmet. 'Here we go.'

'Shhhiiittt . . .' Rick Bonicelli replied, barely able to talk during the catapult stroke.

Karns felt the powerful G-forces pressing him harder and harder into the seat back as the F-14 raced off the end of the giant carrier.

Karns popped the gear lever up, trimmed the nose down, and watched the airspeed indicator. Accelerating through 220 knots, Gunfighter One selected flaps and slats up, then waited for the wings to sweep back.

'Okay, baby,' Karns said to himself passing three hundred knots indicated airspeed, 'here we go.'

The Tomcat smoothly rotated skyward, climbing vertically in afterburner as Karns looked back over his shoulder. Gun Two was just beginning to raise the nose of his fighter.

Back on the gauges as the accelerating F-14 penetrated dense clouds.

'You with me, Two?' Karns asked his usual flying mate, Steve Hershberger.

'Yeah, but I lost you in the clouds,' Hershberger radioed. 'I'll ease off a bit and catch you when we're on top.'

'Okay, Hersh,' Karns replied as his Tomcat shot through the top of the cloud layer. 'You'll be out in a couple seconds. Switch to button seven.'

Karns turned on his scrambler, then tuned to the E-2C Hawkeye's frequency. 'Stingray, Gun One up, flight of two, standard ordnance, squawking. What have you got?'

'Turn right, heading two-three-zero, and climb to angels three-one,' the Hawkeye controller ordered. 'Two Air Force F-l5s tangled with a division of MiG-29s due east of the Iceland MADIZ (Military Air Defense Identification Zone). Four MiGs jumped 'em, just outside of the zone, and the Fifteens dropped one of the MiGs. The Eagles had to disengage because of low fuel, so we're vectoring you for an intercept.'

'Roger,' Karns radioed, as he slowly lowered the nose, pulled the throttles out of afterburner, and turned to the southwest heading. He looked over his right shoulder in time to see Hershberger slide smoothly into a nice, loose parade position.

'Two's aboard,' the lieutenant (junior grade) radioed. 'Looks like we're going to have some more fun with these assholes.'

'Afraid so,' Karns responded. 'Let's arm 'em up. Switches hot, and goin' combat spread.'

'We're hot and moving out,' Hershberger replied in a calm voice, flipping his Master Arm switch to ON. 'My man "Gator" says it's time for a little yankin' and bankin' today.'

'Yeah,' Karns replied, 'but cover your ass. These guys are a lot better than the Libyans.'

The 'Miniwacs' controller spoke. 'Guns, your bogies – looks like three of 'em – are one hundred and twenty at angels two-niner, crossing left to right.'

'Copy,' Karns replied, then switched to ICS. 'You got 'em, Bone?'

'That's affirm; we've got a sweet lock.'

The *Eisenhower*'s Combat Information Center broke in.

'Gunfighter flight, you have permission to engage. Repeat, you have permission to engage. White House authority.'

'Roger, Tango Fox, Gunfighters engaging.'

Karns shoved the throttles full forward again. 'Goin' burner, Hersh.'

'We're with you,' Hershberger responded, advancing his throttles to the stops.

The Tomcats accelerated through Mach One, as the two opposing flights rapidly closed on each other.

'Forty miles,' Gordon 'Gator' Kavanaugh, breathing hard, said to Hershberger over the ICS.

'Guns, Stingray. Bogies are jinking back at . . . turning into you.'

'We've got 'em,' Karns radioed. 'Stand by, Hersh.'

'Roger.'

Both pilots watched the MiGs close rapidly. The Russians had already cost the Ike two Tomcats. Karns and Hershberger had a score to settle with the Fulcrum drivers.

Karns keyed his ICS. 'Centering the T . . . come on. Centering the Dot.'

'Lock him up, Frog,' Bonicelli said in a strained voice. 'Lock him up.'

'I'm trying . . . No tone,' Karns said, then added, 'I've got it. Got a tone.'

'Tally – ten miles,' Karns radioed to Gun Two. 'Stand by . . . FIRE!'

Both pilots squeezed off AIM-7M Sparrow missiles and prepared to counter the Russians' evasive maneuvers.

'Fox One,' Karns yelled as he watched the two missiles track straight for the Soviet fighters. He could see the MiGs snap into a high-G turn at seven miles. 'Bogies breakin' right!'

Karns had barely finished the sentence when the lead Fulcrum disintegrated in a mushroom of orange and black explosions.

The second Sparrow missed and flew out of sight.

'Let's go high,' Karns ordered, seeing the MiGs turn hard to his left. 'Switchin' to guns.'

'Two!'

Karns rolled almost inverted, pulling the nose down to the horizon, then further below to track the second MiG.

'Check six, comradski,' the Top Gun graduate said under his breath. He was almost in the perfect firing solution . . . almost.

'Aw . . . shit!' Karns swore, watching the wily Russian simultaneously 'dirty-up' and pull into his Tomcat.

'Idle and boards!' Karns warned. 'He's trying to get me to overshoot. This son-of-a-bitch is good.'

Gun One yanked his throttles to idle, extended his speed brakes, dropped the flaps, allowed the F-14 to decelerate, then slapped the gear lever down. The big Tomcat dug into a 7-G, gut-twisting turn as Karns cross-controlled to pull inside the MiG-29.

'We're droppin' anchor, Ivan,' Karns groaned under the punishment he was imposing on the straining F-14. He could hear Bonicelli grunting in the back seat.

Karns pulled even harder, feeling the stall buffet, as he closed inside the Russian. He had a perfect gun shot.

'Say goodnight, comrade,' Karns said as he squeezed the firing button on the 20-mm M61 Vulcan cannon. The aircraft vibrated as three short bursts erupted from the forward fuselage of the F-14.

Karns and Bonicelli watched, fascinated, as the Fulcrum trailed oily smoke, then fire, as the entire tail was engulfed in flames. The MiG then slow-rolled to the left as the nose fell through the horizon.

'Good hit!' Karns radioed. 'Good kill!'

The MiG pilot ejected as the aircraft continued to an inverted, nose low position.

'Ivan stepped outside,' Karns said over the radio. 'Splash two!'

'Watch it, Frog!' Hershberger yelled over the radio. 'The other asshole is bouncing you – low at your eight o'clock.'

'Tally!' Karns shouted as he snapped his head as far to the left as possible. His left hand shoved the throttles into full afterburner, retracted the speed brakes, then slapped the gear lever up. A split second later the flaps were retracted as Karns turned into his adversary with a 7-G effort.

'Goddamnit,' Karns groaned as the Russian pilot, going at Warp speed, pulled hard into the vertical. 'Going for separation.'

'I've got him . . . rolling in,' Hershberger radioed in an excited voice. 'Meat on the table . . . bear meat.'

Karns hauled the screaming Tomcat around in a painful high-G turn as Hershberger fired his Vulcan cannon.

Karns could see debris being blasted off the Fulcrum, but the MiG continued to fly.

'Don't get too close!' Karns warned Gun Two. 'You're almost up his ass!'

Hershberger didn't answer as he continued to hose down the MiG driver with his smoking Vulcan. The Russian pilot kicked in a boot full of right rudder, then cross-controlled the Fulcrum, which resulted in the fighter departing controlled flight.

The MiG-29 tumbled right in front of Hershberger as he snatched the stick into his gut, sending the Tomcat out of the tracking and firing envelope.

'Ho . . . shit!' Hershberger said in amazement. 'These bastards are crazy!'

'I'm in,' Karns replied, snap-rolling the F-14 to catch the MiG in his sights. 'He's got it recovered. One of his burners is out.'

Doug Karns then talked to Bonicelli over the ICS. 'Okay, just a few more seconds and we can break for lunch.'

Karns stared through the HUD (Head Up Display) and placed the gun sight on the nose of the Fulcrum, then squeezed the trigger two short times. He couldn't believe the impact the cannon had on the MiG. The canopy disintegrated in a shower of sparkling fragments as the pilot slumped forward.

'Good kill! Splash Three!' Karns radioed exuberantly as he rolled his Tomcat 180 degrees, passing over the MiG canopy to canopy. The Russian's torso was shredded and his lifeless face was smashed into the instrument panel.

Gunfighter One watched the MiG nose over, then disappear through the clouds in a classic graveyard spiral. Karns rolled the F-14 right side up and noticed Hershberger closing for a rendezvous.

'Bring it aboard, Hersh,' Karns said, then addressed the carrier. 'Gun One and Two comin' home.'

'Copy,' Captain Greg Linnemeyer responded. 'We've got it on tape, Guns. Really super.'

'Thanks, Captain,' Karns replied, loosening his oxygen mask and rubbing his sweat-soaked jaw.

'We're breaking out the medicinal spirits on your arrival,' Linnemeyer radioed, 'so stroke the burners.'

SCARECROW ONE

Brad Buchanan watched the radar altimeter warning light blink on and off. 'Keep an eye on me, John.'

'Gotcha covered,' the copilot responded, concentrating on the airspeed, compass, INS inertial navigation, and radar altimeter.

The three Sikorsky S-70 Night Hawks, painted in Russian camouflage, raced across the Gulf of Finland, due south of Helsinki. Rain showers had plagued the flight for the past thirty miles.

Buchanan, call sign Scarecrow One, had his hands full maintaining exactly fifty feet over the turbulent ocean while traveling at 170 miles per hour.

The black, overcast sky made contact flying extremely difficult, if not impossible. The intermittent showers caused a feeling of vertigo in the command pilot.

Without the aid of a definable horizon or light source, Buchanan had to rely solely on his instruments.

'Coast coming up in seven minutes,' John Higgins, the copilot, announced to Buchanan.

'Thanks,' the pilot replied, not moving his eyes from the instrument-panel. 'Let me know when I can go visual.'

'Will do.' Higgins looked through the spray-soaked

windshield. 'Should have the shore lights in four or five minutes, according to the box.'

The Night Hawk combat rescue helicopter carried two other crew members behind the cockpit. 'Blackie' Oaks, the crew chief, and Steve Lincoln, paramedic, listened to the pilots over the intercom. Both Oaks and Lincoln doubled as door gunners, using two M60 machine guns pintle-mounted in the open side doors.

'I sure hope Two and Three aren't having any problems,' Buchanan said to Higgins as they neared the first set of coastline lights.

'Yeah, should be okay,' the copilot responded, thinking about the night vision goggles the other two copilots were wearing. Higgins had decided against using the special vision aids.

The three Night Hawk crews had briefed to keep radio silence, except in the case of an emergency, during their run to the rendezvous point near Novgorod.

Buchanan and Higgins were startled when the radio crackled to life. 'Interrogative, Crow.'

Buchanan recognized the voice of the number two gunship pilot, Pete Barnes. 'Go, Pistol.'

'We lost you in the shore lights, Buck. Say position.' Barnes sounded cool, relaxed.

'Two clicks right of the big, lighted boat, heading zero-two-zero, feet dry,' Buchanan answered the number two pilot, adding, 'Copy, Three?'

'Scarecrow Three . . . ah . . . we've got ya.'

'I've got the pad in sight,' Buchanan informed his crew, then banked slightly to the right.

Everyone knew this would be a quick turn, engines running, then back into the air for the dash to Novgorod. The Night Hawks would traverse the entire route at an altitude of two hundred feet or lower. The only hitch would be towers or power lines not on their charts.

The general secretary removed his shoes and stared at the crackling fire. The warm glow reminded the Soviet leader of the hunting lodge he had enjoyed for so many years. The lodge, located in the central Ural Mountains near Krasnovishersk, was a favorite retreat for the Russian political hierarchy.

Light snow continued to fall as the temperature plunged with the onset of nightfall. Zhilinkhov, relaxed, spilled an ounce of his drink on the thick bear rug as he observed his coconspirators refresh their vodkas. The evening was young and the six men had much to discuss.

'It is good to be home, comrades.' Zhilinkhov smiled, inwardly pleased with his progress.

'It is good to be with you, Viktor Pavlovich,' the elder statesman replied, proposing a toast. 'We salute your efforts, Comrade General Secretary. To the Motherland.'

The six men joined in a toast, spilling more vodka as the glasses loudly banged together. A discreet chime interrupted the group as Zhilinkhov unwrapped a cigar and sat back in his chair.

Yevstigneyev, responsible for party discipline, went to the massive doors leading to the general secretary's private quarters.

Zhilinkhov tipped his glass to his lips and swallowed deeply, closely watching the heavy doors. He was surprised to see Colonel General Vranesevic, the GRU commander, standing at the entry.

'Come in, Comrade General,' Zhilinkhov yelled across the room, motioning with his arm outstretched. 'You have good news for us, eh?'

Vranesevic, clearly pensive, entered the large, warm room and stood at attention. 'Comrade General Secretary, I regret to inform you – '

Zhilinkhov stopped the GRU boss. 'Relax, General. Have a seat,' Zhilinkhov said, pointing to the large couch directly across from him. 'You will have a Stolichnaya with us, General?'

Vranesevic looked nervous, obviously shaken, as he replied. 'Sir, I am afraid I have unpleasant news to report about the two American – '

'What unpleasant news?' Zhilinkhov bellowed, blood vessels bulging from his neck and temples. 'Speak out, General! You cannot find the spies?'

'Sir, we have the spies contained.' Vranesevic squirmed uneasily, then continued in a more confident manner. 'It is only a matter of time before we kill them.'

'The unpleasant news, General,' Zhilinkhov said more quietly, then raised his voice again. 'What is the problem?'

Vranesevic coughed, clearing his throat. 'We interrogated the two women at the restaurant where the spies made initial contact – '

'Give me the news, General,' Zhilinkhov ordered. The general secretary had a threatening look on his face.

'The old woman overheard the two spies talking in the kitchen. She speaks reasonable English. The kitchen is very small and it is easy to – '

'What is it?' Zhilinkhov yelled loudly, totally enraged at the GRU commander. 'Get on with it!'

Vranesevic looked pale, almost in shock. 'She testified, under pressure, that your domestic, the Kremlin resident, reported to the American,' Vranesevic swallowed, 'of your intention to bomb the United States.' A rivulet of sweat rolled down the general's forehead, glistening in the firelight.

Zhilinkhov shoved himself forward in the big easy chair, knocking his drink over. 'Who else knows about this?' The general secretary had a malicious look on his face.

Vranesevic looked at the floor, then back to Zhilinkhov before answering. 'Only two of my men, sir, and the two restaurant workers, the women.'

Zhilinkhov stared at Vranesevic with piercing eyes. 'Are you positive, General? Absolutely positive?'

'Yes, sir,' the GRU officer replied, slightly relieved. 'All four are in my office now. They have not talked with anyone, I assure you. My office is under guard until my return, sir.'

'You had better be right, General,' Zhilinkhov said in the low, guttural, vehement voice.

The room was silent as Zhilinkhov contemplated this latest surprise. He picked up the fallen glass and motioned to Yevstigneyev for a fresh drink. He could see the uncertainty in the GRU officer's face.

'Comrade General,' Zhilinkhov began, smiling, 'you will terminate the two women, immediately, and confine your two men in isolation until you hear from me.' Zhilinkhov watched the unblinking general. 'Do you understand, clearly, General?'

'Yes. Your orders will be carried out immediately, sir.' Vranesevic started to rise.

'Sit down, General,' Zhilinkhov ordered, beckoning the other Politburo members and the defense minister to join Vranesevic.

The aging politicians, along with Minister Porfir'yev, had been startled by the general secretary's order to kill the women. The men, hesitant, sat down with Zhilinkhov and the GRU commander. The Politburo members exchanged dour looks but remained quiet.

Zhilinkhov fixed his cold eyes on Vranesevic again, raised his glass to his lips, and talked over the rim.

'Comrade General, you must know how sensitive this

278

information is to our country. Do you not?' Zhilinkhov lowered his glass, then relighted his thick cigar.

'Yes, sir. I fully understand the magnitude of your endeavor, sir,' Vranesevic answered, shifting uncomfortably in his seat.

'Good,' Zhilinkhov answered, staring into the general's pale blue eyes. 'Then there won't be any misunderstandings between us, General.'

Vranesevic looked perplexed. 'Misunderstandings, sir?'

Zhilinkhov leaned forward again, exhaling smoke in the officer's face. 'Only the seven of us in this room know, or will know, about our operation. Correct, General?'

'Yes, sir,' Vranesevic replied, 'I understand completely, sir.' The rivulet of sweat had returned, gleaming anew.

Zhilinkhov had reserved his harshest obloquy.

'Not completely, General,' Zhilinkhov responded, the vehement voice returning. 'You will rue this day if the cowardly spies are not dead by this time tomorrow. Use everything at your disposal, including the *spetsnaz* commandos, but capture and kill the Americans. Twenty-four hours, General,' Zhilinkhov continued in the menacing tone, 'or I will personally see you executed!'

Zhilinkhov leaped out of his chair, mouth quivering. 'DO YOU UNDERSTAND?'

Vranesevic, visibly shaken, replied with a hoarse croak. 'Yes, Comrade General Secretary. I will take my leave and personally see to the – '

'Twenty-four hours, General!' Zhilinkhov pointed his pudgy finger in Vranesevic's face as the GRU officer quickly rose from the couch and rushed for the two huge doors.

The GRU commander didn't want to tell the general

secretary that he was already using a *spetsnaz* commando unit.

As the massive doors closed, Zhilinkhov turned to his coterie. 'We will be okay. Our plan is intact, my friends.'

The room remained quiet a few seconds as the fire crackled, popping occasionally. Aleksandr Pulaev spoke first.

'We have been compromised, Viktor Pavlovich. We simply don't know if this information has leaked out somewhere bef – '

Zhilinkhov interrupted, feeling the need to instill confidence quickly. 'We have not been compromised, my friends. The only possible obstacle, in my view, would be the escape of the American spies.'

'That is the point, Viktor Pavlovich,' the friend of many years explained. 'If they are allowed to escape, you, all of us, will be ruined.'

Zhilinkhov looked at Dichenkovko, then the defense minister, then the three current Politburo members. He stared into the fireplace for a long moment, then spoke in his menacing tone.

'They will not escape me!' Zhilinkhov never flinched as the crystal tumbler shattered in his powerful grasp.

DIMITRI AND WICKHAM

Both agents lay sprawled on the riverbank, shivering and gasping for air. They had broken through twelve feet of thin ice to reach the muddy shore.

Wickham's right arm, though useless to him, was completely numb and caused very little pain now.

'Dimitri,' Wickham asked, 'can you make it up to the brush line?'

Dimitri rolled his head over, tilting it back to see up

the steep slope. Light snowflakes fell on his face, hampering his vision.

'Y-yes,' Dimitri shivered in reply. 'I can m-make it to the top okay.'

Dimitri and Wickham pulled themselves up the muddy incline, inch by inch, digging their fingers deep into the soggy ooze. Wickham, using only his left arm, struggled to keep his balance.

As they reached the top of the muddy bank, exhausted and covered with slime, the GRU point patrol sounded a shrill whistle.

'Hear the dogs?' Wickham whispered to Dimitri.

The young agent cocked his head, shaking uncontrollably in his freezing clothes. 'They've . . . the d-dogs have found our c-circle?' The response from the frightened young man came out as a question.

'That's right,' Wickham responded, then added, 'w-we've got to get into t-the brush.'

Dimitri, wondering if he would ever see a sunrise again, crawled after the American.

The barking seemed to intensify as the dogs ran back and forth around the false trail left by the CIA agents. A large Soviet armored personnel carrier arrived at the scene and disgorged a dozen elite GRU troops.

Dimitri was shaking violently, teeth chattering loudly, as he stared at the scene across the river. His mind was unable to deal with the harsh realities of his situation.

'Come on, Dimitri,' Wickham encouraged, 'j-just a little longer. You've g-got to hang on –'

Wickham stopped in midsentence, sensing something threatening. 'Oh, Jesus . . .' The American's voice trailed off in weariness, then resurged. 'Dimitri, t-the choppers are returning.'

The distinct sound was clearly the two Mil Mi-28 Havocs.

Wickham felt he was in the grasp of defeat. If the Night Hawk rescue team roared into this ambush, which seemed inevitable, no one would survive.

Dimitri tensed. He too could hear the rhythmic beat of the Soviet gunships approaching the growing contingent of GRU troops. The helicopters' bright halogen spotlights turned the scene into a surrealistic nightmare. A deadly nightmare, Dimitri thought as he turned to face Wickham. 'We aren't going to get out of – '

'Dimitri, listen to me,' Wickham said, trying vainly to rekindle the young agent's spirit. 'We've got to k-keep it together.'

The former Marine Corps captain yanked Dimitri's collar. 'LISTEN. Your message has got to reach the president . . . We've got to get it to the White House, even if we die in the process.'

There was no response from the lethargic agent.

Wickham didn't have the strength to push or prod Dimitri much further. 'Dimitri,' Wickham said quietly, 'do you want to die? Just lie here and give up?'

No response.

'They're going to kill us,' Wickham stated in a matter-of-fact tone. 'Execute us right here.'

'I d-don't care,' Dimitri responded, shaking spasmodically in his soaked clothes.

Wickham knew it would require an insuperable effort to save Dimitri at this point. He had to get the agent's adrenaline pumping again. He had to get him back to Washington to give credence to the incredible situation that could destroy the world.

'Dimitri, if you die, I die with you,' Wickham said in a harsh, low tone, 'and I d-don't intend to go out whimpering!' Wickham paused, then growled into Dimitri's face, 'Suck it up, for Christ's sake!'

Dimitri moaned in response, hugging the ground. 'I've

got to rest.' He couldn't control the spasms shaking his body.

Wickham stopped talking when a bright spotlight suddenly played across the river. Both Soviet gunships had been circling the scene, lighting a large area for the Soviet ground troops.

The American watched as one Mi-28 Havoc started down the river, away from their position, sweeping a powerful searchlight from shore to shore. His relief was short-lived when the second gunship crossed the river, then proceeded up the shoreline, sweeping from bank to bank with the stunningly bright spotlight.

Wickham turned to the inert young operative. 'Dimitri, we've got to get back in the water.'

The debilitated agent tilted his head up, vainly trying to focus on Wickham. 'Y-you are crazy,' he sputtered, breathing heavily.

The American slapped Dimitri across the face with his left hand, almost losing his balance as he sat upright in his stiffening coat. 'Goddamn it,' Wickham spat in Dimitri's face, 'th-they've got infrared! We've got to dissipate our body heat until the chopper passes over us.'

Wickham was more frustrated than frightened. His mind knew what had to be done, given the exigencies of the current situation, but dealing with Dimitri was exacting a high toll.

Dimitri didn't respond to the slap or verbal abuse. He looked at the American and slowly moved his head back and forth, shaking violently.

'Bullshit,' Wickham barked under his breath. 'You're going to move it. NOW.'

The American grabbed the young agent by his collar.

'We'll only be in the water a minute or so,' Wickham explained, dragging Dimitri down the muddy bank. 'You'll have to hold onto me. I can't move my right arm,'

Wickham continued, skidding on his buttocks while he pulled his heavy burden down the bank and into the frigid, ice-packed water.

The Russian gunship was rapidly closing on their position as Wickham, dragging Dimitri, stumbled into the river. The American hoped the Russian chopper crew wouldn't notice the broken ice. The two agents were standing in five feet of water, surrounded by large slabs of ice.

'Dimitri, when I tell you NOW, I want you to hold your breath and duck under the water with me.'

Wickham waited for a response, but received no answer, only unintelligible moans.

'You've got to duck under the water, Dimitri. Understand? For just a couple of seconds.'

Wickham glanced over his shoulder at the approaching Soviet gunship, engines pulsating in the black night. 'You can whack it!' Wickham firmed his grip on Dimitri, then gave the command. 'NOW,' Wickham yelled, sucking in his breath and submerging with Dimitri in his grasp.

Wickham opened his eyes to a completely void, black world. He continued to grasp Dimitri with his left arm, then felt the young agent grab his arm, gripping tightly with both hands.

Time seemed to pass in slow motion. Wickham, eyes still open, could feel the pain mount in his lungs. Just a little longer, he continued to tell his oxygen-starved mind.

The seconds became eternity as Wickham's lungs ached in searing pain. His mind, disciplined by years of training and conditioning, told him to hang on for a moment longer.

The water suddenly seemed to glow, then turned bright, as Wickham realized the gunship's spotlight was sweeping their position. He could see a multitude of particles and organisms, minuscule in size, drifting lazily in front of his eyes.

Wickham was caught unprepared when Dimitri wrenched his arm loose and lunged for the river's surface.

15

SCARECROW FLIGHT

The three Sikorsky S-70 Night Hawks, completely blacked out, raced across the Gulf of Finland. Snow and freezing rain reduced the forward visibility to less than a quarter mile. The weather conditions forced the pilots to fly solely by reference to their instruments.

Navigation was the easy part. The crews relied on their inertial navigation systems to supply the heading, distance remaining, and time of arrival at Novgorod. The INS navigation gear would place the Night Hawk pilots within one-sixteenth of a mile of their destination.

The pilots, concentrating intensely, watched their radar altimeters and scanned the flight instruments continuously. The radar altimeters, set at seventy feet, would be reset to one hundred feet when the helicopters passed the Russian shoreline.

The Night Hawks had passed between the Soviet-held islands of Gogland and Moshchnyy. Landfall would be in eleven minutes, thirty-five seconds, according to the soft, green glow of the INS unit in Scarecrow One.

Brad 'Buck' Buchanan checked his fuel gauges, then focused on his engine instruments. He noted everything in the green as the powerful General Electric turboshafts, delivering over 1,700 shaft horsepower, generated a deep, pulsating roar.

'Look clear between here and the coast, John?' Buchanan asked his copilot.

John Higgins, without taking his eyes from the radar screen, replied. 'Don't see a thing, Buck.'

'Good,' Buchanan answered, then checked with his other crewmen. 'Blackie, you and Steve ready?'

'You bet, Major,' the former Marine gunnery sergeant replied, then added, 'just like old times.'

Buchanan and Higgins laughed quietly at the forced bravado of their crew chief.

All three flight crews, including the crew chiefs and gunners, had been Marine Corps helicopter pilots and crew members. The Night Hawk crews worked in harmony and retained their military roots, including rank at the time of discharge. Every crew member, whether former officer or enlisted, had been handpicked by the CIA from the best in the Marine Corps.

Buchanan thought about the mission, especially the last-minute briefing, as he continually scanned his flight instruments. He realized this was going to be a tough, if not impossible, extraction. Too many obstacles between here and the recovery ship.

Buchanan's thoughts were interrupted by his copilot, former captain John Higgins.

'Buck, looks like a possible, two o'clock, eight miles,' Higgins reported, adjusting the intensity of his radar scope. 'Yeah. Don't know what it is.'

'Christ,' Buchanan replied, 'just what we need.'

'Yeah, Buck, it's a ship alright,' Higgins replied. 'We better come left . . . let's see . . . twenty degrees and see if we can skirt around it.'

'Okay, left twenty,' Buchanan answered. 'Sure hope Two and Three are paying attention.'

'Stop worrying, Buck,' Higgins said, grinning, 'they're going to be just fine.'

The crew of Scarecrow One remained quiet, listening to the powerful throb of the big turboshaft engines.

Suddenly, Higgins gasped. 'Uh-oh . . . Oh, shit! They've got a radar lock on us.'

Buchanan heard the same electronic warning tone in his helmet. 'The ruse may be over, gents.' Buchanan looked back at his crew. 'Hold on . . . we may have to do some violent maneuvering.'

'Major,' Oaks said, 'ten to one that sumbitch is a Russian trawler.'

'Probably so,' Buchanan answered, knowing Oaks was right. The Night Hawks had been discovered.

THE *GANYUSHKINO*

The Soviet intelligence-gathering and surveillance vessel had been headed for the island of Kronshtadt, forty kilometers west of Leningrad, when the radar operator detected the unidentified helicopters.

The captain of the Soviet ship confirmed the sighting, then broadcast a mandate for the low-flying craft to identify themselves.

After repeated efforts to communicate with the suspicious intruders, the captain of the *Ganyushkino* radioed the Soviet Air Force Northwestern Air Sector Control. The Soviet Air Defense Force and surface surveillance ships enjoyed a close relationship in thwarting intruders.

The Russian Air Defense commander, hampered by the inclement weather, couldn't launch his potent jet fighters against the low-flying helicopters. Instead, the Soviet commander elected to launch seven gunship helicopters from the Coast Aviation Brigade. Within minutes of the sighting, four Mil Mi-28 Havocs and three Mi-24 Hind-D combat helos were airborne.

The captain of the *Ganyushkino* continued to relay position and heading information to the Air Defense

Command Post until the unidentified helicopters disappeared in radar ground clutter after crossing the beach.

Two of the Soviet gunships, based at Narva, twenty kilometers west of the Night Hawks, were already airborne when Scarecrow Three raced low across the Russian shoreline.

THE WHITE HOUSE

The Soviet deputy foreign minister, trailed by the Russian ambassador, walked briskly into the Situation Room. The atmosphere was cold and aloof, without pretense of convivial posturing. Both Soviets looked extremely uncomfortable.

Herb Kohlhammer, as secretary of state, was the only member of the president's staff to offer a greeting to the Russian politicos.

'Please have a seat,' Kohlhammer gestured to the end of the expansive table.

The Soviets, looking pensive, sat down holding their coats. The deputy foreign minister nervously ran a handkerchief over his forehead, then cleared his throat.

The president spoke to the Soviet deputy foreign minister first.

'Mister Shcharansky, your country, your government has elected to place the United States in an awkward and very delicate position.'

The president paused, waiting for a response. Both Soviet officials remained quiet, avoiding the American leader's eyes.

The president, becoming visibly irritated, continued.

'Your government . . . No, Soviet leadership, General Secretary Zhilinkhov, has plunged our two countries into a combative posture.' The president stared at the Soviets. 'Does that concern either of you?'

The president fixed his gaze on Shcharansky, then turned to the Soviet ambassador, Krikor Gerasimov. Both Russians remained silent, glancing down at the surface of the table, then back to the American leader.

The president, showing restraint, lowered his voice and spoke to the Soviets. 'Do you understand English?'

'Yes, of course,' the shocked Russians responded in unison.

'Good, goddamnit,' the president boomed, surprising his own staff and startling the Russians.

'This is not a pleasant time for us, I can assure you,' the president continued. 'Your government is responsible for placing the United States in a position of imminent nuclear confrontation.' The president was livid.

'In addition, General Secretary Zhilinkhov is responsible for the deaths of twenty-three American servicemen. He is also responsible for causing severe damage to our space shuttle and for the death of one of our astronauts!'

The president glared at the Soviets. 'Do you deny those facts?'

Shcharansky blinked his eyes several times before responding. 'Mister President, I am not at liberty to discuss those issues. We have been informed that . . . that our government is only responding to American aggression. We . . . have no comment.'

'Then why the hell are you taking up space here?' The president, catching Wilkinson's eye, calmed himself before continuing.

'I am formally requesting that you contact General Secretary Zhilinkhov, here and now, on our direct line, and explain our position.'

The president lighted a cigar, then outlined his ultimatum to the surprised Soviets.

'Very simple, gentlemen. We are not budging another inch. You understand?' The president was pleased to see both Russians nod in acknowledgement.

'General Secretary Zhilinkhov, and the Soviet government, have six hours to turn everything around. Everything, for your clarification, includes bombers, submarines, tanks, and troops – everything!'

The president placed his cigar down and folded his hands on the table. 'If Zhilinkhov doesn't comply, the Soviet Union can anticipate immediate retaliation.'

The room remained silent until the president spoke again.

'Do you have any questions . . . either of you?' the president asked, staring intently into the Soviets' eyes.

Shcharansky, unsure of himself, spoke first. 'No questions, Mister President.'

The deputy foreign minister, fidgeting, continued, 'But I do not have the authority to conduct such discussions directly with the general secretary and I have never attempted to cir – '

'I don't give a damn,' the president responded. 'I'm giving you the authority! We're out of time and options, Mister Shcharansky.'

Everyone in the White House Situation Room knew this was an unprecedented move by the president. Forcing the Soviet hand was a departure from normal relations.

'Mister President,' Shcharansky responded nervously, 'I have been ordered not to enter into any discussions without the express consent of the foreign minister.'

'That's probably true, sir,' Wilkinson interjected. 'Zhilinkhov is not a solo player, as we've witnessed.'

'Well, the rules are changing,' the president stated,

motioning to Kohlhammer. 'Herb, get the Kremlin on the line, and make Mister Shcharansky comfortable.'

DIMITRI AND WICKHAM

Grasping frantically with his good arm, Wickham managed to impede Dimitri's sudden thrust toward the surface of the freezing river. The CIA agent yanked violently on Dimitri's pant leg, slowing the panicked agent from surfacing until the spotlight had passed over their position.

Dimitri surfaced, coughing and gagging, as the Soviet Havoc gunship continued to sweep the river with its powerful halogen lamp. Wickham surfaced a second after Dimitri and began tugging the gasping agent toward shore. The sound of the two helicopters masked the splashing and coughing of the two soaked agents.

'Come on, Dimitri,' Wickham pleaded. 'You've got to hang on. Think about your girl – Svetlana.'

Wickham paused, sucking in air as the two men lay on their backs, feet still in the river.

'Think about her, Dimitri.' Wickham slowed his breathing, glancing at the supine form next to him. Dimitri struggled, chest heaving, as he tried to catch his breath in the gently falling snow.

'Dimitri, if you'll give me every last ounce of strength until we get out of h-here,' Wickham shivered, 'I promise to do everything possible to reunite you and Svetlana back in the s-states. In America.'

Dimitri turned his head toward Wickham. 'Svetlana,' Dimitri half-choked, 'you w-would help my Svetlana?'

'Anything,' Wickham responded, 'in my power. Just hang in th-there . . . for both of us,' Wickham breathed deeply, 'and your girl . . . Svetlana.'

Wickham struggled to his knees in the mud and broken ice, then helped Dimitri to his hands and knees. Both men crawled up the muddy embankment, shaking from the numbing cold, and rolled into the shelter of the shrub trees.

Wickham could see the Soviet troops gathering around the area where he and Dimitri had circled across the road. It would be only a matter of time until the Russians discovered the point of entry into the river.

'You will h-help my Svetlana?' Dimitri asked again, crawling further under the shrubs.

'Yes,' Wickham responded. 'I give you my word. But you've got to help me, Dimitri. We've got to get out of here. Alive, Dimitri.'

Wickham jerked around, not quite sure of what he had heard. The night was ink black. He listened intently, senses keyed in frightened anticipation.

'You hear that, Dimitri?' Wickham asked. 'There it is again.' Wickham waited a couple of seconds, listening. 'That was a splash.'

Dimitri strained to hear but couldn't make out anything. It was too dark to see well and his ears ached from the ice-cold water.

'Let's go!' Wickham nudged Dimitri, then pointed downstream. 'We've got to m-move out . . . get farther away. They're gaining on us.'

Dimitri shoved himself up to his hands and knees, crawled from under the shrubs, and focused down the river. His heart received a shock when he saw what was happening on the opposite bank.

'Come on, Dimitri,' Wickham yelled softly. 'Move it! Follow me.'

'Okay,' Dimitri replied, looking over his shoulder at the inflatable rubber boat being placed in the water at their original point of entry into the river.

SCARECROW FLIGHT

The three Sikorsky Night Hawks were twenty kilometers west of Gatchina when Scarecrow Three detected two fast-moving radar blips approaching the S-70s.

Capt. James E. 'Jungle Jim' Charbonnet decided it was time to break radio silence.

'Scarecrow Lead, Three,' Charbonnet said into his microphone.

'Lead,' came the brief reply from the flight leader. The pilot was concentrating on the terrain rushing under his helicopter.

'Mother-in-law at sixteen hundred,' Charbonnet responded, referring to bogies approaching from the four o'clock position.

'Okay,' Buchanan replied. 'Two and Three, go high and engage.'

'Two with a copy,' Pete Barnes radioed.

'Three.' Charbonnet said, rechecking his armament panel.

Buchanan looked at Higgins. 'How long 'til we get to Novgorod?'

'Ah . . .' Higgins punched three buttons, then waited a second. 'Fourteen minutes, Buck.'

'Looks like the visibility is improving,' Buchanan said, then noted the overcast. 'We've got four hundred, maybe five hundred over now.'

'Yeah,' Oaks responded. 'Hope the zone is cold.'

No one answered as the Night Hawk gunship raced toward Novgorod. The radar altimeter continuously chimed warnings as the S-70 oscillated above and below one hundred feet of altitude. This was contour flying on the ragged edge.

'John, double-check the ADF,' Buchanan instructed,

'and go ahead and broadcast Scarecrow identification for our agents.'

'Now, Buck?' Higgins asked. 'We're still a ways out.'

'Can't hurt,' Buchanan replied. 'Sooner we make contact, the better off we'll all be.'

'Roger,' Higgins said, then pressed the transmitter key on the discreet frequency radio. 'Scarecrow calling Sandman. Scarecrow One to Sandman.'

The copilot waited three seconds, then tried again to reach the CIA agents. 'Scarecrow One to Sandman.'

The receiver remained quiet, emitting occasional broken static. Higgins adjusted the volume.

'Try every thirty seconds or so,' Buchanan ordered. 'We gotta have contact.'

'Will do,' Higgins answered, fine-tuning the radio receiver. 'Should be in range in a minute or two.'

Buchanan scanned his instruments, then looked at the soft glow under the overcast. A small town or village was providing enough light to see the bottom of the low-hanging clouds clearly. Light snow continued to drift slowly from the thick overcast.

Scarecrow One was looking at the settlement, wondering whether or not the CIA agents were still alive, when his headphones came to life.

'Buck, the cat is out!' Pete Barnes radioed his leader as he initiated a 'stern conversion' to jump the Soviet helicopter gunships.

'Roger, Pistol!' Buchanan replied excitedly. 'Pump the bastards and rejoin ASAP!'

'Comin' to ya,' Barnes groaned under the G-forces as he pulled up steeply, performed a wingover, then dove into an attack position on the nearest Russian gunship.

The Soviet pilots, caught off guard by the frontal assault, countered with a steep upward spiral, oblivious to Scarecrow Three.

Charbonnet raised the nose of his S-70, turned into and under the Soviet Mi-28 Havoc combat helos, then loosed a salvo of air-to-air missiles.

Both Russian gunships exploded, one spiraling down in ever-widening circles. The other helicopter, trailing orange flames, plunged straight into the ground, exploding again on impact.

'Goddamn, Jungle,' Barnes yelled over the radio. 'How about a warning next time! You almost took us out.'

'Sorry, Pete,' Charbonnet responded, apologetically. 'I forgot to holler.'

Buchanan broke in. 'Clear the radios and smoke it up here.'

'Roger, Buck,' Barnes answered. 'We splashed both intruders and we're on our way.'

Buchanan checked the INS again as Higgins continued to transmit to the CIA agents.

'Scarecrow to Sandman.' Higgins waited ten seconds.

'Scarecrow calling Sandman. Copy, Sandman?' Higgins waited, then tried again. 'Scarecrow to Sandman. Do you read, Sandman?'

Intermittent static was the only sound Higgins heard from the small transmitter.

'Blackie' Oaks keyed the intercom system. 'Sounds like Cap'n Charbonnet got a kill.'

Steve Lincoln, sitting across from Oaks, pressed his intercom. 'Two kills, gunny.'

Buchanan interrupted. 'Cut the chatter. Too many distractions right now.'

'Yessir,' Oaks replied in a respectful manner.

Wilkinson watched Shcharansky tentatively accept the Moscow 'directline' telephone. The deputy foreign minister was clearly nervous, eyes blinking continuously.

The Soviet ambassador, Krikor Gerasimov, normally verbal and animated, sat quietly in his chair. He hadn't said a word since the president had issued his order.

While the White House staff and Russian officials waited for the Kremlin call to be completed, Wilkinson leaned over to the president. 'Sir, do you want the carrier air groups to launch some leverage?'

'Let's see what develops from this effort first,' the former carrier pilot quietly answered. 'If your hypothesis is correct, Zhilinkhov may use this situation to break the logjam he developed.'

Wilkinson nodded his head in agreement.

The president suddenly snapped his fingers, then turned to Herb Kohlhammer. 'Get the linguist, the Russian interpreter, in here.'

'Yes, sir,' Kohlhammer responded, pressing a code into his console. 'She is in the waiting room.'

Shcharansky winced when a burst of Russian shot through the phone receiver. The deputy foreign minister attempted to speak – several times, openly flinching at the rebukes, then loudly exclaimed that he was at the White House. At the White House with the president. A very upset American president.

Shcharansky explained the extreme situation in Russian to the Soviet general secretary, then fell silent.

The interpreter, skipping the profanity, repeated both sides of the conversation.

The deputy foreign minister was taking a severe tonguelashing, knowing his career was over. He, too, thought the general secretary of the Communist party, psychologically, was not a well person.

'Comrade General Secretary,' Shcharansky said as forcefully as he dared, 'I am making an attempt to convey the situation as it sta – '

The telephone line went dead as a chagrined and humiliated Boris Shcharansky, former Soviet deputy foreign minister and rising political star, hung up the phone. He spoke slowly, haltingly.

'The general secretary will comply . . . with the wishes of the United States.'

No one responded as the two Soviets, now standing, placed their coats over their arms.

The president stood up, followed by the rest of the White House staff, then spoke to the Soviet delegates.

'Thank you for your efforts, gentlemen. You may have made a significant contribution.' The president, unsmiling, stepped forward to shake hands with the Russians. 'Thank you, again.'

Both Russians nodded in acknowledgement, then quietly walked out the door.

'Well,' the president exhaled, then sat down, 'we'll see what the next few hours bring.'

Wilkinson and Cliff Howard, hearing the vice president gasp, turned to see what was happening. An Army lieutenant colonel, serving as a White House aide, was conferring with Blaylocke. His face was a grim mask of pain.

The president, noticing the exchange, spoke to his vice president. 'What is it, Susan?'

Blaylocke thanked the officer, then turned toward the president as the aide left the room.

'Gentlemen, you better have a seat. I have some bad news to report.'

No one said a word, including the president, as every-one sat down.

'We have lost the shuttle,' Blaylocke said, squeezing one hand with the other. '*Columbia* crashed into the water off southern California. They are launching search and rescue efforts at this time, but the SAR people, and NASA, don't have much hope of finding any survivors.'

The president sat back and closed his eyes. Fifteen seconds elapsed before he opened them again, turning to the secretary of defense. 'Cliff, I want the Navy to sink the three Soviet submarines off the coast of Florida.'

Kohlhammer and Howard, both shocked, tried to respond at the same time. The secretary of state deferred to Howard.

'Mister President, the general secretary is backing off. I am not sure we want to send the wrong message at this crucial time.'

'Yes,' the president said, staring into Howard's eyes, 'and Zhilinkhov knows our shuttle crashed because he ordered it attacked, along with the *Tennessee*, the *Virginia*, and our fighter planes. Order the attack.'

DIMITRI AND WICKHAM

The snow had begun to fall more heavily as the two CIA agents struggled along the edge of the riverbank. Slip-ping, stumbling, and occasionally falling, the operatives slowly distanced themselves from the group of *spetsnaz* commandos in the inflatable raft.

Overhead, the Russian gunship helicopters continued to orbit in ever-widening circles. Their spotlights looked like dancing luminous spheres, darting at times, against the dark overcast.

Wickham, feeling sluggish, slipped and fell sideways

on his limp right arm. Stifling a loud groan, the American felt Dimitri trip over his legs, then watched him fall headfirst down the muddy embankment.

The opposite side of the river was teeming with Soviet special forces troops, each carrying a powerful flashlight or spotlight.

Dimitri lay completely exposed to the light beams arcing randomly back and forth across the partially frozen river.

'Oh, God,' Wickham pleaded in frustration and weariness, 'please help us.'

The CIA agent first crawled, then slid down the muddy slope of the riverbank, inadvertently kneeing Dimitri in the side. Fortunately, Dimitri was only frightened by the unexpected fall, not hurt.

As the two men struggled back up the slippery incline, Wickham was startled to hear his miniature radio receiver transmit a message.

'Sandman, do you read Scarecrow?' There was an urgency in the voice. 'Do you copy, Sandman?'

'Hurry, Dimitri, they're here!' Wickham encouraged the young agent to move up the embankment faster, so they could conceal themselves and communicate with the rescue helicopters.

'Scarecrow calling Sandman,' Higgins called, annoyance in his voice. 'Come in, Sandman.'

Buchanan looked at his copilot, then spoke without using the intercom. 'If they aren't there . . . Shit! We may get gamarooshed for nothing.'

'Yeah,' Higgins keyed the intercom, 'they may already be dead, and we're going – '

'We're goin' into a trap,' Buchanan finished the grim statement for his friend.

'Scarecrow One to Sandman!' Higgins said into the radio. 'Copy, Sandman?'

Wickham pulled on Dimitri's coat sleeve as hard as he could with his left arm. The young operative finally struggled over the lip of the riverbank and rolled under a clump of low shrub trees.

Both agents could clearly hear the excited barking of dogs in the inflatable boat. The Russians were almost across the river, slowed only by thin ice along the bank. Time was rapidly running out for the two CIA operatives. The Russians were closing fast, aided by the highly trained attack dogs.

Wickham tugged at the combination radio/homing beacon, folded out the antenna, flipped the automatic direction finder to the on position, then transmitted over the radio.

'Scarecrow, Scarecrow, this is Sandman, over!' Wickham's voice quivered from the freezing cold and adrenaline rush through his body.

'Sandman!' the surprised voice responded immediately. 'Stand by one.'

'We can't stand by!' Wickham angrily transmitted back. 'We're surrounded by Russians!'

'Okay, Sandman,' Higgins radioed, 'we've got a sweet beacon. Hang on. We're seven out and rapidly closing on your position.'

Wickham could hear the sound of the engines and beat of the rotors over the radio. He turned the volume down as far as it would go. The American agent knew the real worry was the Soviet gunships.

The senior agent turned to Dimitri and spoke reassuringly. 'Seven m-miles out. Three minutes at the outside. Sweet Jesus, w-we're going to make it! We're going to make it, Dimitri.'

Wickham, using his left arm in a backwards motion, slapped the young agent across the shoulders in a gesture of friendship and elation.

Dimitri, half smiling, tears streaming down his cheeks, turned to Wickham. 'W-we're going home, we're going home,' he choked.

'Snap out of it, Dimitri!' Wickham ordered, then continued. 'Take off your coat and get ready to run. Your s-sole mission is to concentrate on getting into the chopper, okay?'

'Y-yes,' Dimitri replied, shaking violently, 'that's all I want to do.'

Wickham looked down the river at the inflatable raft. They had reached shore and the two dogs were leaping from the boat to the muddy edge of the river.

Wickham pressed the radio transmit key again.

'Scarecrow, Sandman. Urgent!'

'Copy, Sandman,' Higgins instantly replied. 'Go!'

'Be advised,' Wickham paused, counting, 'there are approximately forty, maybe fifty, ground troops around us, plus two helicopters.'

Wickham waited, without hearing anything, not even an acknowledgement, for ten, then fifteen seconds.

'Say type of helicopters,' Higgins said.

'Gunships. Havocs, I believe,' Wickham responded. 'I think they're low on fuel.' Wickham looked up at the Russian Mi-28 crossing the river. 'They've been out here for quite a while.'

'Good,' Higgins replied. 'Hang in there, Sandman. We're almost there!'

'We're tryin' to,' Wickham said, watching the six advancing *spetsnaz* troops and their dogs.

16

SCARECROW FLIGHT

Buchanan and Higgins rapidly scanned the ADF, then back to the INS. The ADF needle pointed straight ahead, not wavering. The inertial nav showed 3.4 nautical miles to the rendezvous point.

Buchanan glanced at Higgins with a look of resignation, then pushed his intercom switch. 'This is for real, guys. Don't screw the pooch.'

'You got it, skipper,' Oaks replied, looking at Lincoln, the paramedic-turned-door gunner.

Buchanan leaned toward Higgins. 'Ask Sandman his exact position, and see if he can describe the disposition of the ground pounders,' Buchanan said, as he started slowing the agile Night Hawk.

'Sandman, Scarecrow,' Higgins radioed, watching the mileage wind down in the INS.

While Higgins awaited the information from Wickham, Buchanan talked to the other pilots and crews over a separate radio.

'Scarecrow Flight, listen up!' Buchanan ordered the other two command pilots. 'I'm slowing to ninety knots at this time, going to approach from one mile upriver. We've got two gunships and approximately fifty grunts on top of our troops.'

'Two,' Barnes replied in clipped fashion.

'Three!' Charbonnet responded, highly charged from the airborne engagement.

'Two, you jump the gunships,' Buchanan ordered, 'and Three, you strafe the troops.'

'Two,' Barnes replied, rechecking his cannon.

'Three will take the troops,' Charbonnet responded, adding power to close on his leader.

'Two, you break off now and hit the gunships broadside,' Buchanan instructed his old friend.

'Copy, Buck,' Barnes said. 'Here we go.'

'Three, you stick with me and keep their heads down while I go in,' Buchanan ordered Scarecrow Three.

'Right on your tail,' Charbonnet replied.

Higgins pressed the intercom switch. 'Most of the troops are on the east side of the river between the road and the riverbank.'

'Beautiful,' Buchanan replied. 'Are the gunships in the air or on the ground?'

'Our man says they're airborne, apparently circling the area at a leisurely pace,' Higgins answered, then remembered the important part of the message. 'The spook confirmed there are two of them, but they're on the opposite side of the river from the planned pickup point.'

'How the hell did that happen?' Buchanan didn't wait for an answer, knowing it was category three information at this stage of the rescue. 'We'll just have to grab 'em the best way we can. I may not be able to land, so we better prepare to haul 'em in from a hover or use the ladder.'

'Yeah, no problem,' Higgins answered. 'Ah . . . one other detail, Buck. They've got troops and dogs closing on them on their side of the river.'

'Jesus!' Buchanan replied. 'This is turning into a major cluster-fu – '

The pilot's statement was cut off as Scarecrow Two, traveling at a high rate of speed, flashed into view spewing cannon shells at the Russian helicopters.

304

Buchanan and Higgins were stunned, not expecting Barnes to engage the Russian gunships as quickly as he had. The sky seemed to glow brightly under the overcast as various weapons opened up amid the confusion.

'We're coming up to the river now, so let's pick it up,' Buchanan radioed Charbonnet.

'Three is accelerating. Got you in sight,' Charbonnet replied as he lowered the nose of his Sikorsky to gain more speed. 'I've got the river.'

Scarecrow Two rocketed between the two Soviet helicopters in a hail of ground fire.

'Okay, Jim, check your switches,' Buchanan ordered. 'I'm goin' to need a lot of suppression.'

'We're hot,' Charbonnet responded, rechecking his arming switches. 'I see the major concentration of troops.'

Buchanan keyed his intercom. 'Gunny, you engage the troops on the far side of the river while Steve handles the guys closing on our agents.'

'Will do, Major,' Oaks replied, giving Lincoln a reassuring thumbs up gesture.

'I've got a tally!' Buchanan said over the radio. 'Pete, try to work 'em on the east side!'

'Best . . . we . . . can . . . Buck,' Barnes groaned, obviously under stress from the violent maneuvers he was performing. 'Bastards. Pretty quick!'

Higgins was yelling over the discreet frequency to Wickham. 'You'll have to guide us over your position, copy?' The copilot couldn't hear amidst the clattering of the machine guns. 'Speak up! We can't hear you! You'll have to guide us in!'

PING!!

THUD!

Two rounds hit the aft left side of the main cabin. One

305

penetrated the fuselage, missing Lincoln by three inches, while the other ricocheted upward into the rotor blades.

'We're takin' rounds, Major!' Oaks said over the intercom. 'Big stuff.'

'Better slow it down!' Higgins told Buchanan, pointing to a spot across the river from the planned rendezvous point. 'There they are . . . I think.'

'Yeah, I have 'em,' Buchanan responded. 'Shit! The grunts are almost on top of 'em.'

'Buck,' Higgins glanced at the commander of Scare-crow One, 'this don't look so good.'

USS *SARATOGA*

'Launch the Vikings. Launch the Vikings,' blared the flightdeck loudspeakers as the catapult crews hustled out from under the two S-3B ASW aircraft.

The twin engine jet on cat number one roared down the pitching deck, lifted off, and started a turn to the right as the landing gear retracted. Seconds later, engulfed in a cloud of catapult steam, the second Viking streaked into the air and turned to rendezvous with the leader.

Two additional Lockheed S-3Bs taxied into position on the forward catapults. The four VS-30 'Sea Tigers' would join up five minutes after the last sub-killer was airborne.

Each Viking carried four depth bombs internally plus two bombs on the wing pylons.

'Hummer, Fishhook Seven-Oh-Seven, flight of four,' Lt Cmdr Spencer Rainer radioed the Hawkeye.

'Fishhook, we've got the coordinates and the clearance. CINCLANT authorization.'

'We're ready, Hummer.'

Rainer listened to the controller while his copilot

copied the coordinates for two of the three Soviet submarines, then read them back.

'That's affirm, Fishhook,' the Hawkeye controller said. 'Seven-Oh-Seven and Seven-Oh-Four will take target one. Seven-Oh-One and Oh-Six take target two. We are vectoring two P-3s at the third target.'

Rainer keyed his radio. 'Four, let's come starboard one-zero-five.'

'Roger.'

'One and Six,' Rainer continued, 'we'll see you at the boat.'

'Ah . . . roger,' the second section leader radioed, leading his wingman to the second submarine. 'Good fishing.'

Rainer clicked his mike twice in acknowledgement, then keyed the ICS. 'I don't know what the hell is going on, but we're stepping into deep shit.'

THE AGENTS

Dimitri lay spread-eagled in the shrubs as Wickham frantically gave instructions over the small radio.

'You're about a hundred fifty yards away! Straight ahead, along the shore,' Wickham yelled into the radio. He looked around at the advancing *spetsnaz* troops. They had spread out and were firing at the approaching Night Hawk.

'Dimitri,' Wickham shouted, 'fire in the vicinity of the troops! The ones off the boat!'

Wickham pulled out his Beretta and aimed in the general direction of the advancing Soviet troops. Even if the agents didn't hit the Russians, the rounds whining overhead would keep the troops at bay, or at least slowed.

'You're only a hundred yards away,' Wickham shouted into the radio. 'Straight ahead!'

P-ZZZING!!

The high-powered round ricocheted off a tree two yards from the agents, causing both men to drop prone on the frozen ground.

'Dimitri,' Wickham barked, 'start crawling toward the chopper. GO! GO!'

Dimitri dropped his weapon and started crawling on his hands and knees.

Wickham turned toward the Russians, then froze in panic when he saw one of the killer dogs snarling twenty feet away. The animal had hesitated for a split second.

'Oh, shit,' the agent said quietly as he gripped the Beretta with both hands, aimed at the middle of the dark, growling canine, and squeezed the trigger.

The Doberman staggered backwards, emitting a mournful howl, then fell over a stump and died.

Wickham fired the remaining rounds at the advancing Russians, then dropped the Beretta and started crawling after Dimitri. 'Keep movin'! GO,' Wickham yelled to the struggling figure in front of him.

Wickham caught the flare of an explosion, then felt the concussion, as a helicopter thundered into the ground next to the roadway. He fervently hoped it wasn't an American chopper.

'Sandman! Sandman!' Higgins urgently radioed, trying to expedite the rescue effort. 'We've got to set down here. It's the only clear spot. Can you make it?'

Wickham looked up, judged the distance to be sixty yards, at most, then frantically keyed his transmitter. 'Yeah! On our way. We need cover fire!'

The CIA agent grabbed Dimitri by the collar. 'Come on! GO! GO! RUN,' Wickham shouted, racing for the settling Night Hawk. 'Run, Dimitri!'

Fifty yards, Wickham judged as the two men stumbled through the low shrub trees. Their numbed appendages refused to respond in a coordinated fashion.

'Forty yards! Just forty yards,' Wickham shouted to Dimitri. His arm and shoulder shot excruciating pain through his body every time his right foot hit the ground. Wickham forced his mind to block the pain as he stumbled through the shrubs, limping, in a crouch to reduce the target area.

Buchanan saw a stream of fire trailing along another helicopter on the far side of the river. He took his eyes away to orient himself, then glanced back to see tracer rounds continue to pour from the stricken gunship as it slowly rolled over and flew into the muddy river.

'RUN! RUN,' Lincoln screamed as Wickham fell over the back of Dimitri.

'Move it! GO,' Wickham cried breathlessly as parts from the crashed helicopter rained down amid the chaos.

'Twenty yards,' Wickham shouted to Dimitri, then forcefully shoved the young CIA operative.

An automatic weapon opened up from the far side of the river, kicking up pieces of shrub tree immediately behind Scarecrow One.

Blackie Oaks returned fire with his M60 machine gun, silencing the heavy weapon, then sprayed the entire riverbank with tracer rounds.

'Major,' Oaks shouted over the intercom. 'Three is in the river! Some got out!'

Buchanan yelled over the intercom. 'Keep 'em covered, Gunny!'

Oaks answered with a hail of machine-gun fire directed back and forth over the downed Night Hawk.

Wickham and Dimitri reached the side of the Sikorsky as Lincoln jumped out to assist in boarding. The rotor wash was like a hurricane, whipping everything into a blur of dust and weeds.

Dimitri fell, picked himself up, then reached for the door as Lincoln thrust him bodily into the cabin. Wickham shoved on Dimitri, too, as the young agent rolled sideways into the fuselage.

Wickham reached up, grabbed the door, lifted his leg, then stopped in mid-stride as if someone had hit him in the back with a sledgehammer. He fell into the side of the fuselage, then rolled on his side, moaning.

Lincoln grabbed the agent and yelled for Gunny Oaks. Buchanan was shouting into the cabin as Oaks leaped out to help Lincoln get the CIA operative into the helicopter.

'What about Three?' Higgins shouted to Buchanan as the pilot added power and pulled up on the collective. 'We can't leave them here.'

'Goddamnit! I know that,' Buchanan shot back, raising the Night Hawk into the air, then pivoting around to face the river as Oaks scrambled aboard after Lincoln. Wickham was lying face down on the floor, bleeding profusely from the back wound.

'Pete, cover me while I try to get Jim's crew out,' Buchanan ordered as he eased the Sikorsky toward the far riverbank.

'Roger,' Barnes replied. 'We've got a Hind down. The other is running.'

'Stay in there,' Buchanan said, turning the Night Hawk so Lincoln would have a better view of the downed crew. 'Pete, spray the shoreline left of the gunship wreckage, the one you bagged.'

'Will do,' Barnes radioed as he swept low over the river in a forty-five degree bank, then pulled up steeply in preparation for a strafing run.

Buchanan could clearly see the crashed S-70 as he

crossed the riverbank. 'We've got survivors in the water. They're on the side of the Hawk.'

'I see them,' Barnes replied, then fired a stream of cannon fire down the length of the riverbank, concentrating the barrage where Buchanan had asked.

'Lower the chair,' Buchanan commanded, inching closer to the twisted wreckage. 'Keep up the fire, Gunny!'

'You got it, Major!' Oaks replied, raking the shoreline with his M60. 'Cap'n Barnes is givin' 'em some kinda hell.'

Buchanan didn't reply as he maneuvered the nimble Sikorsky over the downed sister ship. He could see three people hanging from the side of the overturned helicopter, clinging to a twisted rotor blade.

'We're going to be heavy, Major,' Lincoln said over the intercom.

'Who gives a shit,' Buchanan barked. 'We aren't leaving anyone.' The pilot waited a second, then added, 'Just keep firing, Linc, and I'll handle the decisions.'

THE WHITE HOUSE

Grant Wilkinson walked into the Oval Office, followed by Susan Blaylocke. The president was sitting in his recliner next to the crackling fire. Snow mixed with sleet fell steadily outside the warm office.

The Joint Chiefs of Staff, except Air Force General Ridenour, airborne in the 'Looking Glass' command post, sat across from the commander-in-chief.

'Have a seat,' the president motioned to the vacant divan facing the military commanders.

'Thank you,' Wilkinson replied as he waited for Blaylocke to sit down, then joined her.

The president looked at each individual in the room,

studying them at times, before speaking. 'Anyone have any questions, or, for that matter, suggestions, in regard to my actions thus far?'

'Sir,' Blaylocke paused, composing her words, 'there are some members of Congress who are less than pleased with the lack of information fr – '

'The bottom line,' the president interrupted. 'Please, Susan.'

The vice president, controlled, replied, 'They have been demanding an audience with you.'

'You know my feelings about that. You handle them, at least for the time being. I don't have the patience to endure any congressional pontificating at this time.'

The president shook his head in disgust. 'They all want more face-time on the evening news, so let them belly-ache for the time being. I've got enough problems.'

'Yes, sir,' Blaylocke answered, formulating a response for the congressmen.

'Any word on the Soviet submarines, Cliff?'

Howard turned toward the chief of Naval Operations, Admiral Grabow. 'Admiral?'

'The *Saratoga*'s ASW aircraft should have been over their targets five minutes ago.'

The president sat back.

'Your thoughts, Grant?' the president asked. 'I need some objective opinions.'

'Mister President,' Wilkinson said quietly, 'I would like to make a couple of observations before I suggest a possible course of action.'

'By all means.' The president reached for another cigar. 'We have a lot at stake, and I want everyone in this room to speak his mind honestly and openly. I want us to be perfectly candid with our thoughts, and, more to the point, our suggestions. Go ahead, Grant,' the president said, unwrapping his rum crook.

Wilkinson leaned forward slightly, as he always did, when he addressed a serious matter.

'Time is short. The point is, in my estimation, that it is finally time to stop placing any faith in the Soviet system. We have been made to look like fools again and again, sir, and I strongly believe we need to stand our ground. Even push a little, if we have to. I support your decision to sink the Soviet submarines.'

The president remained quiet. He looked over to Susan Blaylocke. 'You must have some feeling about our response.'

'Sir, I have never advocated using force to seek solutions with the Soviets.' Blaylocke smiled at Wilkinson in a friendly manner, then continued her conversation with the president.

'However, I agree one hundred percent with Grant. We are dealing with a stubborn, belligerent, and probably deranged Soviet leader. Zhilinkhov is threatening our future, our survival, and I endorse standing our ground on this issue. I don't see any other reasonable choice.'

The chairman of the Joint Chiefs raised his hand slightly, indicating he wished to respond.

'Go ahead, Admiral,' the president said, relighting his cigar.

'From a military standpoint,' Chambers looked at the other Joint Chiefs, 'we are on the razor's edge now. Sinking their submarines is a major step toward declared war.

'As Mister Wilkinson suggested earlier, sir,' Chambers continued, 'we could continue to press the Soviets with our carrier groups. However, I personally believe that would lead to open hostilities on a global basis.'

The president thought for a while, then asked the chairman a question. 'If that becomes the case, Admiral, do you believe we could contain the skirmishes to conventional weapons?'

Chambers looked uncomfortable. 'The members of the Joint Chiefs are in agreement that a regional conflict could be contained. Nuclear weapons, most likely, would not be used, although there is no guarantee.'

'But since this situation is global in nature,' the president responded, 'I assume you believe it would escalate into a full nuclear confrontation.'

'No doubt about it, sir.' Chambers paused, glancing at Wilkinson, then back to the president. 'Especially with Zhilinkhov at the helm.'

Wilkinson leaned forward again, addressing the president. 'Perhaps we should wait and see what Zhilinkhov's reaction will be after losing his submarines.'

'I agree,' the president responded, 'but I am going to press harder if he doesn't back off within the time frame I set. I am convinced Zhilinkhov will be quelled by the Politburo when they realize we are deadly serious. Serious enough to start sinking submarines.'

The president frowned. 'If not, I will order conventional strikes aimed at their airborne bomber forces, in addition to striking any Soviet submarines we feel are a threat to national security.'

An aide stepped into the office, unobtrusively carrying a message.

'Yes, Colonel,' the president said, surprised.

'Sir, General Ridenour is on the scrambler.'

'Thank you, Colonel,' the president responded, picking up a receiver to one of three phones at his side. 'General, how is everything?'

The Joint Chiefs, along with Blaylocke and Wilkinson, spoke quietly among themselves while the president listened to the Air Force general in the airborne command post. The group fell silent when the president placed the receiver back in its cradle.

314

'Well,' the president turned to Wilkinson, 'good and bad news. The submarines – all three – apparently have been sunk. No confirmation on one of them, but General Ridenour believes it went down.'

'The bad news?' Admiral Chambers asked, knowing the answer.

'We lost two aircraft. One crew did manage to get out safely. They're picking them up now.'

No one said a word in response, thinking about the scenario painted by Grant Wilkinson. Was this the prelude to a massive nuclear strike on the United States?

'Also,' the president said slowly, 'the two Navy fighters we cleared to engage the MiGs near Iceland – the MiGs that attacked the Air Force pilots – they shot down three, without any losses.'

Wilkinson sighed, then addressed the president in a firm manner. 'Sir, I recommend that you continue to send Zhilinkhov a strong message. It's time to follow up the submarine attack with a strike to the Soviet bomber group approaching Alaska.'

The president remained quiet, chin cupped in his left hand, studying the surprised looks on the faces surrounding him. No one said a word to the chief of staff.

'I agree, Grant,' the president replied, turning to Chambers. 'Admiral, order the attack.'

SCARECROW FLIGHT

'The Gunny's hit,' Lincoln shouted as Oaks slumped to the floor, holding his stomach, then fell forward in a heap. Blood had splattered over Lincoln, warm drops in the frigid night air.

'Take his place,' Buchanan yelled. 'Keep firing; keep the pressure on!'

PING!

A round hit the cockpit, slightly behind the copilot's head, causing him to jump.

'Jesus!' Higgins exclaimed, sliding down and forward in his seat. 'That was too damn close.'

'John,' Buchanan ordered, 'help Lincoln get 'em aboard before we all go in.'

Higgins nodded, unfastened his seat restraints, then crawled back into the cabin of the S-70.

'Linc,' Higgins shouted, 'you work the winch and I'll take the sixty!'

'Yessir,' Lincoln yelled in return, then moved across the cabin to the rescue winch.

Buchanan could see the three-pronged seat banging into the side of the downed Sikorsky. He couldn't believe anyone could have survived the crash impact. The gunship was a twisted wreck, split open like a watermelon dropped from fifty feet.

'Come on, guys,' Buchanan said under his breath as he stabilized the Night Hawk over the crew in the freezing water. 'Move it!'

Lincoln could see Charbonnet helping someone onto the chair. Time seemed to pass in slow motion as the Night Hawk's rotor blades whipped the surface of the muddy river into a frothy gale.

'Uh . . .' Higgins coughed.

Lincoln looked at Higgins a split second after the copilot took a round through the neck. The paramedic watched, horrified, as Higgins dropped to his knees, clutched his bleeding throat, then fell through the open side door. Higgins's body bounced off the tail rotor of the downed gunship, then disappeared under the surface of the churning water.

Lincoln pressed the retrieval switch on the hoist, then contacted Buchanan. 'Major, Captain Higgins is dead!'

316

'WHAT,' Buchanan shouted, concentrating on the rising rescue chair.

'The captain's dead, sir,' Lincoln yelled, looking at Dimitri. 'I'm gonna put the CIA guy on the sixty.'

'Do it,' Buchanan barked, then glanced back down at the chaotic struggle going on below the Sikorsky.

Lincoln motioned to the machine gun and ordered Dimitri to take the position. 'Start firing! Aim for the far bank. Just keep it moving.'

Dimitri responded slowly, inching toward the M60, as Lincoln grasped one of the gunners from Scarecrow Three and pulled him to safety.

More rounds impacted the hovering helicopter as the shocked paramedic quickly lowered the rescue seat into the maelstrom below.

THE KREMLIN

Zhilinkhov smiled maliciously, then reached for the decanter of vodka. 'The final steps are in . . . motion,' the general secretary slurred.

The Politburo members and the defense minister were not smiling, afraid of the consequences of this unprecedented action against the Americans.

They regretted endorsing Zhilinkhov as successor to the previous general secretary. The men knew the futility of trying to stop the momentum created by Zhilinkhov. They were implicated too deeply to salvage their credibility or their political positions. They had to rely on Zhilinkhov at this point.

'The Americans will relax, as I . . . predicted,' Zhilinkhov stammered. 'I will crush them . . . destroy them . . . very soon, my friends.'

The general secretary laughed, tossed down another

vodka, and exhaled sharply. 'To our future, comrades. We will control . . . finally control the world,' Zhilinkhov loudly proclaimed, motioning to Pulaev for another vodka.

'To the Motherland!' Zhilinkhov proclaimed, reaching for the tumbler offered by his friend. The general secretary poured a generous amount of the clear liquid into his glass, then held it up. 'To our victory, our future, comrades.'

Zhilinkhov laughed heartily, then sank back in his chair.

NEAR NOVGOROD

Buchanan watched the rescue chair descend to the water again, then added a small amount of power as Charbonnet helped his copilot onto the platform.

PZZING!

Buchanan involuntarily flinched as the small-arms round ricocheted off the side of the cockpit. He already had two holes in the windshield and one near his right foot.

'Come on, goddamnit, move it out,' Buchanan swore, feeling the perspiration running down his neck into the collar of his flight suit.

Dimitri fired at the riverbank in wild bursts. He was too cold to hold the machine gun steady, too tired to care. Finally, after the ammunition ran out, Dimitri stopped pulling the trigger and looked at Lincoln.

The paramedic, busy operating the hoist, kicked a loose M16 across the floor, hitting Dimitri in the shins. 'Use it,' Lincoln yelled at the agent.

Lincoln pulled the slightly injured copilot into the cabin and immediately tossed the rescue seat out the door.

'One to go, Major!' Lincoln reported, glancing down at 'Blackie' Oaks.

'Hang in there, kid,' the former gunnery sergeant said in a raspy voice, choking from the blood in his throat.

'Pete,' Buchanan shouted over the radio, 'I need more fire on the riverbank, north of the gunship!'

Buchanan heard static, then the reply from Scarecrow Two as the S-70 turned on its side in preparation for another strafing attack.

'Rolling in now, Buck,' Barnes reported, sweeping low over the elite *spetsnaz* troops. Two rockets landed in a concentration of Soviet soldiers as Barnes pulled up sharply, completing a modified hammerhead turn. Racing back down, Barnes switched to guns, leveled out, and sprayed the entire group of Russian troops, slowly walking his pedals back and forth.

Buchanan turned the hovering Sikorsky ninety degrees to the right, which pointed the tail toward the Soviet troops. The cockpit was already damaged from small-arms rounds and he was the only pilot controlling the gunship.

'Come on, Jim,' Buchanan said to himself as he watched Charbonnet embrace the rescue seat, then push off the side of the downed Night Hawk. There was no sign of the fourth crewman.

Buchanan, breathing a sigh of relief, added more power in preparation for the transition to forward flight.

Buchanan scanned his instruments, then looked down at Charbonnet. The pilot was slowly revolving on the rescue seat, framed by the turbulent rotor wash and foaming water.

PZZINNNG!

Another round caromed off the side of the cockpit, creating a crack in the windscreen directly in front of Buchanan. The scene was unbelievable.

319

'We're goin' to move out,' Buchanan shouted to Lincoln. 'I'll slow down so you can get him in when we clear the fire zone.'

'Yessir,' the paramedic replied, pushing the hoist cable away from the door as the S-70 began to accelerate and climb into the darkness.

Buchanan looked down at the same instant Charbonnet, fifteen feet below, slumped forward into the cable, rolled off the seat, and plummeted seventy feet into the riverbank. The pilot was dead before he impacted the thick mud.

'Pete,' Buchanan radioed, 'we lost Jim. Cover us. I'm off two-six-zero.'

'Gotcha in sight,' Barnes radioed. 'We've got company. Gunships – four or five – closin' like bats outa hell!'

'Stick tight, Pete,' Buchanan ordered, then concentrated on flying as low and fast as humanly possible.

'Rog,' Barnes replied, twisting the throttle to the limits. He watched the engine gauges closely, noting the powerful turboshaft engines were beginning to overtemp.

'They're closin' on us, Cap'n,' the crew chief of Scarecrow Two yelled, knowing his pilot was nursing every ounce of horsepower from the screaming, straining engines.

'Buck, they've got a runnin' start on us,' Barnes radioed. 'I'm gonna have to slow them down.'

Silence followed the radio transmission.

'You copy, Buck?' Barnes asked.

'Yeah,' Buchanan answered, knowing his friend, along with the crew of Scarecrow Two, would be annihilated if they engaged the division of approaching Soviet gunships. 'I copy,' Buchanan answered, feeling his stomach twist into knots.

'You owe me a beer!' Barnes radioed back, then pulled up hard into a high yo-yo.

Buchanan didn't answer, thinking instead about the letter he would have to write to Cindy Barnes.

Scarecrow Two rolled out of the steeply banked maneuver, facing head on to the three Mi-24 Hind-Ds, trailed by two Mi-28 Havoc advanced gunships.

Barnes fired the remaining air-to-air missiles, then switched to his Gatling gun.

'Open up,' Barnes shouted to his gunners as a Hind-D exploded directly in front of the Sikorsky, lighting the night for a mile in every direction.

'Holy shit,' Barnes yelled, pulling hard on the collective. The S-70 shot skyward, silhouetted in the flaming explosion, then rolled almost inverted. Barnes lined up a shot at another Hind-D as the Russian gunship raced past him.

'Steady on . . .' Barnes said to himself as he prepared to squeeze the firing button.

That was the last thought 'Pistol' Pete Barnes would ever have. The Russian gunner in the lead Havoc had placed his second SA-14 missile into the inlet particle deflector of the S-70's right engine.

The ensuing explosion decapitated both pilots, sending the Sikorsky Night Hawk out of control. The spinning helicopter plunged straight down, plowing into the ground in a thunderous fireball.

Steve Lincoln watched in total disbelief as Scarecrow Two exploded on impact. 'Captain Barnes went in, sir,' Lincoln shouted into the intercom.

'I know,' Buchanan replied, straining to see through the snow shower they had encountered.

Dimitri, shivering uncontrollably, crawled next to Wickham, who was breathing in shallow, quick gasps. The senior CIA agent was lying in a pool of his own blood.

'We're on our way out,' Dimitri said to Wickham. 'You'll be okay as soon as we – '

'Dimitri,' Wickham interrupted, 'tell the pilot . . . to get your . . . message out. Top priority . . .'

'Okay,' Dimitri responded quietly, covering the agent with a thin medical blanket.

'What'd he say?' Lincoln asked, glancing back and forth between the cabin and the pursuing gunships.

'The pilot . . . can he send a m-message? An important message to the – to Washington?' Dimitri asked, shivering violently in the cold cabin.

'Yeah,' Lincoln replied, glancing back to the Soviet helicopters. 'But now ain't a good time. Wait 'til we shake these guys, then I'll ask.'

'Okay,' Dimitri responded, then looked at Wickham. The young agent was stunned by what he saw. Wickham looked dead. His eyes, still open, had rolled back almost out of sight.

'No!' Dimitri cried, wringing his hands, totally devastated. 'Oh, no . . .'

The agent, tears rolling down his cheeks, slowly pulled the blood-soaked blanket up over Wickham, covering his head.

Dimitri, in the dark cabin and shivering with shock, couldn't see that his friend, Steve Wickham, had only passed out but was still breathing.

'You might as well cover the gunny, too,' the rescued copilot said as he struggled to enter the cockpit. 'He died a couple of minutes ago.'

Suddenly, two bright streaks raced past the Night Hawk, lighting the interior.

'Christ,' Buchanan shouted, popping off containers of metallic chaff. 'Here come the missiles.'

'Use some help?' the copilot of Scarecrow Three asked, climbing into the vacant seat.

322

'Damn right!' Buchanan answered, noticing the trickle of blood on the pilot's arm. 'You okay?'

'Think so,' the former Marine first lieutenant replied. 'Nothing too serious.'

Two, three, then four more streaks of light went flashing by the racing Night Hawk. A fifth missile tracked into a burst of decoy chaff, exploding fifty yards behind the Sikorsky.

'Linc,' Buchanan shouted, 'can you get a shot, any shot, at those bastards?'

'I think so, sir,' Lincoln replied, leaning out his side door as far as he dared without a restraint.

CRACK!!

The S-70 slewed sideways, then righted itself as Buchanan frantically scanned the engine gauges.

'We've been hit,' Lincoln groaned as he fell backwards, stumbling over the body of Blackie Oaks.

Dimitri could see that Lincoln was bleeding profusely from chest and head injuries. The paramedic had taken a good deal of the impact explosion from the Russian missile.

'Get back there and see what we have,' Buchanan ordered the copilot, then glanced at the blinking radar altimeter. 'Goddamn!' Buchanan quietly admonished himself. 'Pay attention, you stupid shit.'

THE KREMLIN

Two kitchen-staff servers gingerly placed large platters of zakuska on Zhilinkhov's dining table, then hastily exited the room. The brutal interrogations by the KGB had left deep psychological scars on the servants.

'Come, comrades,' Zhilinkhov said to his ill-at-ease friends. 'Let us enjoy these fine delicacies.'

The general secretary motioned for the men to take a seat, then half-fell into his large chair at the head of the massive wood table.

'Viktor Pavlovich,' Dichenkovko, his oldest friend, said softly, 'we need to talk with you about this plan.'

Tension hung in the air, pressing from every corner like walls converging on the individuals present in the dining room.

'What do you – wish to talk about?' Zhilinkhov stopped smiling, squinting menacingly. 'You do not like – you do not have the stomach for – this plan? For world dominance?'

Deadly silence filled the room, making it very uncomfortable for Dichenkovko and the other members. They knew their friend and leader had changed drastically in a short period of time. The five men were frightened, frightened for themselves and the future of the Soviet Union.

'Well,' Zhilinkhov said loudly, banging both fists on the table. He growled again, 'Say what you mean.'

Aleksandr Pulaev cleared his throat. 'We think now is not the opportune time to attack the Americans. Their allies will counterattack us, too. We have aroused a sleeping giant, along with his friends. We must allow time for a return to normal.'

'Left to you, my friend,' Zhilinkhov smiled crookedly, 'there would never be an opportune time!'

'Viktor Pavlovich,' Dichenkovko intervened, 'let us discuss this matter when we are refreshed and have a better assessment of the – '

'We will discuss the matter now,' Zhilinkhov said heatedly, then downed his vodka. 'You surprise me, my trusted friend. All of you. Look where . . . what I have accomplished. I am on the brink of . . . of global conquest . . .'

Zhilinkhov suddenly stopped, rising from his chair, tumbler in hand, to fix another drink.

'Now you tell me you have no stomach, no desire to fulfill our destiny, our commitment to the Party,' Zhilinkhov said as he turned around from the portable serving bar and waited for an answer.

'No, Viktor Pavlovich,' Yevstigneyev, the Politburo member responsible for party discipline, explained, 'we believe, like you, in the Party, our goals for the Motherland, our sense of respon – '

Without warning, an aide urgently rapped on the door and stepped into the room.

Zhilinkhov, surprised, knocked his drink into the sunken ice container, then turned around in a rage.

'Damnit, Colonel, what is it?' Zhilinkhov yelled, causing the senior officer to flinch.

'General Secretary,' the colonel pursed his lips, 'the spies have escaped.'

Zhilinkhov turned crimson, then hurled his tumbler at the wall, shattering glass across the room.

'OUT,' Zhilinkhov bellowed, enraged. 'Get out! Get me Air Marshal Khatchadovrian – NOW!'

The colonel, eyes wide in terror, backed toward the open door, barking orders to a subordinate.

The 'Inner Circle' members were stunned and frightened by the behavior of their general secretary. He was clearly out of control.

Zhilinkhov turned toward his fellow conspirators, talking softly at first. 'General Vranesevic is . . . he is dead,' Zhilinkhov yelled, then clutched his chest and staggered to the couch.

'Call the doctor!' Yegoery Yevstigneyev shouted to the colonel as he was closing the door. The senior Politburo member then went to the aid of his stricken friend, the general secretary of the Soviet Communist party.

325

17

SCARECROW ONE

Buchanan, half-turned in his seat, yelled to his new copilot. 'What's the damage?'

'The right gear. The missile took out the right gear and damaged the fuselage,' the young pilot answered, trying to help the wounded paramedic.

Buchanan turned around and looked down and back from the cockpit. What he saw made him realize the helicopter might roll over on landing. The entire wheel and structural mounts were missing. Fuel streamed along the underside of the S-70's fuselage, vaporizing as it departed the tail assembly.

The copilot donned a headset, then switched to 'hot mike', freeing his hands. 'Major, we're in for a rough landing.'

'Yeah,' Buchanan said grimly, inspecting the damage, 'if we have anything left to land.'

The coast was only minutes away for Scarecrow One and her crew. Buchanan glanced quickly at his engine instruments, still overtemped, then looked at the small chart strapped to his thigh. The map was highly detailed, narrow, and folded accordion style to facilitate monitoring.

Buchanan's flight path was clearly defined, including known obstacles circled in dark rings. The chart extended only five nautical miles on either side of the planned egress route.

'How close are those – ' Buchanan was cut off as

another missile flashed by the right side of the helicopter. The pilot punched the chaff button again, then watched the missile arch into the ground with a brilliant flash and explosion.

'Ho, Sweet Jesus,' Buchanan swore out loud. 'How close are those bastards?'

The copilot leaned out the side door as far as he dared, holding onto the overhead. The windchill was rapidly numbing his appendages, and he couldn't see clearly in the haze of snow whipping by his frozen ears. 'Can't tell for sure. Maybe a half to three-quarters of a mile.'

Buchanan looked at his chart again, then casually spoke to his new copilot-gunner. 'Well, I guess now is a good time to let 'em close up.'

'What?' the young pilot responded, shocked by Buchanan's intention. They would surely die if the Russian gunships got any closer. 'You gotta be kiddin', Major.'

Buchanan checked his chart again, adjusted the cockpit map light, then dropped the nose of his gunship to descend even lower into the black, snowy night.

'Just watch,' Buchanan answered the bewildered copilot. 'Stand by with the sixty, and hang on to your jockstrap!'

There was no reply as Buchanan started a turn to the right. The maneuver would allow the Soviet gunships to turn inside the S-70, closing the range between the combatants in a matter of seconds.

'Here we go,' Buchanan said soothingly, then rechecked his chart. The INS indicated only seven-tenths of a mile to the four eight-hundred-foot communications towers. Towers with many supporting guy wires fanning out in every direction.

'Come on, you Communist bastards,' Buchanan said quietly over the intercom, concentrating deeply on the task at hand. 'Come to the bait.'

Buchanan looked at the INS, then glanced quickly at the knee chart. Three-tenths of a mile. Seconds away in the racing gunship.

'Be there,' Buchanan said softly as he momentarily flicked on the landing lights.

'Hot damn!' the pilot said over the intercom, while watching the INS. 'Perfect!'

Buchanan stared to his right, counting. 'One-thousand-one,' he said under his breath as he waited for the S-70 to be precisely abeam the towers.

'One-thousand-two,' Buchanan continued, looking at the faint image of the steel towers. He could barely see the bases of the structures and their associated buildings in the blinding snow.

'One-thousand-three,' Buchanan said as he began to slowly tighten his turn around and in front of the massive towers, almost invisible under the dark, snow-laden clouds. The blinking lights on top of the tall towers were obscured in the low coastal overcast.

'Major,' the copilot shouted into the intercom, fingers flexing on the M60 trigger, 'they're closin' in fast!'

'Good,' was the only reply from Buchanan as he concentrated on flying the arc around the tower complex. 'They'll have a real sweet surprise.'

Six seconds passed as Buchanan's mouth turned dry. 'Come on . . .' the pilot said to himself, beginning to have a shadow of a doubt.

A brilliant flash, followed in a nanosecond by another blinding flash, marked the end of two Russian gunships. They had flown into the first two towers and supporting guy wires.

The thundering roar of the dual explosions reached Buchanan's ears as night turned into daylight. Wreckage from the two Hind-Ds was tumbling across the ground, igniting everything in reach, including the support buildings.

'Goddamn,' the copilot yelled, inadvertently firing a short burst into the towers speeding past one hundred feet away. 'You knocked two of th – '

A deafening report interrupted the copilot.

Another Soviet gunship, the crew shocked and blinded by the first two explosions, flew into the guy wires of the fourth tower. The third explosion added flaming wreckage, raining down with secondary explosions, to the huge conflagration enveloping the complex. The tall towers were collapsing in a slowmotion ballet.

Buchanan twisted around and saw another chopper pull straight into the vertical, narrowly missing tower three, and enter the overcast at a high rate of speed.

'We're out,' Buchanan whooped, turning back on course. He looked down at his shaking hands. 'Calm down,' he said to himself, then eased off the power from the straining engines. 'Stay together, baby,' he coaxed. 'We're going to make it to the ship.'

A bright flash shocked Buchanan back to the moment. 'What the hell . . .?'

'Another one,' the copilot shouted. 'Another chopper went in! Think it was the guy who pulled up in the clouds. I mean he went straight in.'

'No doubt,' Buchanan answered. 'They don't receive much instrument training.' The pilot looked back at his copilot. 'Probably got vertigo in the overcast, goin' straight up, and fell through the bottom out of control.'

'Jesus, Major.' The copilot paused. 'I've seen a lot, but I've never seen anything to top this. Unreal . . .' the copilot remarked, then added, 'I don't see any more gunships, sir.'

'Well, we ain't home yet,' Buchanan responded, eyes darting to the instrument panel for the thousandth time.

'Damn,' Buchanan shouted over the intercom. 'We're losin' gas at a hell of a rate.'

The copilot, stepping over the shocked Dimitri, leaped forward to the cockpit. 'Bet a line got punctured when we took the hit.'

'Yeah . . . Shit!' Buchanan swore again, mentally calculating the distance to the recovery ship compared to fuel-loss rate. The gauges were dropping rapidly.

Dimitri clambered to his feet, then approached the cockpit. 'Sir?' Dimitri asked tentatively.

Buchanan, having forgotten about his passengers, was startled by the agent.

'Yeah,' the irritated pilot said in a harsh tone, 'what can I do for you?'

'Sir, I need . . . I have been ordered to send a priority message to the White House, or . . . to the Central Intelligence Agen – '

'Christ,' Buchanan interrupted tersely, 'which is it?'

'I guess I better send it to the White House,' Dimitri stammered, still shivering.

Buchanan leaned closer to his copilot. 'You gotta be kiddin' me. This guy was a CIA agent in Moscow?'

The copilot cracked a small grin, then busily strapped himself into his seat.

'We'll send it Top Secret, scrambled.' Buchanan looked over at Dimitri. 'Best we can do from the helo.'

'Yes, sir,' Dimitri replied earnestly. 'That will be great.'

The young agent was exhilarated at being – alive, but deeply saddened by the death of his friend, Steve Wickham. Dimitri knew he would have died, on more than one occasion, if it had not been for Wickham. The senior agent had sacrificed himself for the Kremlin operative.

'What's the message?' Buchanan asked Dimitri.

The president and his staff, along with the Joint Chiefs, had reconvened in the Situation Room. The fatigue was felt by everyone, gnawing at their patience.

Ted Corbin had been summoned to the room and looked nervous, hands together, head down. He sensed everyone believed his subordinates had screwed the entire effort in the Kremlin.

'What is the status of the rescue effort, Ted?' Wilkinson asked gently, trying to remain steadfast to the CIA director.

'We haven't heard anything as of yet,' Corbin answered without looking the chief of staff in the eye. 'My people expect to have an update very soon. The helicopters, according to our estimate, should be on the way back. They should have departed Novgorod by now, if they didn't meet any resistance.'

The president, looking through his update folder, addressed Wilkinson. 'Grant, where do we stand?'

'Sir,' Wilkinson said, standing up and turning to the global situation display facing the president. 'Our Teal Ruby satellites indicate numerous Soviet missiles and launch vehicles in the final stages of launch preparation. Same with the submarines, sir.'

Wilkinson tapped a button, then waited a second until a more graphic overview lighted the screen.

'Soviet conventional forces are making a show of standing down, but the nuclear forces are still poised for a strike in these areas.'

Wilkinson pointed to strategic centers in Russia, under the ice cap in the Arctic Ocean, and to the Atlantic Ocean near the Newfoundland Basin.

'The carrier *Baku* has joined the *Kiev* in the North Atlantic. They are in a position to strike anywhere in

Europe or England. Sir, they've got us encircled,' Wilkinson pointed to the display, 'along with our NATO allies.'

'Goddamnit,' the president said angrily. 'The son-of-a-bitch is going to force us to remain in a high defense posture. Well, by God, his time is up. We'll push back and see if Zhilinkhov wants to turn up the heat,' the president said, standing up. 'Admiral Chambers, have the carrier groups launch fighterbomber sorties to stand off Soviet airspace.'

'Yes, sir,' Chambers replied, turning to Admiral Grabow.

A soft buzzer sounded, interrupting the oppressive tension spreading through the room.

'Yes,' the president responded, irritation written on his face, 'what is it?'

The four ceiling speakers came to life. 'Mister President, we have a Top Secret, scrambled message from Scarecrow One.'

The president, bewildered, looked at Grant Wilkinson. 'Who the hell is Scarecrow One?'

Corbin looked up, surprised. 'Scarecrow One is our rescue commander. He has the capability to send satellite direct anywhere in the world.' The CIA director appeared very tense, tapping his pen on the face of his watch.

'Patch him through,' the president ordered, then sat back down in his seat.

'Yes, sir,' the soft voice replied. 'The feed is open, Mister President.'

Everyone waited, anxiety written on each face. Time seemed to have stopped.

'Mister President, Brad Buchanan, commander of Scarecrow One,' the pilot said clearly.

'We hear you,' the president responded calmly, 'loud and clear.'

332

'Sir, the surviving agent we have on board has an urgent message to relay to – '

The president interrupted. 'What do you mean, surviving agent?'

'The other agent died from his wounds, sir,' Buchanan explained, not knowing Wickham was still alive. 'We have him on board.'

'Please continue,' the president asked, glancing at Wilkinson, then Admiral Chambers.

'The surviving agent was the Kremlin operative.' Buchanan paused. First formulating his words silently, he then spoke slowly and clearly. 'Mister President, the agent states, categorically, that the Soviet general secretary is going to launch a preemptive nuclear strike – a first strike – against the United States.'

'What?' the president almost shouted. He was incredulous, staring up at the speaker as if it were human in form. 'Let me speak with him.'

'I'll put him on, sir,' Buchanan replied, not knowing what else he could say to the commander-in-chief of his country. 'It will take a few seconds.'

During the ten-second pause, every person in the room, with the exception of the president, looked at each other, stares meeting blank stares.

A tentative voice came over the speaker, halting in manner. 'Mister President, my name is Leonid Vochik, and I have been – '

'Yes, go on,' the president responded brusquely, reaching for a rum crook.

Dimitri inhaled deeply, then spoke. 'I heard General Secretary Zhilinkhov say he is going to strike America with nuclear missiles.'

'Who did he say that to?' the president asked.

'Three of the Politburo members, and a former member,' Dimitri said, gaining confidence in himself.

333

'The defense minister was there, too, and the chief of the general staff knows about the strike plans. No one else knows anything. Only the seven of them, sir.'

'Wait a moment,' the president ordered, then turned to Corbin, speaking in a low whisper.

'How reliable is this agent?' the president asked. 'Can we believe him, really trust him?'

'Sir, he is considered extremely reliable,' Corbin said defensively. 'Dimitri was handpicked and has done an excellent job. He isn't a quick study, but he is absolutely loyal to the United States. He wouldn't make up something like this. Dimitri has no reason, no motive, to lie, sir.'

'Okay, son,' the president continued, 'when did you hear him make the comment about striking the United States?'

'Before he left for Lajes,' Dimitri answered, 'to see you, Mister President.'

'That sonofabitch!' Wilkinson seethed, knowing his hypothesis about Zhilinkhov's plans had been right. He never anticipated his thoughts would be so shockingly confirmed.

'What, precisely, did the general secretary say?' the president asked in a tense voice.

'He said that when the Soviet Union withdraws its forces, America would relax, and Russia would strike with nuclear and chemical missiles. He said it would be very soon, Mister President.' Dimitri was relieved to get it all out.

The president still had doubts. His mind was reluctant to comprehend this astonishing disclosure.

'Okay, son,' the president continued in a cordial manner. 'Glad we got you out of there. You have performed well.'

'Thank you, Mister President,' Dimitri responded with pride in his voice.

The speakers fell silent as the president stood up and walked around the table.

'Go to DEFCON-One,' the chief executive said, trembling. 'We'll go with a second attack to the Soviet bombers to get Zhilinkhov's attention.'

MOSCOW

Zhilinkhov had been placed in bed, his speech distorted by the massive stroke he had suffered only minutes before. The news had spread rapidly through the Kremlin hierarchy but had been contained within the confines of the building. No one outside the Kremlin was to know anything.

'Comrade Doctor,' Pulaev, the elder Politburo member, asked, 'what are his chances for recovery?'

'Too early to tell,' replied the portly physician. 'Next twenty-four to thirty-six hours will tell us much. He needs rest, and this medication, for the time being.'

The doctor handed Pulaev a small container of capsules. 'I'll be just down the hallway, in the clinic, if the general secretary needs anything.'

The Kremlin clinic had every imaginable piece of medical and emergency equipment available, courtesy of Western generosity. A complete operating theater was staffed around the clock, seven days a week, by three doctors and four nurses.

The Politburo members and the defense minister gathered around Zhilinkhov. Dichenkovko patted Zhilinkhov's limp hands. 'Viktor Pavlovich, the doctor says you will be fine.' Zhilinkhov's pale lips twitched in response. 'You must rest for now. We will be with you.'

Zhilinkhov rolled his eyes upward to focus on his friends. His face continued to look menacing, twisted in anger and pain, while he stared at his fellow comrades. Zhilinkhov willed his left hand to move slightly, grasping his oldest friend around the wrist. The general secretary still had a powerful grip.

'Strike . . . America,' Zhilinkhov gurgled, 'or I will order . . .'

'Yes, Viktor Pavlovich,' Dichenkovko replied, then encouraged the weakened leader to take a capsule.

Zhilinkhov swallowed the medicine sluggishly, then looked up. 'Now . . . strike now.'

The youngest Politburo member, Nikolai Velekhin, discreetly motioned to his friends to step across the room. The bedroom fireplace, providing a variety of continuous noises, would conceal their conversation from the general secretary.

'Viktor Pavlovich is going to carry out his plan,' the newer member whispered. 'It is too soon to strike the Americans. They are well prepared and could strike first. Their spies – what do they know? Where are they? We must do something before it is too late. For all of us. Viktor Pavlovich has the power to launch the strike by himself. The military commanders will not question the general secretary.'

'Calm yourself. We must have patience,' Yevstigneyev said nervously. 'He will sleep for a while, then we can discuss this matter with him. We must remain silent, my friends. We cannot act on our own.'

Zhilinkhov lay quietly as he listened to the conversation of his coconspirators. His mind, although medicated, was clear in his purpose, his goal. He would not be denied in his quest. The general secretary of the Soviet Communist party would indeed strike a massive blow to the United States.

Zhilinkhov knew it would be only a matter of hours before the course of world history would be altered forever. He would recover from his stroke and rule the entire planet.

The general secretary dozed off as Colonel General Vranesevic quietly entered the room. He remained by the door, beckoning the group.

Dichenkovko led the men to the door. 'What is it, General?'

'The Americans,' Vranesevic swallowed, 'have sunk three of our submarines, off the Florida coast.'

Dichenkovko, along with the other members, turned toward the sleeping Zhilinkhov. 'We must not disclose this to Viktor Pavlovich.'

18

The president, vice president, chief of staff, close cabinet members, and the military Joint Chiefs of Staff crowded into the White House Situation Room. The walls were covered with various screens, maps, projections, and satellite data.

Grant Wilkinson had been in private conference with Cliff Howard, secretary of defense, and the Joint Chiefs for the past twenty minutes.

Wilkinson spoke first. 'Mister President, Admiral Chambers will speak for the Joint Chiefs.'

Chambers looked uneasy. 'Sir, I know I was skeptical about the scenario painted by Mister Wilkinson. I'm still apprehensive about this whole affair.' Chambers inhaled, breathing deeply. 'However, after analyzing all the data we currently have, along with the present Soviet nuclear status, I would conclude, I would have to say a Soviet first strike is a very real probability.'

The president sat quietly a few seconds, turned to his right, then addressed the Joint Chiefs. 'Gentlemen, how do you view this revelation?'

General Hollingsworth, the Marine Corps commandant, spoke first. 'Sir, you met Zhilinkhov. What does he have to lose?' Hollingsworth didn't wait for an answer.

'His country is in shambles and rapidly eroding. Their only grasp, as far as power, is their military. Especially their massive nuclear capability.'

The general reached for his water glass, sipped a small amount to moisten his throat, then continued.

'SDI would render them almost impotent. The entire picture is a very real and very frightening situation. Sir, I believe we need . . . Well, I'll let Mister Wilkinson explain our position.'

'No, you say whatever is on your mind, General,' the president said, lighting his rum crook.

'Well, sir,' Hollingsworth replied, 'as I'm sure you're aware, we've had options in the plans for just such a situation as a worst case – '

'What kind of situation?' the president asked, puffing lightly on the sweet cigar.

'Possible first-strike scenarios, sir,' Hollingsworth said, darting a look at Wilkinson.

The president remained quiet. The room was totally void of noise, tomblike.

'Grant,' the president said, sitting upright in his chair.

Wilkinson eyed the president, took a deep breath, then spoke directly to him, ignoring the remainder of the staff members.

'Mister President,' Wilkinson began, 'we've been together, politically, and as friends, for what would we say . . . twenty-three years?'

'That's right.'

The president placed his cigar down, clasped his hands, fingers entwined, then looked Wilkinson in the eye. 'Explain your position.'

'Sir, we,' Wilkinson spoke very slowly, 'the Joint Chiefs, Cliff Howard, and I, believe the United States should initiate a preemptive strike, a nuclear first strike against the Soviet Union.'

The room remained quiet as the stunned president and vice president stared at Wilkinson, not quite seeing the chief of staff in their shock. Herb Kohlhammer, slowly shaking his head, was speechless.

'For God's sake,' the president exploded, looking appalled at the thought. 'You're serious! All of you!'

Grant Wilkinson stretched both arms on the table, palms down. 'Sir, we are in a position from which we can't extricate ourselves.' Wilkinson looked down for a moment, then returned his scan to the president. 'Grid-locked, sir. Checkmated.'

'Jesus, Grant,' the president said, exasperation written on his face. 'You can't be serious.'

'Sir,' Wilkinson continued, 'we have finally reached a point of no return. We can't go back to yesterday and put another Band-Aid on the problem. We have finally been placed in a no-win position.' Wilkinson looked at Chambers, then back to the president. 'No recourse.'

'Grant, we are the leaders of the United States of America,' the president said. 'Your proposal is absolutely unthinkable.'

Wilkinson spoke slowly and forcefully. 'Sir, we have no other choice. They've provoked us to the brink of war to test our reactions. They've attacked our space shuttle and SDI satellites. Their nuclear forces, en masse, are waiting for the order from the Kremlin, and we –'

Wilkinson stopped abruptly, looking down the table at the chairman of the Joint Chiefs, then focused his eyes on the president.

'We have a trusted and loyal Kremlin operative, in direct contact with Zhilinkhov, corroborate our worst-case situation.' Wilkinson thought for a second. 'The agent could have had no idea we had reached the same conclusion.'

Wilkinson leaned forward, then spoke quietly. 'The Soviets, sir, are going to blow us off the face of the earth.

Zhilinkhov doesn't need the endorsement of anyone to order the strike. You know that.'

Wilkinson leaned back, then stared at the president. The chief of staff had to hold his hands together to keep them from shaking.

Wilkinson spoke again. 'Sir, the Soviets . . . Zhilinkhov . . . is doing exactly what our Kremlin agent – '

'Dimitri,' General Hollingsworth quietly provided.

'What Dimitri said. Precisely. This isn't coincidence, sir. Our operative broke the absolute rule of contact to get this information to us. He went through hell to escape after the KGB disaster, then saw his mentor killed. Yet, he remained rational and got the message to us.'

The chief of staff waited a few seconds. 'Mister President,' Wilkinson drew in a breath, 'I believe him. We've been exposed to Zhilinkhov. I don't have a doubt in my mind.' Wilkinson paused, composing his thoughts. 'Sir, the picture is absolutely clear.'

'Wait a minute,' the president said. 'Zhilinkhov isn't going to live forever.'

'True,' Wilkinson replied. 'There are seven people, at the top, involved in this. We don't have any way of knowing what the other six would do with Zhilinkhov out of the picture. We aren't in a position to wait and see, sir. Zhilinkhov has only to give the order and it will be carried out.'

Wilkinson looked at Admiral Chambers, then back to the commander-in-chief. 'Mister President, you have the same prerogative.'

No one spoke a word.

'Sir, we don't have much time,' Wilkinson said gently. 'Zhilinkhov is a very mercurial person. We have no idea what he'll do next, or when. We only know he is going to pull the trigger.'

Wilkinson waited a moment, then continued, 'I understand how you feel. Until I analyzed this situation, bombing the Soviets first would have been the last thing on my mind.' Wilkinson looked at Blaylocke. 'Unthinkable. Reprehensible.'

'Americans, Grant,' the president said, 'we're Americans, for the love of God.'

'Sir, we can sit here extolling the virtues of the American way of life and watch two hundred million Americans be annihilated,' Wilkinson paused, 'or we can render the Soviet Communist party helpless, with minimal damage to the United States.'

The president didn't reply.

'Sure, we'll take some damage,' Wilkinson said, becoming more forceful, 'but it won't be a Pyrrhic victory.'

Wilkinson waited a few seconds, anticipating questions. No one said a word as startled minds tried to comprehend the magnitude of the suggestion before them. Bomb the Soviet Union.

'Our other option,' Wilkinson continued, 'is to do nothing, remain in DEFCON-One, and wait for the eventual onslaught. We'll lose tens of millions of lives, at the least, and the America we enjoy will be gone forever.'

The president had a blank look on his face as he leaned back in his seat.

'Mister President,' Wilkinson said in a pleading manner, 'you do have an obligation to the American people. An obligation, sir, to protect them.'

The president looked at Blaylocke. 'I want to hear from Susan, Cliff, and Herb.'

'I'm in shock,' the vice president began, looking around the table. 'But I can see the logic in what Grant is telling us, regardless of how horrible it is.'

Blaylocke looked at the president before speaking

again. 'If I'm honest, gentlemen, I must say I've thought about this concept more than once, even today, privately. It was just a shock to hear someone voice the possibility, the unthinkable, as the president said.'

The president interrupted. 'We just can't arbitrarily push the button and destroy the Soviet Union!' The president looked perplexed. 'We have to apprise members of Congress and – '

'Sir,' Wilkinson interjected, 'if we get Congress embroiled in this, you will be facing impeachment proceedings.' Wilkinson almost shouted. 'We'll be waist-deep in rubble before Congress even gets the hearings underway. Mister President, Zhilinkhov has the power to destroy us, and he is going to use it.'

'Cliff,' the president said, ignoring Wilkinson, 'what is your position in this matter?'

Howard, very controlled, addressed the president. 'Sir, I can only reiterate what Grant said. We're going to take battle damage regardless of what we elect to do. The question is, in my opinion, how much damage do we intend to take? Are we willing to risk losing everything? Are we willing to see America, as we know it, gone forever? Our hard-won freedom, sir, tossed away, along with millions of lives? I don't think so.'

The president glanced at Wilkinson, saw him move his head slowly back and forth.

'The choice has been made for us,' Howard said, sadness in his voice. 'I urge you to initiate a preemptive strike on the Soviet Union.' Howard waited for a response from the president.

When he didn't receive any acknowledgement, he continued. 'Now, Mister President, while we have a choice in the outcome. The future of this country, this nation and its people, rests on your decision, sir.'

The president, stunned, stared at the defense secretary with unfocused eyes.

THE KREMLIN

A quiet knock on the heavy doors preceded the entry of the somewhat stout Russian physician, followed by a nurse and a military aide.

The doctor examined the general secretary, noting that he was conscious but not attempting to speak. He seemed to be in very stable condition and resting well.

'Comrade General Secretary,' the doctor said, 'you are making excellent progress.' The cardiologist smiled in a perfunctory manner. 'Can you move your fingers for me?'

Zhilinkhov responded weakly, appearing irritated, or in pain. The doctor knew he had to be careful not to agitate the party boss. Two more hours would see him off duty, relaxing with a vodka, and letting that slob, Doctor Pyadyshev, take the hot seat. No one wanted to be on duty if something happened to Zhilinkhov.

'Do you have any pain?' the cardiologist asked, checking Zhilinkhov's vital signs.

Zhilinkhov moved his head very slowly, indicating no. He still had not attempted to speak.

The military aide remained quiet, but nervous, as the doctor patted Zhilinkhov's shoulder and gathered his instruments. He gave the nurse instructions, then turned back to Zhilinkhov.

'I will check on you in another hour, comrade,' the doctor said unctuously. 'Rest well, and try to sleep, if possible.'

The doctor walked across the room, opened the huge door, and, relieved, quietly exited the private quarters of the party general secretary.

As soon as the massive door shut, the military aide leaned over Zhilinkhov. 'Comrade General Secretary, I am pleased to inform you that Colonel General Vranesevic reports the spies have been killed.'

Zhilinkhov rolled his eyes back toward the top of his head and attempted to speak. 'Con . . . firm . . .'

'Sir,' the aide said, delighted to bring the general secretary good news, 'all three American helicopters were downed, with no survivors. This has been confirmed, General Secretary.' The aide stepped back a pace, reflecting a high degree of military discipline.

Zhilinkhov, a faint smile spreading across his sallow, craggy face, nodded. He was obviously pleased by the good news. His secret was safe, and the Americans would be destroyed.

Colonel General Vranesevic had used the holocaust at the communications towers to conceal the spies' escape. The carnage was unrecognizable as either American or Soviet, thus sparing his life and career.

Zhilinkhov whispered to the aide, deeply slurring his words. He wanted his coconspirators in his presence immediately.

'Yes, Comrade General Secretary,' the aide replied, standing erect at attention. 'Immediately.'

19

THE WHITE HOUSE

The president had taken off his suit coat, opened his collar, and donned a white cardigan sweater. He looked haggard and his stomach was causing him great discomfort.

'Herb, what is your opinion, your honest opinion, about this preemptive attack?' the president asked, gently rubbing his temples, elbows resting on the shining table.

'I can't comprehend it, sir.' Kohlhammer exhaled, his body seeming to deflate. 'I don't agree with the proposal. It's sheer madness. We would be the terrorist of the planet . . . if we survived the retaliation.'

'Susan.' The president turned lightly to face his vice president. 'I want it straight.'

'I'll tell you straight,' Blaylocke answered with a serious look. 'I always have, sir.'

'I know, Susan,' the president replied. 'Sorry. I'm tired, and confused.'

Blaylocke turned toward the chairman of the Joint Chiefs of Staff. 'Admiral Chambers, before I go on record about this preemptive operation, I want to understand the details, the plan of action, if you will.'

Every eye turned to the highest ranking officer in the military services.

'We – the Joint Chiefs have reviewed this scenario from a tactical standpoint and conclude, unanimously, that a preemptive nuclear strike against the Soviet Union is feasible. We will prevail, no question about it,' Chambers said in a controlled voice. 'I am not in a position to address the political or economic ramifications.'

The president spoke to Chambers. 'What about Milt Ridenour? Is he in concurrence with this . . . action?'

'Yes, sir. Unequivocally,' Chambers replied, feeling the president was beginning to respond to the inevitable. 'You can confirm that, sir. He is immediately available in the "Looking Glass".'

'I will, Admiral, if this continues in the developmental stage.' The president, jaw set, looked into Chambers's eyes. The face of the chairman reflected a grim determination.

'Continue your brief, Admiral,' the president said, rubbing his temples.

'We can inform our theater commanders, via secure net, to prepare for an imminent nuclear strike. This will allow us to place our missiles closest to the Soviet Union on the primary targets in the least amount of time.'

'What about the Warsaw Pact nations?' Blaylocke asked, jotting notes on her legal pad.

'We will confine their involvement, as much as possible, to conventional weapons. The major strikes – nuclear strikes – will be confined to the military installations, manufacturing plants, cosmodromes, and other strategic locations.'

'Cosmodromes?' Blaylocke asked, a quizzical look on her face.

'Yes, ma'am,' Chambers replied politely. 'We have to take away any residual capability to launch space vehicles of any kind, including their two space shuttles, *Buran* and *Ptichka*. We will eliminate the Baikonur Cosmodrome at Tyuratan, along with various other launch sites, including the cosmodrome at Plesetsk.'

'What about the Soviet submarines?' the president asked.

'We will be able to eliminate perhaps forty to fifty percent of their submarines before they can respond, sir. Our hunterkiller submarines and ASW aircraft are dogging them now.'

'I'm afraid, Admiral,' the president interrupted, 'that I don't share your confidence in our ability to track Soviet submarines.'

'Excuse me, sir?' Chambers responded in a surprised voice. The president had never been so caustic in a meeting with the Joint Chiefs.

'If you will recall, Admiral, the incident in late 1986,' the president leaned forward across the table, 'when one of our attack submarines – the USS *Augusta* – while cruising underwater off Gibraltar, collided with a god-damn Russian submarine.'

The president sat back in his chair and waited a couple of seconds. 'They never even heard it!'

Chambers cleared his throat. Only a privileged few knew about the embarrassing incident. 'We can't destroy all the Russian submarines, sir, but we anticipate our antimissile systems will be able to eliminate most warheads that do get airborne.'

'That still leaves warheads that are going to impact the continental United States.' The president paused, reflectively. 'Not to mention Alaska and Hawaii.'

'Yes, sir,' Chambers said, feeling a dampness under his uniform blouse. 'That is true, no question about it.'

'And the Soviet bombers?' the president asked, staring intently at the chairman of the Joint Chiefs. 'The ones we don't get in our strike?'

'We'll be able to down the majority, but ...' Chambers slowed, looking tired, 'we'll receive some impact damage. Primarily from cruise missiles.'

'Any projections as to the Soviet priorities, Admiral?' Blaylocke asked, noticing Grant Wilkinson had not said a word during this question-and-answer session.

'Only speculation,' Chambers answered in a cordial manner, ever the gentleman. 'Military primarily, then secondary targets. We simply can't project that information with any degree of accuracy.'

'What amount of damage can we expect to sustain?' Blaylocke paused, writing continuously on her legal pad. 'Realistically?'

'We'll receive considerable damage. Probably greater than our projections, to tell you the truth,' Chambers answered, holding up his hand to indicate he wasn't finished. 'However, I can tell you it will be a fraction of the damage we will receive if the Soviets strike first.'

Chambers stopped for a moment, then added a serious warning. 'You must consider the difference. Think about it. We have been given a warning. An opportunity to control our destiny.'

The room remained quiet while everyone digested what Chambers had said.

'The Joint Chiefs,' Chambers continued, 'are convinced, as are the chief of staff and the secretary of defense, that a Soviet preemptive strike is imminent and inevitable, Mister President.'

The president looked at his vice president. 'Okay, give me your decision, Susan.'

'Sir, I have been trained for years to gather all the information, analyze the material, then make a clinical, unbiased, objective decision.' The vice president looked around the room. Every eye met hers.

Blaylocke continued, confident, clear of voice. 'As I see it we are faced with doing nothing with every warning light flashing, and accepting the consequences, whatever they may be.'

349

Blaylocke looked at her yellow pad. 'Or we can follow the course presented by Admiral Chambers and – '

'On the word of a Soviet emigrant? A neophyte in the CIA?' the president asked, a surprised look in his weary, bloodshot eyes.

'Please, let me have the floor,' Blaylocke asked in an even, pleasant voice.

'I'm sorry, Susan. Please continue,' the president replied, clearly distraught over the possibility of nuclear warfare.

'Or,' Blaylocke continued, 'we can follow the suggestion of the military experts, with the support of Grant and Cliff, and preempt the Soviets.'

Blaylocke removed her glasses before speaking again. 'We control the situation, not the Soviets.'

Susan Blaylocke looked at Chambers, then Wilkinson, before concluding her remarks. 'That is about it, my considered judgement, Mister President,' Blaylocke said. 'I'm satisfied that we don't have a choice. The bell has sounded, and we're waiting to see who throws the first punch.'

Chambers replied, 'A very astute analogy, ma'am. This is, in fact, a first-punch fight. There won't be another chance for the runner-up.'

The room remained hushed while the president of the United States of America digested the proposed action. It was unprecedented.

Grant Wilkinson broke the silence. 'Sir, TASS, *Izvestia, Moskovskii Komsomolyets*, along with various other Soviet media, are reporting the death of the American spies. We know that Zhilinkhov believes that blatant lie, or heads would have rolled by this time.'

'Please make your point, Grant,' the president said, impatience beginning to show on his strained face.

350

'Zhilinkhov is insane, desperate, sir,' Wilkinson continued. 'Now he believes his plan is still safe because the Kremlin operative is dead. We don't know when he will strike. We only know he intends to blast us into oblivion.'

Wilkinson exhaled sharply, looked at the ceiling, then back to the president. 'We either strike first, Mister President,' Wilkinson waited a long four seconds, 'or we become a nation that was.'

'I just need more information, more intelligence before I can make a decision affecting the future of this planet,' the president said, as much to himself as to anyone around the elaborate table.

'With respect, sir,' Wilkinson said in a soothing tone, 'the next piece of information you receive will most likely be a Russian warhead penetrating the roof.'

'Goddamnit, Grant,' the president shouted, shocking the entire staff, 'I need time, time to think this through and arrive at a logical conclusion.'

The room returned to silence, tension straining nerves to the breaking point. Fear began to grip the minds of the staff members.

'Sir,' Susan Blaylocke leaned over to the president, talking gently, 'would you consider taking a short break?'

'No, Susan,' the president replied in a calm voice. 'We need to resolve this. Now.'

Wilkinson started to speak, then fell silent as he saw the president raise his pencil and start pointing, running the pencil back and forth, at the chairman of the Joint Chiefs.

'Admiral,' the president began slowly, once again in control of himself, 'the lives of millions of people, let alone the future of this country – the future of the world – are on the line.'

The president grabbed his pencil with both hands,

351

holding it in front of his face. 'You are convinced, along with the other military chiefs, that we have no other choice: we must launch a nuclear strike against the Soviet Union? You are totally, unequivocally, convinced this course of action is in the best interest of the United States?'

Chambers sat up straight, shoulders squared, and looked into the president's eyes. 'Yes, sir.'

SNAP!!

The broken pencil sounded like a rifle shot in the quiet, tense room. Every person in the room flinched or jumped nervously.

'Grant?' the president asked, holding both ends of the severed pencil.

'We have no choice!' Wilkinson exclaimed sharply, then replied quietly. 'Mister President, I fully endorse the proposed preemptive strike. I will undoubtedly have nightmares for the rest of my life, but I have a responsibility. The choice has been made for us, sir, and that is a significant point. We must act to preserve our country and our freedom.'

'Susan?' the president bluntly asked his second-in-command.

'As painful as this is for me, for all of us, I agree with Grant and the Joint Chiefs, sir.'

'Cliff?' The president looked across the table at his secretary of defense.

'No other plausible choice, sir.' Howard cleaned his glasses, then replaced them on his nose. He adjusted the fit and met the president's stare. 'Time is running out, Mister President.'

'Herb?' the president placed the broken pencil pieces on the table, then looked at his friend, the secretary of state.

'You will have my resignation within the hour, Mister

President.' Kohlhammer appeared saddened, as if he were grieving.

The president, surprise and pain written on his face, replied quietly, 'I understand, Herb.'

'Thank you, sir,' Kohlhammer said in a low, dejected voice. 'It has been a pleasure serving you these past years. I would never have dreamed that . . . I wish to be excused, Mister President.'

'Absolutely, Herb,' the president responded, standing to offer his hand. 'Your efforts have been splendid, and I wish you every success in the future.'

'If we have a future,' Kohlhammer replied, shaking the president's hand.

The remaining members of the staff stood in unison as the secretary of state left the room. Kohlhammer's sudden resignation had surprised everyone. He had always taken a hard line with the Soviets in previous matters.

'Well, gentlemen, Susan,' the president said, still standing. 'I wish I could resign, too. But I can't do that, you see.' The president looked around the table before speaking again. 'And do you want to know why?'

No one made a sound, not sure if the leader of the American people was in the process of becoming unbalanced under the strain. 'Because if I resign, my successor, the first female president of the United States, is going to step up and blast the Soviet Communist party off the face of the earth.'

Grant Wilkinson glanced at Blaylocke, then back to the president. 'Sir, you – '

'Can it, Grant,' the president replied testily, 'and start the plan in motion.'

Wilkinson turned to Chambers. 'Admiral?'

'Yes, sir,' replied the chairman of the Joint Chiefs. 'We are prepared to execute the strike in minimal time.'

Zhilinkhov smiled slightly when his closest friend, and 'Inner Circle' cofounder, Boris Dichenkovko, entered the massive room. The former Politburo member, followed by Minister of Defense and General of the Army Trofim F. Porfir'yev, approached the general secretary's bed.

'You are feeling better, Viktor Pavlovich?' Dichenkovko asked, taking a seat in a large, stuffed chair next to Zhilinkhov's bed.

'Da, much better,' the stricken leader replied slowly, haltingly. 'Our wonderful news has strengthened me, my friend.'

'Yes,' Dichenkovko responded, looking up at Porfir'yev, then back to Zhilinkhov. 'The spies have been killed.'

Aleksandr Pulaev and Yegoery Yevstigneyev joined the group. Their faces reflected apprehension.

'I told you,' Zhilinkhov said, slurring his words, 'that everything would be . . . fine.'

'Yes, you did, Viktor Pavlovich,' Dichenkovko said without emotion. 'Now, you must rest, my good friend.'

The general secretary attempted to smile again, but the result showed only on the right side of his face.

'No, comrades,' Zhilinkhov said in a strained voice, weakly motioning for the minister of defense to step closer. 'Now we launch the strike . . . on the United States.'

Porfir'yev, unsure of how he should respond, looked to Dichenkovko for guidance. No one said a word.

Zhilinkhov's cold eyes hardened. 'Give the order, General Porfir'yev. This minute!'

Dichenkovko hesitated, then inhaled deeply. 'Viktor Pavlovich, we must suspend our plan for – '

'Enough!' Zhilinkhov spat through clenched teeth.

'You have your orders, General. Carry out my command, or you will be relieved this moment.'

Porfir'yev, pale and wide-eyed, again looked to Dichenkovko for help. Pulaev and Yevstigneyev turned aside, speechless. Dichenkovko remained quiet, avoiding the defense minister's unspoken plea.

'General Secretary,' Porfir'yev said slowly, 'as the ranking member of the Soviet armed forces, it is my duty to counsel you not to launch a strike at this ti – '

'The strike will be launched . . . now,' Zhilinkhov hissed, mustering his waning strength, 'with or without you, General. Give the order, or I will have Colonel General Vranesevic place you in custody.'

Porfir'yev blanched, then stepped back in shock, his face contorted in rage. He paused, then found his voice. 'The order will be carried out.'

Dichenkovko stood up and turned away from Zhilinkhov, slowly shaking his head in resignation. 'Viktor Pavlovich, you – '

'Give the order!' Zhilinkhov threatened, lamely pointing his finger at Porfir'yev.

The defense minister walked across the room to the private communications console and picked up the handset. Porfir'yev tapped in the number to Marshal Nicholas Bogdonoff, then waited for the chief of the general staff to answer.

Porfir'yev stared out the window at the gently falling snow, then heard Bogdonoff's aide.

'Porfir'yev. Give me General Bogdonoff.'

The defense minister glanced at Zhilinkhov, then back out the window. Eight seconds passed before Bogdonoff was on the line.

'General Bogdonoff, Porfir'yev. Launch the strike, Operation Galaxy. General Secretary's orders. Launch the strike.'

'Has this been authenticated?' General Matuchek asked, unbelieving.

Canadian Lt Gen. Jonathan Honeycutt, NORAD vice commander, slowly nodded his head. 'I'm afraid so, J.B.'

'Prepare for imminent strike?' Matuchek asked Honeycutt. 'I don't understand, John. Are the Soviets preparing to strike us, or are we going to launch a preemptive strike on Russia?'

'We,' Honeycutt paused, looking left and right, 'are going to launch a first-strike, all-out effort.'

Matuchek turned pale, gripped the side of his command console, then slowly sank into his chair.

'What the hell is going on here?' the NORAD commander absently asked his vice commander. 'Have they gone insane at the White House?'

'I'm afraid I don't know, J.B.,' Honeycutt responded, glancing at the Top Secret Nuclear message in his hand. He read it again. 'All we can do is comply. It is authenticated. White House, Presidential.' Honeycutt placed the message folder on the console in front of Matuchek. 'We're about to hit the marbles, I'm afraid,' Honeycutt said in a halting voice.

Matuchek placed his head in his hands. 'Read it to me again, John.'

Honeycutt picked up the red folder, put his glasses back on, then read the Top Secret message to his boss.

021745ZFEB
TOP SECRET NUCLEAR
FROM: WHITE HOUSE. COMMANDER IN CHIEF
           AK42766/57CC
TO   : CINCSAC
SUBJ : NUCLEAR PREEMPTIVE STRIKE – SOVIET UNION

356

REF : JCS OPTIONAL STRIKE CRITERION
INFO : CINCNORAD
CINCTAC
1. NUCLEAR PREEMPTIVE STRIKE TO SOVIET UNION
SCHEDULED 021820ZFEB. EXECUTE PRIORITY ONE
TRACKING AND TARGET ACQUISITION. MANDA-
TORY CONFIRMATION ALL COMMANDS.
2. IMPLEMENTATION SUITABILITY VERIFIABLE AT
021815ZFEB. VALID AUTHENTICATION AT
021819ZFEB.
3. THIS IS NOT AN EXERCISE.

Matuchek rubbed the back of his neck, then slowly
stood up from his console. 'Have the field commanders
submit their status reports every five minutes, John.'

'Yes, sir,' Honeycutt responded quietly, reaching
across to his phone.

'Oh, God,' Matuchek said, suffering from acute
anguish, 'Alice has no idea.'

The NORAD commander was oblivious to the frantic
activity taking place around him. Frightened faces looked
up at the two generals, then to the twenty-four-hour clock
over the status boards.

USS *TENNESSEE*

The Trident II fleet ballistic missile submarine, ninety-
seven nautical miles due east of Karaginskiy Island,
Union of Soviet Socialist Republics, cruised silently at a
depth of four hundred feet.

The submarine was operating as the right flank of the
carrier task force headed by the USS *Constellation*. The
aircraft carrier, on full alert, had been flying sorties
around the clock.

'Ken,' Capt. Mark McConnell said to his executive

officer, Cmdr Ken Houston, 'have the officers and Chief Booker report to the wardroom.'

'Yes, sir,' Houston replied, simultaneously flipping the overhead PA switch. 'This is the executive officer. Captain McConnell requests all officers and the chief of the boat to report to the wardroom, on the double.'

The captain and his XO sat in stunned silence as the officers and Booker hurried into the wardroom.

'Ken,' McConnell said quietly, 'have the stewards go to the general mess, then secure the hatch when the last man is out.'

'Aye aye, skipper,' Houston replied, stepping into the galley.

'Sit down, gentlemen,' McConnell instructed in a subdued, almost inaudible voice.

Houston stepped back into the wardroom, dogging the hatch behind him. 'All secure, sir.'

McConnell nodded his head in acknowledgement, then spoke to the assembled men. 'Gentlemen,' McConnell started slowly, 'I have a message – an order, if you will – from the president of the United States. Our commander-in-chief.'

The captain looked around the table at the blank expressions. The officers knew something strange was about to take place. McConnell was more serious than anyone had ever seen him.

'I'm going to read it to you.' McConnell looked down at the message, then back to his officers. 'Then I will take questions, one at a time, beginning with Lieutenant Commander Lewandowski, proceeding clockwise around the table.'

When McConnell finished reading the shocking message there was a look of bewilderment on every face gathered around the table.

'We took an oath in order to join this service,'

McConnell said. 'We have been ordered, by our commander-in-chief, the president of our country, to strike the Soviet Union with every available missile on board. I don't know why, or what provocation brought this about . . .'

McConnell waited a few seconds before continuing. 'Does anyone in this room have a problem – any problem with our orders? The orders I have to carry out?'

No one uttered a sound. The officers were speechless, each trying to grasp the magnitude of the message.

'Actually,' McConnell placed the message on the table, 'you know as much about it now as I do. The strike is scheduled within the hour.'

The engineering officer, Lt Cmdr Samuel Woolf, indicated he had a question.

'Sam?' McConnell responded.

'Skipper, what about the men? Are you going to inform them?' Woolf looked anxious, not sure what to expect after the stunning news.

'Yes, absolutely,' McConnell responded. 'After you return to your duty stations, I'll make the announcement. If we have any dissenters, or individuals who have philosophical differences, they will be placed in confinement until further notice.'

McConnell looked at the shocked officers. 'If there are no further questions, you are dismissed.'

The group rose to their feet, confusion written on every face. The shocking order, along with the consequences, were difficult to understand in such a short time frame.

McConnell turned to his XO as the officers and Chief Booker filed out of the wardroom. 'Well, Ken,' McConnell said with sadness in his eyes, 'the unthinkable is going to happen in forty-three minutes. Our world, as we knew it when we left port, is going to be changed forever.'

Houston didn't respond. He couldn't trust his voice, or his emotions.

20

COBRA FLIGHT

The two F-15 pilots had eaten a snack and rested while their fighters were refueled. Their relief pilots had returned to Flight Operations for assignment to other aircraft. Air Force Maj. Enrico DiGennaro was not about to give up his fighter if the balloon went up.

Likewise, his wingman, Capt. William 'Wild Bill' Parnam, wasn't about to leave his flight leader. American fighter pilots had an unwritten contract. Breaching flight integrity was a cardinal sin, punishable by banishment from the brotherhood.

After a quick flight line brief, the fighter jocks were airborne again.

Climbing through thirty-eight thousand feet, Cobra One checked in with the Airborne Warning and Control System aircraft.

'Pinwheel,' DiGennaro radioed, 'Cobra Flight is back with you.'

'Roger, Cobra,' the AWACS controller responded. 'Switch to tactical suppress, ah, tango, romeo, alpha, seven.'

DiGennaro and Parnam were surprised. The AWACS secret tactical radio code, changed on a daily basis, was used only in the event of war.

'Roger, Pinwheel,' DiGennaro answered. 'Copy tango, romeo, alpha, seven.'

'Affirmative,' the controller replied sharply.

DiGennaro and Parnam checked their authenticator codes, then switched to the discreet frequency.

'Pinwheel, Cobras up your freq,' DiGennaro radioed to the orbiting control aircraft.

'Cobras, listen up!' the new controller said in an emphatic, no-nonsense command voice. 'Prepare to engage hostile aircraft. Prepare to attack Soviet aircraft. CINCTAC authorization. Acknowledge!'

DiGennaro was momentarily taken aback. His mind raced, trying to formulate a logical explanation for the startling order. Attack the Russians?

'Acknowledge, Cobras!' The AWACS controller was adamant.

'One, copy,' DiGennaro absently responded, distracted by the sudden turn of events.

'Dash Two with a copy,' Parnam said in a questioning voice.

The AWACS controller waited three seconds, then radioed further instructions to the F-15 pilots. 'Cobras, come left zero-seven-zero, climb to angels four-seven. This is for real, boys. Play time is over.'

'Roger,' DiGennaro acknowledged for both pilots. He quickly glanced at Parnam's F-15, then mentally prepared himself for aerial combat with the Russians.

'Report weapons hot,' the controller ordered. 'You have bogies twelve o'clock for sixty nautical. You are cleared to engage the Soviet aircraft. Switch to Strike – my code eight.'

'Lead is hotel, switching Strike,' DiGennaro responded, checking his armament panel and radio switches.

'Two's hot,' Parnam reported in a clipped manner, adrenaline surging through his body.

The AWACS combat controller keyed his microphone in answer. 'Good hunting, Cobras.'

'You bet,' DiGennaro replied. 'Where are the other flights?' DiGennaro could hear a lot of chatter on the radio.

The AWACS controller hesitated before responding. 'Eleven Fifteens are closing from your ten o'clock, seventy out, and, we've got eight Tomcats and six Hornets about to intercept the tail end of the Soviet group, the same formation you are engaging.'

'We'll be damned lucky if we don't shoot each other down,' DiGennaro replied sarcastically, knowing the attack would be like a nighttime figure eight destruction derby.

DiGennaro again looked over at Parnam's Eagle. 'Cobra Two, let's spread out. We're going for the bombers first.'

'Roger, lead.'

The two F-15s slashed through the cold night sky, poised to assault the Soviet bomber group in less than three minutes. Both pilots remained silent, rehearsing the tactics they would use in the melee.

Suddenly two bright lights flashed off to the right, followed by a number of fiery red explosions.

'Fight's on!' radioed one of the Navy Tomcat pilots.

The aircraft radios erupted like the fast-paced chatter of a dozen horse race announcers talking at the same time.

Total confusion reigned as the Arctic night turned a reddish yellow, reminding Parnam of a Fourth of July fireworks display. Only something was different. The rockets were not going upward, they were traveling horizontally.

DiGennaro and Parnam saw the lead group of Blackjack bombers at almost the same instant. Both pilots fired two AIM-7M Sparrow missiles and then pulled straight up, continuing over on their backs to prepare for another missile attack. Coming down the backside of the loop, DiGennaro and Parnam could see the aerial destruction mushrooming.

'Cobra One is going for the "Jack" pulling up!' DiGennaro yelled to his wingman, hoping Parnam could hear him over the congested radios.

The two McDonnell Douglas F-15s bottomed out of the loop and almost collided with a MiG-29. DiGennaro yanked the fighter's nose up, tracked the Blackjack for three seconds, then fired two AIM-9M Sidewinder missiles.

'Jesus, Joseph, and Mary,' DiGennaro said to himself, sucking oxygen in the high-G turn, 'this is like kicking a gunnysack full of wildcats.'

DiGennaro rolled wings level, switched to guns, and placed the pipper on the Backfire bomber. A split second before he squeezed the firing button the Russian aircraft disintegrated in an arc of falling fire. The Navy F-18 that had bagged the Russian pulled straight into the vertical and disappeared.

The dully lighted sky was a chaotic jumble of aircraft traveling in every imaginable direction, some at supersonic speeds.

DiGennaro tried to block out the radio garble. He had already heard two calls of 'Mayday', and three 'Eject'. DiGennaro eased the nose up, then rolled the Eagle to give himself a better view of the Soviet bombers. They were spread wide, some turning back toward their bases. The Soviet bomber group had been decimated.

DiGennaro found his next target, another Backfire, and wrapped the F-15 into a face-sagging 7½-G turn. Two MiG-29s and a Tomcat flashed in front of DiGennaro, causing him to yank the throttles to idle and deploy the speed brake for an instant to avoid a collision.

Streaks of red lightning crisscrossed the night sky in

every direction as DiGennaro slammed the throttles forward again and retracted the speed brake. The powerful Pratt and Whitney F100 turbofans, blazing in afterburner, thrust the air-superiority fighter beyond five hundred miles an hour as DiGennaro set up a shot. He gently eased the pipper slightly ahead of the Backfire's nose, then squeezed the trigger and rudder-walked the F-15's cannon down the Russian's fuselage.

A stream of molten lead erupted from the M61 cannon mounted in the starboard wing-root. DiGennaro held the trigger down for two seconds, spewing over one hundred rounds a second into the fast-approaching bomber.

'Come on,' DiGennaro said, triggering another two-second burst.

The Russian Backfire seemed to come apart in slow motion. First the left wing folded upward, then the nose dropped downward, followed by a roll to the left.

DiGennaro was watching the bomber's descent when he felt the Eagle shudder. He checked his instruments and warning lights. Nothing appeared wrong.

Glancing over his left shoulder, DiGennaro saw the cause of the vibration – a MiG was spraying cannon fire into the aft fuselage of his F-15.

'Mother of . . .' DiGennaro groaned under the snap 8-G corkscrewing maneuver. He violently unloaded the F-15, going for speed and separation, then snatched the stick back and slammed it hard to the left.

'Pull . . . pull, burners lit, more G,' DiGennaro said to himself, straining to breathe. His chest felt crushed from the high-G loads. He looked back to the left, then slapped the stick hard to the right, snap-rolling the agile fighter into a tight turn to the right. 'Where . . . is . . . that . . . sonofabitch?'

DiGennaro saw the MiG at the precise instant the Eagle's canopy exploded.

The stunned pilot, his plane buffeting in the cold hurricane-force wind, pulled the throttles to idle, trying to slow the F-15 in preparation for an ejection. The instrument panel was a dark blur of flickering warning lights.

DiGennaro looked to his right as the Fulcrum shot by, burners lit, going supersonic. He tried desperately to bring the Eagle's nose around for a cannon shot at the MiG. But something was wrong, terribly wrong.

The F-15 wouldn't respond. DiGennaro tried harder to grasp the control stick as the fighter slowly rolled to the left. His right hand felt completely numb and he couldn't grip the stick. DiGennaro looked down, then recoiled in shock.

His right hand was almost severed, hanging limp from his wrist. DiGennaro moaned, then grasped the stick with his left hand. Feeling light-headed, he released the stick and raised his hand to his oxygen mask. It was secure, but he couldn't breathe. He ran his hand down the connecting hose and discovered the problem. The hose had been ripped apart. He also felt the moistness of his chest wound.

DiGennaro, in desperation, shoved the nose over in a futile attempt to reach a lower altitude where he wouldn't need the life-sustaining oxygen. He watched the altimeter rapidly unwind through thirty-two thousand feet, then drifted into unconsciousness.

The gallant fighter pilot never knew when his F-15 slammed into the dark, cold water.

Capt. Bill Parnam was already sinking to the bottom of the Bering Sea. He had rammed head-on into a Navy F-18 while trying to evade the MiG that had downed his flight leader.

Rear Adm. Donald S. G. McKenna, task force commander, accompanied by Capt. Greg Linnemeyer, walked into the ship's closed circuit television station.

'Greg,' McKenna said under his breath, 'this is it. I never thought we would take the plunge.'

'I have been thinking the same thing, sir,' Linnemeyer answered with a sadness in his voice.

Station technicians snapped to attention as McKenna and Linnemeyer, removing their covers, stepped over the hatch coaming and into the broadcasting compartment.

'As you were,' McKenna said in a friendly tone. 'Are we ready to go on the air?'

'Yes, sir,' the chief petty officer in charge of the studio replied. 'Just need to alert the decks, Admiral.'

McKenna nodded and stepped behind the podium adorned with the ship's seal. His features looked grim through the eye of the television camera.

The public address system came to life. 'The task force commander is prepared to speak to the crew. Stand by.'

'This is Admiral McKenna. There have been many rumors filtering through the ship the past few minutes. I am here to clarify the situation as we know it at this time.'

McKenna waited for the noise to subside before he spoke again. 'We are preparing, as I speak, to launch conventional and nuclear strikes against the Soviet Union. These strikes will take place in less than forty-one minutes.'

A hushed foreboding embraced the entire ship as all activity came to an abrupt halt.

'We are faced,' McKenna paused, 'with a tremendous responsibility. Each of us.' McKenna cleared his throat, swallowing hard. 'A responsibility to our country, to our families, and to the United States Navy.'

McKenna waited a moment before continuing. 'But most importantly, men, is our responsibility to each other.'

McKenna looked at Linnemeyer, then back to the camera. 'I know each and every one of you will do your job well. Good luck, and may God be with us.'

The Admiral stepped to the side, motioning for Linnemeyer to join him. 'Now, your commanding officer, Captain Linnemeyer, will fill you in on the details.'

Greg Linnemeyer stepped to the podium as the sound of jet engines being started reverberated through the huge supercarrier.

THE WHITE HOUSE

The president walked into the War Room and spoke to his chief of staff. 'One thing, Grant.'

'Yes, sir,' Wilkinson replied, staring at the lighted situation display.

'What if we told the Soviets that the Kremlin operative is safe and we know about Zhilinkhov's plan?' The president continued without waiting for Wilkinson to answer. 'That we are prepared to retaliate?'

Wilkinson turned toward the president. 'They'll back off, tell the world our accusation is insane, wait until we eventually relax, then destroy us.'

After seeing the pained look on the president's face, Wilkinson spoke more softly. 'Sir, it's only a matter of time. The difference is measured in minutes, Mister President, between annihilation and survival. We're better off if Zhilinkhov does believe our Kremlin operative is dead.'

'I know you're right, Grant,' the president said in frustration. 'I'm having a very difficult time absorbing this situation. You must understand.'

'Sir,' Wilkinson said in a different, serious vein, 'I share your grief. I'm blocking my feelings the best I can in order to make the correct decisions.'

The president didn't respond as the rest of the staff, except Susan Blaylocke, joined the two men. The vice president, acting on instructions from her boss, was en route to join Air Force Chief of Staff, General Ridenour, in the 747 'Looking Glass' command post.

The big Boeing was on final approach to Andrews Air Force Base as the president sat down in the War Room. Blaylocke, aboard *Marine Two*, would land next to the 747 when it rolled to a stop on the runway. She would be airborne in the flying command post in less than five minutes.

'Okay, Admiral,' the president said in a weary voice, 'the strike goes in fourteen minutes. Tell me, again, what our priorities will be.'

'Yes, sir,' Chambers replied, appearing pale and strained. The JCS chairman stepped forward to the lighted display map. 'We're going to preempt the biggest weapons first.' Chambers pointed to various Russian missile sites deployed west of the Ural Mountains.

'We're going after the SS-20s here,' Chambers said, tapping each site with his pointer, 'at Pervomaysk, Yedrova, Yurya, Verkhnyaya, and the Caspian Sea area.'

A phone, chiming softly, interrupted the brief. Wilkinson picked up the receiver, listened for a moment, then replied quietly. The chief of staff placed the receiver down and swiveled around to face the president. 'The vice president is airborne, sir.'

'Very well,' the president said, staring blankly at the

lighted display map of the Soviet Union. 'Please continue, Admiral.'

Chambers pushed a button on his hand-held control unit, then raised his pointer again.

'We've got over fifty percent of their submarines, including the big boomers, under our thumb right now,' Chambers said, pointing to isolated areas in the Bering Sea, Pacific, Atlantic, and Arctic Oceans.

'We will dispatch them,' Chambers looked at the twenty-four-hour clock, 'in eleven minutes, sir.'

The phone chimed again. Wilkinson raised the receiver, nodded to Chambers, then spoke to the president.

'All commands report ready and standing by, sir.' Wilkinson darted a look at Cliff Howard before speaking to the president again. 'Mister President, the fighters have engaged the Soviet bombers over the Bering Sea.'

'Okay,' the president replied, wiping perspiration from his hair line. He couldn't take his eyes off the clock as it slowly ticked off the final minutes to Armageddon.

Wilkinson listened to further information, then gently replaced the receiver in its cradle. 'Four missile sites – two at Grand Forks, one at Malmstrom, and one at Whiteman – have malfunctions. They'll be unable to launch, sir.'

The grieving president, holding his head in his hands, didn't respond.

'Won't make any difference,' Marine General Hollings-worth said, standing to stretch taut muscles. 'We've got triple overkill built into every target.'

USS *DWIGHT D. EISENHOWER*

Captain Greg Linnemeyer stepped into PRI-FLY in time to watch the first of eight A-6F Intruders hurtle down the forward two catapults. The Grumman all-weather attack aircraft were laden with conventional bombs, bound for Soviet Air Defense radar installations.

Admiral McKenna entered the ship's control tower as the F-14s prepared to launch.

'Attention on deck,' the senior petty officer said in a loud voice.

'As you were,' McKenna replied, then turned to Linnemeyer. 'We're already in the soup, I'm afraid. I just received word that Air Force and Navy fighters shot down at least twenty Russian bombers, fighters, and tankers over the Bering Sea.'

Linnemeyer looked shocked. 'How did we get into this position so quickly?'

'I wish I could give you an answer, Greg. It's too soon for an accurate account of what preceded this tragedy.'

Linnemeyer turned slightly to catch an F-14 rushing down the number one catapult. The Tomcat left the end of the deck, sank precariously low to the water, then began to climb. The heavy fighter, afterburners howling, had kicked spray off the water.

'I know you're right, sir,' the CO said sadly. 'What bothers me at the moment isn't global. It's knowing half these kids won't be returning to this deck . . . ever.'

ELLSWORTH AIR FORCE BASE, South Dakota

The Minuteman II nuclear missile silo felt like a cold burial vault to Capt. Kevin Brostrom. He glanced over at his friend and fellow launch officer, 1st Lt Teresa Kay Langenello.

'It's authenticated and cleared,' Brostrom said in a shaky voice. 'Stand by to insert keys.'

Langenello looked pale, almost chalky white. She paused a moment, reached into her breast pocket, extracted two pills, then swallowed both without benefit of liquid. The prescription tranquilizers would help her face the realities of the next few minutes. She was not the only launch officer who had the prescription.

The two officers, members of the 44th Strategic Missile Wing, had practiced this situation hundreds of times. They had grown accustomed to believing a real launch order would never happen. Their minds couldn't cope with the destruction they were about to unleash.

'Insert keys,' Brostrom said in a weak voice. 'Stand by to launch on command.'

Langenello responded to the order, crossed herself, then began praying quietly.

WHITE HOUSE WAR ROOM

'Three minutes, Mister President,' Wilkinson reported in a halting, dry voice.

The president didn't respond, staring morosely at the top of the table. He hadn't said a word, or looked up, for over two minutes. The commander-in-chief of the United States appeared to be in a trance.

General Hollingsworth slowly turned his head, meeting the looks of General Vandermeer and Admiral Grabow, then glanced at Admiral Chambers, his immediate boss. 'Steady,' was the only word out of the Marine's mouth.

All eyes turned to the clock. Two minutes, forty

seconds before the biggest tragedy in the history of mankind would begin.

The president choked, then suppressed a sob. 'God, forgive me. I have no other choice. The choice . . . was made for me . . .'

Wilkinson quickly moved to the side of the president. 'Sir, you must rem – '

'Do you understand, God?' the president interrupted. 'Oh, God, help us . . . Oh, Lord, I'm sorry . . .'

Wilkinson took the president by the arm, not saying a word. He knew his friend and boss, the leader of a free America, was losing his grasp. He was breaking down under the strain of guilt.

'Launch the strike,' the president said weakly, collapsing in his chair. His mind, reeling in a haze, refused to comprehend the finality of his unprecedented command.

The shock and trauma of the situation engulfed the room as the president slumped, resting his face on the polished table.

Cliff Howard made the first move to comfort him. The rest of the staff stared at each other with fixed looks, slowly realizing the end – the final act – was irreversible.

The president, barely able to walk, was led out of the War Room to a heavily fortified underground bomb shelter. His staff, with the exception of the Joint Chiefs, accompanied him to the reinforced quarters.

As the entourage reached the bunker area, an aide, out of breath, rushed down the corridor.

'Yes, Colonel,' Wilkinson said, holding the shaking president by the arm.

'Sir,' the senior White House aide said breathlessly, 'Moscow is on the hot line!'

'What?' Howard replied, shock registering on his face. 'Couldn't be this soon.'

The aide ignored Howard as he addressed the commander-in-chief. He could see the president was pale, but he was clearly in charge of the White House.

'Sir, the Soviet general secretary is dead! The message said the acting general secretary implores us to downgrade our alert status. They are de-escalating their military posture at this time. They want to speak with the president – with you, sir – immediately!'

The news stunned the president and his staff. The gravity of their blunder was only beginning to register in their minds. No one spoke as they stared, transfixed, at the breathless aide.

'Zhilinkhov passed away about ten minutes ago, and the acting secretary wants – '

'Oh, Christ in Heaven!' Wilkinson exploded. 'The chiefs don't know!'

Wilkinson raced down the hallway, almost falling as he rounded the corner leading to the War Room. The short distance seemed like miles to the panicked man.

WAR ROOM

General Hollingsworth, Marine Corps commandant, looked at the wall-mounted twenty-four-hour clock, then picked up the red phone. 'Delta One Strike. I repeat, Delta One Strike. Presidential authority. Launch all missiles. Launch all missiles. Condition One Sierra. I repeat, Condition One Sierra. Code Able.'

Hollingsworth caught the eye of Admiral Chambers, who nodded yes.

'Authentication,' Hollingsworth continued, 'Baker, Tango, Victor, one, niner – '

'STOP, GODDAMNIT,' Wilkinson shouted, gesturing wildly with his arms. 'Cancel the order. Cancel the strike!'

Hollingsworth hesitated a fraction of a second, uncomprehending.

'NOW,' Wilkinson yelled. 'Cancel the goddamn strike!'

'Cancel, cancel,' Hollingsworth shouted into the phone as the other chiefs stared in shocked relief.

'Cancel the strike. All commands reply immediately. Repeat. Cancel the strike, per presidential order.'

Epilogue

The cold, bundled-up tourists walking along Pennsylvania Avenue had not the slightest inkling their lives had been spared by a measure of seconds. Their futures would not end in thirty-five minutes. Washington, District of Columbia, would not become a smoldering mass of uninhabitable rubble.

Cameras clicked in the frosty air, children played in the snow, and businessmen bantered over martinis, oblivious in their naïveté.

Thus, on a cold day in February, the beginning of an end, as civilized people, had come precariously close. The unthinkable had almost happened.

Millions of innocent people, in Russia and North America, would continue to enjoy their lives on the planet Earth, unaware of the fragility of their existence.

The order to rescind the preemptive nuclear strike against the Soviet Union halted all the major missile launches. However, preparatory measures to neutralize Russian submarines, fighter aircraft, bombers, surface ships, and early warning radar installations had commenced two minutes before the scheduled strike. A number of skirmishes escalated until the 'cease-fire' order was communicated to on-site commanders.

The United States military, after assessing the damage reports, had lost three submarines and four surface ships. A final tally listed an additional thirty-one aircraft destroyed, including two B-2 Stealth bombers.

Soviet losses included seven submarines, two surface ships, and over sixty-five aircraft destroyed.

An extreme state of readiness remained in effect for seventy-two hours. The global tension rippled through every country, sending the economic balance into an upheaval.

Three weeks after the aborted nuclear strike, the Trident II submarine USS *Tennessee*, heavily damaged, limped into the port of San Diego, California. Three members of her crew had been buried at sea off the Hawaiian Islands.

The operative known as Dimitri, along with the crew of Scarecrow One, autorotated onto their rescue ship. The S-70 had run out of fuel as Buchanan slowed to flare the Night Hawk over the ship's deck. The gunship was destroyed, but the crew, along with Dimitri and Steve Wickham, survived.

Wickham endured a lengthy and grueling recuperative process, aided by daily visits from his friend Dimitri, before returning to full duty with the Central Intelligence Agency.

The president of the United States worked tirelessly with the British prime minister, along with other heads of state, to reach meaningful agreements with the Soviet leaders. He convinced the new Communist party general secretary that it would be in everyone's best interest to have semiannual summit meetings at alternate sites. The twice-a-year gatherings proved to be beneficial to all the participants, and helped establish the president's tenure as one of strong, aggressive leadership.

Glossary

ADF: Automatic Direction Finding, using radio signal strength.

ADI: Attitude Direction Indicator, a primary flight instrument.

APU: Auxiliary Power Unit.

ASW: Antisubmarine Warfare.

AWACS: Airborne Warning and Control System.

Ball: The optical landing device on an aircraft carrier. Also referred to as 'meatball'.

BARCAP: Barrier Combat Air Patrol. Generally used to protect vessels at sea.

Bogie: Unidentified or enemy aircraft.

Bolter: Carrier landing attempt in which the tailhook misses the arresting gear, necessitating a go-around.

CAG: The Commander of the Air Group. Oversees all the squadrons embarked aboard an aircraft carrier.

CAP: Combat Air Patrol.

Check Six: Refers to visual observation behind an aircraft. Fighter pilots must constantly check behind them to ensure an enemy aircraft is not in an attack position.

CIC: Combat Information Center. The central battle management post in Naval surface combatants.

CRT: Vacuum tube used to display computer information in writing or pictures.

Departure: Refers to an aircraft departing from controlled flight.

DME: Distance Measuring Equipment. Distance information provided to a pilot in nautical miles from a known point.

378

Elevon: A control surface used after the space shuttle enters the atmosphere. It is a combination of an aircraft elevator and aileron, controlling pitch and roll.

EVA: Extravehicular Activity. Refers to activity outside the space shuttle.

Fox Two/Fox Three: Pilot radio calls indicating the firing of a Sidewinder or Phoenix missile.

Furball: Multiaircraft fighter engagement.

G-force: The force pressed on a body by changes in velocity. G is measured in increments of earth gravity.

Gimbal: Attachment to allow rocket nozzles to move in two or three axes. Helps control direction of flight.

Gomers: Air combat adversaries.

HUD: Head Up Display. Transparent screen mounted in front of the pilot's normal line of vision. HUD is used to display flight data and weapons systems information so the pilot doesn't have to look down into the cockpit.

ICS – Internal Communications System.

INS: Inertial Navigation System.

Knot: One nautical mile per hour. A nautical mile equals 1.1 statute mile.

LOS: Loss of signal. Shuttle radio signal loss during atmosphere re-entry caused by shock waves and ionization.

LSO: Landing Signal Officer. Specially qualified squadron pilot responsible for assisting other pilots in landing aboard a carrier.

Mach: Term named for physicist Ernst Mach. Used to describe the speed of an object in relation to the speed of sound.

MAD: Magnetic Anomaly Detector. Used to locate submerged submarines.

NATOPS: Naval Aviation Training and Operations

manual. Provides rules and regulations for the safe and proper operation of all Navy and Marine Corps aircraft and helicopters.

OMS: Orbital Maneuvering System.

PRI-FLY: Control tower on an aircraft carrier.

RCS: Reaction Control System.

Retro-fire: To fire engines in the direction of motion to reduce forward velocity. Allows gravity to pull a space craft back toward earth.

RIO: Radar Intercept Officer. Back-seaters in F-14 Tomcats and F-4 Phantom aircraft.

RMS: Remote Manipulator System.

SAM: Surface-to-air missile.

SAR: Search and Rescue.

SRB: Solid Rocket Booster.

Tally: Derivative of Tallyho. Target in sight.

Telemetry: Data transmitted to earth from the space shuttle.

Trap: Arrested landing on a carrier or runway.

UHF: Ultra-high frequency radio.

Unload: Release pressure on an aircraft control stick to ease the G-load.